QUEEN OF BEDLAM

QUEEN OF BEDLAM

Laura Purcell

MYRMIDON

Myrmidon
Rotterdam House
116 Quayside
Newcastle upon Tyne
NE1 3DY

www.myrmidonbooks.com

Published by Myrmidon 2014

A catalogue record for this book is available from the British Library.

ISBN 978-1-910183-01-4

Set in Requiem by Ellipsis Digital Limited, Glasgow
Printed in the UK by CPI Group (UK) Ltd, Croydon, CR0 4YY

1 3 5 7 9 10 8 6 4 2

For Anna

✣ FAMILY OF GEORGE III (SIMPLIFIED) ✣

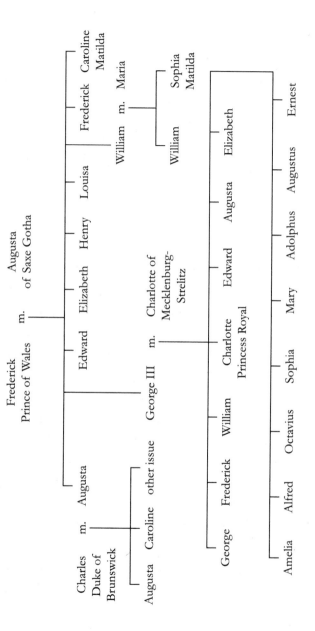

PROLOGUE

Windsor Castle
ᐱ 1812 ᐱ

This would be the last time; Charlotte had made her decision. Now she just had to go through with it. All her life, she had been able to force herself into unpleasant tasks. But this was different. A visit always disturbed the cold composure she worked so hard to preserve. This had to be the last time.

She walked with a step much steadier than her heartbeat. The regular click of her heels gave her a feeling of comfort, of order. The wind whipped violently around the courtyards of Windsor Castle and it took all her strength to remain on course, sailing like a great ship in her gown with its plentiful train.

With her attendants, she wound her way to where he was kept under lock and key like an animal. Would he be violent today? She added her sigh to the greater groan of the wind. She was growing too old to bear these trials.

At last they reached the dreaded apartments, haunted rooms that Charles I had occupied on his way to trial and execution. Now they housed the culmination of Charlotte's nightmares.

Doctor Willis met her at the door. She loathed the very sight of him now – his forced expressions of calm and competence.

'How is he today?' she asked.

'Getting on very well, Your Majesty,' the doctor told her. 'Nice and quiet.' His tone was overly sympathetic – a false, hushed voice that made Charlotte feel like a child.

'No talk of sinking you into hell?' she enquired. 'Or raising people from the dead?'

Doctor Willis flashed a smile that seemed alien in the surroundings. 'No, madam. He talks only of Hanover. He believes all his loved ones have gone to Hanover, where they will never age.'

Why should he have that comfort, when she did not?

The doctor led her into the room and she walked as if in a dream, following the ghostly glow of his candle. Slabs of grey brick surrounded her, decorated with threadbare tapestries. A spider scuttled across the wall into a corner of drifting cobwebs.

The patient sat by a stuttering fire. While the top of his head was bald and shining, hair grew from behind his ears in long tendrils that flowed into a silver beard. He stared at Charlotte with glazed eyes, his pupils dilating uselessly.

Once, the sight would have made her weep. But all her tears were spent.

She sat down opposite him. In the dark well of his rolling pupils, she saw reflected her own grey hair and lined face. Her mind struggled to comprehend that this was them, aged. It was like waking up in an unfamiliar room.

Where was the handsome King of old, with his drooping eyelids and sensuous smile? Where was the bright little wife who inspired his devotion?

If she had been there, that other Charlotte, things would have been different. She would have made his dry, cracked lips break into a grin and cast a sparkle in his dull eyes. She would have known what to do. She would have saved him.

CHAPTER ONE

Upper Lodge, Windsor
~ 1783 ~

'Keep your eyes closed!' She giggled as she slapped him playfully on the hand. It was all in place, all perfect. Everything was just as she imagined.

'I can't see a thing, I swear!' He was lying. Although she had blind-folded him with a blue sash, there were gaps at the bottom where he could peep out.

They reached a marble staircase that swept upwards into darkness. No one else was there; all was silent and still.

'Come, there are steps.' She clutched the warmth of her husband in one hand and a tapered candle in the other. With no attendant to hold her train, she stumbled and tripped up the steps, screeching with laughter.

'Good God, what are you up to?' George groped helplessly with his free arm for a banister. 'I'll have to keep you in order, madam.'

The candle swung around, its circle of light illuminating a gilded frame, a chandelier, a damask wall.

As they reached the landing, he took another step into thin air. She caught him as he plunged. Another peal of laughter rang from her lips and her husband echoed it with his own.

'Through here,' she led him on, not really needing the light of the candle; she had learnt this route by heart.

The door opened softly on its hinges. Charlotte peered into the room, focusing on the window at the far end. Colour slivered between the gaps in the shutters. It was ready.

'Where are we?'

Hastily, Charlotte laid her candle on the nearest table and unbolted the shutters with a clang.

'It had better be pretty spectacular, after this,' George warned her.

With one deft movement, she pulled off his blindfold. 'Don't you worry – it is.'

The night sky burst open with the light of fireworks. A terrace, perfectly manicured lawns and a long canal shimmered. Lantern flames rippling off the water and sparkling on every spot of glass. Below them, a violin sprang into song. The familiar tune built and swelled, playing in canon with the pop of fireworks. The sound of George's favourite composer, Handel, reverberated around the park.

'Happy birthday!'

George put out a hand and caressed her cheek, making her skin tingle as if she were a girl again. All the planning, all the preparation was worth it for the look on his face. 'Every hour I spend with you convinces me: I have a treasure.'

Suddenly embarrassed, Charlotte turned him around. 'Never mind that, you're missing it. Look!'

Boats glided down the river, each ablaze with colour and light.

Reflected in the swirling dark water, their lamps stretched into the heavens, outshining the stars. Charlotte wheeled George around again.

'Look here!' A crocodile of small creatures wound its way out of the gardens onto the terrace. They came two by two, like animals in the Ark, with the tallest at the front and the smallest at the back.

'Why, it is the children!' he cried.

Their fourteen offspring were dressed in elaborate costumes as cupids, sultans, warriors and concubines. From the eldest George, the Prince of Wales, to the youngest, little Alfred in the arms of his nurse, they shone in dazzling jewels and fabrics.

'Oh! Let's go to them!' George grabbed Charlotte's hand and set off at a run.

Her feet barely touched the ground. The stairs, portraits and flagstone floors blurred before her eyes. All at once they spilled out into the cool of the evening, surrounded by the heady scent of flowers.

Their children swarmed about them. At the forefront, baby Alfred held out his stubby arms to Charlotte with a look of pure ecstasy. She seized him impulsively and clamped him to her chest, brushing her lips against his soft clean skin. He tensed. What was wrong? Perhaps he wanted the nurse back. Charlotte looked up for the attendant but then realised her baby was not struggling to get away; he was trying to cling on. Terror stretched his cheeks and his eyes were enormous, swelling with tears.

'Alfred!'

His warm body slipped from her grasp. Something with an inhuman strength was dragging him from her. Her fingers trembled – she knew their grip would not last for long. Gritting her teeth, Charlotte held on with every ounce of strength. Her baby wailed.

'Alfred!'

Against Charlotte's will, her fingers fell slack. With a sudden jolt, the boy flew from her grasp and she was falling, falling . . .

Charlotte awoke with a jump, her heart beating wildly. She let out a breath. It was only Windsor after all.

Her boudoir materialised around her with its fine paper hangings and gilt frames. The party she saw in her dream was a long time ago. And Alfred was dead. She clenched her muscles and leant forwards on the sofa as a deep vibration quivered inside her. Of course, it was the child in her belly that woke her; it kicked strongly now. She picked up some needlework, hoping concentration would banish the images of her dead son. It was futile. Wherever she looked, Alfred's chubby face rose before her, fresh from her dream. Her baby, her boy. Blond hair, a shining, wet mouth.

The memories drifted through her mind like a dark mist. Alfred inoculated against the smallpox on her command, blisters erupting on his tiny eyelids. The carriage taking him away to Deal for sea air. His strength failing, his tender frame shrinking. Then little Octavius, just six months later . . .

Thumps upstairs startled her from her reverie. Her husband's furious voice came muffled through the floorboards. She knew what his shouting meant: Britain's precious colonies in America were slipping through his hands. It was America that drove George to her bed; he came seeking comfort, not another child.

The stranger inside Charlotte's womb flinched. She was seized by an emotion so violent that she wanted to ball up her sewing and shriek. But she had always scorned weak, hysterical women and so instead she laid down her tambour frame and rose to her feet, ready, like any good Queen, to repress her feelings. She needed to bury them as deep as her poor little boys.

Her attendants, Lady Harcourt and Lady Pembroke, stood up but she waved them back down. She waddled across the floor, adjusting her belly. Again, her husband shouted above her head and for a moment her fear rose up to mirror his. What hope was there for this child, conceived at a time of rebellion and grief?

She stopped beside the royal cradle. Her worn face looked back at her in the gleaming wood: the long countenance that had never been beautiful, a sharp nose and a wide mouth. She had put some gorgeous children into this crib – seven surviving heirs and five blooming daughters. But this one felt cursed.

Charlotte laid a jewelled hand upon her swollen belly. *Live. Please, please live.*

A door slammed and shook the floorboards. Charlotte buried her face in the cradle's satin curtains, despising her own weakness. With the cool material pressed against her skin and her eyes firmly shut, she tried, tried with all her strength, to forget. But in another minute she dropped to her knees with a pain she recognised all too well.

Upper Lodge, Windsor

Royal gathered her four sisters together: Augusta, Elizabeth, Mary and the tiny six-year-old Sophia. She made sure their gowns hung straight and the powder in their hair stayed away from their faces. She knew if one tiny thing was out of place, her mother would blame her.

'Come on! Make haste!'

Royal turned to her father. Praise God, he was happy once more! Colour tinctured his cheeks and he walked with a bounce in his step. She had watched him anxiously over the past weeks as he jabbed pins into maps and shouted at his ministers. The calamitous events in America had taken their toll. But now he was calm, with a sleek wig on his head.

'We are ready, Papa.'

Royal followed him along the corridors, her little sisters trailing behind her like ducklings. Time to see yet another new baby.

Yet something was different. The King moved quickly, almost desperately. He had visited the baby twice a day, more often than any of Royal's young siblings. Jealousy whispered in her ear but she pushed it aside. She would always be his favourite daughter.

Guards threw open the double doors. 'The King, the King!'

It was a tall, gilded room flooded with light. The

Queen's state bed glowed from the centre, its golden curtains catching every ray of August sun. Embroidered flowers ran along the tester, their pattern echoed on two chairs at the foot of the bed.

In a honeyed pool beside the chairs stood the cradle; mahogany and swaths of silk. Silver rocking threads hung from each corner. Royal's mother toyed with one as she watched the baby. At the sound of their footsteps she turned, dropping her thread, and curtseyed to the King. Despite her recent confinement, she was impeccably elegant in a taffeta gown of dove grey. Profusions of lace flowed from her half-sleeves like miniature waterfalls. A choker of pearls stretched taut around her neck, bobbing when she swallowed.

A cold feeling of inadequacy crept up Royal's torso as she bent her knees and returned the curtsey. Seventeen years had been insufficient to calm her nerves in her mother's presence – she was unlikely to conquer them now.

'Girls.' Her mother's soft, foreign tones. 'Come and meet your sister.'

They walked as they had been taught: eyes on the floor, their steps small and delicate. Little Mary's face quivered as if she wanted to sneeze. Royal felt a throb of horror but then, somehow, Mary managed to hold it in.

Her mother twitched a curtain aside. 'Look. This is Amelia.'

Royal peered cautiously over the silk coverlets, careful not to knock the crib with her hoop. Her lips parted in surprise. Her mother had presented a string of new

7

siblings to her, but never one as beautiful as this. Amelia was a doll, all ivory skin and wispy curls of blonde hair. A terrible emptiness tugged at Royal's breast and belly – it was high time she had a child of her own. Royal put out a finger to touch the soft, baby skin and Amelia grabbed it, holding it tight above the coverlet in her dimpled fist.

'She looks like Octavius.'

Royal wished the words back at once. Her throat grew hot and thick with fear. How could she forget herself like that? They did not speak of these things. It was not dignified to show emotion.

The Queen glared, a muscle twitching in her jaw. Silence pressed on them painfully.

The King bustled forward. 'Yes, very like, very like. There is no resisting her.'

Royal let out her suspended breath.

The smallest princess, Sophia, edged forward and pushed past Royal's skirts. She was so short for her age she could barely see over the cradle.

'Papa,' she said innocently, 'this baby won't die too, will it?'

Royal's stomach plummeted. The Queen would pull her up for this indiscretion later. But her father remained cool and bent down to Sophia's level, the tails of his blue coat trailing on the floor.

'No, my darling. Of course not.'

Royal did not listen to him; she looked into her mother's pale face and realised she was not so sure.

CHAPTER TWO

The White House, Kew
~ *March 1784* ~

Heat from the warming pan crept up Charlotte's legs into her aching back. At thirty-nine, her body was slow to recover from childbirth. Still, it was blissful to be out of confinement and back in George's bed.

She gave a dreamy, contented smile and turned over to face her husband. She was heavy with sleep, but not ready to surrender to it yet. This was precious time. Here, in the hush of night, with only candle flames lighting their faces, they could be alone at last.

'You are quiet tonight, my love,' he said. 'You haven't touched your gruel.'

Charlotte rolled over reluctantly and picked up her bowl. Of course she had been quiet. A secret gnawed at her conscience – one she didn't want to share with him.

'I've been thinking.'

He stirred the mess of oats in his bowl. 'Oh? And what is my Charlotte thinking about, eh?'

She hesitated. He looked too peaceful to disturb, but she could never lie to him. She half-whispered the name. 'Marie Antoinette. The Queen of France.'

George paused, a spoon half-way between his lips.

'She wrote to me, you see,' she explained. 'But I haven't replied. I wouldn't, without your permission.'

George placed the spoon in his mouth and swished gruel around his cheeks. He did not look at Charlotte. 'Do you want to write back?'

She put down her bowl, cold under the weight of his displeasure. He was testing her and she knew it. 'My darling, I will do whatever you wish.'

He sighed. Wrinkles, extenuated by the shadows, furrowed his high forehead. 'Reply to her if you must. I have no objection. But she must be an impertinent sort of woman, to approach you after the role her country played in the American war.'

She scolded herself for sending him down this path of thought again. He seemed to have aged ten years since the loss of America.

'I thought I would rather have died than seen my colonies lost,' he continued. 'But America is gone and here we are, forced to carry on.'

'Such things are sent to try us. We'll come out the other side stronger and happier. You'll see.'

He put a morsel of bread in his mouth and chewed on it meditatively. 'I thought—' he shook his head, batting away some dark cloud. 'I tried. I tried to make the Crown respectable, as my father told me to. But there have been so many riots since I came to the Crown: about the silk, about the Catholics, about John Wilkes. Do the people hate me?'

'Oh, George!' Charlotte gathered him to her and leant his head against her shoulder. 'You must not despair,' she whispered into his scalp. He looked so vulnerable without a wig, the hair cropped close, sticking up in little tufts that put her in mind of a baby bird.

'The Americans called me a tyrant!' He laughed grimly into her nightdress. 'Does that describe me, Charlotte? Does that describe your husband?'

'No,' she said firmly. 'I am married to the best man alive.'

They remained silent for a moment, holding one another. Nothing but touch could heal the pain of the past few years. They had struggled on, surviving only for each other. Charlotte clung onto him, watching the candle as it burnt low and started to spit.

'Well! At least you love me, eh?' George chuckled. 'Even if the Americans loathe me, even if those damned Whigs try to storm my Parliament?'

'I will always love you,' she said earnestly. 'And I will always be here.'

He looked up into her eyes. Just then, the candle guttered and blinked out.

⤶ *Lower Lodge, Windsor* ⤷

'Now, what part comes next?' Royal looked encouragingly into the face before her, with its big blue eyes and flaxen curls.

'The German provinces!' Sophia declared.

Royal smiled. 'That's right! Clever girl! These bits here.'

Royal sorted a few small, irregular shapes from the jigsaw chest and spread them on her lap. Each one was a reproach to her – another place she had failed to visit. When would her turn come? When would she see more than shapes on a map? It made her sad to watch Sophia sorting through jigsaw pieces. Her little sister would be trapped in the palaces too, with nothing but dull days ahead of her.

Sophia picked up one of the smallest shapes and inspected it in the candlelight. It was the province of Mecklenburg-Strelitz.

'That's where Mama comes from,' Royal told her. 'Isn't it tiny? Can you guess where it goes?' Sophia puzzled over the spaces left on the floor. Royal sighed. She knew the layout of the entire globe like the back of her hand, but she had yet to set foot outside of England.

Mary sat plucking a doll in her hands. 'Let's stop doing this. It's boring.' Royal despaired of her. If Mary found the games of childhood boring, she would be in for a great shock when she grew into a young woman.

The clock chimed on the mantelpiece, reminding Royal that it was time to visit their parents in the castle. The customary feeling of dread pulled at her, a chain coiled about her chest. She was never free. Always ordered here and there, always at the beck and call of another.

Mrs Cheveley scratched on the door with a rattle and the three princesses rose to their feet. It would be another evening of dramatic readings, watching the Queen for permission to laugh or applaud. Together, the governess and Royal wrapped Sophia and Mary up against the cold and ushered them into the night air.

The moon rode full and round. A light wind fluttered the ribbons in Royal's hair. She took a deep breath and gazed out into the distance, trying to imagine she was in another place. Somewhere out there was the land she would travel to and claim as her own, and the lover who would woo her under starlight. She needed them now; she needed to get away.

Restricted by her gown, she fell a little behind Mrs Cheveley and the girls. Sophia's head bobbed in the distance, a rogue curl escaping her cap and floating on the breeze. But then another movement flickered in the corner of her eye.

Crossing the park, far from the castle torches, was the figure of a young man. He saw Royal and stopped. For a moment, she thought she had wished her future husband into life and summoned him there. The silhouetted figure hesitated. Then it moved toward her. The towers and turrets of the castle threw black shapes against the night sky. With every few steps, the man glanced furtively at the windows, like a prisoner fleeing the dungeons. But as he came closer, Royal saw he was no fugitive: he was her brother. She cried out his name and started to run.

'George!' she embraced him. 'What are you doing here? Have you come to see Mrs Siddons play for us?'

'The deuce I have!' He reared back. His face was florid, his abundant hair even frizzier than usual. Apprehension settled beneath Royal's ribs like a stone. Not another quarrel.

'I wouldn't go in there to save my soul,' he vowed. 'I'm just going to dine at the inn, then I'll be back on my way to town.'

Royal recoiled, stung. If only he would try, just try, to keep the peace. 'Were you not going to visit us? We see so little of you.'

'That's not my fault. The old man hates me, you know he does.'

She pressed her lips together. There it was again, the ripping feeling inside as she tried to reconcile her love for her brother with her loyalty to the King. She looked away toward the grey hulk of the castle. George's eyes burned into her. He wanted her to agree, to complain about the King – but she would never speak against her father.

'I suppose you've heard about my allowance?' His voice

dripped with bitterness. 'Parliament granted me a hundred thousand a year. He made them reduce it to fifty.'

'The taxes are so high . . .'

'Do not try to talk of politics,' he scoffed. 'That's not his real motive and you know it.'

Royal clenched her hands. How could she make this young man, addicted to luxury, understand the hardship of royal policy? It wasn't as if their father lived a sumptuous lifestyle. He would manage very well on fifty thousand a year.

'What does Mama say?'

George leant both hands on his cane. 'She says I must behave well enough to deserve the King's friendship. You know that's not her talking. He is behind it all; he poisons her against me.'

Royal sighed. There was no arguing against his paranoia. She wanted to grab him by the shoulders and shake some sense into him. If even their mother, who adored George beyond reason, was on the King's side, he should listen. But he never would.

'What will you do then?'

He grunted and straightened up. 'If he wants me to be in debt, I will be in debt. I have Carlton House now. I can re-decorate the whole place.'

Why must he behave like a child? A man of twenty-one, the eldest of them all! She knew she could not stop him. It was like chasing a horse that had already bolted.

'Do not run up more debt,' she whispered feebly. 'Please. Mary asks for you every day. Forget Carlton House and come back here. Ignore the parents – come back for us. We need you.'

They really did. Of all the brothers, George was the only one who remained in England. Frederick, William and Edward all fought in the armed forces, while Ernest, Augustus and Adolphus studied abroad. George was the princesses' only hope for the future, their only advocate with the Queen. But he was also selfish.

Ignoring Royal's appeal, he adjusted the beaver hat on his head. He gave her a cold peck on the cheek and stalked away.

'George! Please!' Her voice rang shrill and panicked in the night air. She could not believe he would be so heartless. But he kept walking, thrashing the grass with his cane. The lights of Windsor town glowed faintly in the distance.

Empty with despair, Royal watched him reach a slope and start to climb. A dark cloud glided across the moon, obscuring her view. In another moment he had disappeared over the brow of the hill and Royal was alone in the dark.

CHAPTER THREE

Kew Gardens
1785

A milky heat haze hung over the gardens. Bluebells stretched out in a carpet before the cottage, winding round the menagerie and off into green shade. Sweat trickled down Charlotte's neck beneath her lace lappets. She blotted at her forehead with a handkerchief.

'Where are we up to?' she asked Royal.

A gazebo sheltered them from the sun's fierce rays. The table in front of them was littered with Charlotte's projects; unanswered letters from the French queen, a catalogue of furniture, Lord Bute's botanical tables and a herbarium.

Royal sanded her writing and turned to another book. Running her finger along a column, she stopped halfway down the page. '*Strelitzia reginae.*'

Charlotte lifted her flushed cheeks in a smile. She was still flattered they had named this flower from the Cape of

Good Hope in her honour. 'Ah, you haven't seen this yet, have you? Fetch it,' she ordered a servant.

Royal put her pencils in order and checked her paint brushes while she waited. Charlotte glanced at Augusta and Elizabeth over by the menagerie, sketchbooks in hand. The animals, tired by the heat, stood still and allowed them to make detailed studies.

The servant returned carrying a bright orange flower, spiky and bird-like, with an azure blue nectary. Charlotte took it reverently in her hands and stroked the waxen petals. 'Look. Have you ever seen anything like it?'

Royal shook her head. 'Can I draw it, before we start?'

'Of course. But don't knock it. I want a perfect pressing – stem included.'

Royal sifted through her books until she found her sketch pad. Opening it, she flicked through the pages. Flowers, cupids, ladies, cattle . . . Charlotte's breath locked in her throat as an image shot before her eyes, as quick as a blink.

'What's that?'

'Sorry?'

Charlotte reached out for the sketchpad. With shaking hands, she pushed the pages back until she found the drawing. There. It was like staring into the past. Flaxen curls, peachy skin. A little pouting mouth. Suddenly the sun was unbearably bright. Charlotte squinted. 'You drew Octavius.'

Royal nodded, fear carved on her face

Charlotte did not want to worry her daughter, but it took all her strength not to slam the pad back on the table and burst into tears. Every time she came close to forgetting, to being happy again, a ghost reared up. How did other mothers cope with loss? The pain was unutterable.

'It is good.' She squeezed the praise out of her dry mouth. 'Very like.' It was torture to put the pad down; like having the child wrenched from her arms all over again. But she managed to place it before Royal and turn over a new page.

'I wanted to give it to Papa,' Royal explained. 'For his birthday.'

Charlotte swallowed. If the drawing had this effect upon her, it would destroy George.

'Wait a while,' she advised. 'He has enough to try his nerves with the Danish and American ambassadors visiting.'

'I thought they seemed nice.'

Sometimes Royal was so oblivious that Charlotte wanted to hit her. Nice had nothing to do with it. She struggled for the right words. 'Your aunt's terrible marriage in Denmark . . . the loss of America . . . the loss of Octavius . . . it is pulling too hard on one painful chord.'

Royal nodded. With a sigh, she positioned the flower and began to draw, her pencil scratching across the page.

Charlotte used the silence to regain her shattered

composure. The air was hot and close, stifling the scent of flowers until she could only smell leather from the books and the faint tang of animal dung. Picking up her cup of orange tea, she took a sip of the bitter liquid and exhaled. It failed to calm her nerves. She wished she had some snuff.

She was painfully aware that little Amelia, so small and vulnerable, was not beside her. Wild fears galloped through her mind: the baby might suffocate in her sleep, or choke on pap. Her gaze drifted in a semi-circle, back to Augusta and Elizabeth. But they were not sketching now. Elizabeth leant against the fence, one hand on her side.

'Eliza?'

Royal's pencil came to a halt. Charlotte set her cup clattering down and took off toward the menagerie, dread snapping at her heels.

'What is it?' Charlotte demanded.

'Oh, Mama, you will make her listen.' Augusta removed her straw hat and wiped her sweating brow. 'Elizabeth's been getting this pain in her side for days. She has to sit and rest.'

Charlotte forced Elizabeth to lean on her shoulder. Her daughter's face constricted with agony and Charlotte's heart clenched with it.

'It will pass in a moment, Mama. It always does.'

'I don't care. You are going to sit down.' She dragged Elizabeth away from the fence. Servants ran to help. A donkey in the menagerie jumped at the noise and brayed.

The wheezing, heaving sound stopped Charlotte in her tracks. Limp with fear, she yielded Elizabeth to the servants and watched them take her into the shade of the gazebo.

Augusta placed a hot, sticky hand on her shoulder. 'Mama? What is it?'

Charlotte shook her head. She couldn't tell Augusta what she feared. She couldn't tell the girl that she had a taint in her blood.

The donkey's laboured, grating bray called up unwelcome images of Charlotte's mother-in-law, withering in a state bedchamber. A cancer of the mouth, the doctor had said. Charlotte could still hear the rattle in her old, wrinkled throat, could still see her skin turning blue as she struggled for air. It was only after the funeral that Charlotte heard the rumours: scrofula lurking in the blood. A fatal inheritance of scars, swelling and consumption. Now it was in the veins of her children. Had the Saxe-Gotha blood killed Alfred? Octavius? Charlotte shuddered and took Augusta's hand.

Under the gazebo, Royal dabbed lavender water at Elizabeth's temples and waved smelling salts under her nose.

'Will she faint?'

Elizabeth brushed them away. 'I'm well, I'm well. I need a moment to catch my breath is all. I've spent too long in the heat.'

Charlotte sat beside her daughter and poured her a cup of orange tea. Her trembling hands made the china chink. 'If you are unwell, I will cancel the concert.'

Elizabeth cocked an eyebrow. 'And offend all the ambassadors?'

'I would. You know I would.'

Elizabeth screwed up her face and lifted the cup. The movement clearly hurt her. 'We must go, Mama,' she gasped. 'Papa needs us.'

George. Lost in motherly worry, Charlotte had almost forgotten about him. She pictured the strutting American and the cool, insinuating man from Copenhagen. Elizabeth was right. The King needed them. Everything must bow to that.

She nodded reluctantly. As she gave her silent consent, uneasiness trickled down her chest and settled deep in her stomach.

⤚ Windsor Castle ⤙

Boredom. It was the constant spectre through Royal's life: a heavy, suffocating oppression, tighter than any corset.

It was half-past nine; the ancient music concert had droned on for half an hour and showed no indication of stopping. Royal tried to block out the whine of the strings, wondering why her mother and father looked so entranced. It all sounded the same as last month.

The King tapped his foot in time to the tune, holding the Queen's hand. Only the two of them had seats; the courtiers stood around drooping and trying to switch feet inconspicuously.

A cough tickled Royal's throat and it would have to scratch away there unrelieved for at least another hour. She was not just trapped in the castle – she was trapped in her own body. No noise, no sign of humanity could escape her.

There were many people pressed close about her – smart young men in spangled waistcoats, with breeches down to their knees and shapely calves. They raised quizzing glasses to their eyes and tossed back the queues of their wigs as she wavered, but they dared not speak to her. Royal saw her old friend Lady Harriot, newly married and growing a prominent bump beneath her purple lute gown. Envy almost choked the breath from her.

All of a sudden, a mighty crash jarred her back into the room. Royal's fan flew to the floor as the music screeched to a halt. She looked up and saw the orchestra frozen, hands paused in mid-air. What was it? Before Royal could turn, a mass of white-powdered wigs, feathers and flowers blocked her view. The courtiers, hitherto so silent, buzzed like flies. Apprehension stole along Royal's flesh and she shivered.

'What is it?' her father's voice sliced through the hubbub. 'What has happened?'

His presence parted the courtiers like the Red Sea. A low whisper rippled through the room. Royal strained her neck, trying to see. Papa would make it right. Papa would solve any problem...

'Your Majesty!'

A figure lay prostrate, twitching against the hard stone

floor. Pearls and shimmering taffeta settled around it in a pool.

The bodies before Royal shifted; she made out another lady kneeling at the girl's head, dabbing away with scented water. The restorative had no effect.

'Dear God!'

The King plunged to his knees in time with Royal's heart. In that instant, she saw her.

The crumpled figure, falling into spasms on the castle floor, was painfully familiar. It was her sister Elizabeth.

⌁ *Lower Lodge, Windsor* ⌁

It was horrific. Charlotte sat perfectly still, concentrating on the pain shooting through her head.

Every migraine was crippling, but she welcomed this one – it overpowered her senses and swept away her thoughts. She didn't want to think tonight; her reflections appalled her.

First there were the spasms. Then, Elizabeth erupted in scrofulous abscesses. The doctors murmured about an inflammation of the lungs, but it meant nothing to Charlotte. Would Elizabeth live? That was all she wanted to know.

At the last count, Elizabeth had lost two and a half pints of blood, yet she was not purged of the sickness. Still the physicians opened fresh veins and blistered her sweet, soft skin. Charlotte could only beg God not to take her daughter, her best girl. Not Elizabeth. Any of them but Elizabeth.

The court buzzed with the old whispers that had flown about when Octavius had sickened, just as suddenly as Elizabeth. Gotha blood. A dark enemy, poisoning the veins, threatening to strike down her children at a moment's notice.

With her head throbbing, Charlotte tried to wind herself in and become the serene Queen she needed to be. Whatever happened, she would have to carry on. She could not fail her husband.

Her old friend and servant Madame Schwellenberg entered the room with a basin of warm elderflower water. She sat beside Charlotte and pried her hands from her face. In small, circular motions, she bathed her forehead and eyelids. The rash that ailed Charlotte in moments of stress had erupted all over her skin.

'Has the doctor been out?'

Madame Schwellenberg hushed her. 'Time for that later. You rest, now.'

A wooden rattle scratched on the door. Charlotte's eyelids sprang open and she rose to her feet, nearly knocking the basin from Madame Schwellenberg's hands.

'Enter,' she called, in a voice unlike her own.

A page opened the door for the King. George looked tired and anxious. Charlotte's stomach plunged at the sight of him. *No. No. She can't be dead.*

Caring nothing for Madame Schwellenberg, he threw his arms open and Charlotte flew into them. His solidarity was like a harbour in a storm. She could not look up — she only wanted to remain safe, buried in his chest. If she never came out from the lapels of his coat, they could never tell her the awful, awful news . . .

He caressed the back of her head, knocking her lace cap askew. 'She is safe,' he whispered, tears choking his voice. 'The doctor has told me she is out of danger.'

Charlotte's knees gave way but George's arms held her up. Tears spilled from her eyes, stinging her rash, and soaked into her husband's cravat.

'I thought we were going to lose her,' she sobbed. 'I thought — I thought it would happen again.'

'I know, my love. I know.'

She raised her face to his. 'I couldn't bear it, George, if we lost another child. I wouldn't survive it.'

His blue eyes filled with tears. 'Neither would I,' he admitted. 'Neither would I.'

CHAPTER FOUR

The White House, Kew
1788

Charlotte couldn't sleep for the infernal heat. Muggy air pressed against her body like the thoughts pressing on her mind.

She dozed on and off, feverish images running past her eyelids. Although Elizabeth had made a full recovery over the past three years, fresh worries sprang up to torment Charlotte.

The harvests would be ruined by this heatwave; she imagined desperate farmers wielding pitchforks, withered plants and black corn.

George groaned and turned over, shifting the mattress and snapping Charlotte awake. The covers swished and rustled. Suddenly there was a jerk, and the frame of the bed creaked like a thing in pain.

Charlotte rolled onto her side, her heart thudding. George thrashed beside her, clutching at his stomach. Immediately the curse of Gotha blood, the blood of her mother-in-law, flew into Charlotte's mind.

She sat up and put her arm around him. 'My love?'

He gasped and looked at her with pleading eyes. 'A pretty smart bilious attack. Feels like a spasm in my stomach.' He clenched his teeth.

The nightmares were still fresh in Charlotte's mind. She clung onto George, her fingertips digging into his shoulders.

'It's the dryness and the heat,' she said, more to reassure herself than him. 'Everybody is troubled with it.'

He writhed in the bed. 'I daresay you're right. But it hurts like the devil.'

Charlotte's bleary eyes groped in the darkness for a clock, wondering if it was too late to summon a physician. She could barely distinguish the hands in the gloom, but it looked about three in the morning.

'I fear I'll stop you sleeping,' said George. 'Why don't you go to the couch in the dressing room? I'd go myself, if I thought I could.'

As if she could abandon him! But it was like him to be ill and think of her first. A surge of sweet love flowed through her, so intense it almost hurt. Her hands gripped his nightshirt.

'I wouldn't leave you,' she said softly. She turned and put her feet on the carpet. 'I'll ring for Madame Schwellenberg. She can send for Baker. At the very least, he'll give you something to ease the pain.'

'I don't like to cause a fuss . . .'

Charlotte pressed a finger to his lips. She was taking no chances. 'I insist. You are precious. We cannot be too careful of you.'

George kissed her finger. 'I've always said it: you are a treasure, Charlotte. A treasure.'

But his kind words were cut short by a sudden howl of pain. Charlotte ran to the bell and jangled it until the lever broke.

∽ *Kew* ∼

Royal paced outside the cabinet. She heard the soft tones of the Queen rise and fall behind the door, but she could not make out the words.

Tension pulled sharply at her shoulders and her neck. The King's spasm had lasted from three o'clock in the morning to eight o'clock at night. Surely that was not normal? Royal pressed her ear against the door and Sir George Baker's voice rumbled back at her. She heard the word *gout*.

Just gout? Royal wanted to believe it, but doubt tugged in her mind.

A scrape of chairs warned her the physician was leaving. She scuttled down the hall and round the corner, nearly tripping on her skirts.

The short, thick-set figure of Sir George Baker appeared in the doorway. He walked backwards and bowed on the threshold before closing the door. Royal watched him retreat down the hall until, a few moments later, the Queen and her ladies drifted out of the cabinet.

Arranging her hair, Royal turned the corner and walked toward them, her head down. When she was level with her mother, she fell into a profound curtsey. She would humble herself – humiliate herself – for news of her dear father.

'Ah, Princess Royal! You may stand. I've just been speaking with Baker.'

Royal raised her eyebrows, her body still sunk on the floor. 'Indeed? What does he say about Papa?'

'He recommends the Cheltenham waters. We are to leave tomorrow at five.'

Royal leapt to her feet, concern blaring in her head like a horn. 'Tomorrow? Is the King fit for such a journey?'

'Oh, yes. He thinks it will do him a world of good. Lord Fauconberg has lent us his house, only a quarter of a mile from the wells.'

'Baker says it is safe to move him?' Royal asked doubtfully. 'Surely the movement of a carriage—'

The Queen tapped her with a folded fan and laughed. 'Calm down, my dear, the King will be well. He's in good spirits now and he wants to go.'

Royal was flabbergasted. How could her mother laugh at such a time? Unless . . . Something was not right. The Queen was too bright, too vivacious. She was hiding something.

'But—' Royal started.

'Look, here is a book for you.' The Queen thrust a small leather volume into her hands. 'I borrowed it from Miss Burney especially for you. I want you to read this. Stop worrying and concentrate on your studies instead.'

Royal nodded, disconsolate. Once again she was being treated like a child, kept out of adult secrets. Resentment burned within her.

'The King was exceedingly ill in 'sixty-five,' the Queen told Lady Harcourt. 'Worse than this, I think. He was so feverish, and had this shooting pain in his chest that gave him no peace by day or night. He recovered from that quickly enough. This will be nothing, you mark my words.'

The ladies-in-waiting responded with reassuring chatter and ushered the Queen down the corridor, recounting anecdotes of their own husbands' ailments. Royal's eyes followed the swishing trains of their gowns. Of course, none of them spoke about the husbands who had died. No one mentioned Lady Charlotte Finch's spouse, gripped by mania.

Royal leant her back against the wall, clenching her book in both hands. She realised she had no trust whatsoever in her mother's judgement. It was unbearable. She knew more than her mother: about people, about life – about everything. Yet she was subject to the Queen's will – a will she knew was misguided and wrong. Normally, she could swallow her pride, but where Papa was concerned? Impossible.

Royal opened the cover of her book and stared at the fly leaf. *The Present State of Music in Germany*. This was what the Queen gave to Royal – Royal, who hated music. She slammed the book closed with a snap.

⌢ Cheltenham ⌣

Charlotte lay in bed, refusing to open her eyes to the sunlight that danced upon their lids. She was unusually drained. The night had been nothing but six sleepless hours, worrying about the news from France. The printing presses there were frantically busy, running off pamphlets and treaties demanding a new constitution. And if the Paris coffee-houses buzzed with sedition, it wouldn't be long before London followed suit.

Outside, there would be crowds of people to wave at, important men to meet, and – most exhausting of all – the constant need to look cheerful. She genuinely didn't have the energy. Her body felt sapped, her brain sluggish. It was not just France she was worried about – there was George.

This was not the restful holiday he needed. The English people came to see their King in the fiercest torrents of rain and the cruellest glares of the sun, singing the national anthem with all their might. They came, but they didn't go away. When the family arrived at Bays Hill Lodge, they could hardly get inside the building for people pressing their noses up against the windows.

Inside the house, it was barely more comfortable. A cramped warren of rooms, living cheek by jowl with a skeleton staff. And to top it off, Royal was laid up with influenza.

'Your Majesty.'

Charlotte groaned, pulling herself up in bed. She opened her bleary eyes and paused. Something was wrong about the scene in front of her. For a moment she couldn't make it out. Then she realised: George was not beside her in bed. It was as if someone had thrown a pale of cold water over the sheets.

'Forgive me, Your Majesty.' Lady Weymouth stood before her, stark fear on her face. 'It's before your usual time – I would not presume to wake you, but the King ordered me. I could not refuse – he said I must fetch you immediately.'

A thump of panic drove off all Charlotte's sleepiness. She threw back the covers. 'Good God! What's happened?'

'I – I don't know, Your Majesty.'

Charlotte tried not to let Lady Weymouth see her apprehension. 'Very well. Tell the King I will be down immediately.'

Lady Weymouth dropped a relieved curtsey and shut the door.

Once Charlotte was alone, fear possessed her. Was he unwell? Was it Royal? She had seen influenza kill before. She ran to the basin and splashed water over her face.

With a shaky voice, she summoned Miss Burney and demanded to be dressed. The woman was maddeningly slow, fumbling with the hoop and her gloves. Charlotte did not wait for her to fasten the last button – she charged out the room, carrying her hat, strands of hair caught in her necklace.

She sped down the tiny staircase, holding her skirts up as high as she could, stumbling down every step. When she reached the bottom, she flew through the entrance hall toward the door and bumped straight into the equerry, General Garth.

'Oh, General, forgive me!'

Charlotte looked at his face and realised her pulse was right to hammer hard in her chest. Large bags sat under his eyes and crusts of sleep formed in the corners of them. He was pale, hastily dressed in his scarlet uniform, and he had not shaved.

'Your Majesty.'

Charlotte moistened her lips with her tongue. For a moment, she was too afraid to ask him questions. But she could not be cowardly – she could not flinch from this.

'You must tell me: what is the matter? Why has the King called me down so early? Where is he?'

Garth shifted awkwardly, his boots squeaking on the

floor. 'Don't worry, Your Majesty. The King is a little – flurried, is all.'

'Flurried?' she gasped. 'How so?'

'Well, he ran into the equerries' room at goodness knows what hour this morning and woke us all with a holler. We scrambled to get up and dressed, but before we could, he was off again. I ran and found him down by the riverbank – he was asking the people to huzzah for Worcester Bridge.'

They shared a long look. George had always been a little eccentric – it was one of the things Charlotte loved about him. But this felt different somehow – as uncomfortable as a full-throated fire on a midsummer's day. She frowned.

'I will go and see him – thank you, General.'

Charlotte didn't appreciate how early it was until she stepped through the door into chilly air. The sun, although strong, had barely passed the horizon and a ghost of the moon hovered in the sky.

George appeared at once, running. Thank God, he was safe and whole – but charging at her like a bull. Before she had time to speak, he seized her by the waist and carried her across the street.

For the first time, it did not feel natural and safe to be in George's arms. His muscles were taut, his skin unbearably hot. She stuttered a fearful laugh. 'My love? What are you doing out here? Why are the carriages all getting ready to leave – what has happened?'

George set her on her feet and smiled. 'We are going on a day trip!' he announced. 'Gloucester. Model jail. Inspect the hospital. Day trip to Gloucester.'

Charlotte nearly snorted in his face. Gloucester? Had he woken at the crack of dawn and terrified the whole household for a trip to Gloucester? She might have felt relief, but there was something unsettling about George. A fine mist of estrangement sat between them – he had the distant, occupied look of one in a fever.

'I would – yes, I'd like to go to Gloucester,' she said carefully. 'But is it not a little early? Do we need to leave right now? I didn't think Gloucester was so very far away . . . The children will not even be awake.'

'They *should* be awake!' he gestured with his arms – large, sweeping motions that scared the pigeons roosting on the roof behind him. 'They're missing a beautiful day. Wake them up! No idleness here! Wake them up!'

Charlotte was used to following and trusting George implicitly, but now she looked into his prominent eyes and felt uncertain. Was it really him talking, or was it the illness? His temperature was high and he was confused – he needed a bed and bleeding, not a trip to Gloucester. She took his arm gently within her own. 'My dear, remember what the doctor said. You must make sure you are careful and rest.'

He laughed and patted her on the head. 'Ah, such a good girl. Always so worried. I *am* resting. I would usually ride thirty miles in a day – this is a rest. A good rest.'

Charlotte hesitated. She was unaccustomed to saying *no* to him. But when she thought of dragging poor, snivelling Royal out of bed and putting the delirious King into a carriage, she knew in her heart that she could not go through with it. 'We'll go later. Rest awhile. There's no need to set out so early.'

George clapped his hands together in delight. 'Yes! Yes there is. We need to get back before Fred comes up from London.'

It was a lifeline. Fred. Of course! That explained so much. George was always wild with joy to see his favourite son. Charlotte sagged with relief. 'I did not realise he was joining us. I will look out a good hotel for him.'

'My dear, I've already seen to it. I've got wood and glass and all sorts of things, and the men are going to build a house on the grounds today.'

Charlotte's muscles solidified. She couldn't have heard right. 'I'm sorry – did you say build a house? On – on Lord Fauconberg's grounds?'

'Yes.'

She gaped at him. He had no more reason than a poor man doused with gin. She could not help one final remonstrance, one final appeal to his latent good sense. 'Will he not mind?'

George brought his face close to Charlotte's, as if he was going to kiss her. She shrank back.

'Mind?' Confusion was branded on his forehead. 'Of course not. Mind! We're building a house for Fred. What else would we do?'

He shot his wife a bemused glance, as if she was going completely mad.

CHAPTER FIVE

Upper Lodge, Windsor
Autumn 1788

Royal stared at her reflection in the dressing-table mirror. Perhaps if she looked hard enough, she would see her future written there.

There was so much she could do, so much she could become – if she was only given a chance. Her mother underestimated her – they all did. She was worth more than this. She knew she could be a great ruler in her own right. Not a slave, not a princess at the whim of her parents. She could reign and do it well. The knowledge sizzled inside her until it hurt. Marriage was the only way out. But beside her sisters, she was like a crow in a cage of canaries. She had hoped to grow into her looks by now, to suddenly become as dazzling as Augusta or Mary. But still there was no sign of a bloom in her face; she was born to be plain. Her friends were marrying, pledging their betrothals and giving birth to children. So far, Cheltenham had been the only exciting thing to happen to Royal, and she had caught the flu.

The weather was grey; a blank sky bearing down through the windows. With a great sigh, Royal waved off her ladies, straightened her necklace and adjusted her frizzed hair around the moulding cushion placed on her scalp. Her reflection lacked so much. The enormity of it was overwhelming. She shook her head dolefully at the square face, long nose and jaded eyes. It would have to do.

As she rose from her stool, there was a tap on the door. Lady Waldegrave opened it to reveal Miss Burney beaming.

'Happy birthday, Your Royal Highness. The Queen has sent me to bring you and Miss Gouldsworthy down – if you are ready?'

Royal painted on a smile. 'I am at the Queen's pleasure.'

The governess and the princess shared the same birthday, Saint Michael's day. Royal hoped ardently, as she met Miss Gouldsworthy on the landing, that they would not share the fate of spinsterhood.

They descended the stairs arm-in-arm, just as the Queen wanted. Everyone was gathered in the hallway, foremost among them the Queen, her face radiant as she clapped her slim hands together.

'So! Here are my two Michaelmas geese!' To Royal's astonishment, her mother wrapped her in a light embrace and brushed dry lips against her cheek. Such a careless show of affection in public was highly unusual. 'Come, come.

Your presents are all laid out in my morning room.' The Queen laughed feverishly, and with one dizzy movement, turned and swept down the corridor. Royal raised her eyebrows at her sister Augusta, who laughed and shrugged. The princesses fell into line, walking sedately in the wake of their mother. With the tact she had learnt from the cradle, Royal took Elizabeth's arm, moved her head close to her hair and whispered through the corner of her mouth.

'Why is Mama so merry?'

'She has not stopped all day. Early this morning she found out Mrs Siddons cannot come to read the comedy she promised you. She has been running about like a thing possessed, making alternative arrangements.'

'What is happening instead, then?'

Elizabeth pulled a face. 'You won't like it much. A concert. But you must try to seem grateful. She's made Fischer come down to play the oboe, and all the Windsor singers. She tried very hard.'

Royal groaned. 'The usual set up I expect – eight till midnight with only one tea interval?'

'I wish it was shorter. I think Papa needs to rest.'

'Papa?' Royal's whisper came out a pitch higher than she intended. All worry about the concert was obliterated instantly. 'Is he all right?'

'I trust so – I hope so,' Elizabeth said dubiously. 'He showed me this rash on his arm. Royal, it looks like it has been scoured – great red wheals breaking up through the skin – I never saw anything like it. I told him to take care, but you know what he's like. He's been out walking all morning in the damp grass. Mama is very worried. That's why she's so – well . . . you know.'

Royal nodded. This would not be a very happy birthday. She managed to conceal her worries as she opened presents – taking care to gasp and exclaim over each one. None of her family could buy her what her soul craved. She would give all the diamond rings and enamel watch-chains to be married and free. But for now there was only tea and cake.

The ladies of the family had just finished their refreshments when her father came into the room. With all his usual good humour, he threw his arms around Royal and hugged her close.

'Twenty-two years – eh? How did that happen? Can you believe it, my love – twenty-two?'

'Indeed I cannot,' said her mother. 'How soon they grow – and we grow – old!'

The King laughed and released Royal. She slunk back down in her chair. If so much time had passed, why had they not arranged a marriage for her?

'I'm not *too* old,' insisted the King, 'not so old that I cannot do a bit of farming, what? I've been hard at it all morning. Best to plant now for the spring. When I'm a little better and we get back to Kew, I'll have to make a start there too, what?'

Concern clouded the happy atmosphere of the room.

Cold needles pricked Royal's neck. She turned to the Queen, who looked uneasy, but only compressed her lips.

Elizabeth was brave enough to contradict him. 'If you do not rest, Papa,' she said, 'you shan't get better. Have you had breakfast? There is some tea left . . .' She stood to fetch it, but he dismissed her.

'Oh, I've had a biscuit. I'll have something else later. Can't stop now – I've come to take the Princess Royal for a drive on her birthday!'

Royal laid a hand on his arm. His skin burned through the layers of his shirt and jacket. 'Really Papa, I am in no hurry. Sit and have a drink. Or at least go and change your stockings. It looks damp out there.'

Now the King was close to Royal, she saw that the whites of his eyes were custard yellow. Light-red patches mottled his face and put her in mind of the rash Elizabeth had mentioned. He needed a doctor. Why did the Queen not say something?

'No, no, no,' he growled. 'Lots to do today. Must attend to business. Can't make your Mama late for her concert.'

The girls turned to their mother expectantly, knowing only she would be able to stop him. With the greatest composure, the Queen dabbed the sides of her mouth with a napkin and laid it back on the table in silence.

Royal nearly cried out in disbelief. Before she could speak, the King dragged her up and pulled her from the room. His grip bit into her arm.

'Come! Come!'

Royal looked desperately back over her shoulder at the Queen, unable to believe she would let her husband go out in this feverish state. She gave Royal a weak smile and took a pinch of snuff.

⤙ *The White House, Kew* ⤙

The time for pretence was over. Charlotte had endeavoured to block out the truth but it was a labour all in vain. George was not himself, whatever she told his ministers to the contrary. She had to acknowledge he was beyond even her reach – and the thought made her feel like a lost child.

He paced up and down in the candlelight, his bare feet slapping against the boards. Charlotte was in bed and ready to sleep, but he didn't notice her. He was a being of another world – an odd, ghostly figure in the dark room, one hand resting on his mouth and fiddling with his lips. Back and forth, back and forth, his nightshirt flapping at his knees. Stripped of his wig, boots and spangled jacket, he appeared frail and diminished.

Charlotte had seen him upset, distracted and angry before, but never quite like this. An icy fear inside her stomach forbade her from asking what was wrong. Paralysed by anxiety she could only sit, uselessly, her eyes following him around the room. What was happening to him? Without warning, he spun on his heel and marched toward her. He threw up the covers, sending a cold draft across Charlotte, and hit the bed hard, making her bounce.

He did not look at her. For once she was glad of it. 'I beg you will not speak to me,' he said, his voice muffled into the pillow. 'You must not speak to me. I've heard a dreadful rumour about George and a Catholic woman. But we cannot discuss that tonight. We must not talk of it, for if we do I will not sleep. I never sleep anymore – no, hardly one minute, and talking will only make it worse. No talking, no talking. Make sure you do not say a word. We will talk tomorrow – tomorrow. Now sleep.' With a violent jerk, he sat up and blew out the candle.

Charlotte remained immobile in the pitch black, trying to understand. She did not want to move. She knew it was ridiculous, but the prospect of settling down in bed and laying her head on the pillow beside George scared her. She had the premonition that if she closed her eyelids, if she fell asleep, something bad would happen. Something very, very bad …

A guttural, animal noise woke her. Charlotte thrashed her limbs, completely disorientated, until she sensed the pressure of a pillow against her cheek.

The cry came again, a horrendous blend of a gasp and a scream.

George.

Fully awake in an instant, she crawled up on her knees and turned to face her husband.

He sat beside her, bent double and clutching his stomach. As she leant toward him, she heard him rasp for breath.

'George?'

Pain ripped across his features. Just like her baby boys, as they drew their last gasps. Charlotte froze, staring at him, lost in the horror of the moment.

A sudden spasm shook the bed and George kicked out, screaming. She jumped down and stumbled wildly across the dark floor.

She hurled herself into the corridor and ran, a startled deer blinking in the harsh light. She fell into the pages' room, relieved to see five solid men in this frightful nightmare.

Help me.

George's page Stillingfleet stammered at her; a young man with sandy hair whom she did not recognise went red and cast his eyes down.

'Retire, for God's sake retire!' Murray said, and the others turned, retreating from the scandal of their undressed Queen and filtering out through the door.

No! No! Stop! Charlotte lunged to grab the sleeve of embarrassed young man. He didn't meet her frantic eyes. 'The King!' she shrieked. 'A surgeon! You must go for the surgeon – go to Richmond!'

Stillingfleet stopped in his tracks. His face grew pale. He whispered hurriedly to Murray, who nodded and sped through the door.

'Of course, Your Majesty, of course.' Stillingfleet returned to her side, gentle now. 'Will you not sit down?'

Charlotte could not loosen her grip on the boy's coat. As Stillingfleet gestured to a chair, clarity hit her like a bowl of water thrown over her face. It was night, it was cold, and she, the Queen of England, was standing in a servant's room wearing nothing but her nightdress. She crossed her arms over her chest. 'Yes,' she said, trying to sound more composed. 'Yes.' She sat on the very edge of the chair, leaning forward. Terror shook her limbs. *Gotha blood.* It had to be. The diseased blood of the King's mother had come to claim him. She stared at the intricate pattern on the carpet as something solid to hold her gaze. The coloured shapes swirled and merged. Time passed.

It was only when a shawl touched her goose-pimpled shoulders that she came back to life. She looked up to see Lady Courtown and Lady Townshend bending over her. She had not noticed them come in.

'The King . . .'

'Mr Dundas arrived about ten minutes ago,' Lady Courtown told her, fluffing the cushions behind her back. 'God knows it took him long enough. Can you imagine dawdling for half an hour before coming to the aid of your sovereign?'

Charlotte only absorbed a handful of words. 'He is here? What does he say?' She set her teeth against a dreadful diagnosis. Dear God, he could not die. What would become of her?

'The gout, probably,' said Lady Courtown with a sage nod. She took Charlotte's hand and chafed it. 'Cramps in the legs, shooting pains in his stomach. Dundas managed to get some senna into the King but nothing else. He won't swallow the strong stuff.'

Charlotte could not accept her ladies' brisk optimism – it stuck in her gullet.

'He is no better,' she said. It was a statement, not a question.

Lady Courtown sighed. 'No, Your Majesty.'

'Then you must fetch Frederick. Frederick will make him swallow the medicine. The King will do anything for him.'

'Sir George Baker is already on his way to—'

'No!' Charlotte yelled. Her companions flinched at her side. How could they be so calm, so foolish, when death stalked her husband? 'Do you not see it must be Frederick? You must get him. You must!' Her chest heaved, smothering her words, and tears cascaded down her taut face.

It was a sweet relief to cry at last. A moment – just a moment – to be a wife instead of a Queen. But she knew it would not last for long. With George indisposed, every duty would fall on her, no matter how her heart ached. She would need to sign papers, order servants, watch his doctors with a hawk's eye. She must not fail him now. She would not.

CHAPTER SIX

The White House, Kew
❧ *Winter 1788* ❧

Steam rose from the tea urn. Cold meats, cheese and bread sat on the table. Even the scent of them made Charlotte feel sick.

In the few days since George's fit, a swarm of doctors had descended on Kew, soberly dressed, leather bags in hand. It was abundantly clear to Charlotte that they did not know what they were talking about. The truth was, they had never seen anything like this illness. It was not colic, not gout, not fever – but it had symptoms of them all. And if the doctors did not know what it was, how could they cure it?

Madame Schwellenberg placed a cup of bone china before her. Charlotte screwed up her nose as another lady poured in dark, sharp-smelling tea. She didn't drink it, but sat, cradling the cup in her hands.

She was utterly lost. Without her husband to lean on,

the court felt like a stark, lonely place. It was all in her hands. She had decisions to make and she could only pray they were ones that George would approve of when he was well again.

Bumps sounded on the floorboards upstairs, followed by raised voices. Charlotte's ladies froze.

'He is insisting on going to Windsor,' she told them. 'He will not be put off.'

Lady Pembroke pursed her lips. 'It is difficult. He is the King. They cannot just tell him what to do.'

'They should. They should insist on him staying. He is not well enough for the journey.' Charlotte rubbed her itching eyes. She had pleaded with the doctors to keep him still. The suggestion could not seem to come from Charlotte – George would think she was undermining him – but he had to stay put. She dreaded to think of the reaction in London, when he was seen in this state.

'Have you heard from the princes?' Lady Courtown asked.

'My sons say they will meet us in Windsor. I wish they would come here instead. Frederick would persuade the King to stay put, I know it.'

'The Prince of Wales is coming too?'

Charlotte met Lady Courtown's troubled expression. They were all fearful of the meeting between father and son. On the best of days, the King found the Prince of Wales's presence irksome. His debts, his dabbling in foreign politics and his friendship with the radical, unkempt politician, Charles Fox, were all triggers to the King's temper. Would the sight of the prince bring on more spasms? She tightened her grip on her cup. 'Yes. I need the Prince of Wales by me.'

Where else should the heir to the throne be, except at his parents' side in a time of crisis? If the worst were to happen, and the King were to die . . . A tear ran down her cheek and dropped into her untouched tea.

What if the rumours were true? Gossipmongers said her beloved eldest son had married a Catholic widow. A papist called Mrs Fitzherbert could never be Queen. Young George would lose all claim to the throne with such a union.

The sound of feet pounding down the stairs startled her. She stood, sending her cup flying. It bounced off a plate, shattered, and clattered to the floor in jagged fragments. A brown tea stain trickled down the tablecloth and spread across the carpet. Shouts and screams tore down the hall. As Charlotte's pulse accelerated, she sped toward the door. She was about to put her weight on the handle when it swung outwards, knocking her off balance.

The King caught her and pushed her back into the room. 'I knew it! I knew you hadn't left me!'

What had happened to him? The transformation was sudden and complete. He wore nothing but stockings and a nightshirt, revealing peppered, blotchy skin. Reeking of mustard and body odour, he fell on his knees before Charlotte and clung to her legs. Before she could speak, doctors and equerries streamed into the room. They dragged the screaming King to his feet. Charlotte's ladies backed right up against the walls, crushing their gowns and curls. She was left alone in the melee of grappling men. As she watched them dive and swoop at her dishevelled husband, anger eclipsed her fear. 'Stop it! Stop it! Let him be. He is your King.'

Sir George Baker reached the threshold, panting. His fat face was scarlet as he straightened his wig. 'My apologies, Your Majesty. A fever took him and we couldn't control him.'

'*Control* him?' Charlotte cried. 'His Majesty does not need to be controlled like an animal!'

To prove her point, she turned and took a step toward George. Catching sight of her, he fell limp in the arms of his pages. What were they putting him through? She had a mind to dismiss them all instantly. As she edged forward, George hunched, like a cat raising its hackles. His eye gave no gleam of recognition – he was the quarry, awaiting its predator. Beads of sweat stood out on his mottled forehead. How could this be?

'There now,' she said. It was the tone she used to soothe her dogs. 'Your Majesty can sit and be calm. Can't you?'

In a heartbeat, George launched himself from the hands of his servants and grappled Charlotte to the floor. She screamed as her head knocked against the carpet. A hairpin stuck painfully into her scalp. Suddenly, George's lips were upon hers and his tongue forced its way into her mouth. It was a desperate, sickly kiss.

'They're trying to take you from me,' he whispered. 'They want to separate us.'

It was hard to breathe. Charlotte gulped in air but it didn't inflate her lungs. 'No!' she gasped. 'You are ill. They are keeping you in bed to recover.'

He clasped her hands; wrung them so hard it hurt. 'Don't believe it. They have sent the little ones away.'

'No, George. *I* sent the girls to Windsor. I didn't want them to worry about their Papa.'

Shock, and something like displeasure, flickered across his face. But in the next instant, the pages, Murray and Stillingfleet, hauled him from her. Her ladies moved in to put her on her feet and straighten her gown. She stood still as a doll and let them do it. Her thoughts were paralysed, smashed onto the floor with her pearls and headdress.

'Don't let them take me from you, Charlotte! Don't let them.'

Charlotte's heart lurched. He was as piteous as a child. A wave of tenderness brought her to life and she called out across the wall of people between them. 'You are safe, my love, you are safe! I will come and sit with you later.'

Sir George Baker gestured for Lady Pembroke to follow him to the door. He whispered something in her ear, and she replied with a nod. She was about to return to Charlotte when the King's sweating hand darted out and grabbed her. The force of the action whirled Lady Pembroke round. Her throat worked convulsively against a pearl necklace.

'Your Majesty?'

The King stared at her, mouth ajar. He breathed out in a wheezing hiss of air. 'My dear Lady Pembroke. I thought it was you.'

'Yes, Your Majesty.'

'You are well?'

Lady Pembroke looked at Charlotte for help. She had none to give. This man wasn't the husband she could read with a glance.

Lady Pembroke stuttered. 'Yes, I thank you, Your Majesty.'

'Good. Good. You are a good girl. I know you will look after the Queen.' He strained in the pages' arms and kissed Lady Pembroke's hand. His lips lingered over her trembling fingers for an instant. Charlotte watched him, unable to believe her eyes. Then he dropped Lady Pembroke's hand and let his pages sweep him from the room.

Windsor

Sophia, Mary and Amelia stood shivering on the drive in their capes, awaiting the King's carriage. Sophia stamped her feet to force blood back into her toes. No one would tell her anything. The tight-lipped silence of her governess, Miss Gouldsworthy, was frustrating and Sophia resented being kept in the dark. It was her own father, for God's sake – had she not some right to know?

Wasted leaves clung to the trees around her, ready to drop. Sophia felt equally suspended, waiting for the fall. She'd only received a few letters from her sisters, cautiously worded. They said the King had gout and went to the levee with his swollen legs wrapped in flannel. Sophia had no more information. She knew that mere gout would not cause the Queen to send her, Mary and Amelia away. She thought of the newspaper discarded in the housekeeper's room and wished she had stolen it.

Wheels rattled in the distance and, gradually, the chopping of hooves could be heard. Sophia held herself rigid, breathing in shallow puffs. They were coming. The carriage appeared and the gates peeled open with a metallic grate. The vehicle coming slowly up the drive looked more like a hearse. It drew to a halt in front of Sophia, throwing a shadow over her.

The King, the Queen, Royal, Augusta and Elizabeth sat crammed in together with no attendant. Sophia peered in through the curtains at the window, struggling with her short-sightedness. The minute she saw her father's face, she fell back with a cry. Swollen veins made a purple web of his skin. Only one cheek was clean shaven; a grey fuzz crept up the other. Her mother used all her strength to hold him back in his seat. In her ten years, Sophia had never seen her parents like this and it took the breath from her. It was a forbidden, obscene glimpse into an adult world she knew nothing about. She didn't want to see any more.

The footmen opened the carriage door and let down the steps with all their usual ceremony. The King broke free and half-hobbled, half-fell onto the pavement. Looking up at the terrifying, alien figure, Sophia, Mary and Amelia performed their curtseys with shaking legs.

'Papa?' Sophia took a step forward and put out a hand. It quivered but she kept it there, reaching toward him. Her real father must be in there somewhere. A gentle touch, a kind word, would revive him. It had to. But he stared at her with eyes warped from their usual blue to something like blackcurrant jelly. He opened his damp mouth as if to speak – and began gasping for breath. Sophia couldn't move. She couldn't take back her hand. Her heart threatened to break through her ribcage as she sensed this was very wrong . . .

Without warning the King burst into hysterical sobs and clutched at his body. He looked as if he was being attacked by a swarm of bees. Sophia stepped back, pulling Amelia with her. The Queen had been right to keep him away. He was dangerous.

He threw off his hat and gloves. Noticing the cane in his hand, he hurled it like a spear, forcing Miss Gouldsworthy to dive away, screaming. He paused for an instant. Then he ran. The tableau around Sophia leapt into life; her sisters jumped out of the carriage and scooped the younger girls into their arms. Sophia fell into Augusta's embrace. Her sister's soft touch was the only thing she could relate to. The world had changed in an instant. Without her parents' authority and self-control, there was no order – she was lost.

The Queen took off down the drive in the wake of her husband, pearls and jewels falling from her head as she ran. Sophia sobbed. For the poised, proper and elegant Queen to make this spectacle of herself, it must be the very end of the world. At last the Queen caught him, her determination and speed triumphing over his confused fears. Sophia saw her place a hand on each of the King's shoulders and draw his forehead to her own.

'It's all right,' she said. Her face belied the words. The King said something Sophia could not hear, but whatever it was, the Queen shook her head at it emphatically. 'We must bear up under all afflictions,' she told him. 'God will not test His servants beyond what they can bear.'

The stance of the King softened. Sophia dared to hope. Her mother would cure him. Her mother could do anything. 'Ah!' he replied sadly. 'My Charlotte. I see you are prepared for the worst.'

And he took the Queen in his arms.

✎ *Upper Lodge, Windsor* ✎

They could not keep him still. If he would remain in the Upper Lodge and submit to the purges, he might get better. But he was too strong for the doctors. Camphor julep did nothing to sedate him. If all else failed, they would have to tie him down. Charlotte covered her mouth to stifle a sob.

It had happened so quickly. One day she was obeying his orders, the next planning how to restrain him. *To restrain George.* The reality hadn't sunk in, but Charlotte thanked God for it. When the truth really hit, she knew it would crash her against the rocks. Determined to bring him back to the sickroom, she asked for her stout boots and a fur-lined pelisse. Her ladies received her delicate silk gloves, which she exchanged for woollen mittens.

'You cannot go alone,' said Lady Courtown.

Charlotte rubbed her thumb over the cross at her neck and raised it to her lips. 'I would not put any of you through such scenes.'

A hand rested on Charlotte's arm. She turned to face Lady Pembroke.

'Your Majesty, let me attend you. The King knows me of old. He will not be violent with me.'

Charlotte faltered. The idea of a friend by her side, a hand to steady her, was tempting. 'My dear, he is not . . . he is not like himself.'

She watched the lines deepen in Lady Pembroke's face; little claws around the eyes, stripes across her forehead. 'Your Majesty, you know what my husband was. A drunkard and a villain. I bore that. I can bear an ill King.'

On impulse, Charlotte kissed her cheek. 'Thank you. Thank you.'

Madame Schwellenberg placed a hat over Charlotte's hair and wound a calash around it, muttering in German. She'd noticed a white streak in Charlotte's hair a few days ago. It didn't matter. Charlotte had never quite been a beauty – and what good were looks without George to see them?

Charlotte and Lady Pembroke walked down the wide stone staircase, their heels clicking in unison and echoing through the hall. Tension held them mute. As the men in livery, standing either side of the double doors, threw them open, Charlotte bowed her head and pulled Lady Pembroke out into the bleak autumnal day. A light, persistent rain worked its way through her veil and under her sleeves. Her insides slithered like fish in her belly. What would she say to him?

Windsor smelt earthy and damp. Green, slick trees shed drips from the ends of their leaves like tears. Drops of water speckled the last of the dying flowers. The castle towered over them, grey and unchanging, blending into the leaden clouds above. Charlotte shuddered as they stepped across the threshold. She had never liked the castle. It wasn't like her lodge, with dimity curtains and allegories painted on the ceiling – it was musty and rank with the scent of wet stone and mouldering wood. There were no fine sconces and tapered candles here, only a soupy, half-light.

A draught blew them forward and Charlotte realised she was colder than she had been outside. George's voice drifted above the air whooshing through the corridors. They found him in one of the better apartments, which had been repaired for his music concerts. A dark, rectangular patch on the wall caught Charlotte's eye the minute they stepped into the room. Something was missing.

'My Zoffany,' she murmured. 'Why has he moved my Zoffany painting?'

A warm breath against her cheek. She jumped round to find George peering over her shoulder.

'I got rid of it. I hate it. I will put some real art there.'

Every syllable was a needle pricking her skin. His voice carried a venom she had never heard before. She fumbled for words. 'What . . . whatever you wish.'

Doctors lurked warily at the sides of the room. She noticed that one of the pages sported a black eye. George prowled around her. Her breath accelerated as fear burned through her chest. This was not her husband – it was some beast ready to pounce and tear her limb from limb. She froze, her eyes fixed on the spot where her painting used to be.

'My dear . . .' Instinctively, she turned her head to his softened voice – and saw him offer an arm to Lady Pembroke. Lady Pembroke had no choice but to take it. She tried to keep hold of Charlotte with her other arm, but the King was too strong and wrenched them apart. 'It is a treat to see you. How well you look today.'

Charlotte felt sick. It wasn't the words, but the expression on his face, that wounded her. She'd seen it before: glowing eyes, soft features. It was the look of ardent love he reserved only for Amelia.

'Your Majesty . . .'

He laid a hand over Lady Pembroke's mouth. 'Hush, hush.'

Lady Pembroke's bosom heaved beneath her fichu. She stood stone still as the King caressed her cheek, her hair. He let go just as the doctors moved toward him. But he kept looking at her with his heart in his eyes.

'Your M—Majesty,' Lady Pembroke stuttered. 'You are mistaken. I am not the Queen.'

His face twisted. 'No. But you should be.'

Charlotte's knees gave way. She put out her hands and caught herself just before her face hit the floor. 'George!' The name was wrung from her heart. 'George! I have come to fetch you back to the lodge. To your family.'

He shook his head at her as she scrambled on the ground. There was no concerned look, no loving arm to help her stand. 'No, no. Poor thing, you are mad and have been so these twenty years.'

'George . . .'

'You are not safe. I will not let you into my bed again until seventeen ninety-three.'

Through misty eyes she saw his face, as hard as flint. He didn't even know her.

Charlotte couldn't remember how she got back to the Upper Lodge. One minute, she was weeping at George's feet, the next, spread out on a daybed with a pounding headache. She stirred, putting a hand to her tender forehead. She tried to sit, but hands pushed her down. Madame Schwellenberg, Lady Holland and Lady Courtown appeared, leaning over her.

'The King . . .'

'They have sedated him,' Madame Schwellenberg told her in German. 'He is gentle as a lamb. They told him he made you faint and he wept at the thought of it.'

Charlotte didn't understand. For a moment in the castle she was sure, absolutely sure, that he hated her. She closed her eyelids and groaned. 'Where is Lady Pembroke?'

'In her room. She was very distressed.'

Charlotte saw it again: her husband, fawning over her friend. The image raked up all her misery and she opened her eyes, forcing her way into a sitting position. She had never been jealous before. The idea of George with another woman was so devastating, so unthinkable, she had hidden the fear of it in the back of her mind. But now it was here, in front of her, and she had no charms to win him back.

'Are my sons here yet?'

'They will be soon,' Lady Holland told her. She hesitated. 'They have been kept in town by . . . business.'

'What business?'

Lady Holland sat down beside her – a presumption Charlotte would usually take offence at, but she didn't have the energy to scold. 'Your Majesty . . . Surely you must see . . . If it should happen that the King is indisposed over a long period, there must be . . . arrangements. For the country.'

Charlotte hugged her knees to her chest. 'No,' she whispered. 'No, don't tell me the doctors have given up hope.'

'Of course not, Your Majesty. But they must prepare for every eventuality.'

'Treasonous talk,' Madame Schwellenberg huffed. She plumped a pillow behind Charlotte with particular gusto.

Lady Holland looked penitent. 'I'm sorry, Your Majesty. It may just be gossip. But I thought you deserved to know.'

Charlotte swallowed. 'What – what other gossip have you heard?' She watched Lady Holland's skin redden beneath its porcelain paint.

'I have heard that the Prince of Wales is very eager to do his duty. But nobody wants him to serve a Regency . . .'

'I should hope not!'

'. . . they want you.'

Everyone fell still. The logs ticked behind the fire-screen.

'Me?'

Lady Holland nodded. 'The people do not trust the Prince of Wales. They think he has married a Catholic.'

'Mrs Fitzherbert,' Charlotte murmured.

'I tell you before,' Madame Schwellenberg ventured to use her terrible English. 'Nobody like your son.'

Charlotte's head reeled. She couldn't even cope with running the household – with living – without her husband by her side. How did the people think she could manage a country?

'Do not worry.' Lady Courtown rubbed her back. 'It may not happen. The King is sure to recover.'

There was no conviction in her voice.

CHAPTER SEVEN

Upper Lodge, Windsor
∼ *Winter 1788* ∼

'You do not understand, George. Your father will not see a Whig doctor. Tell him to go away.' Charlotte ran beside her son as he strode down the corridor to the drawing-room. His step was long and confident; he walked as if he were King already.

'Warren is the best, Mama. Doesn't the King deserve the best doctor?'

Of course he did. But a staunch supporter of the opposition party was hardly likely to calm his nerves. Doubt and regret feasted on her. She had made a mistake. She should never have invited the prince. She thought her son would have the ability to forgive and forget the King's harsh fathering. But he was not here to comfort – he was here to serve his own agenda.

Her heel turned on its side as they rounded a corner at speed. She righted herself and hurried on. 'Why will you not stand still and talk to me?' she cried.

He pulled up abruptly. Charlotte nearly skidded into the back of his perfectly tailored coat. 'Mama.' The prince placed a finely manicured hand on hers. 'You invited me here. You said you couldn't manage all the business. I have come to help you, and all you tell me is that I'm doing it wrong.'

Charlotte looked into his florid face. For the first time in her life, she was truly ashamed of him. It was only too clear that the prospect of ruling excited him. His eyes sparkled as bright as the diamond pin in his cravat. It should not have shocked her, but it did. She should have known the long-baited prince would seize his chance for revenge. 'When the King recovers, he will judge all we have done,' she reminded him. 'I know your Whig friends help you, but they do not have your best interests at heart. They are all grasping for power.'

He scoffed. 'You know nothing of these things.'

Resentment stained her cheeks. 'I know the King will be furious to hear of Whig doctors and Whig politicians in his house.'

'Mama, when the Regency comes . . .'

'*If* it comes.'

'Oh Mama.' George lowered his head and put his hands beneath his coattails. 'You don't really believe he will recover, do you?'

The compassion in his voice was worse than the anger;

it told her there was no hope. She backed away from her son as if he had pulled a pistol on her. He was wrong. Of course her husband would recover. He had to.

'You can keep your politics.' Her words came out in a wet, furious whisper. 'But where the King's health is concerned, I hold the power.'

George shrugged. He looked at her with tender melancholy, like she was a thing to be humoured and pitied. 'I will tell Warren to report to you, when he's done.'

She forced what little dignity she had left into a stately nod. There could be no truth in his words. It was just wishful thinking, a longing for power.

Suddenly they heard heels skittering across the floor. They turned to see a cloud of blue satin flying toward them. Lady Pembroke's skirts were ripped and crumpled. Beneath the torn lace at her neck, branded on her throat, was a bright red hand mark. Letting out whooping sobs, she pushed past them and turned down another hall.

'Good God!' the prince stepped forward, a hand on his sword. 'Guards! Guards, Lady Pembroke is attacked!'

Charlotte slumped back against the wall. The world pulsed around her. With a colossal effort, she bit back the bile in her mouth. 'George, we don't need the guards.'

'What do you mean?'

He watched her. It took him a moment to hear the words behind her silence. 'You can't mean ... No. Not the King?' He hushed his voice but it was incredulous, harsh in her ears.

'Yes.' She tipped her head down, ashamed. 'Yes. Your father.'

⤚ *Upper Lodge, Windsor* ⤙

Royal wandered through the deserted hallways of Upper Lodge in search of her shattered mother. If past experience was anything to go by, she would find her locked up with mournful thoughts or hovering around the King's rooms like a tormented spirit.

They could not rely on the Queen any longer. The reins of control fell slack in her hands, now that the love of her life was entombed in an ill, confused man. Royal had compassion for her mother's misery – but she also blamed her. Now was not the time to drop beneath the arrows of misfortune; it was the time to fight. The Queen only added to her children's woe. Two ailing parents to care for: a King lost under a roiling fever and a Queen eclipsed by melancholy. Responsibility bore down heavily on Royal's shoulders.

Outside, rain fell thick and fast, lashing the trees. As a terrified little girl, Royal had run to her father for comfort whenever thunder cracked over the palaces. She could not lean on him now. This time, she had to face the storm alone.

Royal slowed her pace as she saw her mother's scrawny back. A blade of pity cut through her. The Queen had grown so thin that the bones of her spine stuck out. She hung around the corner, listening to the King scream. Why did she torture herself like this?

The physicians were blistering his scalp and legs with mustard, applying leeches to his forehead to draw out . . . whatever it was. This strange, unspeakable illness that tore the core from her world.

The Queen jumped when Royal placed a hand on her shoulder. 'Oh, Mama.' Suddenly she was nothing but a quivering girl. Fear and unshed tears sparkled in her enormous eyes. 'Don't listen,' Royal urged her. 'What good can it do?'

The Queen looked away and tightened her grip on the wall. 'I must be with him somehow. They won't let me in. They say – they say I am too emotional, and I upset the King.'

A low noise swooped down the hallway – eerie, chilling to the blood. It took Royal a moment to realise it was her father, howling like a dog. The sound struck her motionless.

'He keeps slapping the pages,' the Queen whispered, 'then he begs them for forgiveness a hundred times.'

Royal shook the image from her mind. She couldn't let her mother drown her in a pool of horror. 'It's painful, being blistered,' she explained. 'The shock would make anyone lash out.' She laid an arm around her mother's shoulders. 'You wouldn't really want to be in there, watching him in pain, would you?'

The Queen stared into her face, all guards down. Her features contorted as emotions chased across them. She was still for a moment, letting Royal see it. Then she burst into tears. A freezing torrent ran across Royal's skin. Her mother never cried. The sight of a weeping queen sliced through the last mooring holding Royal to the shore of normality; she was speechless.

'Oh, Royal!' With a sudden, irritated motion, the Queen drew out a handkerchief and mopped up the traces of her tears. 'How nervous I am! I am quite a fool! Do you not think so?'

Royal thought she was like a wilted rose trodden on the ground; she thought her opinion had always been the King's opinion and she didn't know what to do now his judgement was clouded.

A scream rang out and they winced. A voice called after it, as ghostly as tree branches groaning in a high wind. 'Oh Amelia, little Amelia! Why won't you save your father?'

'He always asks for Amelia,' breathed the Queen. 'Never for me. It's always Amelia.' The corners of her mouth twitched down. Every word, every noise from the King drained more colour and life from her.

'Go and sit with Miss Gouldsworthy,' Royal suggested. 'Papa has said he will take me for a drive later. I'm sure that will do him some good.'

The Queen wrung her hands. 'He is too ill. A drive indeed! Madness!' She heaved a shuddering sigh. 'But how can we stop him? You must be very careful. And come to me at once, as soon as you are out of the carriage.'

'Of course I will.' Royal reached for her mother's hand and kissed it. Her palm was cold and light like a breeze passing through the castle.

Royal could not bear to stay with the shell of her mother a moment longer. She turned on her heel and strode away, kicking out her skirts. The mingled sobs of her mother and her father throbbed against her ears.

'I am not ill. I'm nervous. If you want to know what is the matter with me, I am nervous.'

Royal shied back against the upholstery of the carriage, dodging a spray of spittle from the King's lips. Cushioned doors barred all escape and brocade curtains half-shielded her from the outside world. She was hemmed in with him – and alone.

Compassion and fear fought for dominance within her. Her handsome, kind Papa – reduced to this. Hunched in his seat, still crippled by the doctor's blistering and bleeding. Fierce red skin crept around the edges of his wig. He infused the carriage with the vapours of his sickroom; hot, sticky scents of calomel and turpentine.

Tears pricked Royal's eyes as she admitted the bitter truth: he must be dying. Every day he slipped further away, dropped another inch from the pedestal she had kept him on. The realisation threatened to undo her but she couldn't give way. She took his swollen hand. 'You have been very nervous and suffered many painful treatments today. Do you think you are well enough for a drive? Or had you better rest?' She gestured out of the window at the miserable November landscape.

He shook his head vehemently. His wig slid to one side of his scalp, revealing bulbous, peeling blisters. 'No, no, no, a drive is just the thing.' He raised his voice and hammered his cane against the ceiling. 'Go on there, you! Twice round and keep it slow for the princess.'

It was not a voice Royal recognised; his words were so rapid that she wondered how he drew breath. Instinct urged her to revoke his command – stop the drivers at once and get him back to bed. But then there was a jerk beneath her and the carriage set off at a lively trot.

'You mustn't worry about me,' the King said. 'The Queen is my physician and no man needs a better.'

Unable to reply, she concentrated on the trees gliding past her window, holding tightly onto the leather strap. The moments passed in silence.

'Do you suppose we'll pass by Lady Pembroke's house?'

The change of subject disorientated her. She cleared her dry throat and sought for words. 'I thought her house was at Richmond?'

'Yes, yes, I forgot. Lovely lady, Eliza Pembroke. You should've seen her at court in my youth! A queen of hearts, that's what we called her. For God's sake, what's wrong with these coachmen?' Another hammer at the ceiling. 'Speed up there you! Don't dilly dally!'

The carriage lurched forward. Royal clenched the strap, racking her brain for a normal, grounding subject – something to bring him back to the here and now. 'Will Fred and George join us for dinner?'

He looked at her as if he understood, but his reply was at a complete variance. 'I know, I know you want to travel. What are you now, twenty-two? Ah, it comes around so fast. I have been lax in getting you a husband. I know you want a husband, but I haven't been able to part with you and that is the truth. My poor sisters! I wish I'd never married them off! But enough, enough – you must have a husband, of course you must. You, me, the Queen and Augusta, we'll go to Hanover this summer and make our court gay. I will invite all the German princes – all of them! And you may have whichever you like best. How's that for you?'

Royal had the sensation of being outside her body, looking on at the scene. She had waited so long for her parents to plan her marriage, but now the prospect didn't make her happy. 'It would be . . . wonderful. But we mustn't think of it until you are better.'

He pulled his hand from Royal's and stuck his head out of the window. 'I didn't tell you to go this way! What is the matter with you today? Stop, stop!'

The horses pulled up sharply, sliding Royal forward on her seat. For an instant, she took her attention off the King.

A bolt slid and a blast of cool wind whipped across her

face. She looked up to see the door swinging open and her father gone. *Oh God, no!* She leapt up and flew after him, hopping as she landed with one foot tangled in her skirts. 'Papa!'

His blue Windsor coat retreated into the distance as he hobbled across the grass. She felt sick with horror.

'Papa!' she screeched.

He slowed at the sound of her voice. Royal tottered forward a few more steps, everything in her willing him to stop.

'Papa?'

He halted; a thin, shrivelled silhouette against the darkening sky. For a moment he stood still, staring out across the park. Then he dropped his shoulders, let out a breath and trudged back. Relief washed Royal's tension away, weakening her limbs. She struggled to remain upright. He returned, flushed from running, dragging in breath. Mud and grass stains splattered up his stockings.

'I thought I saw . . .' He closed his eyes and massaged the bridge of his nose. 'There is this floating mist before my eyes, you know? I worry I'm going blind.' His wig hung on his ear and several strands of it had come loose from the ribbon tie. This was the father Royal had idolised. This was the man all England had to rely upon. Gently, she put an arm around his shoulders and guided him toward the carriage. 'Come on Papa. Let's go home.'

*

The gong boomed. Royal's nerves vibrated to the deep, metallic sound. She needed to give the Queen an account of the outing before she went up to dress for dinner, but she didn't know if she could face her. How could she speak truthfully without breaking what was left of her mother's heart? It was painfully complex, like performing a step in a cotillion – and Royal had never been a good dancer.

The Queen sat in her closet, huddled together with Miss Burney. Her fingers worried at the embroidery on her chair. 'How was he?' she asked at once. Her hungry eyes searched Royal's face. 'None of that . . . unpleasantness we had on the way from Kew?'

Royal longed to unburden herself and confess what she had been through. She wanted to kneel at the Queen's feet, throw her head into her lap and sob. But she saw her mother's haunted face and the way her hands trembled and realised she could never tell the truth.

'He's . . . lively.' She heard how false and hollow the words sounded on her lips. 'The blisters do not seem to have hurt him. He is still a little – confused. But he is looking forward to the future. He talks of going to Hanover in the summer.'

Royal feared the Queen would spot her lies with those sharp, boring eyes. But she straightened in her chair and looked pleased.

'Hanover? He often promised to take me there and then travel up to see my family.'

'That is probably why he thought of it.' Although it was

cruel, although it was false, Royal yearned to give her mother some comfort. 'He wants to thank you. He is full of praise for you and your care of him.' Royal's mouth tingled at the dishonesty.

The Queen narrowed her eyes and bit her lip. 'Did he . . . did he talk to you of Lady Pembroke?'

Royal shuddered; she could almost taste the Queen's bitterness. 'A little. Something about her house at Richmond.'

All the light in her mother's face blinked out. Her expression soured. 'I see. Well. You had better go and dress for dinner.'

The clock ticked on the marble mantelpiece as they waited for the King without saying a word. He had never been late for a meal before in his life. Royal sat opposite George and next to Frederick. She focused on the plate before her, tracing its markings over and over again to hold her mind steady.

'The King!'

They stood as one body. The sound of chair legs scraping across flagstones made Royal wince.

He came in leaning on a stick, clicking across the floor. The eyes within his purple face were inflamed and bloodshot. Royal's heart lurched. She yearned to look away from the pitiful sight, but her eyes were like trained dogs, following him around the room. He limped straight over to Prince George and – astonishingly –embraced him.

'You have made me so happy in coming to see me. I

knew you had a heart. I always said you did. You've been a vexatious son, I won't pretend otherwise. But I love you and I forgive you. Dear boy. Dear, dear boy.'

George gaped at him. 'I love you too, Papa. How are you today?'

The King kicked his feet together. 'They would make me believe I have the gout. But if it was gout, how could I kick the part without any pain? You see me all at once, my boy, an old man.'

'Surely not, Papa,' George said smoothly. Royal felt a surge of grateful love toward her brother, the consummate performer, full of easy charm. 'Science improves every day. Do none of your treatments help?'

'Mmm, perhaps, perhaps.' The King's attention wandered and he ambled away from his chair at the head of the table. It took him some time to realise he was going in the wrong direction. With painful slowness, he halted beside the Queen, looped round her, and started down the other side of the table. Royal's side.

Her every sense stretched to hear the tick of his walking cane, the wet rasp of his breath. He passed behind her like a cold draught. The crucial moment came – and went. He was near the head of the table, she had escaped his notice. She let out her breath between pursed lips.

But then, catching sight of Frederick, the King made a sudden dive and threw his arms about his favourite son. Royal jumped and knocked her soup bowl against a glass.

'Yes, Frederick is my friend! Oh, my boy!' he croaked.

He hid his head upon the prince's shoulder and wept bitterly. Stiff and awkward, Fred put his arms around the King, looking alternately to George and Royal for help they could not give.

'There, there, Papa. There's no reason to cry!'

The King raised a wet face to Fred's ear. In a voice so low Royal could just make it out, he said, 'I wish to God I may die, for I am going to be mad.'

The ground tilted beneath Royal. She put out a hand to steady herself against the table as black spots skipped across her vision and threatened to take over. She should have known Papa would have the courage to say the forbidden words; put a name to the fears that leapt and danced inside each one of them. But to hear it out loud, at last, sapped every hope from her breast.

With difficulty, Fred coerced the King into his chair. 'Have a bit of roast beef. That'll set you up for anything. A bit of barley water too – you'll feel a new man.'

The King sat down, looking wary. 'I've always been prone to fatness. Like George.'

'You're thin enough at the moment, Papa, that you could eat a whole cattle herd with no ill effect. It will give you strength.' Fred nodded encouragement and returned to his place.

The farce of a family dinner began. The soup came out, cold and skinned. Royal pushed it around her bowl, trying to ignore the ceaseless flow of her father's words. He spoke until he was out of breath, took another gasp and began again. There was no sense or meaning in it; his voice was a dull babble, pierced only by the scrape of knives and forks against china. The old, caged feeling pressed around Royal. She set her teeth against the welling panic and drank deeply from her wine glass. She wanted her head to swim on the oblivious seas of alcohol, but it didn't happen, no matter how many sips she took.

Her brothers kept up a show of conversation – whether it had any pertinence to what the King said, they could not possibly know. George turned the topic to the morning papers. A ghoulish Old Bailey trial had caught his attention: a mother accused of smothering her own child. Royal felt queasy. Didn't they have enough horror around them without invoking the spirits of dead infants?

'Well, I don't care what this Garrow says,' George told Fred. 'If she murdered her baby, she should hang for it.' Without warning, the King leapt to his feet. Royal's head snapped up at the sudden clatter of plates. Augusta dropped her cutlery. Quick as a bullet, the King flew to George's side. The prince widened his eyes and leant back in his chair, away from the steady, menacing gaze. He stuttered words, but the King didn't stop to listen; he seized his eldest son by the beautiful lapels of his coat and flung him across the room like a rag doll. There was a nauseating crack as George's head collided with the wall. As he slumped to the floor, a mirror fell and shattered over him. The Queen screamed.

Everyone swarmed away from the table but Royal could only watch, pinned to her chair in disbelief. Augusta and Elizabeth dashed over to George, propped his head in their laps and dabbed his bruised temples with Hungary water. The Queen stood, shoving her chair to the floor with a bang. Her wide mouth hung open, her lips as pale as ivory. Royal understood the look on that raw, broken face. The worst was done. Some thread in her parents' marriage had been irrevocably snapped by this violent assault on their eldest child. Her family was shattered, like the shards of glass littering the floor.

The Queen hovered a moment, looking from her son to her husband. She lurched, and Royal thought she would faint, but instead she picked up her skirts and dashed from the room. As soon as his wife fled, the King gave chase. With a cry, Frederick darted after him. Only Royal sat at the dinner table, viewing the devastation.

Nothing would be the same again: this was the one clear thought in her churning mind. Everything had changed the instant George hit the ground. Restraining her tears, she plucked the napkin off her lap and threw it on her plate. Much as she wanted to scream, sob and grieve, there was no time. The Queen needed her. Slowly, she pulled herself up. Her legs wobbled beneath her. George still howled inconsolably, but her sisters would take care of him. The Queen would be all alone.

Royal took a few tentative steps, heaved in a deep, steadying breath and forced her legs to propel her. She ran, half-tumbling down the stone passages, falling helplessly on after the commotion that rang out through the halls. Nothing looked familiar – low light-distorted shapes and shadows crept across the walls. Reaching a fork, Royal turned on instinct and came up against a group of people crowding outside the Queen's dressing room.

The first person she saw was her mother's Keeper of the Robes, Madame Schwellenberg, hands planted on her immense hips. She was a formidable woman who barely flinched as she blocked the raving King from passing her again and again.

'I tell you once, the Queen ill. She see no one,' Madame Schwellenberg barked in her terrible English.

The King howled and slumped into Frederick's arms. 'Oh Fred, they said the King was ill. He was not ill. But now the Queen is ill, he is ill too!'

'Don't fret Papa. She'll get better.'

It grew dark. The castle fell into a grey gloom as Royal remained motionless, unable to draw her eyes from the shadowy figures in front of her. If only she knew how to help. She ached for Fred, who bore the terrible responsibility of being the King's favourite. What could he do with this person who was no longer the father he knew?

Madame Schwellenberg lowered her arms, watching the King weep into his son's coat.

'They will not take her from me!' Suddenly shoving against Fred's chest, the King freed himself and pushed past Madame Schwellenberg.

They flew after him.

The whole convoy burst into the Queen's darkened room. Shapes moved in the dusk: the Queen, snivelling with her face in the pillow, Royal's lady-in-waiting, Elizabeth Waldegrave, and the governess, Miss Gouldsworthy. There was a hiss and a flare of light as the King lit a candle from the dying embers of the fire and marched toward the bed. He thrust the flame forward and Royal gasped. If his hand trembled, he would set her mother's hair alight. Gingerly, the Queen lifted her red and blotchy face from the pillow. Her jagged breath made the candle flame waver. She eyed the King like an animal in a trap.

He squinted, waving his candle. 'Is this the Queen, Miss Gouldsworthy?'

'Y – yes, Your Majesty.'

'Then I must take care of her myself.'

He threw the candle aside – Royal jumped, but as it fell to the ground, a rush of air extinguished the flame. The King leant forward and lifted the Queen into his arms like a child. She didn't struggle – she seemed more dead than alive. Incredibly, the King, who needed a stick to walk with only an hour before, left the room with a steady step, carrying his wife.

CHAPTER EIGHT

Upper Lodge, Windsor
Winter 1788

Charlotte would not move; she would never move from this bed. Terror could not penetrate through her warm sheets.

Her pillow was wet with tears, but it didn't stop her entering the precious oblivion of sleep. She didn't dream; there was only the relief of a great, black void.

In the insufferable minutes she spent awake, she heard him. Not George – that man was not her George. His words appalled her. He thought London was under water, that his pillow was Charlotte's poor dead baby Octavius. The heavy curtains tied round her bed and two doors separating them didn't hush the noise.

Once, in the still of the night, she heard rattling and his pathetic cry.

'Surely one door is enough to stop me? We have been

married twenty-eight years and never separated a day. Now you abandon me.'

It was a lie: she had not been married to that man for twenty-eight years. She didn't know this stranger who howled at the moon and tried to jump from windows. She wanted her real husband back.

Charlotte's thoughts flew out of the dreary November skies, back to the muggy summer evening of her marriage. She saw herself suffocating in bridal finery; velvet, ermine and gold. The bridesmaids were prettier, all white silk encrusted with jewels, but George didn't spare a look for them. He had kept his eyes firmly upon his new queen and promised to love her for all of his life with his hand on his heart.

Bumps came from the hall. Charlotte raised the pillow and buried her head beneath its soft warmth. The cold, sharp world outside was pressing in on her, trying to enter her sanctuary. She heard the doctors in her dressing room and the whispering pages lining the corridors. They couldn't help her; the only person who could console her for the loss of the King was the King himself.

Even her eldest son George was no comfort now; after the attack his concern had evaporated, leaving only a shard of cruelty. He summoned his own doctors, his Whig friends whom the King despised, and mocked his father in public, sure of his imminent accession.

They were all waiting for her husband to die. Every

courtier jumped from the sinking ship of George III and climbing aboard the gaudy new conveyance of George IV – even his favourite son, Frederick. After all he had done for them! She wouldn't think of it. She wouldn't surface into that unbearable world. As long as she remained in bed with her eyes closed, she was safe.

Except her shelter wouldn't remain secure for long. Soon, the prince would move them all to Kew, to freeze the winter away in a summer palace.

Hot shame spread through Charlotte. They had to hide the King. They had to conceal the terrible possibility that he was going – that he *was* – mad.

∽ *The White House, Kew* ∼

Sophia had never understood before when old people said they felt damp chills in their bones, but since coming to Kew she'd experienced it first-hand – an icy knife that passed right through her as if she was a strip of gauzy material.

The tremors of her body propelled her down the hall. Sandbags sat propped against the windows, but they didn't keep out the cold. The windows trembled in their frames. There were no carpets or thick curtains to retain heat. All comfort was gone – emotional and physical. Wind whistled and creaked through another part of the palace. How quickly it had all fallen away – peace of mind, smiles, sunshine, a family. At the age of eleven, all was lost. What would become of her now?

'We won't see Papa, will we?' she asked Mary. 'I don't think I could bear to see him.'

'The idea is for *him* to see *us*. I think they will try to keep him away from the windows as much as possible. In case . . .'

Sophia looked at her feet and willed the warm teardrops to stay in her eyes. If she was weak and cried, the Queen would be angry.

Royal, Augusta and Elizabeth met them on the landing. Mary pounced on them with questions. 'What's happening upstairs?'

Royal and Augusta exchanged a knowing look. Sophia bristled with frustration – they were her parents too. She had a right to know.

'Mama is upset,' Augusta told her. 'She was distressed that Dr Willis had to come.'

'But why? Surely he will make him better.'

Another pained pause. 'Dr Willis is a – *special* – doctor. He has his own – *facility* – in Lincoln.'

Mary looked at Augusta blankly.

'He's a mad doctor. He comes from an asylum,' Elizabeth said.

Despite Sophia's best efforts, a tear escaped and splattered on her satin shoe. Maybe they would take Papa away. Maybe she would never get a chance to hug him again.

They walked together, down the halls and out the doors,

with slow, measured steps. The purblind sun struggled between clouds and cast a sickly light on the landscape. It was silent; no children chased hoops with sticks along the paths, no boats raced on the river, no cows lowed on the green.

Suddenly a cry rent the air – something between a howl and a screech. The girls froze.

'It couldn't be . . .' Augusta started.

Royal looked off into the distance. A breeze stirred the short curls at the back of her neck. 'An animal in the menagerie,' she said.

For once Sophia was thankful to be short, hidden behind the poufs and false hair on her sisters' heads. Tension made it difficult to breathe or even see straight as she walked on, trees flashing around her. She didn't know where she was until her nose caught the scent of damp grass. They had reached the garden – they were approaching the house. Somewhere, behind the expressionless stucco walls and darkened windows, lurked her father. Sophia held herself rigid, fearful one movement in the wrong direction would make him worse, not better. Mary gasped beside her but Sophia didn't look up; she kept her eyes trained on the muddy hem of her gown. She heard a bang.

'Who is that?' Amelia squealed.

Sophia stared down resolutely, ignoring the snatched breaths and suppressed moans that beat against her eardrums. Everything was hazy, blurred . . .

'For God's sake catch Sophy, she's going to faint.'

Images spun as Augusta swept Sophia into her arms. She hadn't passed out, but she was too weak to stand.

'We can't stay.' Augusta said. 'Go back, go back.'

Augusta's body shifted beneath Sophia in retreat. Overcome with relief, she looked up. Splintered pictures slotted together. Her vision cleared, like fog rolling off the hills. She choked on a scream.

Pressed against the glass was a haggard old man wearing a dirty nightgown and cap. Foam swam in his long beard. He banged at the window, gesticulating wildly.

Hands grasped the old man's arms and hauled him, screaming, out of sight. The curtains flapped wildly, and then settled into a gentle wave.

CHAPTER NINE

Kew

～ 1789 ～

The deputation from the House of Lords and the House of Commons had finally departed, leaving Charlotte in a darkened room with three dogs and the low hum of her own misery.

She tried to digest what they'd told her about the trusts conferred by Parliament. The detail made her head swim. Her ladies were right: the people looked to her. They did not want the Prince of Wales in charge if there was to be a Regency. How could she explain she was utterly incapable? Without George's love, she was like a cutting in the greenhouse: deprived of nutrients, shrivelling up and rotting. She wanted to curl up and cease to exist. She put a cool hand to her sore eyes, swollen from hours of tears. She must look a fright. Even her auburn hair had dribbled out its colour, leaving only a blank, stark white.

She sent for hourly reports on the King, but hope was

drying out. Deep down, she knew he would not recover. She had never felt so alone, not even when she first came to England speaking a different language. Now her last hope, her eldest son, had abandoned her. He avoided her room, knowing full well she deplored his plan to pass a Regency Bill. His betrayal blistered.

Charlotte doubted her son would give her the respect due to a Dowager Queen when he stole the throne; he was suspicious of her, jealous of her popularity with the people. He no longer kissed her hand when he retired for the night and he had stolen precious jewels from her keeping, the diamonds the King wore in his hat – relics of happier days – calling her a *damned magpie*. He would probably throw her down and put that Mrs Fitzherbert, the Catholic everyone said he had married, into her place. Unloved. Bereft of both her Georges. How could she tolerate a life like this?

Footsteps pattered outside the door. Charlotte inhaled; it would be the page, reporting back from Dr Willis.

'Enter.'

The door creaked open, admitting an agonising shaft of light as Stillingfleet shuffled into the room.

'You are late. Did you give the King the grapes I sent him?'

Stillingfleet held up the bunch sheepishly. Dismay settled round Charlotte like a dark cloak.

'He would not take them?'

'No, Your Majesty.'

'Why not? What did he say?' She steeled herself for another blow.

'Just ravings, madam.'

'Ravings about me. I will hear them.'

He coughed awkwardly. 'He did not mean a word, Your Majesty.'

'Then it can do me no harm to listen to them.'

He hesitated. 'He asked – he asked if the grapes were from Lady Elizabeth Pembroke.'

Barbs of jealousy pierced Charlotte's heart. She struggled to keep the venom from her voice. 'I see. And when he heard they were not, he sent them away again?'

'Yes, Your Majesty.'

It was bad, but no worse than she expected. 'What else?'

'The King said he would be much obliged to Your Majesty if you would send the dog Badine to him. He has a fancy to tie a blue ribbon about her neck.'

Charlotte's little spaniel twitched her ears at the sound of her name. Badine and the Pomeranians were Charlotte's last comforts; she would not part with them.

'Why? I sent his own spaniel, Flora, to him last week.'

He cringed. So there *was* something else. She would know of it. Now Charlotte had felt pain, she wanted it in a torrent. She had a frightful compulsion to hear all the abuse her once loving husband hurled her way. 'You do me no service by concealing things. I will dismiss you if you do not tell me what the king said this instant.'

'He said . . . he said that Badine was very fond of him and that she . . . well, that she didn't like you. Which, of course, Your Majesty, is nonsense . . .'

'Of course. What else?'

'I hardly know how to tell you, Your Majesty – but you must remember, he is talking gibberish.'

'Still, I will hear the nature of it.'

'The King – the King said that indeed, he did not – he did not like you himself. He said you had a . . . bad temper, and that the children are . . . are afraid of you.'

Good God. Charlotte hadn't realised pain could be so exquisite, so severe. This, from her husband! From the one for whom she had given up, sacrificed, smothered everything!

'I see,' she said stiffly. 'That will be all then. Get someone to bring me the daily report. Those idiots Warren and Baker send everything to the Prince of Wales.'

'Yes, Your Majesty.'

He retreated, scraping from the room. The moment the door shut, Charlotte slumped to the floor and hid her face in Badine's fur.

CHAPTER TEN

Kew
1789

Royal, Augusta and Elizabeth walked arm-in-arm across the gravel, bleak wind dishevelling their hair. The harsh winter had melted into a dull new year. Most of the trees were still bare and twig-like. Here and there, a few evergreens peeked out. The snow had melted to a thick sludge that stained the princesses' slippers as they stole toward the White House.

Once more, Royal saw that terrible window where the demented King had banged and gestured to her. Today it was empty; white curtains hung demurely either side. There was no trace that the nightmare had ever happened. Could she believe what the doctors told her? Had Dr Willis performed a miracle?

They slipped inside and climbed the stairs. Royal held the bannister with a wet, slippery palm. Everything in the palace looked exactly as she remembered it. For some reason, her imagination had transformed it into a scene of horror. At last they arrived at the door to his room. Only a few planks of wood separated them from the King. But which King? The frenzied patient, fit for Bedlam, or their father? Royal balled her hands into fists, preparing for disappointment.

As the door glided open along the carpet, Royal had an absurd impulse to close her eyes. But all was tranquil within. Her fingers unclenched. The room was a large, bright square, plainly decorated in peach with white mouldings. A fire sizzled and Royal noticed with approval that the pokers and other implements were not kept out beside it. There were no ornaments or pictures to catch the eye, not even a looking glass. The furniture consisted only of chairs and tables, flanking the walls of the room.

In the far corner lurked a large seat with bulky fastenings on the arms and legs; it glowered at Royal, casting a high shadow on the wall. This must be it: the chair where they restrained him. The sight of it burned her eyes and she snapped her face away.

There he was. Her heart turned over.

The King slouched at a table patched with sunlight. He stooped over a pack of cards, laying them down in neat rows. He had an aura of tranquillity that took Royal's breath from her lungs. Hope bustled forward, pushing against all restraints. Dare she creep closer and steal a look at his face?

'Your Royal Highnesses.' Royal jumped and saw a grave-looking man, dressed in black and white like a parson. 'I am Dr Willis,' he said. 'Will you allow me to take you to the King?'

So this was the man; the doctor who had done so much. Royal understood why her Papa feared him. He had a dampening presence, an air of complete control. As witness to a world of madness, he exuded a dreadful calm.

Royal nodded, unable to speak without letting out a stammer. Dr Willis escorted them across the room, his stride masterful and strong beside their fearful, mincing steps. The King looked up from his cards when they approached. The light fell full upon his face. Flesh had dropped off him in great swags. He was drawn like an old man, with seamed cheeks and lines bracketing his mouth. Illness had shaken him up, extinguished his vital spark.

'Your three eldest daughters, Your Majesty. Come to visit you.'

Recognition dawned on his sallow face as he stared at them. He paused, then smiled.

'My dears! My dear girls, sit down.' He looked at Dr Willis to judge if this was acceptable. 'I hope you will not feel it wrong – me playing cards on a Sunday. I think it is excusable now, since I have no other way of entertaining you.' His bony hands shook as he took up his deck once more.

A bolt of love and pity struck through Royal. His words

made sense. There was no foam, no flaming red blotches on his skin. She collapsed into her chair, overwhelmed with gratitude.

'We don't need entertainment,' Augusta said softly, as she took her seat. 'We're so happy to see you.'

Something like a smile tugged at his lips. His muscles quivered, having forgotten the action. 'Very kind of you, my dear. You will forgive me, but I *do* need the amusement. So much silence and loneliness. For so many months, nothing but – hush! Hush!'

The princesses started as their father clamped his hands to his lips and turned his head away. A few servants stirred; the King closed his eyes. Dr Willis did not comment, but paced the room with the sharp gaze of a hunter.

Augusta fluttered her hands in her lap. 'Of course, Papa. Carry on. Don't mind us.'

They let him continue his game in peace, placing card upon card.

Royal knew why he didn't speak. Words beat against the wall of his face; he had the jaded, tormented look of a war veteran with no one to understand what he had seen. He would never be able to discuss the past few months. There was no way he could start; the language did not exist.

Long minutes passed before he put his deck aside and addressed them. 'Perhaps Augusta would sing for me?'

Augusta raised a hand to her throat. 'I will try, if that

would please you.' She turned beseechingly to Dr Willis. 'What shall I sing?'

'Anything cheerful, but not too rousing.'

'Rule Britannia?' she suggested. With her wide, doe eyes, she looked as if she feared one false move would lead Dr Willis to put her in the restraining chair.

'Very suitable.' Willis decreed.

'*When Britain f-first at Heaven's command, arose from out the – the azure main . . .*' Augusta's feeble, shaking voice made the patriotic song sound more like a funeral dirge. '*This was the charter of the land, and guardian angels sang this strain.*'

All at once, the King's booming voice rose up to join her for the chorus. '*Rule, Britannia! Britannia, rule the waves . . . Britons never, never, never will be slaves.*' He fell back in his chair laughing and clapped, delighted.

Royal sensed the presence of Dr Willis at her side before his shadow fell over them. 'That will be enough for today,' he said with decision.

The King paused mid-laugh. He pulled himself straight in his chair, smoothing out his jacket. 'Surely, I might spend a few hours with my family – when I must stay with so many footmen all day long?'

The stony face of his captor didn't flinch. 'Not today.'

The King sighed and collected his cards. 'You will tell the Queen how good I have been, will you not? And say I am quite well enough to see my younger daughters. I do not think I will frighten Amelia anymore.'

'I will judge when Your Majesty can receive more visitors. You must continue to improve.'

The princesses swept their curtseys and retreated backwards with practised steps, managing not to collide or catch one another's skirts. The servant opened the door behind them and they tumbled back into the real world. Augusta, Elizabeth and Royal blinked at each other. They were all pale and tear-stained, but strangely jubilant. The dreaded first meeting was over. What now?

'What did you think?' Augusta asked in a whisper.

'I think,' replied Elizabeth, with something like her usual twinkle, 'that George won't be getting his Regency Bill after all.'

⤙ *The White House, Kew* ⤚

It was the news Charlotte had dreamed of for so long. Only now, she comprehended the distance between her dream and reality.

A recovery didn't blot out the past few months. It did not cleanse the bitter images from her mind or remove the thorns from her heart. She wanted her old George back, but she would never get him. He was lost in the mists of time. This would be yet another George; one drained by madness, inured to suffering. Would he like her any better than the madman had?

She hovered in the doorway, clinging on to Amelia for

dear life. The child was her shield, her talisman against his dislike.

'Are you certain?' she whispered.

Dr Willis's son, John, nodded. 'My father is only next-door. He can come straight away if there are any problems.'

Charlotte buried her face in Amelia's hair. It smelt of roses and nutmeg – comforting, homely.

She knew she could not do it. She could not go into the room. They were urging her to jump over a mountain precipice, assuring her the plunge was safe.

'He shall not hurt you, Your Majesty.'

Perhaps not physically. She saw him out of the corner of her eye, a wiry form bent over the table with a combed wig on his head. It was not his physical presence that worried Charlotte – it was his words; those cruel words that had nipped and scratched over the past months.

'Come, I will walk with you.'

Keeping Amelia's arms round her neck and her face half-hidden in the child's curls, Charlotte edged into the room.

He looked up at the sound of her skirts brushing the floor. 'Is that the Queen? Praise Heaven!'

Not that harsh, hoarse roar. George's voice – familiar tones that went to her heart. She curtsied as he scraped his chair back and rose, shakily, to his feet.

Dear God, he was so changed. At least there were no swollen veins or blotchy patches now, but the features she loved were equally gone; the cheeks hollow, the skin wizened. Grieved beyond words at the wreck of her idol, she cast her eyes down to Amelia's slipper.

'How are you faring, Charlotte my love?'

Mingling pain and joy robbed her of her voice. She worked her mouth, but no sound left it.

He went on. 'I have hated this room. You have no idea how I have hated it. But now, it houses the two things I love most in all the world.'

Oh, George. She wanted to believe it. Yet the memory of Lady Pembroke was fresh before her eyes. What if their marriage had been a mere pretence all this time? A patched-up job to tear him away from the unsuitable Lady Sarah Lennox, as the gossips said. What if, in his madness, he was giving vent to his true feelings?

When she failed to speak, George reached out and took Amelia into his arms. Charlotte let go of the little white gown with reluctance, but her fingers were too weak to cling on.

'My beautiful girl! Oh, how I missed you!'

Amelia let out a high, girlish scream. Involuntarily, Charlotte looked up and met her husband's eyes. They were pale blue. Finally – not bloodshot, not purple, not streaked with yellow. A cool blue iris against white. George's eyes. But Amelia didn't recognise them. She writhed in his grasp.

'You're scaring her,' Charlotte said. 'Let me take her.'

George stared at his daughter, appalled by the tears

drenching her chubby cheeks and the balled up fists that pounded his waistcoat. With a mournful expression, he passed her to Charlotte. Their hands touched briefly in the exchange. Charlotte flinched.

'I'm sorry. I suppose she's forgotten me.'

Charlotte positioned Amelia's face in the folds of the fichu at her neck, safe from fearful sights. Her heart panged for George, looking on helplessly at his own family. It wasn't his fault – but she couldn't see how he would ever heal the breach. It was like he had returned from the dead, a second Lazarus, after they had made up their minds to bury him.

'Amelia will remember,' she said with artificial brightness. 'You must give her time.'

He nodded, sadly. 'I understand. You all need time.'

Charlotte did. She was torn. She needed to be alone, to twine her contradictory feelings together. Fear and love suffocated her as they struggled for supremacy.

Amelia whimpered, her breath hot and damp through Charlotte's fichu.

'I must take Amelia out. I'll come back later.'

He nodded again. How bony his neck was. His cravat seemed thicker than the skin it encased. 'Please do. To see you again . . . I cannot tell you what it means to me, Charlotte.'

No, he couldn't. And she could not tell him what she had been through. Out of habit, she folded down her head and dipped into a curtsey. Then she put her hand on the back of Amelia's golden hair and sped away in a flash of red brocade.

CHAPTER ELEVEN

London
~ *April 1789* ~

London was on fire. Lights blazed from every wall, every coach, every rooftop. Even the poorest houses had rush lights in the windows to mark the occasion.

It was official. Willis had cured the King. Sophia waved from the royal carriage as it wound its way through the glittering streets in triumph. She smiled so broadly that it hurt. Surely now her life would carry on as it had before? This sudden flare of light would scatter the dark clouds the last year had brought. All she had lost was restored.

The princesses had new jewels and fine silks in recognition of the great event. Light from outside reflected in their diamonds and sparkled stars over the ceiling. Transparencies – paintings on gauzy paper, lit from behind – bore glorious inscriptions: *Health to One and Happiness to Many*, *When We Forget Him May God Forget Us* and *God Save the King*. Faces pressed against the windows, smiling and cheering. Sophia's cheeks stung from grinning back but she couldn't stop. Irresistible smiles broke free at every fresh reminder: he was well again.

Back home, Amelia would show the King transparencies in the garden and recite the charming poem Miss Burney had composed at the Queen's command.

'Look! Look!' squealed Mary.

Sophia craned her head. A parade of sedan chairs bustled past. As they cleared, she realised what Mary pointed at: a corner building with lights glinting in every one of its many casements.

It was Brook's Club, the stronghold of the Whig party. Even those who tried to persuade Prince George to take the throne from the King were forced to celebrate tonight for fear of window-smashing mobs. The sisters smiled at one another, unable to say a word. Pure glee spoke for itself.

⌒ *Queen's House, London* ⌒

People gathered about the courtyard, twitching with anticipation. Charlotte hovered by the window, concealing herself in the folds of the curtain. Her fingers clung so tightly to the blue material she was afraid she might pull it down. She hadn't felt this knotted with nerves since her wedding day.

The horses waiting by the carriage shifted their weight as a light wind fluttered their manes. Looking past them to

the black iron gates, Charlotte saw the tattered, weather-
beaten announcement flapping back and forth: *A Complete
Recovery*. She stepped back from her vantage point and let
the heavy curtains fall back into place. Was that it, now?
Was it all over? A nightmare to be dismissed in the cool
light of day? The King may be healed, but she was not. His
cruel words were branded on her heart. She could not
pretend he never lavished attention on Lady Pembroke, nor
could she erase the feelings of revulsion and horror she had
conceived for him. But what choice did she have? Duty
called, merciless and insistent.

Charlotte pulled a snuff box from her pocket and took a
pinch of the brown powder. She inhaled it sharply, relishing the way it kicked her senses into action. This stuff was
keeping her alive, of late. Her fingers, heavy with rings,
struggled to close the box's delicate lid. Diamonds weighted
her neck, sparkling like ice. She was coated with every piece
of jewellery the King had given her on their wedding day.
The solid gold, the translucent fire in the gems, made her
feel safe. These jewels had seen her through her wedding
and they would see her through this – a second marriage.
She and George were two different people now and they
would have to learn to get along all over again. It would not
be as easy at this stage in her life as it had been at the age of
seventeen.

A light scratch at the door made Charlotte look up; it
would be Princess Royal, obeying her summons. She

stashed the snuff box away and wiped the powder from her hands. They trembled. This wasn't going to be an easy conversation.

Royal shimmied into the room, a white satin dress accentuating her figure. A purple bandeau arched over her hair with *God Save the King* embroidered in diamonds. Good. Exactly as Charlotte had designed it. There was some comfort in these small, aesthetic pleasures. They would look the part of a happy royal family, whatever fear and blame roiled beneath the surface. Royal curtsied, careful not to crush her gown.

'Princess Royal, this event is very important. I will not have any scenes upsetting the King. I'm relying on you to watch the girls. Remind them they are not to speak to their brothers today.'

Royal raised her eyebrows and made a moue with her mouth. 'All of them?'

Damn her, why could she never take a simple instruction? 'You are not to speak to any of them. Not after the way they behaved.'

Royal gave her a curious look; something like reproach mixed with pity. 'I will try,' she mumbled. 'But – but Mama, Fred nearly died the other day.'

Charlotte grunted; she was not in the mood for back-chat or Royal's youthful, foolish judgements. 'Nonsense. There's no harm done. A reckless duel, that is all.'

'Captain Lennox shot off one of Fred's curls, you know!'

Charlotte wheeled round at her. 'Why should you defend them? Do you know what your precious brothers have been doing? Do you?' She should have stopped there, but anger throbbed in her head and flashed behind her eyes, demanding satisfaction. 'They have spread a scandal that you are pregnant! They think if they taint you it will discredit us. They mock your father in public! And none of your darling Whigs wear *God Save the King* in their caps!'

A deep blush covered Royal's cheeks.

'Even now, they want your father out of the way and your brother on the throne! Don't you know how close he was to getting that Regency Bill passed? To overthrowing the government your father worked so hard for?' She stopped for breath. Royal's lip trembled. Charlotte felt a stab of remorse and reached for her snuff box.

'H – he was very wrong,' Royal stuttered. 'I h – hope you will forgive him, eventually.'

'What is the use in talking about this? Have you distributed the prayer of thanksgiving to all the servants?'

Royal nodded. Her throat moved up and down convulsively.

Guilt itched at Charlotte as she took a long, hard pinch of snuff. Of course, Royal was not responsible for her brothers' perfidy. But she should have known better than to poke and needle Charlotte on this point.

'Royal . . .' Charlotte thought for a moment, then took both her daughter's hands in her own. 'I've been meaning to talk to you. The little princesses . . . The doctors tell me I must devote myself to the King's needs from now on. I shall not be able to attend to their studies. I thought you the proper person to oversee it.'

A small ray of hope appeared in Royal's face. 'I would like that,' she said. 'I will do everything I can for them. For as long as I am here.'

Charlotte caught her meaning. A bitter stone lodged at the back of her throat. Must she be the one to deal this blow? She had hoped the girls would figure it out for themselves. 'You must not be in a hurry to marry, Royal,' she said softly.

'But I am almost—'

Charlotte cut her off; it was kinder to nip the bud before it grew. 'It would be very unwise to mention such a thing to your father.'

Royal pulled herself up, as if she had walked into a wall. A shade of sadness fell over her young face and with it, understanding. 'No great changes,' she murmured. 'Nothing to disturb his composure.'

Charlotte nodded. 'No. There is nothing for you to do but get in the carriage.'

The state coach gleamed at Charlotte as she came out of the Queen's House, its golden fretwork double gilded by the low spring sun. Its magnificence caught her breath – it was still as splendid as the first day she climbed into it. The intricately carved figures stared blindly at her, their faces smooth and unchanged by time. She ran her eyes over each golden shape; shells, cupids, fruits, flowers, dolphins and angel wings. All this luxury just for her. It was time to be Queen again.

Charlotte glided down the stairs, a floating figure in her panniers and trained gown, and felt her spirit lift for the first time in months. All the degradation and humiliation of the past weeks melted under the carriage's bright golden sparks. She could do this. Pageantry and show were second nature now. She had come to England as the unimpressive princess of a poor duchy and made herself into a model queen. She could crawl back from the position of wronged wife. She must.

The King waited for her, wearing his favourite Windsor uniform; a navy blue coat with red lapels and white piping. It hung strangely from the new angles of his shrunken body. Although the air was warm, he wore a greatcoat that reached his ankles, as if the slightest puff of wind might knock him down. A sudden deluge of pity for the poor, weak man doused Charlotte's resentment. She gave him her best smile and laid a hand in the crook of his thin arm.

It was all she could do. Her heart thumped in her throat, blocking any words. They proceeded toward the coach in silence. Charlotte remembered the day they first met. She had been thoroughly tongue-tied — as she was now. She remembered seeing George in the low September sun, haloed by autumn light. She remembered throwing herself at his feet. Yes, they were starting all over again. And she was still entirely at his mercy, just like that trembling, seventeen-year-old girl.

The great four-tonne coach barely tipped as the slender King climbed in. Charlotte felt enormous by comparison, struggling up the steps to sit facing him, her skirts filling all the space between them. She shoved a swag of lace under her feet. The door shut on them. They were alone.

'You look beautiful.'

The compliment took her by surprise. *Beautiful*. How she had needed to hear that word in the days and nights spent gazing into the mirror comparing herself with Lady Pembroke. There was nothing so empty, so lonely, as having no lover to notice her, to remark on a new jewel. She looked thankfully into his drawn face and saw something of the old George flickering there. *No*. Her blossoming tenderness snapped shut like a rat-trap. She wouldn't give in to it; she couldn't trust it to stay. Relying on him was how she came to be hurt in the first place. 'Thank you,' she said abruptly.

There was a holler outside and the coach stirred into motion. Eight Hanoverian horses, white as a whip of cream, pulled them through the streets of London in splendour. Charlotte leant forwards for a better look and shouted with laughter. It was tremendous.

Men in golden livery and black hats sat aboard the lead

horses, bouncing up and down to the trot. Their fine, powdered wigs were tied back in queues with black ribbons. Behind the state coach, streams of horses marched in their wake, two by two, all the royal guards and Charlotte's children travelling in joyful procession. Crowds poured in around them, leaning out of every window and crushing each other in the streets. Men waved caps and called kind words. Foils, shattered pearls and diamonds littered the pavements as ladies grappled with one another for a better view. Charlotte saw a young woman in a dead faint, lifted over the crowd to safety.

Caught up in the intoxication, Charlotte grinned at the King. 'Do you remember worrying, after America, that the people hated you?' She held her fan up to her lips and shook her head. 'Look at them now.'

He locked eyes with her. This all felt familiar. Edges blurred and melted; Charlotte flew back into her memory, back to another journey in triumph.

Once again, she smelt the herbs cast in her path as she travelled to Westminster Abbey for her coronation. She saw her young self, peeping out beneath the fringe at her window, watching the whole sky turn gold as the soldiers spread a canopy over her head. She remembered the banquet hall plunged in darkness, and stepping through the door to watch a volley of light shoot along a wax string, illuminating thousands of candles one by one. She saw golden plates flare up in the darkness and remembered thinking she was the Sun Queen, with the world lighting up before her.

Ah. How times had changed.

St Paul's smelt of dank stone and carried a chill, despite the sea of people within. Charlotte looked up over the great arches and raised her eyes to the vaulted ceiling, gooseflesh prickling her arms.

She must remember, in this sacred place, all her blessings. Life was not as she wished, but when she thought back to those dreadful days, cowering beneath the sheets and listening to George babble ... She could not be ungrateful. She thanked God for His mercy in giving her back a husband – even if it was not the husband she once knew.

Beams of light filtered through the windows and washed across the cathedral. As Charlotte led her family into the sumptuous royal pew, a shaft of sunshine settled upon the King's head. A benediction. She held her breath, hopeful yet fearing. Could she believe? Was this a sign that all would be well?

A profound hush spread through the congregation. Charlotte closed her eyes and listened, sensing the presence hovering beneath the weighty silence. This was where she needed to be now. This was where she would draw her strength. She could feel it coming to her, like rays from a distant sun.

George's voice darted through her consciousness, shattering the reverie. 'Who is taking the service?' he asked. His words rang, painfully loud, through the quiet cathedral. Hundreds of heads turned to look at them.

Charlotte's cheeks grew warm, but George was oblivious, waiting for her answer. She put her finger to her lips, making a hushing sound.

The clergy emerged, carrying the golden cross of Christ, their robes fluttering across the sanctuary and altar. People stood in respect – but not George.

'Oh, him! Very good, very good.' To Charlotte's astonishment, he pulled out his quizzing glass and peered through it.

She cringed. This could not be. Not now; he was better. Wasn't he? Tears pressed, hard and insistent behind her eyes. Perhaps the doctors were wrong. Perhaps she had been right to doubt them. If she could just keep him quiet for this one service! She could not stand to see him humiliated before his own people.

The congregation sat down in a rippling wave. Charlotte cast her eyes out into the mass of people and they locked, instantly, on her sons George and Frederick, who sat with their uncle. Pointing. Laughing.

She bit back a gasp as their betrayal twisted like a blade in her flesh. More people took notice of the King's quizzing glass.

'What's he doing?' hissed Sophia, but Royal quickly muffled her mouth with a handkerchief. *Good girl.* Charlotte met Royal's eyes and saw they were as wide with fear as her own must be. They were both wondering what he would do next.

A sharp blast of sound filled the stone arches and vibrated in Charlotte's chest. She jumped – then realised. It was the organ. Its haunting music swallowed them, drowning out George's voice and its many questions. She was safe for as long as the hymn continued.

This was how it would be forever, Charlotte realised; she would never relax. She was a sailor in the crow's nest with no end to his shift. The worst of the malady may have gone for now, but she would live her life watching for signs of it, pushing it back. She would spend each day in fear of its return.

Dusk fell and brought Charlotte her hardest trial yet. Ladies washed her with rose-water, sponged her teeth and deposited her, sweet-smelling as an open flower, in the King's bed. Madame Schwellenberg tucked swanskin blankets around her, purposefully avoiding her eye. Charlotte must do this – her duty. They both knew it. But the thought of the door closing on them, shutting her in alone, with him, all through the dark night ... She was sure Madame Schwellenberg pressed her shoulder, ever so slightly, before leaving her to her fate.

There was no comfort in the five woollen mattresses, nor the coverlet of eiderdown. Charlotte forced herself to lie still against them and smile at the King, trying to recall those times she was eager for him, desperate for his touch. All she saw was the vivid red hand mark, bright and hot as shame, pressed on Lady Pembroke's breast.

She held the covers over her chest, embarrassed he should see her in a shift. It did not feel natural anymore. This was not the man that she knew and trusted with her body. Would he be her gentle lover, as he had always been? Or would the sight of a woman in his bed inflame him, bring back the raging monster? He climbed into bed beside her and she stiffened. This was how a fox must feel, hunkered down in the long grass with the hounds sniffing nearby. She had the same desperate impulse to run.

But nothing happened. He didn't reach out and touch her, he didn't force his body on top of hers. Minutes passed, marked only by the sound of her pulse and blood rushing past her ears. She heard him breathe, even and calm. She stole a glance. He lay flat on his back, staring at the dusty tester over their heads. He was serene. He was not about to hurt her.

Relief slowed her heartbeat and sucked the tension from her body. With it went her last thread of energy. She needed to sleep. She needed to close her eyes and be free of this long, emotional day. Behind her eyelids, images twirled and danced. The gleaming carriage, the King's quizzing glass. Maybe she had judged him too harshly. He had been away from the world for so long, he was bound to forget social niceties. And such crowds of people, the pressure of being stared at. His mind couldn't grapple with that yet. But perhaps it would, in time.

She opened her eyes. He had not moved. Still staring up calmly like an effigy in St Paul's.

Nettled by a sense of guilt, Charlotte shuffled closer and stretched an arm across his stomach. Her skin tingled as she felt his warm flesh beneath the nightshirt. She waited for a reaction, but there was none. God, how she had longed for his embrace. She had forgotten the way he stirred her blood, the comfort of holding him.

He turned his head on the pillow and their eyes met.

'If I pay respect to you, why need it affect you?'

Charlotte swallowed. 'Affect me? What should affect me?'

'My loving another.'

It was there again: that queer look from another world. Charlotte bit her lip to stop it from trembling. 'Who do you speak of?'

'Lady Pembroke,' he said. 'I love her.'

Without a word, she drew her arm back from his skeletal frame and rolled over to face the wall. She held the tears in just long enough. She wouldn't let him see her cry; she wouldn't make a sniffling noise or allow her shoulders to shake.

Damn him. Damn his traitorous, ungrateful heart. She would never let him touch her again.

CHAPTER TWELVE

Weymouth
⤚ *Summer 1789* ⤙

There was no Hanover for Royal after all. Instead of creating a dazzling court to catch her a husband, the King took her to an English seaside resort.

She had known, deep down, it would be this way. When he had rambled on about suitors in the carriage, it was only the madness talking. She tried to kindle gratitude in her soul and tell herself it was a price worth paying to have her father well again. But as he improved day by day and life resumed its normal pattern, she felt the shackles chafing her ankles once more. Only this time, there was little hope of escape.

She sat on Weymouth beach, contemplating the waves rolling in and out of the bay, tasting the tang of salt on her lips. Her younger brothers were somewhere out there, over that blue expanse; so was the prince who was meant to come and rescue her. He would never come now.

Once, the eldest Princess of England would have been a prize for any man, but Royal's value on the international marriage market had plummeted. She was tainted by association. No dynasty would risk a hint of madness entering the bloodline. Even if some foolhardy prince did appear and ask for her hand, the Queen would make her refuse. Anything to avoid tipping the King back into a delirious chasm.

She was trapped and the sea kept guard. The blue gulf heaved in front of Royal as her white gown billowed about her like impotent wings, and she threw her hopes down into its depths.

How to resign herself? How to stop the dreams from floating into her head and accept that she would always be a childless spinster? She saw Elizabeth's head bobbing in the water beside the bathing machines and tried to comprehend that this was the furthest she and her sisters would get from England: a few yards into the ocean.

An army of women with burly arms, and skirts tucked up under their legs, helped people into the water. Over where the men bathed, two warrior mermaids escorted the King out of his machine. A cluster of well-wishers coated the shore; ladies with wide-brimmed bonnets and parasols, men in straw hats tapping their canes against the beach. Royal heard a drum, then a trumpet and recognised a tune. Sure enough, there was a band hunched up inside a spare bathing machine, playing God Save the King.

People on the beach caught wind of their national anthem and bawled out the words. Children jumped in time to the music, calling down scolds from their nurses. At the end of each verse, they gave a huzzah.

Royal put her head in her hands, driving her fingers up beneath her bonnet and cap to grip her hair. Saving the King; this was her mission. The people could sing of it with gay abandon – it cost them nothing. But for Royal it was not a song of celebration – it was duty's commanding voice. Grey years of solitude and sacrifice cruelly set against a merry tune.

How would she bear it?

Once they were dry and dressed again, Royal and Elizabeth strolled back to Gloucester Lodge with their attendants in tow. The town they walked through was decorated to receive them; floral arches crossed every road and the women wore crowns of blossom. Crowds of people walked in the clement weather, gawping and pointing at them as they passed. Elizabeth waved at a little boy in his nurse's arms. His round, pink face erupted into a grin and Royal felt a cavity open within her. She would never have one of her own.

By the time the Queen was her age, she'd had five babies. Unreasonable hatred flared inside her at the thought. Five – when Royal would give her right arm for one. She hadn't known, when she played with the infants

Sophia, Mary and Amelia that they would be the only children she would ever have. It was too late to appreciate them now – they were growing up fast.

Still linking arms, Royal and Elizabeth arrived at the end of the terrace overlooking the bay. Their uncle's house, Gloucester Lodge, was a wide redbrick building just across from the sands. It felt incredibly gloomy as they entered, closed the door and blocked out the sunshine.

'Where is the Queen?' Royal asked the maid, who took their hats and gloves.

'Her Majesty is drinking tea. She said you may join her, if you wish.'

Royal did not wish, but she knew it was an order. She shared a look with Elizabeth. They both found it difficult to cope with their changed mother.

They hesitated as they crossed the threshold. The Queen sat before a table laden with pastries, china cups, plates and a shining tea urn. Although the scent of warm, flaking pastry and brewed tea leaves set Royal's stomach groaning, the Queen paid no attention to the feast. Someone had poured her a cup of tea but she ignored it, gazing instead out of the open window with fixed, unblinking eyes. Her lace cuff trailed in her tea. Diamond studs pinned a wispy veil over her head, but it did not conceal the shock of white hair beneath.

Was it kinder to interrupt her thoughts or leave her be? Impossible to judge. Like a spinning top, she whirled between feverish gaiety and periods of gloom. It had been easier to comfort her when the King was ill, but now . . . They could not console her for an unnamed grief. Elizabeth had tried to prompt her with gentle enquiries, but she confided nothing.

A strong waft of currant bun drifted toward them, pushed on by the breeze from the window. Royal's stomach rumbled and the Queen looked up – there was no retreating now.

'Come in, come in!' Before they had time to curtsey, the Queen deposited buns on plates and thrust them into their hands. 'Sit now, both of you sit. I have been for a walk today. Look at this lovely sprig of myrtle I found! I will carry it back to Kew and plant it myself in a pot.' She waved the thin green stem at them, an artificial smile plastered to her face.

Elizabeth swallowed her mouthful. 'It's very pretty, Mama.'

'I thought so.' The Queen held the plant to her lips before returning it to a jug of water. Her hands performed the actions clumsily and the large tea stain on her cuff dripped down her dress.

'Are you well, Mama?' Royal asked.

The Queen turned around. 'Well? Of course I'm well. What should be the matter?'

Royal could not meet her mother's eyes. She muttered into the rim of her tea cup. 'I thought perhaps you were a little fidgety. That's all.'

'Fidgety!' The Queen's shrill laugh sounded forced. 'Bless you, child. I'm not fidgety. The King is well again – I'm the happiest woman in the world. How could I be otherwise?'

Her question dropped into a pit of silence. Unable to respond, Royal took a large bite of currant bun.

Just then, a door closed in the hall. They rose to their feet as Augusta entered the room, followed by Lady Waldegrave. Their appearance acted like a stimulant on the Queen – she was off again, flapping her hands for the servants to fetch more refreshments. 'How was your sailing? What did you learn about the navy today?'

Augusta didn't return her smile. 'I – I've just heard some rather disturbing news, actually, Mama. The French people have stormed the royal prison, the Bastille.'

They looked at one another.

The Queen frowned. 'Why would they do a thing like that?'

'I don't know. Who knows why the French do anything?'

Royal cleared her throat. Her interest in Whig politics gave her a little more savvy than the rest. 'It's a direct challenge to the crown.' They all stared at her over the rims of their cups. 'Is it not?'

'Nonsense!' cried the Queen. 'If it was anything serious, I would have heard from Queen Marie Antoinette.'

'The sailors thought it was serious,' said Augusta, sitting down to receive her cake. 'The news was fresh that minute, just over from France. Maybe Marie Antoinette hasn't sent her letter yet.' She toyed with her fork. 'Goodness, I hope there won't be a war.'

The Queen turned pale. Her saucer rattled as she set her cup down with a shaking hand. 'No. There cannot be a war. Not now. The King—' She didn't finish her sentence. She didn't need to. The parlour fell silent. Outside the birds sang sweetly; there was no sign of another storm rising, but Royal felt it coming. She felt it in her blood.

'I will never forgive the French if they make Papa ill again,' she whispered. 'Never.'

∼ *Gloucester Lodge, Weymouth* ∼

Charlotte awoke to the sound of seagulls calling outside her window.

At first, she couldn't remember why she had a sense of anticipation about this morning. Then it came to her in a flash of cold light: the Bastille. Marie Antoinette. She leapt out of bed, threw a wrapper around her shoulders and slunk out of the door. Although it was early, the corridors of Gloucester Lodge were warm and bright. Housemaids chattered and clanged in the rooms downstairs. Carefully, Charlotte placed one bare foot in front of the other and avoided the creaky floorboard. She didn't know exactly what she planned to do. She simply had to be at the King's desk when the post arrived – prepare him, see the reaction first hand. But perhaps the news from France wouldn't be so bad. Perhaps she wouldn't even need to comfort George. If only she had a recent letter from the French Queen. Until post trickled in from the Continent, the press would exaggerate.

Charlotte tiptoed past a closed door. Behind it, a servant beat something and hummed a tune. She rounded the corner, trotted forward a few steps, and opened another door with a soft click. She glided into the study – and saw the King at his desk.

She leapt back with surprise, but no fear. It was clearly a good day – he was washed, dressed and about his business. He paused in the middle of sealing a letter.

'Oh.' Charlotte shut the door behind her and curtsied. 'Forgive me. I did not expect you to be up.'

He held his golden seal above a pool of melted wax. Its sickly, burning scent reached out at Charlotte from across the room.

'I am rather early.' He pressed his seal down and imprinted the fast-setting wax. 'What brings you here?'

She opened her mouth and shut it again. This was not how she had planned it. She had expected time to sit, gazing out the window at the glistening sea, and choose her words. Her mind scrambled for an excuse. 'I wondered if I had any letters. Brought here by mistake. It sometimes happens.'

'I haven't seen any.' The King picked up his letter, turned

it over, and placed it on a pile in the corner of his desk. 'You are welcome to look. Who do you expect to hear from?'

'The Queen of France.'

She studied him for a reaction.

He grimaced. 'A bad business. So much violence.'

She released her breath in a great whoosh. 'You know?' She couldn't keep the incredulity from her voice. All that worrying, all that anxiety, and this was how he took the news?

'Just frightful,' he said. 'The mob wanted to hang the governor, but the rope broke. Apparently they cut his head off with a pocket knife instead.'

Charlotte's hand flew to her mouth. 'No!'

'That's not the worst. I heard they kept slicing his body in the gutter, even though he was long dead, and scalped him like savages.'

'Good God!' Bubbling panic replaced every feeling inside her. Augusta was right: it *was* serious. What would Marie Antoinette do?

Seeing her distress, George turned his chair and put his hands out to her. Without thinking, she stepped forward to clasp them.

'I thought we lived in modern times,' she murmured. She closed her eyes, but she still saw red, like a splash of blood. 'This is as bad as anything from the dark ages. The poor King and Queen!'

'We know nothing for certain yet. Let us wait and see.

We have had riots enough and come through them, haven't we?'

Charlotte squeezed his fingers. Had they really come through them? She recalled uprisings in the past; clinging desperately to George as silk weavers descended on her palace in a furious mob. His calm had been unbreakable. Had he repressed too much? Had the panic taken its toll, years later, and erupted into a foaming frenzy? 'You always speak bravely, but you must tell me the truth. Are you sure this hasn't upset you? I'm certain it has. You don't feel any flurry, any . . . illness?'

He caught her meaning. Looking her square in the eye, he spoke in a firm, steady voice. 'No. No, I feel well.'

For today, perhaps. Unable to meet the intensity of his gaze, she turned her head toward the desk and saw the letter he had just sealed. The curved, black writing engraved itself onto Charlotte's vision. The world shrank around her, focusing in on the paper and the name. *Lady Pembroke*. In her husband's own hand. She couldn't rip her eyes away from it. Lead filled her limbs, weighing her down. Her hands dropped George's and fell heavily by her sides.

Always the same. Whenever she thought he was returning, that she was gaining ground – a blow that sent her staggering back.

He followed her stare with a quick flick of his head. 'Oh! No, Charlotte – you mustn't think . . .'

But she was already drifting toward the door in a melancholy haze.

George called after her. 'It is an apology.'

She stopped. Outside, the first celebratory band of the day woke its instruments with a muted boom.

'For the attack?'

'For everything.'

An apology for Lady Pembroke, but none for the wife whose heart he broke.

George picked up a pen and twirled it in his fingers. 'I know I behaved badly. So many improper words, so many awful deeds . . . It was like a thick cloud engulfing me. But it's gone. I'm getting better and better every day.'

Silence. She couldn't call him a liar to his face.

'All will be as it was before,' he said. 'You will see.'

Charlotte thought she had seen enough.

CHAPTER THIRTEEN

Kew
∼ *1791* ∼

Royal wandered past the Temple of the Sun, wishing the golden rays emblazoned on its roof could shed a little heat. Her ears and nose stung from the cold as she waded on through the gardens, frozen grass crackling beneath her boots. In the winter, Kew was a trap of bitter memories. It looked enchanting, with its frosted trees and stretches of sparkling lawn, but Royal heard the mad cries of her father on the wind as it whipped through the undergrowth. She could never forget that dreaded winter, nearly three years before.

Birds chattered in the aviary, merry as springtime, hopping around and bouncing off the fretwork of their cage. Royal wondered if her mother was there, feeding them dry rolls. She twisted down a path and skirted the aviary just in case.

She avoided family meetings where she could. They had an undercurrent of sadness, ever present. Although years had passed since the King's recovery, the Queen hadn't regained her cheer. She spread misery where she walked; a censer wafting its sour incense.

Royal's life had been frozen, like the sap in the trees, with no hope of a summer to make it warm and gold again. She looked up and saw a long, low building with arched windows. The Orangery. Relief washed over her as she anticipated the warmth and quiet inside. She trotted stiffly with numb legs, imagining the great stove wrapping its heat around her.

A few gardeners trimmed the plants outside. She acknowledged their bows with a curt nod before diving round to the glass door. She fumbled with the handle beneath her mittens. The hinges were stiff with cold and wouldn't move. With an energy born of desperation, she shook and clattered the door until it gave way and she half-fell into the Orangery.

'Princess Royal!'

She snapped to attention. The Queen stood in front of her, incredulous. A wide-eyed cluster of ladies held their breath.

'What are you doing, roving about on your own?' the Queen demanded. 'I thought you were teaching Amelia?'

The warm air brought blood back into Royal's skin with painful jabs. Her cheeks tingled.

'I've finished,' she said defensively.

The Queen stared at her with that old, judgemental look that made Royal feel like a worm. Now she was for it. She wished she had braved the cold and carried on to the greenhouse.

LAURA PURCELL

Suddenly, the Queen waved her ladies away to a corner and seized Royal by the arm. She dragged her to a tree with tiny, new-born oranges, fresh with the tang of citrus.

'Your political friends . . . what do they say about France?'

The question caught Royal off-guard. Where was the scolding, the demand for responsible behaviour? Her mind churned, searching for the safest answer. 'Their opinions are mixed.'

The Queen chewed her lip. The dark green leaves of the orange tree partially obscured her face. What was she thinking? There must have been bad news.

'You have heard from Marie Antoinette,' Royal guessed.

'Yes. I'm not likely to hear again. They've locked her family away in the Tuileries. She is guarded day and night like a common criminal. A prisoner, in her own country! Can you imagine what that is like?'

Royal thought she could.

The Queen twisted her hands together. 'There is nothing I can do. I am tired of worrying about it. I am tired of waking up and wondering if it will be the first day of war.'

Shadows like bruises sat under her bloodshot eyes. Royal drew on her reserve of reassuring words – she was running low. This was her role now; to placate, to soothe – not just the Queen but her sisters and the King.

'Pitt won't intervene yet,' she said. 'The Treasury cannot afford another war.'

The Queen stepped back and leant on the misty, grey

glass. 'What am I meant to do in the meantime? Watch the King fret?'

'It's all we can ever do,' Royal reminded her sadly. 'At least the weather will improve in a few months. We can come back here and plant seeds. It might take your mind off . . . things.'

The Queen made an impatient grunt. 'I cannot wait that long. I need something now. All I think of is France and the King. I need somewhere they cannot reach me.'

Royal longed for that too: her own space. A place to breathe. Why did the Queen think she was the only one who suffered? Damming the flood of her anger and self-pity, she pitched her voice at a sweet, hopeful note. 'There is one good thing about France.'

'Oh?' The Queen raised a sceptical eyebrow.

'Fox supports the revolution, but George does not. They will drift apart and George is sure to make it up with Papa.'

The Queen digested this for a moment. She looked relieved, but her face twitched to repress the emotion; she would not even allow herself the luxury of a smile. 'And what about you, Royal? Do you support revolution?'

Royal shook her head. She understood the need to kick against oppression and injustice better than most, but she could not justify the means.

'I am for liberty,' she said firmly. 'Not bloodshed.'

CHAPTER FOURTEEN

Frogmore, Windsor
1791

Pink petals flurried over Charlotte and Elizabeth, settling in the rims of their hats. Charlotte raised her face to the blossoming tree and inhaled its floral rain. Spring had come at last. The sun was high in the sky, casting a glow on the land she had purchased. It was all hers now – her sanctuary. Frogmore would be her place of asylum, safely tucked away from the court – and from the King.

Heaven knew she needed it. The landscaping and decoration would gather up her meandering thoughts and lead them away from the darkness that threatened to engulf them. She could expand her new house into a long white building full of glistening windows. She would spread a majestic lake out before it, to cast up a wobbling reflection of the plane trees and chimneys. It would be beautiful, perfect. A place for her to hide and forget.

'Just there.' She pulled off her glove and pointed across

the lawns. 'That is where I thought you could put your gothic ruin.'

Elizabeth followed her outstretched finger to a nook enfolded by clumps of trees. 'It's a good spot. And if you like it, Mama, I can design some more things.'

They wound their way through the formal gardens. Elizabeth put up a parasol to shade her face from the sun, but Charlotte couldn't bear to miss a single ray. For the first time in months, she felt herself relaxing, unfurling to bask in the light. It was as if she had awoken from a deep, troubled sleep, to find the world fresh and budding around her.

The pavement formed a cross through the four sections of the garden and a fountain bubbled at the centre. Charlotte watched the water ripple to the edge of the basin, where it lay stagnant. Its gentle, tinkling sounds hypnotised her. It was like a lullaby – penetrating, soothing her deep within.

'Mama.'

She heard Elizabeth as if from a distance. 'Mmm?'

'You and I have always been open and honest with each other.'

Charlotte started, the fountain's magic instantly shattered. *Open and honest?* This couldn't be the forerunner of something pleasant. She looked round at Elizabeth, willing her to hold her tongue. Just to let her enjoy one day of sunshine and happiness.

She licked her lips, which were suddenly dry. 'Yes, my dear.'

Elizabeth glanced behind to make sure the ladies in waiting were out of earshot. She dropped her voice. 'That being the case, I wanted to ask you – first-hand – if it's true.'

Charlotte heard the resolution in her voice and knew she would have to answer truthfully, whatever the question. She swallowed. 'If what's true?'

'Did you refuse an offer of marriage for one of us from the King of Sardinia?'

'Who told you that?' Before Charlotte could think, the words flew out her mouth, harsh and accusing.

'Does it matter? I only want to know if it is true – and if it is, why did you not tell me.'

Of course it mattered. It mattered if one of Charlotte's ladies was a gossip. 'Do not be impertinent. It is for the King to decide what you do and do not hear of.'

'Mama—'

'But if you must know, yes, the offer was made and rejected out of hand. The man is older than your father!' Charlotte cried. The censorious expression on Elizabeth's face was unbearable. 'Why would we even consider it? There was no reason in the world to tell you such an absurd suggestion had been made.'

Perhaps a cloud had drifted across the sun, or a sudden wind had stirred up. Either way, Charlotte no longer felt the warmth that feathered her face but a moment ago.

Elizabeth took her hand. Charlotte let it lie stiff in her grasp.

'I do not mean to accuse you,' Elizabeth said. 'It is just that we never expected to get any offers at all – after Papa. Now with each one you turn down I worry – I really do worry – that we shan't get any more.'

Charlotte looked into Elizabeth's care-worn eyes, knowing she should feel pity, but instead, a throb of possessiveness asserted itself. 'What then? You do not want to leave me.' She didn't inflect the end of the sentence into a question.

Doubt flickered across Elizabeth's face. 'No. Please God, I will have some years with you yet. But Mama, surely you see it must happen one day? I need an establishment. I cannot live forever on the goodwill of George and his heirs. Surely you see that?'

Charlotte did see it, but she didn't like to have it pointed out to her. It called up a dismal image of her future self, old, sitting alone with the King in an empty room, trying to stir the embers of conversation. A draught of horror rippled over her.

'*I* can only depend on George and his heirs,' she snapped, jerking her hand from Elizabeth's. 'But I suppose what is good enough for me isn't good enough for you.'

'Mama . . .'

Charlotte put up her hand. 'I cannot believe you would be so selfish! Not one of you will think of me, left alone with a poor, deranged husband.'

Elizabeth looked stricken. 'I would never do anything to hurt you, Mama, or my father. But I do mean to marry one day.'

Charlotte gave her a long, hard glare and turned upon her heel. She stomped back toward the house, hearing nothing but the tumult of her own emotions. Fear gripped her so tightly she could hardly breathe. She would be left alone at last. For the children, the King's illness was just an episode to be forgotten, while they moved on with their lives. They wanted to abandon her – even Elizabeth!

The pain of betrayal made her furious, snappish like a wounded animal. So Elizabeth thought she would leave this life, did she? Well, she couldn't go anywhere unless Charlotte let her. And God knew, she would never do it.

Charlotte entered her new house, shaking petals from her skirts. Her pleasant day had spoiled like a rotten fruit tart.

She swept her way down the colonnade into the Green Pavilion, where everything was arranged according to her directions. The sash window hung ajar to let in the sweet spring breeze, which fluttered the red and green curtains. Porcelain vases with silk flowers decorated the tables and baskets of fruit adorned every windowsill. It was beautiful, but it failed to appease her. She paced up and down on the oriental rug, thinking furiously.

Why didn't Elizabeth understand that Charlotte needed her girls? They had to stay – for a few more years, at least.

God only knew what the King would make of it. Would Elizabeth speak so candidly to him? Would she dare to insist on a marriage – or worse, elope?

Charlotte caught herself with a shake of the head. It didn't matter what Elizabeth did. It would be illegal. The King had made a Royal Marriages Act to ensure their children could not marry as recklessly as his siblings. He had them firm in the clutch of his hand.

Charlotte came to a halt. Her feet sank into the rich pile of her new rug. It would work out. She just had to stay calm and breathe.

A door latch clicked and she wheeled round. No one was there. But surely she had heard ... Her heart drummed loud in her ears. Below it came a softer noise. She cocked her head to the side, listening. As her pulse slowed, she heard a low, deep sound, like the first mutterings of a thunderstorm. She closed her eyes, straining to hear.

It was not a storm. It was a voice. In Princess Royal's closet. She crept forward on the very tips of her shoes and pressed her ear to the smooth wood of the door. The noise grew louder and turned into a string of hushed words.

'I'm sure it's all some unfortunate misunderstanding.'

She recognised the voice instantly. Her son, her George! A thrill of hope coursed through her. He was here. Did this mean the King had forgiven him at last?

'No! You don't know what she is like now. It grows worse

every day. Even her ladies say she never laughs and jokes with them like she used to. How do you think she treats me? She hates me!'

'Royal . . .'

'No!' Charlotte winced as a shriek met her eardrum. 'Royal isn't even my name! I'm Charlotte! *Charlotte*! But I'm not allowed it because it's *her* name. I am not even allowed my own name.'

Charlotte fell back from the door, her spine solidifying into a rod of ice. They were talking about her. She knew she should walk away, that it was foolish to go back and hear more, but she could not stop herself.

George's voice again. 'I don't know what you think I can do about it.'

'I need to get married. I'll be twenty-six soon and too old for anyone to want me.' The words tumbled from Princess Royal in a fever. 'You could help me find a husband, you could tell Papa it's a good idea and you could stop everyone from choosing my sisters first.'

'If we can assure the princes you are not mad like Papa, you shan't have a problem. You have a big dowry. Mama was never beautiful and she's married to the King of England!'

Charlotte's head throbbed and lights flashed before her eyes.

'Papa is an angel. I cannot hope to find a prince like that.'

For a moment they fell silent and Charlotte half-feared,

half-hoped they would hear her heart pounding through the wall.

'I need money,' George said, 'and you need a husband. Surely someone out there has money and needs a wife? A princess of England – the eldest princess especially – is a good catch. There are a few people on the Continent from whom I have been trying to secure loans. If I suggest to one of the princes that you might be the reward . . . this could work. This could actually work.'

'Do you have anyone in mind?'

'Fred's in Prussia right now. Is their crown prince not about your age? He would make a fine match. I will write to Fred and see what he thinks.'

No. Charlotte staggered away and gripped the mantel-piece for support. Whichever way she looked, her children dropped away, one after the other, like pearls on a snapped necklace. The only constant she had was the memory of her dead little boys, Alfred and Octavius. They didn't leave her.

She crouched and laid her forehead against the cold marble of the fireplace. It would never do – she realised that now. Frogmore was a sham. A fine new house and elegant gardens would not be able to save her, after all.

<hr>

⤳ *St James's Palace, London* ⤷

Sophia watched the town rattle past the carriage. The sky was peachy-pink as the sun set over London with crimson streaks. She made out silhouettes of buildings and trees in the last light. A rare glimpse of the outside world.

She looked away from the window, over to her sisters. Ribbons and plumes of feathers nestled in their piled-up hair. Long white gloves stretched up to their elbows and their dresses poured out around their hips like waterfalls. This was an occasion demanding all their finery: their brother Frederick was bringing his Prussian bride to St James's for the first time.

Sophia's new court dress made her sit awkwardly against the cushions, the weight of its jewelled satin tugging on her shoulders. Beneath it, her stays bit into her chest.

'What do you think she'll be like?' she asked Mary.

'Fred's wife?'

'Who else? Don't you think she must be very beautiful? He fell in love with her so quickly! I hope she is pretty. That would mean her brothers, the princes of Prussia, are handsome.'

Mary let out a rippling giggle.

Princess Royal cleared her throat. 'The princes of Prussia have not come with her.'

Sophia pulled a face. 'I know that. But Fred's been telling me that the oldest prince would make a very good match for Mary, one day.'

'If there is a war in Europe, no one will be getting married for a long while.'

'And,' added Elizabeth, 'Fred will have to go back to the Continent. He'll have to fight.'

War. The word expanded in Sophia's head until it was full of powder smoke, cannon balls and bloody swords. Had it really come to that? She'd heard the court talking about France in hushed voices or disapproving sneers, but she had not realised that the situation was perilous.

She remembered Royal telling her they had abolished the monarchy in France. How could they even do that? The monarchy was not just an institution – it was real, living, breathing people. Could they abolish Sophia's family? Abolish her? Simply tell her she did not, could not exist any longer?

They shared the rest of the ride in silence.

When the carriage pulled through the Tudor entrance of St James's Palace, Sophia gazed up at the towers, which seemed to reach right into the sky and brush the wakening stars. She suddenly felt very small.

She climbed out of the carriage, wobbling into the night air. A man in livery and a tricorn hat appeared to light her way. They passed through long, oak-panelled galleries, lined with portraits of kings and queens. Their painted eyes followed Sophia as she tried to keep up with her sisters. All the while the one word stalked her, treading on her hem: *abolished*.

By degrees they reached the appointed saloon, and lined up either side of the King and Queen without saying a word. As if on cue, the door opened and Sophia saw the small, handsome features of her brother Frederick, shining with pride. Carefully, he turned to lead a lady through the doorway.

She was not what Sophia expected at all. Frederick's wife was a tiny, stick-thin creature, almost child-like. A powdered wig swamped her head and slender face. The material of her dress, beautiful though it was, hung like a sack from her figureless body.

The newlyweds bowed low before the King and Queen.

'Papa, Mama. Allow me to introduce Frederica.'

As the new Duchess of York curtseyed again, light ricocheted off her jewels; she was dripping with wedding diamonds. Such a shame that her poor figure didn't set them off to advantage.

The King raised her up and shook her by the hand. 'You are very welcome here, my dear. It does me a world of good to see how happy you've made my Fred.'

'We are so relieved you arrived safely,' the Queen said. 'Travelling through France at a time like this . . .'

'It was terrible, Your Majesty,' the waifish princess said. 'People stopped us at Lille. I have never been so frightened.'

'They wouldn't let us pass until we removed the royal arms from our coach,' Frederick explained.

Sophia tried to picture a country where members of the royal family were stopped and abused in the street. The only mobs she had seen were the swarms of well-wishers who followed her recovered father to Weymouth.

Mary placed her mouth close to Sophia's ear and shielded them with her fan. 'Didn't George want Fred to marry a princess and produce heirs for England? So he could stay with Mrs Fitzherbert and not worry about the succession?'

Sophia nodded, afraid to speak or even look at Mary, lest the Queen saw her.

Mary huffed in doubt. 'Well. I don't think Fred picked a good one. They don't look like childbearing hips to me. Wherever they are.'

CHAPTER FIFTEEN

Queen's House, London
1793

The news arrived at last. The ground-shattering, time-stopping news. The people of France had put their King on trial – and sentenced him to death.

Charlotte slumped forward in her chair as the gulf of an unknown future yawned before her. Blood rushed past her ears like water. To kill a King!

How had it come to this? The world was upside-down, warped past her recognition. She could not attend to the messenger's words. All she could think was thank God, thank God she was with George when he heard this. Without her, the force of dismay must have capsized his mind. Perhaps it still would.

'I offered him sanctuary.' George shook his head, his eyes wide. 'Why would they not let him come to England?'

That look. It was there, lurking beneath his features. Ready to take over. A dreadful calm spread through

Charlotte as she realised she had to keep her wits. If she didn't guide and manage him, this strain would set the monster free. 'They are an unnatural people. A savage and unprincipled nation,' she breathed.

'Poor man. Poor man. He *would* give his support to the rebels in America! Did he not realise what he was doing?'

America again. That was the root of the evil. They had started a fire no one could control and now it engulfed the French royals. What must Marie Antoinette be suffering? Charlotte had witnessed her share of trauma, but she couldn't begin to imagine it: having her husband snatched from her arms, wheeled through the streets and decapitated. Did they make Marie Antoinette watch as they led her King up the steps to the scaffold? Did she smell the reek of his blood as it flowed out onto the straw? No – she must not let herself think of it. George needed her full attention.

She watched him, frozen in shock, staring into space. Given time, his memories would form a quicksand and drag him down. It was dangerous to leave him. He needed a flame put beneath his seat, a call to action. 'This revolution is like a pestilence,' she murmured. 'We must remain calm and stamp it out. We must stop it spreading to our people.'

George leant back on his throne, resting the queue of his wig against the golden frame. 'I fear it is too late. Ireland is already demanding concessions for the Catholics. And while there are people like that beast, Fox, poisoning the minds of my subjects . . .'

He was probably right. None of them were safe. The channel of water separating England from France suddenly felt very narrow. Charlotte had been through so much with George's illness – could it possibly be that the worst was yet to come?

She put a hand on his shoulder, letting it tremble against the epaulette of his jacket. She allowed her eyes to fill with tears. It felt strange – she had spent so long restraining sobs that it took a concerted effort to let them show.

He turned to her.

'Will we be next?' she whispered. 'Oh, George. Will they hurt my children? Or me?'

George brought his hand down with a slam. 'By God, I won't let a single person touch you! Do not worry.' All at once, determination animated his frame. He took her hand from his shoulder and pressed it hard to his lips. 'I will never let it happen in England. My father told me to retrieve the glory of the throne. I will not fail him.'

There was no hint of lunacy in his expression; only pure conviction in the righteousness of his cause. For a brief moment, Charlotte cared nothing for the French King. A warm chink of love shone through the wall she had built against her husband and it felt glorious. If this was what it took to bring the old George back, she would endure it gladly.

'Will we go to war?' she asked.

He nodded. 'It will not be my choice to make. But surely even Pitt must see that it is the right thing, the moral thing to do.'

She swallowed. 'Let us pray that England agrees with us.'

War, again, so soon. This time, it had to be won; it could not be a repeat of what had happened in America. They were not fighting for land; the stakes were higher now. They were fighting for their throne – and their very lives.

.

⌒ *Greenwich* ⌒

A heaving mass of humanity lined the docks. Red-faced, sweaty people pushed through the crowd with boxes, barrels and portmanteaux.

Sophia felt a desperate urge to turn tail and flee for some pure air. The waterside odours clawed the back of her throat – a nauseous mixture of excrement and rotting fish. She looked down and saw a poisonous flow of hay, weed and bottles clogging the water.

The warships in harbour looked indestructible, shining and new, with masts rising up into the clouds. But Sophia knew how soon they could shiver to splinters. Her brother William had spent hours telling her of his travels at sea – the battles and the near misses. She ran her eyes over the square windows in the side of the hull, picturing the cannon firing through them, and imagined the metal thud of

a ball in her stomach. Some of these men lining the dock –
officers in their red army coats and the navy lieutenants in
their bicorn hats – would suffer that fate. She wanted to
run and warn them, to make them stop this madness. She
couldn't bear the idea that someone would get hurt.

Gruesome tales of the French, servant's gossip, echoed
in her head. Were her brothers to fight those monsters who
massacred prisoners and took their ears for trophies, who
danced the *Carmagnole* on piles of slippery bodies? What
about that man who pulled the limp heart out of his victim
and squeezed its contents into a glass, so he could drink the
blood of an aristocrat?

'Don't look so glum, Sophy.' Frederick cupped her cheek
in his hand and squeezed it.

Her words tumbled over one another. 'Can't you stay? I
wish you would stay. I wish Papa had not appointed you.
Then you would be safe.'

'Ernest and Adolphus are under arms. Did you think I
would stay here and do nothing?'

'George is staying here,' Sophia pointed out. 'And think
of your poor wife! Frederica is already worried about her
father and brothers. Now she has to fret about you too, in
Flanders!'

Fred bent down to her short height. His lips stretched
in a patient, indulgent grin. 'How could I look her in the
face knowing I had done nothing to help her family? Prussia, Austria, Piedmont, Spain and Holland are all fighting

against France. We cannot lose, Sophy. We *shall not* lose.'

Surely that was tempting fate. She nipped her lip, trying to commit him to memory, just as he was: handsome in a red coat with epaulettes, a blue sash crossing his torso. He kissed her forehead and stood back up.

It was hot, so very hot. The people pressed in close around her. There was no air. Frederick turned to say something to their parents but Sophia couldn't hear it; her ears were muffled. Perhaps she would never get the chance to speak with him again. He could perish in the flash of a flintlock and a cloud of smoke. They might all die out there – Frederick, William, Edward, Adolphus and Ernest. She tried to grip onto Mary but her hands were slick, unable to take purchase. The heat was unbearable. Her eyes sought Frederick. Where was he? She couldn't see straight – there were black clouds rolling in, blotting out his face. Suddenly the bustling dock, and the horses pulling carts aboard ship, slid from her view. She felt the cold pavement press against her cheek. Then it was dark.

Lower Lodge, Windsor

Early in the morning Royal tripped down the corridors of Lower Lodge, leading the reluctant Queen behind her. Rims of frost clung to the windows and a cold, pale yellow light tinted the walls. Royal pulled her shawl tight about her shoulders.

Frown lines around the Queen's mouth and forehead showed that she was not convinced by Royal's story. For once, Royal hoped her mother was right. Royal slipped into a closet adjoining the room where the young princesses studied. As soon as the Queen came in behind her, she shut the door with a click.

'Why can't we just go in and talk to her?' the Queen asked.

'I told you. She is . . . suspicious.'

Royal knew the Queen would rather be at Frogmore, supervising the decoration of her new apartments. It was one thing for her to neglect the little ones' education, but Royal wouldn't let her turn a blind eye to their health. Sophia needed help, yet she fought off all Royal's ministrations with an eye of dark mistrust. Royal didn't know what to do. Without experience of nursing or a voice of authority, she was powerless in the face of her sister's illness.

She eased the door open a crack. The attendant, Mrs Cheveley, knew the plan; she had kept Sophia sewing with her back to them.

Sophia sat composed, embroidering flowers onto a cushion, her golden hair flowing over her shoulder. The Queen poked her nose through the gap in the door and watched her.

'Suspicious, you said? You don't – you don't think she will be . . .' She struggled with the word in her throat and spat it out like a thing vomited, '. . . mad? Like her father?'

'Papa is not mad,' Royal said, with more conviction than she felt. 'He is better now.'

The Queen nodded but the trouble didn't leave her pinched face.

Together, they observed Sophia pulling her needle in and out of the material. She was concentrating hard, making even, accurate stitches.

'I see nothing alarming. She looks well enough. A little thin, perhaps.'

Royal grunted with annoyance. 'It is more than that. She has not been right since she collapsed at Greenwich. Wait, you'll see.'

As the words fell from Royal's mouth, Sophia turned deadly still. Suddenly, the needle dropped from her hand, swinging uselessly by the silk. She slumped back in her chair. It was happening again. Royal put a fist in her mouth to stop herself crying out; she knew what came next. The fit started gradually, little spasms in the arms and face. But the twitching built up like the crescendo of an orchestra, taking on a rhythm of its own. It was as if a demon had possessed Sophia; her slender body contorted and tossed from side to side, threatening to throw her from the chair.

'Mrs Cheveley says this can happen several times a day,' Royal whispered.

A tambour frame clattered to the floor. Sophia jerked convulsively, one last time, and fell limp. There was a moment of profound stillness. Then, Sophia stretched her tumbled limbs, like a kitten waking from sleep. With perfect calm, she sat forward, picked up her needle and started sewing again.

Royal shut the door.

The Queen's knees gave way and she fell onto a chair, crunching her silk dress. Her face was ashen beneath her elaborate hair.

Good. Perhaps she would pay attention now.

'I don't know what to do,' she admitted to Royal. 'We must call a physician – perhaps we should send her away for better air. Make sure Mrs Cheveley is her companion every night; I do not want her sleeping alone.'

'I will arrange it at once.'

The Queen seized Royal's hand and looked at her with eyes full of need. 'We must do everything we can. Sophy was born just before Octavius and Alfred. That end of the family is not strong.'

Royal shuddered. What a foolish thought. There was no such thing as a family curse. 'No, Mama. We will make her better. And remember, Amelia's the youngest child. She's healthy.'

The Queen withdrew her hand and looked away into some dismal memory Royal could not share.

'You do not know what it is to lose a child,' she said in a thick, choking voice. 'I've lost two sons. I cannot, I *cannot* lose a daughter.'

⌁ *St James's Palace, London* ⌁

It was no ordinary drawing room. Charlotte felt every eye pinned on her, like needle-pricks in her skin. Even Sophia's illness flew from her mind. She had been so concerned about losing a daughter, she had not worried about losing a friend.

She cast her wary eyes down the long, white chamber, taking in the sparkling chandeliers, the ladies in their hoops and wigs, the men wearing breeches and embroidered waistcoats. Which of them would turn on her, given the chance?

If a nation could turn against a young, pretty queen, what hope did Charlotte have? She put her hand to her neck and adjusted the ribbon around it, painfully aware of its exposure. Marie Antoinette. Her poor lively, artistic friend. As the pressure of water built in Charlotte's eyes, she turned her head to the windows. The crimson drapes framing them stood out against the walls like streaks of blood. Her heart flipped over in horror and she looked away.

The image was clear in her mind: Marie Antoinette wheeled out through the streets on a tumbrel. Once, she rode in a fine carriage, but she made her last journey on a farmer's cart. Rather than mounting the royal dais, she walked up wooden steps to the scaffold. The woman to whom people used to kneel was strapped to a dirty board and laid her head down for the last time upon the guillotine.

Horror clawed through Charlotte's guts as she pictured the scene: rough wood splintering against her chin, her shoulders tensing for the terrible blow, the roar of people subsiding for the sickening whistle as the blade dropped. Her poor, poor friend. Gone.

'Did you see Adolphus's shoulder?' she whispered to the King. 'It is a miracle he can stand and talk. No wonder they sent him home.'

The King followed his wife's gaze across the floor to their young son. His arm was strapped across his chest and his coat bulged where it covered his injured shoulder.

'Dolly will be well again. Do not fret over those scratches. You must prepare yourself to see Ernest. Apparently his eye and cheek are badly scarred.'

'When will he be back?'

'Soon after Fred.'

The name hung in the air like a foul smell between them. After his exploits in Dunkirk, the Duke of York was coming home in disgrace. He was not fit to command; the Prime Minister had intervened and forced the King to summon him home.

All this worry, swirling about George, like leaves in an autumn gale. He loved Fred the most. Would he be able to bear his shame?

'You must not get upset about Fred,' she urged him. She

heard the desperation in her voice. 'I'm sure he tried his best.'

The King sighed. 'If only we could have frozen time when they were young, eh? The little boys, the girls . . . especially the girls.'

He was right – it would not be a pleasant thing to watch these girls grow into women. Sophia was already drooping under ill health – and what would become of Amelia? She was too beautiful, too clever to be content with the life of an English princess. She would want to marry, but the King would never allow it. Charlotte could see, even now, while she was only ten years old, that he would never let her go.

But perhaps she was worrying too soon. If the revolutionary fever spread, there would be no future for the monarchy. Her daughters would never grow up. The guillotine would ensure that none of them aged a year.

CHAPTER SIXTEEN

Gloucester Lodge, Weymouth
↶ 1794 ↷

'There you are, Your Royal Highness, a nice gentle mare.'

Charlotte watched critically as General Garth lifted Sophia into the saddle. 'Be careful now,' she warned. Sophia was usually a good horsewoman, but today she didn't look strong enough to control a mouse. With her big wide eyes and delicate drained face, she was like a porcelain doll. One spook, one bolt on the horse's part, would surely break her.

Prince Ernest drew up close alongside on his strong bay hunter. George was right to warn Charlotte about his scar. A gruesome, white and pink smile slashed across the cheek of his handsome face. One eye was badly damaged, heavy-hooded and drooping.

'Stop fretting, Mama. She'll be fine. I'll be right by her side.'

Ernest had taken a fancy to his little sister since returning from the war. Charlotte was glad of it; his dry humour made Sophia smile and brought a bit of colour to her wan cheeks.

General Garth clucked his tongue and the horses idled forwards, swishing their tails in time to the slow click of their hooves. Charlotte waved her handkerchief at them, keeping her eyes on Sophia.

When she returned to her rooms, she found her dog Badine in a hurry of spirits. The little spaniel refused to sit by Charlotte's side and rejected the cake crumbs offered to pacify her. 'What is it, dear heart? Are you ill?' Badine padded to the door, where she lay down with a huff. At first Charlotte thought nothing of it, but then Badine sniffed at the crack of air beneath the door and scrabbled her paws against the floorboards.

Uneasiness snaked around her shoulders. What had Badine heard? Animals were always the first to sense something wrong. Charlotte immediately thought of Sophia, but swatted the awful idea away. 'Badine, what are you doing? Come, sit down.' With a reproachful look, Badine slunk back to the sofa. But within a few seconds, hooves clattered in the street and she sprang up with a sharp bark.

Charlotte jumped. 'What is it? Lady Wyndham, do go and see.'

Lady Wyndham stuck her needle in a pin cushion and brushed aside the curtains. 'Why, it's the Prince of Wales, Your Majesty!'

Charlotte's limbs turned to stone. Something was

wrong. The Prince was still at odds with the King, and besides, he would never come to a place as dull as Weymouth without a summons.

She swallowed, hard. 'What a pleasant surprise.'

The main entrance opened with a jangle of locks and chains. They heard an indistinct hum of voices from the hall, then riding boots slapping across the flagstones and trotting up the stairs. The prince had gone straight to the King; this could not be good. It could not be good at all.

Charlotte put her needle aside and scooped Badine onto her lap, gripping her warm, silken fur.

Finally, after hours of delay, Charlotte received her orders to wait on the King.

She stole up the stairs, burning to know why George had come, fearing to hear the answer. What would she find behind the door? The King in tears? Furious? She entered the small room – such a contrast to her palaces in London. A large window opened out onto the Esplanade, where hoards of people rushed to and fro. Beyond them the sea spread out like a cardboard backdrop in a theatre, pushing a flutter of salty air in through the sash.

The King turned to face Charlotte, his features shining with joy. Her breath caught at the fleeting glimpse of her old, handsome bridegroom.

'My dear, what's happened? Was George here?'

He came to her, both hands outstretched, and kissed her cheeks in turn. 'Yes. He wants to get married.'

Married? Her blood tingled with a sense of foreboding. He couldn't – he was already married. Sworn before God. Everyone knew. 'But – what about Mrs Fitzherbert?'

The King nodded and rubbed his hands together in business-like fashion. 'That's all over. They were never legally married; you know my Act of Royal Marriages forbids it.'

So, just like that, years and years of devotion were dismissed. These men were cruel when they wanted to be. She knew she should rejoice that George was finally pleasing his father by taking a bride in preparation for his future role of King. But the idea felt sinful – bigamous.

'I am amazed,' she said.

He threw up his hands. 'A change of heart; he's come to know his duty.' He paused. 'Are you not going to ask me who he wants to marry?'

Jealousy hollowed out Charlotte's insides. This woman would not only replace her in young George's heart; she would be the successor to her role, the next Queen of England.

'He came to you with a specific proposal in mind?'

'Yes. The only proper alliance. One I wanted to point out to him . . . his cousin Caroline.'

Bile rose up in Charlotte's mouth as the room seemed suddenly dark and quiet. Caroline of Brunswick. Daughter of a woman Charlotte despised, the topic of salacious gossip.

'You are not pleased?' He hesitated. 'Oh, of course! Did not you tell me some time ago that your brother Charles was thinking of marrying her?'

'Yes, but I advised him against it.'

He looked at her sharply. 'Why?'

Because Caroline is an indecent, eccentric slut of a woman who has to be kept under constant supervision.

'On account of the age difference.'

He nodded. 'Very true. No such problems in this case, though. There are – what? – six years between George and Caroline?'

The awful things Charlotte had heard about Princess Caroline rang out like mocking cries in her memory. She was dirty, unchaste and wicked. Was such a woman to take her place? Take her son?

The King watched her. 'You like it very little, I fear.'

How could she tell him the awful truth about his own niece? How could she begin to explain that Caroline's mother, the King's sister, bullied her from her first moments in England? Suddenly she was there again, years before, in the antique environs of St James's Palace. Exhausted by the emotion and confusion of her wedding ceremony, fighting to keep her shoulders straight, pulling against the colossal weight of her diamond stomacher.

Women she did not know came forward and kissed her

flushed cheeks, dismaying her with the beauty and elegance of their English fashions. Then another set of blooming girls came to the front and stared at her.

It had been the King's sister, Augusta, who seized Charlotte's hand with a rough motion and held it out for the ladies to kiss. 'For God's sake!' she muttered, just under her breath. 'It's bad enough she's ugly. Did he have to marry a simpleton too?'

Charlotte hadn't understood the language, back then, but she caught the meaning. She could translate the titter that rippled round the circle of prettier, fashionable women. That had been the first hostility. It had only got worse from there. Despite the years that had passed, the bitterness of those taunts and the terror Charlotte felt in the past still ached like a raw wound.

Snapping back to Weymouth and the present, she avoided meeting the King's eye. 'I will treat the Princess of Brunswick very well, I assure you.' She knew it was a lie. She knew she would punish Princess Caroline for her mother's misdeeds.

The King beamed at her. 'Good. I knew I could rely on you. It is what our dear son wants, after all.'

'Yes,' she said wearily. 'I will always do everything in my power to make him – and you – happy.'

CHAPTER SEVENTEEN

Queen's House, London
～ 1795 ～

Royal's thumb had a groove, like a miniature valley, from the impression of her sewing needle. The delicate skin of her fingertips stung. Laying the needle carefully upon her lap, she shook cramp out of her right hand. A circle of intent women surrounded her: the Queen and every princess, embroidering for George's wedding. They'd been working since daybreak – even Sophia, still frail from illness and smothered in rugs with a bowl of gruel at her side.

It was odd to imagine a bride winging her way toward them across war-torn Europe. Royal settled back into her chair and the fire kissed warmth onto her face. Thank God that amidst all this fighting and misery, wonderful things could still happen.

Amelia rubbed her eyes with her fist. 'How many children will George have? Will he have as many as you, Mama?'

A shadow passed over the Queen's face. 'God willing, Amelia, he shall.'

'A son first,' Mary specified with an expert stab into her material. 'Another King George.'

A niece or a nephew. Royal imagined a new-born baby and her arms felt empty; there was a disgruntled tug about her womb. She recalled her little brothers and sisters; their sweet gurgling noises, the wonderful smell of a brand new person. A child growing up around the palaces would change everything.

'How do you get on?' George bounced into the room, excitement animating his portly frame.

The Queen gave him a thin, tight smile. 'Much the same as half an hour ago, my dear.'

He chuckled. 'Well, I have been prodigiously busy in that time. I have told Papa who should be in my wife's household and I've just had a meeting with the architect. All the renovations will be ready when Caroline comes.'

'I rather thought Carlton House was grand enough,' the Queen said in a dampening voice. 'Can you really afford to make such large alterations?'

'Yes, of course. Once Parliament approves my new allowance, everything will be fine.'

The Queen pursed her lips and continued sewing. The union clearly displeased her. Royal couldn't understand why. She thought her mother would be proud, now that George was trying to make himself respectable.

'Show me the picture again.' Amelia stretched out her arms. 'I want to see my new sister.'

George bent over her chair and kissed the top of her golden head. He handed her a small, round portrait. Royal glimpsed large, sloping eyes and a long nose. 'And she is on her way even now!'

'Yes. We must make everything perfect for her.'

'Perfect?' A glob of spit shot out of the Queen's mouth, across the room. 'She is from Brunswick! What do you think she's used to?'

George shrugged and paced around the circle of women, his hands behind his back. The only sounds were the tap of his boots and the crackle from the fire. Royal wondered if, despite the unreasonable quality of her anger, the Queen was right. She often got the hideous suspicion George was making these improvements to Carlton House for himself, not his bride. Of all the topics relating to his marriage, his increased allowance from Parliament was the one he talked about the most.

He slowed as he passed Royal's chair, leaning in as if to inspect her work. With a deft movement, he dropped a note onto her lap. Almost without thinking, she covered it with her fabric, and George continued walking.

Could it be? The scrap of paper burned through her skirt. Blood raced impatiently through her veins. This note could only mean one thing: he had found a bridegroom for her.

From under her eyelashes, she saw the Queen focused on her work, too angry with the conversation to attend it further. Maybe just a little peek. One glance to prove she wasn't dreaming. Royal folded the silk and moved her hand to straighten it out, the note curled in her palm. A scratch of spidery black writing met her eyes. There were four words: *The Duke of Oldenburg.*

It was like the sun had emerged from behind a cloud. Royal struggled to hide her blooming grin. Pure delight flooded her chest and threatened to burst her ribcage.

God bless him.

ᕁ *Chapel Royal, St James's Palace, London* ᕁ

It was just like Charlotte's nightmares about Alfred – she saw the horror approaching, but could not stop it.

Her legs shook on the edge of her chair, urging her to stand and cry out that this was madness. But it took more courage to say nothing. She gripped the arms of her seat, half-expecting her fingers to splinter the wood.

The bride looked just as Charlotte intended in a gown of velvet, silver tissue and lace, festooned with bows and ribbons all the way down the skirt. The candles winked as Caroline waited for her groom, catching on her jewels and throwing out spirals of glitter. She had long, soft curls down her back and a pile of rich material and feathers towering on her head. But she was still ugly.

No art could conceal the vulgar rouge patches slapped on her face, her sloping nose with its sharp end or her wide, sloe-like eyes. Gaps in the teeth and indications of rot marred her bashful smile. Was such a girl to be the next Queen of England?

Charlotte's son, her George, arrived swaying before the altar. The Dukes of Bedford and Roxburghe stepped in to hold him upright. Sweat dripped off his pale, rigid face. King Louis of France couldn't have looked worse on his way to his execution.

Thankfully, the chapel was dark, with wavering candles throwing long shadows down the aisle. No one would see Charlotte clearly and realise she wasn't the image of a proud mother. She took a deep, calming breath, inhaling the cold scent of stone. On her wedding day, this candlelit space looked enchanting and romantic. Now dark corners and the constant hiss of burning wax made it eerie.

She had foreseen this disaster, but there was no satisfaction in being right. George was as revolted by Caroline as Charlotte was. A pile of bank notes might have softened the blow – but there were none. War had drained the Treasury and it couldn't afford to grant George the sum he expected. Now, with a wife and a potential family to support, he was only going to run up more debt.

The ceremony played out with the gravity of a funeral. It was wrong, terribly wrong. They knew, every one of them, that George yearned to crawl back to Mrs Fitzherbert, but they kept patching together this false union of souls, calling on God to approve their actions.

'Therefore, if any man can show any just cause, why they may not lawfully be joined together, let him speak now, or else hereafter forever hold his peace.' The Archbishop of Canterbury laid down his book, staring from George to the King, from the King to George.

Charlotte closed her eyes but the imprints of the figures before the altar still flickered on the backdrop of her eyelids.

He is already married. He is married to Mrs Fitzherbert. She prayed someone would say something, do something to stop it, but no one moved.

The Archbishop was forced to carry on.

Caroline gave her promises in the half-light. George struggled to return the words, cloyed with a combination of misery and alcohol.

At last it was done. The choir swelled in an anthem of rejoicing as Charlotte's son and the Brunswick girl walked arm in arm down the aisle, the bride just keeping her drunken husband stable.

'What is the matter, my prince? You have such a sad face on!'

Charlotte closed her eyes and clenched her hands, remembering she was another bride who was called ugly. The matter, she needed to tell Caroline, was that she was ill-looking and she smelled. And George, addicted to the finer things in life, would never even try to love her.

CHAPTER EIGHTEEN

St James's Palace, London

A low autumn sun illuminated a wood-panelled room: dust on the windowsill, dark tapestries on the wall and a girl, crouched beside them.

A young Charlotte, fresh-skinned and auburn-haired, packed jewellery into a chest. Milky pearls, emeralds and an immense diamond stomacher. She took a cross from around her neck, kissed it, and laid it gently on top of the hoard.

As she went to close the lid, a pair of painted eyes met hers: the pearl bracelet on her slim wrist, bearing a portrait of George. She lingered over this last piece, uncertain. At last she undid the clasp and committed it to the chest.

Her window looked out onto the dirty streets of London, so different from the home she had known. What wouldn't she give to see the sleepy Schloss with its crumbling tower, or the beech tree where she played as a child?

Misery sat awkwardly with her — it had rarely been her companion before.

She caressed Presto, the little dog nudging against her leg, and shut the lid on her treasures. Turning the key in the lock, she scrambled to her feet, weighed down by the cage of whalebone and canvas supporting her skirts. As she put out a hand to steady herself, the sepia light fell upon her little finger. Another ring, with George's face upon it. That, too? She wavered. Perhaps one ornament was allowed. It had no useless finery about it; simply the comforting features of the man who had so quickly become her whole world in this nest of strangers.

'Come, Presto!' She folded her hands and started toward the door. She was about to place her fingers upon the knob, when it flew at her face.

'There you are!' Augusta, the Dowager Princess, her mother-in-law. Her shrewd eyes darted at Charlotte beneath their arching, disapproving brows. 'You're not going to Communion like that!'

The Dowager Princess purposefully spoke English, not the French that Charlotte understood.

She was silent for a moment, translating, before she ventured to reply. 'Like what?'

'Without your jewels! I told your ladies to lay them out for you. Useless women!'

'They did. They dressed me in them.' Charlotte flushed, speaking in French. 'I came here to take them off.'

'Take them off?' The Dowager Princess repeated in disbelief.

'Yes. I didn't think it right to go to a solemn service in them . . . remembering the Last Supper . . . it insults God.'

The older woman guffawed and pushed her back into the room. 'Rubbish, child! Where would you get an idea like that? Put them back on.'

Charlotte saw George's three sisters poke their noses round the door, whispering gleefully at her expense. She set her jaw.

'I will not. I promised my mother I would never . . .'

'Your mother is dead.'

'All the more reason to respect her words!'

'You won't offend the court and dress like a beggar at church. I won't have it.'

Angry tears scalded her eyes. In the past, in every other dream, she submitted to what came next. But not this time.

Presto yapped and jumped about her feet, spurring her on. She screwed her hand into a fist.

'Go on, then! Put them back on. At once! Do you hear?'

Charlotte snarled at the mocking, flabby face, heaved up her fist and swung with all her might . . .

She did not have the satisfaction of completing her punch. The world tilted beneath her and she snapped awake as her head collided with the carriage window.

The King sat beside her, pale and swaying. 'George? What is it?'

She tried to sit up. The cushioned upholstery tossed beneath her like a tempestuous sea. The carriage was rocking. She looked out of the window and screamed. Filthy, angry faces pressed close, baring their teeth. She scuttled back.

'Be still, my love. We mustn't betray fear, whatever happens.'

People surrounded them. The horses shied, scrabbling their hooves against the road with deep-throated whinnies.

A fist thundered at the window. 'Bread! Peace and bread!'

She reached out and clutched George's hands to stop her own from shaking. 'Is that all they want? Bread?'

'War drives the price up,' he explained. 'Do not worry. The guards will come soon.'

Do not worry? He saw all this and told her not to worry? He must be invulnerable to fear.

The dark cloud of people continued to push the carriage and shriek.

'Down with the tyrant!'

'No King!'

Charlotte pictured the shadow of the guillotine, stretching across the channel from France. But George didn't even tremble. Without warning, the window cracked and shivered into fragments of glass. She shrieked and crouched down, covering her head with her hands.

'Was that a shot?'

A smoking hole in the upholstery answered her.

The surly cries of the rabble came louder now. Through the broken glass, dirty hands reached in and scratched at the door. One grimy finger caught on the fichu around her neck. Charlotte sprang into George's lap, letting the piece of material fly loose and sail out of the shattered window.

'We'll be killed!' She buried her head in his shoulder, shutting out the noise.

'No fear, Charlotte,' was all he murmured. 'No fear.'

Sharp flecks of stone flew in through the window and pricked Charlotte's flesh. When she raised a wary eye from

George's coat, she saw her lap covered in grit, the tissue and gauze of her gown torn to pieces. Another violent jolt – this time, from the front. Charlotte heard a horse grunt as its harness jangled. Dear God, they were taking the horses from between the shafts!

'No! Stop it!' A strange, male voice by the window. A broad back appeared and shielded them from the view of the mob. 'Damn it, I've got the coachman's blunderbuss and I'm not afraid to use it. If one of you steps an inch nearer the King, I'll blow your bloody head off.' The crowd hissed and jeered. Their unknown protector fired a warning shot into the air, lighting up the sky outside.

Just then, in the distance, the trumpet blast of the Horse Guards rang out.

Thank God, thank God. They were saved.

Queen's House, London

Methodically, Royal bathed the cut, vivid against the Queen's long, pale cheek. It was a repetitive motion that stilled the flurry of her thoughts. People had hissed at her brothers before, even at the King. But an attack on the Queen was something new. Far too French for Royal's liking.

'My own people . . .' the Queen muttered through white lips. 'My own people throw stones at me! They shoot at the King's carriage! It will be the guillotine next Royal, you mark my words.'

Royal brought out her false, soothing voice and wrung the wad of damp cloth. 'No, Mama. It's healing nicely now. See? Only a very little cut.'

'This time, yes. But what about the next?'

'There won't be a next time.' Royal spoke with a cheerfulness she didn't feel. 'Papa has offered a reward. They will catch the wicked men and that will be an end of it.'

The Queen mumbled something in German about the price of bread and scowled.

Royal placed the sodden cloth back in the bowl and shook drops of water from her fingers. Then she took a soft piece of flannel and dabbed her mother's face. Where was the courage and good cheer that used to define her? Every conversation with the Queen these days was like coaxing a fretful infant.

'Come on, now. It will be Christmas soon and then George's baby is due in January. Think of that! You will be a grandmother.'

The Queen said nothing.

'Perhaps this baby will bring him and Caroline closer together?'

The Queen brushed away Royal's hand and pressed her fingers to her eyelids. 'No, it won't. How could he ever be close to a woman like that? And what if their son is just like her? Imagine that: a Brunswicker King of England!'

Royal sighed and laid a hand on her shoulder. It was a grim thought. She, too, disliked the rowdy and volatile

Caroline, but the King was fond of her and if he could see goodness beneath the exterior, there must be something there.

'Don't worry, Mama.'

The Queen shook her head.

Annoyance throbbed through Royal. Her mother wasn't the only one suffering. How long would she refuse to take comfort, drag them down with her?

A scratch at the door disturbed them. The Queen inclined her head. 'Enter.'

The King's equerry General Garth scraped his way into the room. Royal smiled at him, her eyes avoiding the claret birth mark branded across his cheek and eye.

'Your Majesty.' He bowed low to the Queen, hat in hand. The gold braid on his scarlet coat glistened. 'Your Royal Highness,' he said, turning to Royal. 'The King begs the favour of your attendance in his library for a moment.'

This was it. Her heart flipped inside out like a parasol in the wind. This was the moment for which she had thirsted, ever since George leant over her shoulder and gave her the paper about the Duke of Oldenburg.

Royal looked to the Queen for approval, fighting the muscles in her cheeks that wanted to smile. 'May I go?'

The Queen nodded, looking as dismal as ever.

With a dazzling grin, Royal took the general's arm and set off toward the Octagon Library. The elation of her spirits was impossible to contain; she did not want to walk, she wanted to dance with him through the palace. Just like that, the world was transformed.

When she looked at the walls and realised she might escape them forever, they became beautiful; full of exquisite plasterwork and stucco roses. At long last, the shackles of her imprisonment rattled loose around her ankles. She would go to the King, and he would say . . .

What would he say? He could not possibly say *no*. She thought of the Queen's words after his recovery. *No sudden changes. No separations.* In her desperation to break free, she had forgotten the risks. What if the madness came back? What if she, and she alone, caused a relapse?

Before she had time to plan her defence, she was there. The King's men opened the double doors and let her into the library.

The room was wide and tall, tapering up to a domed ceiling. As she walked forward, rows and rows of books filled her eyes, rising higher with every step. Some of them contained laws, rules binding her to the King's will. Ensuring that she could not marry without his consent. She took a breath. The air was laced with the scent of leather and freshly turned pages.

There he was. Her father looked small in the forest of books. She swept him a curtsey. His skin was pale and sweaty, his eyes dark with thought. 'Come here, my dear.'

She approached the desk cautiously. Of course he would resist the idea of her marrying at first. But she must convince him. She *would* convince him; the whole course of her future depended on it.

'Sit down.'

She leant back into a leather chair. Blades of light fell diagonally across the rows of books, highlighting motes of dust.

'My dear, I've received a letter.'

Something in her soul hardened and steeled itself to her purpose. All at once, she realised she would never surrender. She would have this match if it cost her blood. *What if it costs his mind?* She shook the thought off. He was recovered, now. 'Yes, Papa?'

'It is a proposal of marriage.' He looked down at the paper as if asking it for a prompt. 'A proposal for you,' he specified. 'From the Hereditary Prince of Württemberg.'

Royal baulked at the unexpected name. Surely he meant Oldenburg? *Württemberg?*

'Yes, you may well be surprised. I cannot believe he would think of it, after the dealings he had with your cousin.'

Royal put a hand to her forehead, feeling giddy. Someone else had asked for her. She was solicited by someone who, as far as she knew, had no gentle nudge from her brother. Could it be possible?

'He asked for me?' she repeated stupidly. 'Me first? Not Augusta or Mary?'

'Eh? Yes, he asked for you. But that is not the point. Do you not understand who this is? The brother of that prince who came wooing Augusta. Remember? He was married to your cousin and abandoned her in Russia?'

She did remember. The widower of her cousin, who disappeared in mysterious circumstances only to turn up dead months later. Her stomach should recoil with revulsion at the thought of such a husband, but it didn't. A beggar doesn't refuse a mouldy crust of bread.

'Of course I told his minister I could never send my daughter to a man with such brutal, unpleasant qualities.'

Disappointment soured Royal's mouth. In the set determination of the King's face, she saw her hopes blowing away like bleached leaves in an autumn wind.

'Then why are you telling me this?' she blurted out.

The King sighed. He made a bridge with his fingers and rested his chin upon it. 'Because I am worried about you. You are quiet and withdrawn. We hardly see you. Your brother George says it is because you're not married. He seems to think you want to be settled, more than anything in the world.' He laughed uncertainly.

Don't, Papa, don't. She knew what he was doing; he wanted her to refute it. He was inviting her to say she would stay with him forever, that his love was enough for her. But she had to admit, at last, the simple fact she had known all along: it wasn't.

She had never let her father down in her life. She felt his expectations snake around her like ropes, tying her to England.

'It's true,' she said softly. 'I want to marry more than any-thing.' The words tasted revolting, like a sin confessed.

He did not move. A clock chimed in the distance. 'I thought all six of you would stay here with me.'

Royal picked at her fingernail. Suddenly the wooden desk became a barricade between them, a battle line. If only she could make him understand. She loved him dearly – more dearly than she could ever say. But she could not give up her life for his comfort. She wouldn't.

'Of course you should marry one day,' he explained. 'But there's no rush for these things. Your poor mother had terrible trouble when we were newlywed. She was too lenient with her servants and her maids went on strike. One of them even took her jewels!'

Royal closed her eyes, shielding herself from the pathetic sight of him. 'I must take my chances, Papa. I am twenty-nine. How many children did you have at twenty-nine?'

He paused. Avoiding her question, he said, 'I just – I just don't want any of those horrible things to happen to you, Royal. I love you.'

She bowed her head in shame. The ribbons in her hair drooped and brushed her cheeks. She felt like a villain. A stone cold, heartless monster. But God help her, she would never give in on this one point.

'I love you too, Papa. I really do. But I need to marry.'

His big blue eyes were full of memories. She knew he was

thinking of his sisters, disastrously wed, and his miserable nieces, Augusta and Caroline.

He didn't realise Royal was more capable. Even he didn't see what she could become if she were only free of this palace.

'Perhaps,' he said unhappily. 'Perhaps.'

CHAPTER NINETEEN

Queen's House, London
Winter 1795

The grandfather clock chimed, singing out Caroline's doom. Over an hour late!

Sophia envied her bravado – following her own time, letting the Queen stew. A courageous act, though not a particularly wise one.

She bent over her book, trying to hide in it. If only she had stayed upstairs with Mary, she wouldn't be caught in this embarrassing tiff. The words on the page blurred – she couldn't block out the raised voices of her parents.

'This is outrageous.' The Queen placed her hands on her hips. 'She was due at five!'

'Hush, dear.' The King came up beside her and patted her shoulder. 'I have sent a messenger. I'm sure there will be some explanation.'

'One good enough to keep the King and Queen of England waiting? Without as much as a note?'

The King took the Queen's hand and led her to a wing-chair. 'It is badly done. I'll talk to her. The pace of life is slower at Brunswick. She must learn how we do things here.'

The Queen looked at him doubtfully. 'Is she capable of learning?'

'Of course. She will learn. Won't she, Sophy?'

Sophia started. She knew they would draw her into this, sooner or later. 'I hope so, Papa.'

It would be impolitic to agree with him and antagonise the Queen. Sophia had never seen her hate with such ferocity. What reason could she have? Caroline was certainly coarse, but not a fiend. If anything, her vulgarity was amusing – a breath of fresh air in the stuffy old palaces.

'Be charitable,' the King counselled. 'Imagine she is one of our girls, married into a strange country. Would you not want their parents-in-law to have patience with their faults?'

The Queen's face changed. He had her there. She'd done nothing but fret since an offer of marriage had come for Royal.

If the match took place, Sophia prayed that the Duchess of Württemberg would prove a kinder mother-in-law to Royal than the Queen of England was to Caroline.

A rap at the door interrupted them. A messenger, clothed in gold, announced the Princess of Wales.

'There, now!' said the King. His satisfaction was evident as he pulled on the lapels of his coat.

They stood – the Queen grudgingly – as Caroline entered the room. Her belly went before her. She was enormous with child.

Her dress was buttoned up all wrong, her hair had not seen a comb for days, but it failed to spoil her radiance. Sophia felt a twinge of jealousy as she took in the glowing skin, the becoming plumpness.

'Uncle!' Caroline walked straight to the King and kissed him, her lips making a loud smack against his cheek. 'How good to see you!' She still spoke in French – her grasp of the English language was poor. Sophia received a handshake, the Queen a brusque curtsey. 'Fine weather,' Caroline smiled.

The Queen stared. '*Fine weather?*' she mimicked. 'Is that all you have to say for yourself? You're over an hour late!'

'Am I? Blast it – there's no keeping time in this state! I spend half the day tied to the close-stool.' Laughter welled up inside Sophia; she fought to keep it in. 'Do you know,' Caroline continued, heaving herself into a chair, 'George has put velvet seats on them? Crimson velvet! As if that could make the things pleasant! You cannot polish muck, my mother always says.'

The Queen wrinkled her nose. 'Indeed, you cannot.'

Caroline did not rise to the bait; she simply flashed an infuriating smile.

'And what do you mean by seating yourself? Did the King invite you?'

'My dear – her condition . . .'

'I am so fagged!' said Caroline, stretching her arms. 'Sophy, fetch me that footstool, would you?'

Sophia obeyed, grinning. She had never seen anyone beat the Queen before and it intoxicated her. She swapped a triumphant look with Caroline as she helped her place her swollen ankles on the cushion.

'Well, *you* may have time to waste talking of muck and nonsense – I do not.' The Queen snapped her fingers and a lady rushed over with her gloves. 'I waited because I wouldn't go without seeing you, but you really have made me late.'

'I regret it, Aunt.'

While the Queen prepared to depart, Caroline turned to Sophia and took her arm. 'Sit by me. I have been meaning to talk to you.'

Sophia's chest squeezed. Would it be about Royal's prospective husband? She had heard worrying rumours but Caroline would know the truth. Her deceased sister was the pivot on which all the gossip turned.

The voice of the Queen stopped Sophia dead. 'Sophia has no time. She is coming with me.'

'I am?' she asked, bemused. Why did the Queen make herself so disagreeable? Why could she not be cordial to Caroline, just to please the King?

'Oh, do stay, Sophy,' Caroline urged. 'Just a minute. You can join the Queen later.'

Sophia wavered, trapped between an imploring face and a barbed one. She looked to the King as the only male authority in the room. His furrowed brow and widened eyes only reflected the confusion she felt.

'Come, Sophia. Now. We have errands.'

There were no errands. Her hateful mother had no right, no right at all, to make up these lies. She acted as if a minute's conversation with Caroline would soil her forever.

The King swallowed loudly and fidgeted. Could Sophia defy the Queen and risk an argument with him present? Would his sensitive nerves withstand it?

'I am waiting.'

Sophia coloured painfully. The King's worried expression made up her mind for her.

'No, I really must go,' she told Caroline. 'I am ever so sorry.'

'Oh. Well. Another time, perhaps.'

Sophia turned from Caroline's wounded look. Burning with shame, she let the Queen frogmarch her to the door.

CHAPTER TWENTY

Upper Lodge, Windsor
∿ 1796 ∿

Charlotte surveyed the litter of paper on her desk in dismay. Scrawled writing, blots of ink and globs of wax swam in a pool of light beneath her candle. Only the letter from her son George stood out.

Can you not make Papa agree to a separation? I would be serving my family in the most essential manner by ridding them of a fiend. Otherwise, all of us must make up our minds to submit to her evil influence for the rest of our lives.

Nothing can equal what I go through. No words can paint it strongly enough for your imagination. I abhor her; my aversion and detestation are rooted. I shudder at the very thought of sitting down at table with her.

God bless you ever dearest mother. I am so overpowered with unhappiness I feel light-headed. I know not where to turn for a friend now but to you . . .

*

Every ounce of common sense told Charlotte to leave the situation between George and Caroline be. The Prince of Wales had done nothing to merit her unswerving loyalty. Rather the opposite – she still recalled those dark days when he rode roughshod over her toward the Regency. But alongside that image was another: the new-born baby, suspended over the Christening font as Charlotte reclined proudly on a bed of state. He was her flesh and blood, her boy. She would always be on his side, deep down. Charlotte understood what it was to despair of a marriage; for discontentment to grow up like weeds and smother the blooms. Her boy deserved better than that.

Wind howled around the walls, moaning like a tormented fiend. Maybe it was a warning; a foretaste of the punishment ahead if she continued. If the King were to find out . . . He had been troubled enough by the offer of marriage for Royal. Dare Charlotte cross swords with him over this? She put down the candle and sat heavily in her chair. Scooping her Pomeranian dog, Mercury, onto her lap, she fiddled absentmindedly with his ear.

What had she become? She had spent a lifetime nursing hatred for the mother-in-law who tried to crush and dominate her spirit. But now Caroline was here and Charlotte was falling into the same pattern: she was making Caroline's life hell.

Feeling her discomfort, Mercury wriggled and licked her fingers. The gentle lap of his tongue warmed her cold hands.

Upstairs, the King ran about in high glee. The Brunswick girl had pupped a granddaughter, named Charlotte for the Queen. It would not do to think of that poor baby. If Charlotte dwelt on the little thing, so innocent in all of this, she would not be able to perform her task.

The sound of the King's joy jarred against the lament of the wind. Glasses chinked as he drank to little Charlotte's health. He thought grandsons would follow, blind fool that he was. Charlotte knew better. She took her right hand from Mercury and gave him the left one to lick. Slowly, she picked up her quill and dipped it in the ink. She let the nib hang over the well and watched dark drips fall off the end. Could she really wreck a new-born baby's home to make George happy? It was impossible to weigh her love for her son with that of her granddaughter. But she had to make a choice.

Finally, she laid her wet quill against the sheet of paper and wrote a line:

Dear Mrs Fitzherbert . . .

A stone of guilt sat uneasily in her stomach. What language did a queen use to beg a common, Catholic woman to reurn to her son and make him smile again? If only this false wife of his, this Mrs Fitzherbert, had been born a Protestant and a princess. She was like soothing balm to George's soul. With her, his temper was better and he was seldom drunk. Fitzherbert was more of a princess than Caroline would ever be.

Cheers rang out upstairs; more toasting to the baby. Charlotte pulled Mercury's furry body to her for comfort and continued her letter. It was a betrayal. But her granddaughter would understand, when she had a son.

∼ Queen's House, London ∼

Sophia crept down the deserted passage, shuffling her feet along the skirting board. She edged forward with one hand on the wooden panelling, her chest against the wall, and felt her heart bump back at her.

She should not be here. Her own daring made her nauseous.

Early in the morning, she had dismissed her ladies, pleading a headache. She told the attendants to let her lie down undisturbed on the bed until four o'clock. She was counting on their obedience – if one of them came to check on her, she was undone.

Her shallow breath rasped. She was nearly there now; Ernest's door was in sight. Was she doing the right thing? Even if she got there without being seen this could still go horribly wrong. But her brother Ernest was her only chance. Surely he would help? At last, she faced the door. It stared at her, daring her. She made a fist, closed her eyes and knocked on the wood with a quick rap.

No answer. Her heart sunk. After all that? Where had he gone? She crouched and saw a slant of light glimmering beneath the door. A sign of occupation? She could go in and see . . . but what if it was a servant, tidying?

She sat back on her heels, debating. She was too scared to think clearly. Fear blocked out her desires and told her to flee. But if she ran back to her rooms now, she would never know. She would spend days blaming herself, sick with guilt. She had to take the chance. Climbing to her feet, she put out a trembling hand and turned the cold handle of the door.

Ernest sat with his feet upon the desk, staring at the ceiling. A cigar dangled from his fingers, perilously close to the carpet. The smell of smoke scratched at Sophia's throat and poked her eyes. Gasping, she staggered to the window and threw open the sash.

'God, Ernest, how do you bear it?' She flapped her hands before her eyes to stop them watering. The relief of finding him was diminished by the haze of bitter fumes.

He considered her upside down, over the mop of his sandy hair. 'I don't usually have guests.' He raised the cigar to his lips and drew on it heavily, causing the tip to glow. 'You can sit down if you like.'

She took the edge of a small, hard chair and waited. He said nothing. He merely sat blowing smoke rings into his own abstracted thoughts.

'I suppose you are surprised to see me here,' she started, 'up and about again?'

'Should I be?'

'I have not been very well recently.'

He looked at her and smiled. The white scar on his cheek became ghoulish as it reacted to the stretch of his muscles. 'I hadn't observed. You are not particularly well at the best of times.'

She rolled her eyes at his taunt. 'You really are intolerable. But I will forgive you today – if you take me to see Caroline.' She tried to drop the words casually, but they hung between them, interlaced with the wreaths of smoke. She gripped the edge of her chair.

Ernest crossed his legs at the knee and mashed his cigar into the desk. 'Why?'

Sophia's cheeks blazed with shame. 'She wanted to speak with me when she was here, but I was not at leisure.'

'Well then, wait until she comes back.'

She stared at him, aghast. 'I can't.'

'Look Sophy,' Ernest sighed, tossing away the dead cigar, 'I know why you want to see her. You want to talk to her on your own and the Queen will never allow it. She probably called you away and you did not dare to refuse her. Am I right?'

Sophia drew her shoulders into her body and shrivelled. It pained her to admit her cowardice, especially to Ernest, who was so determined and sure of himself. 'Yes.'

'For God's sake.' He stood up, brushing his hands. 'Why didn't you say so?'

Because I am ashamed. Because she couldn't bear to admit she was terrified of her mother and would hurt someone else, just to avoid the Queen's displeasure. 'I thought you might take me because . . .' she struggled. 'You seem to like Caroline, too.'

Ernest pulled his coat off the back of his chair. 'I will take you, you little idiot, because you're my sister and you asked me.' He shrugged himself into the navy-blue sleeves with a grunt. 'And if it annoys the old woman or Fred or George, so much the better.'

Carlton House

The Prince of Wales was away in Brighton, but his town house remained cool and exquisite, a living monument to his absence. It retained the faint aura of splendour and style he managed to dust over everything he touched. If only he had been able, or willing, to sprinkle that magic over his marriage.

As Sophia and Ernest pulled up in their sedan chairs, Caroline's nursery assistant, Miss Garth, ran to meet them. Sophia knew her of old; she was niece to the King's equerry, General Garth.

'Princess Caroline will be delighted to see you,' Miss Garth said. 'God knows she is dreary enough, poor thing, with her little list of people she's allowed to see. However did you manage to get away?'

Sophia gestured to Ernest, who grunted in return.

'Take her along, Miss Garth. I am staying around here. I cannot be doing with damned women's talk.' He shooed them away and wandered off through the double doors.

Miss Garth led Sophia around the base of the grand staircase and turned left toward the private saloon. It was like being in another country. The style was rich and exotic – a far cry from the restrained décor the King favoured. As they entered the saloon, Sophia blew out her cheeks in wonder. An excess of green brocade, tassels and gimp met her eyes; the loving decorations George prepared before he met his wife, before he knew how he hated her.

A mewl came from the other side of the room. She turned and saw Caroline coming forward to greet her, baby Charlotte nestled in her arms.

'Oh, look at you! She is beautiful, Caroline!'

Charlotte had rosy, dimpled cheeks and a spray of light brown curls. She was the very image of George. Sophia wanted to scoop her up and kiss every inch of her. She was starting to understand, at eighteen, what it was to yearn for a child of her own.

Caroline watched her caresses with strange, sloping eyes. 'You are brave. Coming here.'

'Ernest brought me. He's downstairs.' Sophia found she couldn't meet Caroline's intense gaze. Remembering her audience, she quickly switched to French. 'I wanted to see you. I felt wretched.'

'Why?'

'I never get to speak to you. I'm always running away.'

'Don't be silly. When the Queen calls you, you have to go.'

Sophia pulled her shoulders back; a tight, awkward gesture. 'She's rude to you. Unpardonably rude. I'm sorry for it.'

'Oh, she doesn't scare me.'

Sophia wished she could say the same.

Caroline gestured for her to sit down. As they fell against the green sofa, Sophia put her arms out for her niece. It was easier to speak of difficult subjects with Charlotte's soft warmth to cling to.

'Caro, I need to ask you something, something delicate. I couldn't put it in a letter.'

Caroline raised an eyebrow. For a moment she looked absolutely farcical, with her big red cheeks and untidy hair.

'They're talking about marrying Royal to the Prince of Württemberg.'

An amused snort escaped Caroline. 'Oh! Fat Fritz, is it?'

'Is he fat? I didn't know . . . Wasn't he married to your sister?' Caroline's sister, her dead sister. Her ghost shimmered before them for a moment, cloaked in grief and mystery.

'Yes,' Caroline said thoughtfully. 'His children are hers.'

Once more Sophia felt embarrassed, trespassing on forbidden ground. She looked down at the baby's silken hair.

'Pray, forgive me for asking. I just need to know – is it true? All those things they say about him?'

Caroline smirked, resting her cheek upon her fingertips. 'I didn't think you liked Royal.'

'She's my sister,' Sophia said simply.

Caroline nodded and exhaled. The room seemed to breathe out with her. 'I can only tell you what I've heard.'

Sophia shuffled along the cushions, closer to her, and Caroline grinned; she never passed up the chance to tell a story, however painful.

'Well, Fritz and 'Gusta went to Russia to visit his sister, who is married to the future Tsar. Old Fritz said he left 'Gusta behind for—', she put on a snooty tone and pulled up her nose, '—behaving *licentiously*. He said no harm would come to her there, because she was a favourite of the Empress, Catherine II. But the next we heard, Catherine had tired of 'Gusta and banished her to Lohde. Apparently she died there giving birth to a bastard.'

Sophia winced at the words of scandal. 'But you don't believe him.'

Caroline shook her head. ''Gusta wrote to me – the man was trying to get rid of her. Any excuse would do. He ordered his aide-de-camp to interfere with her one night, just to slur her name. Luckily she had a maid sleeping with her and the blockhead had to go away again.'

The child slipped from Sophia's lap. She made a grab at her as she cried, 'But – but that's horrible!' Was such a man to marry Royal? What if she was to disappear, like Caroline's sister, never to be heard of again? It would kill the King.

'Oh, they were both as bad as each other. But my sister was never stupid. I'm sure she found a way out of the marriage.'

'What do you mean?'

Caroline shrugged. 'People say they've seen her. At the play, in Geneva . . .'

Sophia's head reeled. 'What, seen her alive?'

'Obviously.'

The room became close and stuffy with the threat of sin. If Royal married this man, she would not truly be his wife. Juggling little Charlotte in one arm, Sophia ran her fingers across her forehead and pressed a thumb deep into her aching temple.

'But then – why did you not say something to the King?'

Caroline offered an airy, infuriating shrug. 'Fritz wants a new wife; Royal wants a husband. My sister wants shot of him. It is all very convenient.'

'But – it's bigamy!'

The moment the word left Sophia's mouth, a change came over Caroline. She drew back and took the baby onto her lap. 'My love, I think you are the only one in your family who cares about that sort of thing.'

Suddenly, Caroline's own situation burst into Sophia's mind and struck her speechless. She had forgotten that

Caroline, too, was a second wife; married to George after he made his vows to Mrs Fitzherbert. She withered inside.

'I beg your pardon. I forgot . . .' The baby made a noise and wriggled. 'I need to tell Royal.'

Caroline turned to her with wearied tolerance. 'What good will it do? Someone needs to look after those children.'

It was true; Fritz's three children in Württemberg were Sophia's own kin – orphans without a mother. Royal would be just the person to take care of them. She hesitated. It made sense but it felt filthy, tainted.

'Would it have made a difference, if you knew? About Mrs Fitzherbert, I mean.'

Caroline tilted her head to meet Sophia's gaze. 'I knew enough.'

Sophia felt a surge of pity for her eccentric, forlorn sister-in-law with her odd clothing and musky smell.

'It will get better, you know,' she said hopefully. 'George will come round. I'm sure he will.'

Caroline smiled, sickly sweet, and laid a hand on top of Sophia's. '*You* make it better for me, *mon coeur*. Thank God *you* will never have to go through this yourself!'

There was something in the way she spoke that made Sophia's skin prickle. 'What do you mean?'

Caroline's cheeks glowed a brighter red beneath her rouge. 'Oh. Never mind.'

'Tell me.'

Caroline shook her head.

'Caroline.' Panic built inside Sophia.

'Oh, Sophy . . .' Caroline looked down at the rug. 'You've been very ill, you know.'

'Yes.'

'Ill enough for people to remark upon. On the Continent.'

'Really?' It was hard to imagine herself as the gossip of foreign courts.

Caroline nodded miserably. 'They say you are an invalid. Not capable of marriage. Not the kind of stock to introduce into their family line. Do you see?'

Sophia did see; that is, she understood. But as for her actual vision, it clouded and swirled around her.

Not capable of marriage. Marriage was her only hope of escaping the Queen. Without it, there was none.

When Sophia returned, slinking her way back through the servant's passages, she found a chair propped up against her door. Sitting on the red-and-white striped cushion, with the watchful air of an owl, was Princess Royal.

'There you are.'

Sophia's heart beat thick and fast in her neck as fear mingled with annoyance. She stopped and glared, defiance blazing in her eyes. How dare Royal sit there, judging?

'They told me,' Royal continued, 'you were laid down upon the bed.'

'And so I was. I am recovered.' Even to Sophia, it sounded false.

They were silent, weighing the unspoken words between them.

How smug Royal looked, sitting there. Her new spotted gown opened up onto a pure white petticoat. A portrait of her intended fiancé hung from the neckline of her bodice, grazing her breast. Sophia's jealous resolution to keep Caroline's story a secret set like cement. Let Royal, with all her airs of wisdom, run into disaster.

Royal ran a hand down the length of her face. 'You are delicate, Sophy. A terrible illness has only just left you and there are mobs out against us. You cannot put your constitution at risk by running around the streets to see Caroline.'

There was no use denying it. Sophia stifled her rising panic. 'Will you tell the Queen?'

'I don't know.'

Sophia scoffed with a nervous snort. 'You had better make haste. There is not much time left to debase me in her eyes before you marry, is there?'

Royal rocked back, making the chair creak. 'I only speak to the Queen about your health and welfare,' she spluttered. 'I say this for your own good.'

'I am sure it comforts you to think so.' There was a strange satisfaction in ruffling her sister.

Royal stood up, towering above her, and looked down

with disdain. 'You are changing, Sophia. You must check yourself before it is too late.'

'I have to change!' Sophia jerked the chair away from her door. 'The world is changing! Ernest says I am too weak.'

'Ernest is no role model for a young lady. If you are to have a husband, one day . . .'

Tears pricked Sophia's eyes – Caroline's words were still fresh in her mind. *Not capable of marriage.* 'I am never to have a husband!' she howled and slammed the door.

CHAPTER TWENTY-ONE

Queen's House, London
ᴖ 1797 ᴖ

Royal held the letter to her nose and inhaled. Between the musty smells of ink and paper, she thought she detected the scent of him – her future husband.

Was it really happening? Somehow she had persuaded the King, the famously stubborn King, to say *yes*. And here, at last, was something tangible of her success, a part of the prince to keep. She ran her fingers over the paper and imagined his hands resting there. The hands of the man who loved her.

Once more she pulled out the portrait framed with brilliants and imagined the lines and brush strokes animated with life. She had never nurtured any illusions about Fritz. It was common knowledge that he was a fat, plain man, not the handsome prince of fairy tales. But to Royal, his features were the sweetest in the entire world. This was her saviour, the man her children would resemble.

The clock chimed and startled her. The time for correspondence had evaporated already – it felt like she had just sat down. She fumbled with the mass of papers and ink bottles on her desk before running to the glass.

No improvement there. She tutted at her hair and straightened the fichu around her shoulders. Did it really matter? Fritz considered her perfect, just as she was. Who was the Queen to gainsay that? The thought made her giddy with joy.

She hesitated with her palm on the door handle. Fritz's letter sat on the desk with the forlorn air of an abandoned puppy. With an impulsive movement, she snatched it up and tucked it next to her heart. None of the usual apprehensions snagged at her skirts as she trotted through the palace. Whatever the Queen thought, she had Fritz's love. The future lay open before her, full of endless possibilities.

A weak autumn sun struggled in through the windows of the Queen's room, dappling the walls in spots of pale gold. Light fell over swathes of rich material stretched across the floor – blues, greens, gold; muslins, velvets and taffetas. Royal stopped, amazed. The Queen looked up and smiled – a smile diluted by waves of stress.

'My trousseau?' Royal guessed, breathless.

The Queen inclined her head. 'Do you like it?'

Royal caressed the silky material and then let it run through her fingers like water. '*Like* it? It is beautiful!'

The Queen's ladies swarmed about Royal, petting and caressing her, cooing like doves.

'It is very handsome, Your Royal Highness,' said Lady Sydney. 'Those Germans won't know what has hit them.'

The Queen bent over and shook some creases out of the taffeta. 'I do not think it wise to make up any dresses yet. You had better wait until you get there and see what the fashions are.'

Royal nodded. These rolls of fabric would be her travelling companions, then the costume of that unknown woman, yet to be born: the Hereditary Princess of Württemberg. A chance to reinvent herself.

'It's important to make a good impression and look as they expect you to,' the Queen continued. She glanced up and for the first time, Royal realised her mother was worried. She remembered odd snatches of conversation, hints thrown out about the Queen's unhappiness in the early years of her marriage. It was hard to imagine the imperious figure standing before her as a nervous and vulnerable girl.

'What did you take in your trousseau?'

There was a haunted look in the Queen's eyes. 'Me? Oh, you don't want to know about that.'

'Yes, I do.'

'It was a completely different situation,' she replied, busying herself with a roll of satin. 'I only had one good gown to start with.'

'Did my grandmother choose the material for you, like you have for me?'

'No, she died four days after I became engaged.'

'Oh. Yes. To be sure.' Mortified, Royal fell silent and watched her mother work.

The Queen's every movement filled the room with the presence of her regrets. It was as if she thought, by preparing so thoroughly for this marriage, she would somehow undo the misery that started her own.

The last link to the Queen's youth, Madame Schwellenberg, currently lay above stairs on her deathbed. Royal had not stopped to think, until now, how important the old servant must be to her mother. A support through early marriage, a rock in the King's illness.

Guilt prickled Royal's throat as she considered the Queen's position. Her dearest friend and her eldest daughter would leave her, with only the King for comfort.

And what sort of King? Would the stress of the upcoming nuptials corrode his nerves?

Royal's eye fell upon the trousseau again and she watched the colours shimmer in the moving light. The sumptuous materials went on and on, a sea rippling with colour. In the midst of it all, she spied a patch of white standing out like a sail. 'What's that?'

The Queen followed her gaze. 'Oh, yes! Come and look.'

They walked over to the spot. Tiny dresses, stockings

and caps lay in neat rows, just waiting for an infant to fill them up and bring them to life.

Royal opened her mouth to speak, but her lips stuck together. Her desire and fear were too deep-rooted to voice. *Baby clothes*. All at once it was alarmingly real: she would have to endure childbirth, she would be responsible for the scions of Württemberg. Was she up to the task? Her ambition and habitual assurance in her ability fled at the sight of a tiny white dress.

'One set for a boy, one for a girl.' The Queen smoothed out the minuscule bonnets. 'All the way up to three years old.'

'They're lovely.' Royal's cheeks burned as she pretended to inspect a little shoe. For the first time since her engagement, she felt nervous. Didn't some women die in childbirth?

'It is nice for every woman to have a little boy and a little girl,' Lady Harrington observed. 'Although the Prince of Württemberg has one of each already, does he not?'

'Yes,' the Queen said quietly. 'A blessing. None of the usual pressure to produce an heir.'

Maybe not, but there was pressure enough. Royal could never forget that Fritz had married her cousin Augusta. There was a benchmark to live up to. Would he expect her to know what to do on her wedding night? Was it true she would hurt and bleed at first? The thought of such profound intimacy with a stranger made her cringe. Instinctively, she looked to her mother. The Queen's eyes were veiled. Princesses did not speak of these things. They were not questions she could ask.

'Have you considered what you will wear on the day?'

Royal pulled her tacky tongue from the roof of her mouth. 'A little. I thought white and silver for the embroidery.'

Lady Sydney frowned. 'Is it not white and gold for marrying a widower?'

'Yes, but white and silver for a daughter of the King,' the Queen pointed out. 'She is an English princess first.' She flicked her eyes over Royal. No clearer way of saying she lacked the finesse to make a bride.

'Now, Princess Royal, that is all I want you to think about your clothing. I'll dress you for the marriage cere-mony. No one else will have a hand in it.'

'But Mama, s-surely . . . I w-wanted . . .'

'No.' The Queen laid a cold finger on her lips. 'This is the last time. I will have you dressed properly for once.'

Royal absorbed the meaning. Acid rose in her core to disintegrate all her new-found confidence. That's why the Queen chose the materials: she didn't trust Royal's taste. She didn't want her shaming the family. It wasn't an act of love at all.

Royal's hand fluttered to her bosom. She felt the edges of Fritz's letter beneath her gown, but it was no longer a talisman against the Queen. It was a flimsy, thin piece of paper.

'I will do whatever you think is right. I do not want to disappoint the prince.'

Her nose fizzed and tingled as she held back tears. The prince. Her fantastic image of him was shattered. She thought of his portrait and began to see a man, a real man, made of nothing but flesh. A man who could, and probably would, find fault with her.

∼ *Queen's House, London* ∼

When the time came, Sophia didn't envy Royal at all. The gut-wrenching anxiety was painful to watch.

Royal sat rigid on the sofa, wearing a blue, cut-away over-gown, which showed off her tall and curvaceous figure. Her petticoat was a masterpiece in embroidery, the flowers winding up and around in beautiful patterns. Nerves turned her face alabaster white and tinctured her cheeks with blushes. In her agitation, she looked younger than her thirty years; almost child-like.

What must be going through her head? The most important meeting of her life was about to take place and the success of her marriage could rest on this first impression. Would she like him? Did it even matter? Probably not – the bargain was sealed.

Royal watched the King intently. Sophia flicked her eyes in the same direction and saw him, remarkably composed, hands folded in his lap. Only someone intimate with his mannerisms would spot the tics that betrayed him: the way he squeezed the end of one finger and blinked in rapid succession.

A ripple of apprehension ran through her. It wasn't Royal who would pay the price of her escape. She would not see the aftermath of her wedding. Unless . . . unless the King was so distressed that he ranted and raved in front of Royal's prince. What would happen then?

The moment came upon them. The man on whom everything depended entered the room and Sophia rose to her feet.

They had warned her to expect a fat man, but her definition of fat had been modest. The prince was a beast. His stomach was a swollen, jiggling thing with a life of its own. The material of his waistcoat creased as it stretched over the mound of flesh. His presence was overpowering – he was not just wide but tall, at least six feet.

'Your Majesty.' He bowed to the King and Sophia watched, enthralled, as the ghastly stomach crumpled within itself to his bend.

She swooped down in a curtsey but couldn't lower her eyes to the floor as she should. Unbidden, a horrible thought dropped into her mind: Royal had to share a bed with him. He would crush her.

The King motioned for them to sit down. 'How was your journey? Not too rough, I hope?'

The prince spoke with a thick German accent. 'It was

bad, I am afraid. The crossing was the worst. Do you usually have storms in the spring?'

'Not very often.'

'I had a rough crossing myself,' said the Queen, 'when I first came to England. But that was in the summer.'

'Ah! It is an honour, then, this weather. A greeting from England!'

'You stayed with Sir Joseph Banks, I believe. An excellent man, what?' asked the King.

'Indeed. He was very kind.'

There was nothing missing from the prince's manners or address, and his face, though fleshy, was not ugly: a large forehead, expressive eyebrows and a fine, straight nose. He would look somewhat elegant if it were not for that stomach.

He turned. 'Although he told me my fiancée had been unwell. I was very distressed. I trust she is better now?' His eyes locked on Royal.

There was a pause – a long pause. Sophia heard Royal's throat clench and recognised the painful click of words, caught in the back of her mouth. The old stutter. Sophia couldn't resist; she turned around in her chair to stare. Royal's diaphragm heaved, trying to force out speech. For a moment Sophia met her eyes, wild, hunted and pleading for help.

As smooth as glass, the Queen said, 'You must forgive the Princess Royal, Prince Friedrich. She has a little hesitation of speech, which comes out when she is under stress.'

Royal swept down her eyelashes and lowered her burning face.

The prince looked concerned. 'I hope, my dear princess, this first disturbance will be the last I ever cause you.'

Although Royal could not look up, she moved her head slightly in acknowledgement.

Sophia was flabbergasted. Could this be the man who ordered the murder of his wife? Caroline's story must have been false; she couldn't imagine this prince in a bad temper, let alone laying violent hands on a woman.

'You are very kind, Prince Friedrich. I assure you, the King and I feel your generosity more than words can say.'

'Please, you must call me Fritz. We are almost family.'

Sophia scrutinised his face, his jowls, for a clue. So far, he seemed like a good man, but only Royal would ever know for sure.

Royal took a candle and retired to her room. Guilt pursued her every step. The King had not shown his misery – he was too well bred for that. But she had seen what it cost him to host the man stealing his daughter.

Dear God, what had she done?

Her ladies sat her down and unpinned her hair. Royal looked into the mirror, but didn't see her reflection. She gazed beyond, picturing her prince again.

He had not seemed disappointed with her plain looks.

Even when she humiliated herself with that stupid stutter, he had been kind and encouraging. *The first and the last disturbance I ever cause you.* That was not just generosity; that was sweetness itself.

Still, Royal couldn't shake off her sense of unease. What if the Queen was right all along? A separation, a change, would be the perfect catalyst for the King's illness. She groaned as remorse ripped through her. If her marriage brought on another spate of madness, she would never forgive herself. As her hair tumbled down, Lady Waldegrave picked up a silver brush and worked the stiff pomatum out of the roots. The scratching, ripping sound made Royal wince. It was too late to turn back. Her fate lay with a large, tall stranger. Royal could only pray that as Amelia grew, she would come to fill the vacant place in the King's heart. But then, if Amelia wanted to marry . . .

The tugging on her hair irritated her beyond endurance. She stood up, took the brush in her own hand and waved the ladies away through a side door. When they were gone, she threw herself onto the bed, fully dressed.

She shut her eyes, but she could not block out the faces; their demands, their emotional blackmail. The King, the Queen, her brothers and sisters, her husband, the people of her new country . . . she could never please them all. It wasn't fair. Why must she bear all the pressure alone, feel all the guilt?

She picked up a pillow and hugged it. With a cold, hollow feeling, she acknowledged that the damage was already done. She wasn't betraying her father now; she did it months ago, when she insisted on having a husband. She told him she wanted a bridegroom and, dear father that he was, he gave her one.

The path was set before her. She must follow it.

⤙ *Chapel Royal, St James's Palace, London* ⤚

There were rooms imprinted on Charlotte's memory. In reality, she could walk in and out of them, but in her mind they were locked, without windows.

There were the chambers where her baby boys had died. Part of her would always be caught in them, watching the dreadful scenes again and again. The room in the castle where George spat hatred in her face. The servant's quarter where Madame Schwellenberg passed away, leaving her scared and alone. And now there would be the Chapel Royal. The place where she lost her eldest daughter – the first, no doubt, in a long string of deserters.

Royal sailed into the room with a steady step, looking straight ahead at the altar. Joy transformed her face into something lighter, more beautiful.

Charlotte remembered herself as a bride, recalled the words her brother-in-law said as he led her, trembling, into the chapel: 'Courage, princess, courage.' Royal already possessed it. That was one virtue Charlotte had managed to instil in her, at least.

The bridegroom was stuffed into a silk suit, shot through with gold and silver thread. Embroidery coated his lapels and cuffs. Over his bulky shoulder, he wore the blue ribbon of the Order of the Golden Fleece. A dagger of pity plunged into Charlotte. At least when she went up the aisle, she was heading toward a young, handsome prince with a good temper.

But this Fritz . . . He snapped at her ladies in waiting and complained to Lady Harcourt because he had received no gift from his bride. He was no match for Royal. It was like pairing a dove with a wild hog. But there was nothing she could do. The die was cast and Royal, ignorant of it all, was happy.

Charlotte watched the bride's long pelisse of crimson velvet sweep up the aisle, dappled in patches of colour from the stained-glass windows. The white satin dress, threaded with silver, sparkled and shimmered in beams of spring light. A cluster of long ringlets surrounded Royal's ecstatic face. Little stars bounced off her diamond coronet and reflected in her eager blue eyes. As she reached Fritz's side, she slowed and turned to him. He dwarfed her in height and width. How vulnerable and helpless she looked beside him.

'Dearly beloved . . .' The sacred words droned in Charlotte's ears. Her vision darkened. How would she cope without Royal? Her daughter, her first baby girl. With a war and a sea between them, they might never meet again.

Thirty years of love and care poured into a child and then – gone. Forever. And Royal was only the first. Time and children were slipping through Charlotte's fingers; it was like trying to hold water in her hands.

The King cleared his throat. Charlotte was intensely aware of him at her side, holding himself under rigid control. He was doing all he could to keep cheerful and re-strained for his daughter. One vein stood out on his neck; a muscle at the corner of his eye fluttered every few seconds.

She knew he wasn't seeing this wedding, playing out before them now. He was gazing back to the marriage of his sister, Caroline Matilda, so long ago. The small, fifteen-year-old bride in floods of tears. And another scene, a few years later.

Charlotte remembered it well. A study strewn with dying candles and half-drunk glasses of port. Maps and charts spread out over a table, barely distinguishable in the feeble light. George had bent over them, his finger tracing a line. He wore no wig, no jacket, his waistcoat was unbut-toned and his cravat hung loose around his neck.

'I must get my sister back from Denmark,' he had told her frantically. 'I must. The affair was not her fault. She isn't a bad girl.'

'You think the Count seduced her?'

'I know it! But he has paid for it, by God. Executed by the government. With him gone, they have no right to keep my sister imprisoned. I will launch ships. I will pull her out of there!'

'Away from her children?'

'Yes. They will never let her near them again. Oh, poor girl. Poor stupid, heedless girl! It isn't her fault, Charlotte. She was bound to stray. She married a lunatic.'

Ah, the irony of that.

Well, Royal was no Caroline Matilda. She would conduct herself better. But Charlotte doubted if George would be able to make the distinction. Once he started down a trail of association, there was no stopping him.

Who knew what horrors Charlotte would have to face tonight? She would have no time to nurse her own sorrow. As always, she would put her feelings aside and devote herself to soothing him. It was a pattern she was starting to resent.

How could Royal do it to her? Had she forgotten their conversation when the King recovered? *No distress, no sudden changes.* Perhaps she just didn't care.

Charlotte wanted to shake Royal by her jewel-encrusted shoulders and tell her it wasn't worth the sacrifice. A life-long, happy marriage was a myth. The congregation proved that: George sitting awkwardly beside his hateful wife, Frederick and Frederica, now estranged and barely speaking.

And then there was her own husband, the man she had adored for years. Charlotte ran her eyes over his long, kind features and tried to make her heart flip like it used to at the sight of him. There was nothing.

If even a love like theirs could lose its magic, what could possibly last?

⤙ *St James's Palace, London* ⤚

It was pitch black. Someone shook Royal's arm. 'Your Royal Highness. Your Royal Highness!'

Why couldn't they leave her alone? Her head floated – she needed sleep. She was drunk with weariness.

'Princess Royal! I mean, Princess of Württemberg!'

The new title exploded behind her eyelids like a firework. She forced them open a crack, trying to remember. An unfamiliar room, turned on its side. Where was she? Was the wedding over? A shadowy figure swam into view. She sat up suddenly and everything swirled.

'There, now. Drink this.' A glass of water pressed against her lips. She let the liquid trickle into her mouth and down her chin. Swallowing was a supreme effort. How did she come to be here? A slice of memory was missing from her brain. When the glass disappeared, she put up her hands and rubbed her clouded eyes. She paused, confused. A cold metallic touch grazed her left cheek. She snatched her fingers down and stared at them. There, on her left hand, glimmered a newly-minted wedding band. It felt heavy and awkward on her finger.

So it had happened. It wasn't a dream.

'Why am I here? What happened to my wedding?'

The maid smiled. 'You fainted, Madam. When the King said goodbye.'

Royal pushed the hair from her forehead. Vague strands of memory came back, but she couldn't plait them together. How had her father looked? Proud or distraught? Right now, she couldn't recall his face.

'Is he gone?'

'Oh yes, Madam. They are all gone.'

They are all gone. The words were icy drips down the back of her dress. She was alone. Years and years would pass before she saw her family again. *If* she saw them again. No one to talk to who understood her. Her only company would be a man she did not even know.

What had she done?

A tear slid down her face. Annoyed, Royal brushed it away. She had made her decision and it couldn't be undone. There was no turning back now.

The clock chimed. Royal stared at it, unable to believe the hands were right. 'It's late,' she said, and as the words left her mouth she felt ill. It was night – her bridal night.

'Come on then. Let's get you ready.' The maid crossed to a chest, opened a drawer and unfolded a glorious silk shift, trimmed with lace.

Royal swallowed, grimacing against the painful sensation in her throat.

'Your Highness?'

Reluctantly, Royal levered her body onto its feet, leaving one hand hovering over the sofa in case she fell straight back down. But she was too afraid to faint. She stumbled into the centre of the room. It was unavoidable. She had to lie with her husband. It was her duty – and the only way to get a baby. She had spent years wanting this. Right now, she could not think why.

Her arms quivered, like thin branches in the wind, as she held them up for the maid to undress her. Without speaking, the woman unbuttoned Royal's gown and swept it over her head. The bodice came off, the cage and hoop that held out her skirts. The moment the comforting weight of material left Royal's skin, she shrivelled up. The maid eased the shift down over her body and tied the puff sleeves around her shaking arms. It was a beautiful garment, truly beautiful. But the wispy silk clung to her breasts, barely concealing them, and Royal felt a rush of air between her legs. She was exposed.

God help me. She didn't know what her husband expected, but she was sure she couldn't do it. She hugged her arms around herself as the maid let down her hair and brushed the ringlets into soft waves.

'You're cold,' she said. 'Let's get you into bed.'

The last thing Royal wanted to think about was the bed. Lifeless, she let her attendant lead her toward the enormous four-poster, cold and ceremonial like everything else in St James's Palace.

The maid pulled back the covers and Royal slithered between them. The sheets were cool; icy fingers against her goose-pimpled skin. She lay, stone-faced, as the girl tucked her in.

'Thank you,' she croaked.

The maid bobbed a curtsey and Royal realised, with a stab of terror, that she was leaving.

Stay! Stay and protect me! She tried to cry out but she had no voice. With one soft movement, the maid picked up the candle and retreated from the room. The door closed gently, but Royal winced as if it had slammed in her face.

The room fell into shadow with nothing but the clicking fire to shed any light. Her heart beat so strongly she felt its pulse in her throat. What now? Royal clutched at her covers, trying not to tear them. Like a child, she wanted to crawl down to the bottom of the bed and hide. The maid must have gone to fetch Fritz and tell him Royal was ready . . . Ready for what?

A footstep and the creak of a floorboard. Royal fought the hysteria that clawed against her chest. The door handle moved. She sank down into the pillow, willing it to swallow her. A small chink of light appeared in the doorway, then a flickering candle.

The man who was now her husband eased his way into the room. Even in this dim light, he looked enormous. His white shirt opened at the collar and fell down to his chubby knees. In the shadows, his night-capped head appeared small, a little rock on top of a mountain.

This was not how she had imagined it. She had pictured a muscular, athletic prince who made her giddy like George's handsome friend, the Duke of Bedford. She had thought of herself as a warm and sensuous woman, ready to love and be loved. How stupid she'd been.

'You are well, now?'

She couldn't return his smile with her frozen lips. Instead, she nodded.

He waddled over to the bed and set the light down. The foreign scent of his skin reached Royal's nostrils: clean linen, sweat, wine. He sat down heavily, rolled his fat legs up and crawled beneath the covers.

Hot panic swept over Royal. It seemed a hideous, abnormal thing to have a man in the bed beside her.

'You must not be frightened.' He turned on his side and she rolled helplessly toward him. 'I will blow out the candle, if you like?'

The flame showed a gleam of desire in his eyes that deprived Royal of speech. Gratefully, she nodded again.

He puffed out his cheeks, blew, and darkness enveloped them. 'I will be gentle.'

She could not doubt his kindness. Would she not come to love a man with such considerate manners in the fullness of time? How many princes would understand the fear that beat beneath a virgin's breast?

It was then the gruesome realisation hit Royal like a

musket ball in the stomach: he had done all this before. He was being kind to her, because he knew what it was like for a young woman; he had done the same thing with her cousin Augusta. She tried not to picture them together. Was it incestuous to bed this man, after her cousin?

The bed creaked as he edged toward her. To Royal's absolute horror, his sausage fingers touched her neck and slid sensuously down, grazing her breast. She lay like a slab of ice. He fumbled with the ribbons at the front of her shift – her poor, thin, shift – and suddenly his cold hand was on her torso, cupping the tender flesh around her nipple.

Desperate with embarrassment, she wanted to cry, to push him off and tell him to stop. But in the next second his mouth came down, a wet clamp upon hers. She closed her eyes. His breath, at least, was sweet and his lips were soft. The warmth of his mouth gave her comfort. This wasn't so bad. She sat up slightly and pushed her lips back against his. She would prove she wasn't entirely hopeless.

But her response excited him. Before she knew what was happening, he tore at her pretty shift, pushing it down to her waist. Everything inside Royal screamed, but she knew she had to bear it. *Think of a baby. Think of a baby.* It was the only way to get one.

With a quick movement, he put a knee between Royal's legs and eased them open. She braced herself; it was about to happen – whatever it was. Gasping, Fritz heaved himself on top of her, punching the air from her body. His skin was damp and sweaty against hers. She longed to pull away but she could barely move. The solid, heated part of him felt insanely large.

He kissed her again, arching his back into the air. Thankfully, his weight shifted and Royal drank in a breath through her nostrils. She was about to exhale when his weight crushed her and a searing, white-hot pain jolted through her.

Dear Lord. She had expected it to hurt, but this? Her muscles trembled, unable to cope with the pain. She had been right – she couldn't do it. If she could draw breath she would cry out, plead with him. But his mouth locked firmly around hers and his huge, quivering belly squeezed the life out of her.

Royal could think of nothing, feel no sensation except the ripping, burning shocks inside her. She held on to Fritz's arms, slippery with sweat, and their solidity kept her from fainting. She managed to let out a small whimper, but Fritz was oblivious to her, groaning and pumping away, faster and faster. Tears slid thick and rapid down Royal's face.

Just when she thought she could bear it no longer, Fritz shook all over like a man with the ague. Braying out a long, moaning noise, he reared up and froze above her. She looked on, fascinated and horrified, as he quivered. Suddenly, he let out a breath and slumped, deflated, against her.

It must be over. Thank God.

His lips brushed limply against her cheek and then he fell motionless. Royal became aware of a sticky, slithering feeling between her legs. Little by little, the pain down below abated, as if it was running out of her with the liquid. Finally, the pressure against her private parts eased. Fritz wriggled and rolled off of her. The air smelt foul. Not just sweat, but some other sickly sweet, sharp scent. Royal shifted uncomfortably and gasped. When she moved there was a sudden, sharp pain, different from the horrendous pressure of Fritz's love. It was like a cut or a bad bruise.

Fritz began to snore.

Gingerly, Royal slid her legs off the side of the bed and pressed her feet against the wooden floor. Her whole body shook uncontrollably. Unable to stand, she eased herself onto the ground and crawled toward the fire. Its gentle, warm touch was the closest thing to a hug she could get. How badly she needed her sisters, to throw her arms around them and weep on their shoulders. But they had all forsaken her.

She stopped, exhausted, in a shallow pool of light right by the hearth and looked down at herself. Blood. The defiled shift, tangled around her waist, was splattered with tiny blobs of red. A stream of dark liquid trickled from her, so she pulled her shift round and sat on it. The flow was not bad; a little less than a monthly cycle – but it smarted. So that was it, the great mystery: uncomfortable, embarrassing and almost brutal. That was what poets mused about, that was what made a baby. Royal pulled her knees up and hugged her arms around them. She never wanted it to happen again. Why had her mother not warned her?

CHAPTER TWENTY-TWO

Hyde Park, London
Summer 1797

Moist, fragrant air filled Sophia's lungs. The park stood out in vivid detail; each twig and leaf had sharp, defined edges beneath the lenses of her new spectacles. She adjusted them on the bridge of her nose and leant back in the saddle, leather creaking beneath her. It was unnerving to see the world so clearly after years of squinting at soft, melting shapes.

Officially, the court forbade spectacles, but Ernest said she should intervene and improve her vision in this age of discovery. He was right: it was time to shake off the confines of her weak body and live.

The clack of hooves beat a slow rhythm down the path. General Garth's horse flicked its tail, swatting lazily at flies. Sophia's own mount, Traveller, had a gentle, lilting step that rocked her as he walked.

'Do you think she's there yet?'

Sophia turned to Amelia, riding beside her. 'Who?'

'Royal, of course.'

'Oh. I don't know.'

In truth, Sophia had barely thought of Royal since she'd kissed her goodbye. She didn't want to dwell on her sister's happiness on this bright, warm day and darken it with the remembrance of Caroline's words. *Not fit for marriage.*

Amelia tilted her head to watch the Serpentine flowing on the horizon. 'I wonder what it is like,' she said, 'getting on a boat, knowing you may never see England again.'

'I cannot imagine it.' But of course she could. Sophia dreamed of every detail, fantasising about a marriage she would never have; the thrill of a kiss, warm arms around her, the soft wriggle of a baby on her chest.

Ernest put his reins in one hand and turned in the saddle. 'We're there.'

Sophia nodded. She pulled back on one rein, guiding Traveller's head to the right. Amelia's mount saw and mimicked the action without her command.

'Hey-day! Where are we going?'

Sophia only smiled. She wasn't used to keeping secrets from Amelia, but it felt delicious.

They wobbled as the horses adjusted their step to the uneven turf. Plodding across the grass, they came to a tree with branches spilling out of its trunk and cascading to the ground. It was like a giant green fountain, stopped in time.

Sophia aimed Traveller at a gap in the tangled wall of

branches. After she and Amelia rode through, General Garth took up sentinel duty in front of the opening.

'What's going on?' Amelia asked.

It was cool beneath the drooping foliage. The ground and air, so rarely disturbed by people, held their breath. Sophia patted Traveller's neck, sending up a cloud of dust, then hopped off the side-saddle and took hold of his nose-strap.

'Sophia!' Amelia looked afraid.

Sophia considered her sister, dismayed by how handsome she had grown. Her blonde hair sat in a chignon at the back of her head, held in with combs of silver filigree, while a thin calico dress clung to the growing curves of her body. Healthy. Eminently suitable for marriage.

'Sophy, please!'

Sophia swatted the envious thoughts away. 'We're meeting someone,' she told her.

It was regrettable she had to draw Amelia into this, but there was no other way to protect Sophia's reputation. She couldn't go skulking round bushes alone. Besides, she needed the moral support.

'Who?'

At a crunch of twigs, Sophia swivelled around. It was only a bird adjusting its balance on a branch. She exhaled. 'You can't tell the Queen. Or George.'

Amelia pulled a face. 'Well, if it's such a big secret, why did you bring me?'

'I cannot very well go off riding on my own, can I?' Sophia scuffed the toe of her half-boot against the dirt. 'And you are the only one I trust.'

Amelia leant forward, clutching at the pommel of her saddle. Her plump lips parted with excitement. 'Have you got a lover?'

Sophia laughed bitterly. 'Be serious.'

'I am.'

'I'm riding out with my brother, my little sister and a fifty-year-old equerry. Does it look like a romantic meeting to you?'

Amelia deflated, disappointed. 'I guess not.'

'I'm meeting Miss Garth.'

'She won't be able to find us in here.'

Sophia tutted in impatience. 'She *knows* we're meeting here. The whole idea is that no one *else* will see us. Mama would kill me if she found out.'

Amelia looked down and fiddled with her horse's mane. 'I had better not get involved then.'

A horse snorted. Sophia spun around. Every second, she expected the Queen to sweep in and punish her. It was all very well to talk of defiance and rebellion. The reality was terrifying. A slice of light ripped across their grotto as General Garth moved his mount aside, and in another second a female figure appeared, fighting her way through the branches.

'Frances.'

Miss Garth stumbled over raised roots in the soil, clutching the strings of her reticule in both hands. Sophia let go of Traveller and moved toward her, pressing her lips against her friend's heated cheek.

'How is it with George and Caroline?' Sophia asked at once.

'Terrible. They are talking about separate establishments.'

The princesses stared at her. Surely the King would never allow such a thing?

'They can't,' Sophia said. 'Not a full separation. The scandal . . .'

'It is too late. They will never live together now. She won't even speak to him.'

Sophia took a breath, thinking of poor Caroline. Her hopes were over, truly over. How shaming it must be. A marriage that had failed was worse than no marriage at all. It was degrading, imprisoning. And how would the King take it?

Miss Garth groped in her reticule. 'Here. An answer to your last letter.'

Sophia pulled out a note from her bosom and exchanged it. 'Tell Caroline I love her. God knows I've tried to speak up, but it's no good. Everyone just shouts at me.'

Amelia nodded from horseback. 'It's true. Mama is most displeased with her.'

'My mistress would not want that.'

'I can't hold my tongue while she suffers like this,' Sophia cried. 'It breaks my heart.'

'The Queen will break more than that if she finds you sneaking off to see Miss Garth,' said Amelia.

Miss Garth glanced at the gap in the tree. 'Have you ever thought about my uncle?'

'The General?'

She nodded. 'He can bring your letters to me, and to Princess Caroline. You can trust him.'

Sophia watched the shadowy figure beyond the branches, a man she knew and yet did not. He was a recurring figure from her childhood, but she had never really noticed him behind the uniform. He looked somewhat ominous in silhouette. She felt a cold hand on her nape, warning her against it.

'Will it not get your uncle into trouble?'

'Not with the King.' Miss Garth smiled. 'He's a favourite.'

Sophia bit her lip, thinking fast. It did make sense. 'I suppose even if Papa found out, he would not mind . . . he is very fond of Caroline.'

Miss Garth nodded. 'That's settled, then. It is much less dangerous for you. I will tell him tonight.'

Another conspirator in her growing circle. More and more people, likely to betray her to the Queen. Sophia shivered. What did she know of General Garth after all? Could he be trusted? She wondered if she had done the right thing. Sophia let five minutes pass after Miss Garth left before she pulled Traveller's head up from cropping grass and edged cautiously toward the outside world. The park was still. She signalled to Amelia and walked out of the grotto, dragging the reluctant Traveller back into the light.

There he was; General Garth, the man she must trust with her letters. He dismounted and stood ready to help her back into the saddle. Sophia gave him an uncertain smile as he put his hands on her waist. His grip was firm and warm. Assured.

All those sentiments and opinions lying in his hot, strong hands . . . He could open anything, read anything, tell anything. She would be putting herself completely at his mercy.

The General swung her into the saddle. She felt a little shock as he released her, suddenly aware of him, the strangeness and masculinity of him. She peered down from Traveller's back, considering the man for the first time. He was short, about the height of a regular woman, and had a birthmark that extended down the side of his face like a splash of claret. It lent him a dangerous, fiendish look. Not pleasant but somehow exciting. She was being stupid, of course. He was no fiend. This man was her father's trusted servant, the uncle of her friend, ready to help her contact Princess Caroline. A solider. A man of honour, undoubtedly. Nothing to arouse either interest or fear.

He came forward to check Sophia's girth and stirrup were secure. Through lowered eyelashes, she studied the offensive birthmark. What an odd thing. It varied in hue as it crossed his features, like watercolours washing across a canvas. Suddenly, it reminded her of the sunset, and became strangely beautiful.

'All safe and sound now, Your Highness.' The General looked up and smiled at her. It was a warm smile, the smile of a kind man. She had to turn away from it, feeling a little light-headed.

Yes, she could trust him.

∼ Stuttgart ∼

Royal watched the countryside roll past as her carriage rumbled along the road. They had made it. A sickly Channel crossing, close run-ins with revolutionary soldiers, but they were in Württemberg at last.

A rush of love, almost maternal, coursed through her as she watched the landscape. This was her homeland now: the tall corn, the rich woods, the fat cows – all were hers. She would look after this land. She would do it good, some-how.

Fritz's reflection appeared in the window, silent and thoughtful. She assessed him, her husband. It was still awk-ward between them. A kind of habitual fondness sprang up inside her and she did her best to nurture it, day by day. But she missed speaking freely. She longed for the day when she would know him well, make jokes. Right now, she knew his body intimately: what he looked like naked; the sound he made when he slept; the touch of his skin – and yet she was unacquainted with his mind. It was lonely.

He caught her gaze in the glass. The journey furnished a topic of conversation, at least.

'Are we close?' she asked.

He nodded. 'You will see streets soon. And your people.'

Royal smiled in response, but her stomach turned over. This was her moment. She had to shine. In all her dreams of freedom, she had never imagined the pressure. Important people simpered over her at drawing-rooms and balls, expecting her to say intelligent things. In Hanover, the common people had crowded round her carriage, begging to see the King's daughter, and called out blessings on her head. She hoped they were not disappointed with the shy, quaking princess they saw.

'Will I meet your parents when we get to Stuttgart?'

'Just my *Vater* and the boys.'

Royal shifted in her seat. This was one of Fritz's key attractions: a ready-made family. Now the time had come to meet them, she was petrified. They too would expect things from her, compare her and say: *how different she is from his last wife*.

'Do you think your sons will like me?'

'Of course. I have told them they must call you Mama.'

Her chest throbbed. How many years she had yearned for that name. But she knew the children would be the hardest to win over. 'Oh, you mustn't make them. They might not like to. Their own mother . . .'

Fritz huffed. 'They will like what I tell them to like,' he said shortly. 'Their first mother was nothing to you. They will not have any false loyalties.'

Royal swelled at his favourable comparison. 'And the little girl? When do I meet her?'

'Trinette. She is at Ludwigsburg with my *Mutter*.'

Royal exhaled, disappointment and relief blending within her. The meeting with this little girl was more important to her than any dignitary – more important, perhaps, than her introduction to Fritz. Her own daughter. It was all she had ever wanted.

Gradually, the woods gave way to clover-speckled fields. As the hills dipped and softened, small dwellings appeared on the roadside and Royal knew their journey was coming to a close. She squeezed her hands together in her lap. Stuttgart nestled in a lush valley with hills and woods rising behind it. Vineyards, lakes and cobbled paths sped past her eyes. Medieval architecture filled the streets with wobbly beige buildings. Royal's head swivelled from left to right, trying to take it all in. Fritz chuckled at her curiosity.

'I will show you it all, *liebchen*. Give me time.'

All at once, Castle Square opened up before them, a magnificent horseshoe full of windows and engraved stone. It was a brand new, opulent palace. Royal could not conceal her wonder. Statues peered down at her from the roof as the carriage slowed and came to a stop.

The jolt brought her back to reality. This was no sight-seeing trip. It was time to make her first impression. Royal pushed down the rising nerves. Whatever she did, she must not ruin this one chance.

A flock of footmen scurried toward them and flung open the door. Fritz sighed with satisfaction – this was all normal, all comfortable for him. Royal envied his ease. It was all right for him – no one was here to stare at the prince.

He clambered out. When his weight left the carriage, it rocked, sending her sprawling. Hurriedly, she righted herself and smoothed down the layers of petticoats, linen and silk, just in time to look composed when her husband stretched out his palm to her. She slipped her little hand into his enormous paw, trying to conceal the tremor in her fingers. Her hair was probably all over the place. She closed her eyes as Fritz gripped onto her and guided her down the steps.

A chorus of cheers burst into her ears. Her eyelids peeled back, cautiously, to reveal the city out in fete; ladies, gentle-men, dirty little children and tenant farmers crowded the square. She turned and straightened her hat so she could see them all. At the sight of her face, the crowd exploded like a powder keg. It was overwhelming. Royal thought she'd crossed the threshold into a new world on the day she married, but now she knew she was wrong; she had barely even started.

A fountain played in the courtyard, its musical sound lost beneath the roars of the people. They weren't roaring for peace and bread like the crowds in London. They actually seemed to like her. She saw two great pillars supporting a balcony, marking out the entrance to the palace. As Royal swept her eyes over the stone and down to the floor, her breath caught. It was them: her stepsons.

She knew them instinctively. The taller one, the elder, was the very image of his father, though less stout. The younger was skinny and dark-haired; he reminded Royal of a colt.

Fritz pulled her arm within his. 'Come then, Charlotte.'

She stopped, half-dazed. *Charlotte*. Yes, of course, she *was* Charlotte. She could be Charlotte here, with no Queen to claim her name. Her face split into a beaming smile. The sun broke through a layer of cloud and caressed her cheek. She had done it. She was out of her cloister and life was beginning, truly beginning, for her at last.

It did not take Royal long to discover that the Duke and Duchess of Württemberg were not like the King and Queen of England. They did not want to live in a simple, unpretentious way, with plain dinners of cold meat, salad and stewed pears. They were royalty and determined to live on the fat of the land.

Stuttgart was grand, but it was nothing compared to the palace of Ludwigsburg. Her new home spread out across rich countryside, its cream walls baking in the sunlight. They drove to the entrance under an avenue of chestnuts and limes, and through the branches she saw the sheer mass of the place, its huge white columns and urns on the terrace. The ground sloped down at the front of the house, giving way to a lake with a jet of water bursting from its centre. Beyond that, close to the entrance of the palace, hints of the formal gardens peeked out: neat rows of trimmed hedges, flowerbeds and topiary.

Mine. This is all mine.

Royal looked across at Fritz, incredulous. 'We live here?'

The boys giggled at her stupid question.

'You do not like it?' Fritz teased.

She laughed, a sort of hysterical laugh, drunk with joy, and pressed her nose against the window. Plain old Royal, the mistress of such a palace? How would she ever grow fine enough to deserve it?

The carriage pulled up with a crunch on the gravel. A bevy of servants descended on them, scuttling off with trunks, bandboxes and hatboxes. Fritz helped Royal down the steps.

'Where now?' she asked. She longed for a warm bath, several cups of tea and a soft bed. She needed to revive before she could absorb any more.

'The Great Hall.'

She grimaced. That didn't sound like a place to recuperate. 'What's in there?'

'My *Mutter* and Trinette.'

Her head swam. 'I cannot meet them now! I am all dusty from the road.'

'That does not matter.' He seized her hand and marched her helplessly on through the vast corridors.

The Great Hall was like a cathedral. Fritz's father, the Duke, and the two boys, Wilhelm and Paul, crossed the long, cold floor in front of Royal and Fritz. Their footsteps clicked in unison as they passed under lustrous chandeliers and a ceiling painted with angels.

It was beautiful, but Royal could not take it in. She was like a blinkered horse, staring at the ladies at the end of the room.

If only she'd had time to prepare! Her mouth was dry, her brain tired and unable to form words. What a fright she must look, with wind-matted hair and a dusty, mud-splashed travelling habit. Excruciatingly nervous, she kept her eyes trained on her feet. She was dismayed to see her boots covered in filth.

At last they came to a halt. Royal curtseyed on trembling legs, still not trusting herself to look up. She felt the proximity of her new daughter like a strong tug underneath her ribcage, and sensed the young eyes judging her. It was like being a girl again, under the scrutiny of the Queen.

'My dears!'

Warily, Royal winched her eyes from the floor, expecting to see a mother-in-law just like the Queen of England: slender, cold and austere. But the woman before her melted that image away. The Duchess of Württemberg was pleasantly round; in her mid-sixties with pale grey hair pulled back from her forehead and arranged in curls. She kissed Royal on both cheeks. '*Meine Tochter*, my Charlotte. Come – meet Trinette.' She took Royal by the hand, a motherly scent of lavender rising from her skin, and led her toward a teenage girl. In another instant, Royal faced her daughter.

She was beautiful. Dark-chocolate hair looped up into a loose bun at the back of her head, setting off enormous brown eyes in a pale face. A light dusting of freckles – not enough to look vulgar – and an elegant bow mouth completed the image of perfection. Royal could have wept at the sight of her.

But she wasn't a pet to be stared at and cooed over. Suddenly the brown eyes met hers, questioning, assessing.

'H-Hello.' Royal fought against her stammer to squeeze the word out.

Her heart brimmed with sentiments she couldn't articulate. *I am a friend. I will be your best friend.* She willed Trinette to understand her, but it would take time. For now she was just a strange, travel-worn woman who had turned up on her door-step, trying to take her mother's place.

Trinette looked uncertainly at the duchess. When she nodded, Trinette bobbed a curtsey. 'Hello, Mother.' The name sounded unnatural in her little mouth. Forced.

Royal blazed with the memory of herself at this age, self-conscious before the Queen. The last thing she wanted to do was make Trinette feel like that. But how could she put her at ease, when she was flustered herself?

'I have just l-left your Aunt Caroline in London,' she tried. 'She charges me to send her love.'

Trinette nodded, as if her aunt was of no consequence to her. She was busy dissecting Royal's gown, her hair, her hat. How did she compare to Trinette's mother, cousin Augusta? Unfavourably, she feared. *Give me a chance. Please, let me try.*

The duchess laid an arm around Trinette's shoulders. 'Your new Mama is not just related to you by law. She is family. Your mother was her first cousin.'

This caught the girl's interest. 'Really?' Her eyes seemed to cut straight through Royal's dress and skin to the blood pulsing beneath. Blood that they shared.

The Duchess smiled. 'Charlotte's grandfather was your great-grandfather. You are blood relations.'

For the first time, Trinette's face opened. She turned quickly to her grandmother and hissed in her ear. Though she tried to whisper, Royal heard every word.

'Do you think my mother would like it? Knowing her cousin came to look after us?'

Poor cousin Augusta, long dead. Cold fingers crept up Royal's arms and down her back. She was encroaching on her cousin's territory, walking in her footsteps. Augusta stood where Royal stood now; she slept where Royal would sleep. Then she lost it all, in a puff of smoke that had never really cleared. What *did* happen to her?

The duchess smiled so warmly, and hugged Trinette so close, it was hard to believe anything sinister had ever taken place inside this palace. It must have been a misunderstanding. There was no other explanation.

'I am sure your mother would be very pleased,' the duchess said. There was certainly no guilt in her face. 'I am sure of it.'

Queen's House, London

Charlotte tightened her grip on the King's elbow. 'Please, you must stop encouraging her! Is it not bad enough that the papers take her side? Must George have his own father against him too?'

He patted her hand as if he was calming a fretful horse. 'Peace, my dear, peace! I am not against George! I want the best for both him and Caroline.'

Charlotte made an impotent noise of frustration and bowed her head. It was a glorious day, but the warm weather failed to cheer her. The terrace reflected light back into her face and heat pressed through her clothing, chafing against her skin.

She would have thought that with all the pressures on

the King, George and Caroline could at least pretend to get along. It was not like they needed to spend time in each other's company – there were a thousand and one ways they might avoid being together. But like children, they refused to play nicely. And here was Caroline, running to tittle-tattle on the nasty boy that pulled her hair.

'You must not let Caroline think she can send George's letters on to you!' she exclaimed. 'Of all the childish things . . .'

The King pulled her aside to sit on a white iron bench. The metal seat scorched through Charlotte's thin calico gown.

'My love, I have returned the letters to her. She can be in no doubt that I disapprove of her actions.'

'Good! What did you say?'

The King spread his palms. 'I told her she must try her best to make her home agreeable. I said submission is a woman's greatest virtue and she must practise it if she wants to win George's esteem.'

A wry smile flicked up the corner of her lip. 'That is the answer I would have expected from you.'

'If she meant to enrage me against George, she has not succeeded. His letter seems quite sensible. He's willing to live on terms of civility and good humour, I think. There is just one paragraph that bothers me.'

Charlotte raised her eyebrows. 'Yes?'

He looked at the crowd of courtiers, who had stopped at

a respectable distance from them. 'I cannot speak candidly here. It is enough to say that, if some accident happened to little Charlotte – which God forbid! – he would not insist upon another heir.'

Charlotte shuddered, finding she could not blame her son. Caroline was repellent enough fully clothed and five feet away.

She gazed up at the redbrick palace, its windows glinting in the sunshine. Of all the royal residences, it was the most like her first home in Mecklenburg-Strelitz. She thought of her childhood years and felt an intense pity for little Charlotte, whose infancy was far from happy. Fancy being torn between two parents, each immature and selfish! A thought occurred to her. 'We must get the child here, with us.' It would be perfect – a distraction for the King, to stop him missing Royal, and a balm to Charlotte's heart.

The King looked thoughtful. 'Away from her mother?'

Of course, away from her hateful mother. She was astounded that he would hesitate to separate them. But that Caroline was a worming, serpentine woman; she burrowed inside his head, twisting the truth.

'Away from all of this. I do not trust Caroline to educate her as a queen should be taught. I do not even trust George with that task.'

The King sighed and raised his eyes to the pale blue sky. 'She needs to be with her parents.'

'What an example, though! Even Sophia has been

misbehavung since Caroline came along. She's a dangerous influence, George. A danger to our granddaughter.'

He put out his walking cane and heaved himself up. Once standing, he offered Charlotte a hand. 'I will think on it,' he said, closing the topic.

Time to tread carefully; forcing the issue would only make him ill. But a little hint here and there . . . A little reminder each day . . . She would corrode his defences, as imperceptibly as the sea ate away at the shore. If her daughters were going to leave her like Royal, she would replace them with a granddaughter. An heir to the throne who would never abandon her native English soil. She put her palm in his and rose. 'Of course,' she said, all wifely meekness. 'I will submit to your opinion.'

CHAPTER TWENTY-THREE

Windsor
ᑲ *Autumn 1797* ᑭ

A fine mist lay over Windsor, diluting the scenery. Sophia made her way down to the stables, noticing detail in the landscape for the first time thanks to her spectacles. Beads of dew clung to the leaves and jewelled spider webs stretched across the bushes. A chilly, damp sort of day, but to her it was beautiful. Everything was weirdly focused and alive, as it always was on this one day of the week. The day she got to see *him*.

Her heart thundered beneath her warm cape. Her stomach was a mess of nerves and excitement, but she did not want to turn back. A strange blissful fear coursed through her, pushing her legs forward. She couldn't explain the fascination that had suddenly gripped her. Even in moments of quiet reflection, she did not admit the truth to herself. She attributed the flutter of her spirits to illness, to concern over Caroline.

With her spectacles, she made out the black iron clock standing in the stable yard. The hands pointed to the precise time of her appointment and, sure enough, a short figure waited beneath the clock. Sophia smiled, her breath suspended. He was always punctual.

The yard was warm with the smell of hay. Sophia picked her way over the cobbles, hurdling piles of muck and dodging wheelbarrows. She was acutely aware of General Garth watching her, conscious of every movement she made. It was imperative, for some reason she could not articulate, that she didn't appear foolish in front of him.

When she finally reached General Garth, he doffed his three-cornered hat. 'Your Royal Highness.'

She smiled – too broadly. 'Good morning.'

'I'm glad to see you looking so well. You were a little indisposed last week, I recall?'

Sophia couldn't meet his earnest eyes, full of concern. 'I was. How kind of you to remember.'

'I must remember; my niece presses me for every detail about you.'

No words sprang to mind. She had nothing to say. Every nerve was strained, intent on the closeness of him. They stood a while, silent, listening to the calls of the stable boys and the scrape of grooming brushes against the horses' thick winter coats.

'I have heard some news that may interest you, Your Royal Highness.'

Sophia peeped up and saw him tap the side of his nose, before putting the other hand in his pocket. He drew the corner of a letter over the top. It gave her a sense of guilty anticipation unlike anything she had known before.

'You can tell me later. First, would you be kind enough to take me to my horse? There was a little hobble in his gait yesterday, which I fear may be lameness.'

His face twinkled at her convincing lie, spoken loud for all to hear. 'But of course.'

He led her into the stalls, where the early morning light broke through the wood in anaemic puddles, patterning the straw-littered ground. It was blissfully peaceful. No people, no bustle. The only sound was the constant scratch and chomp of horses eating hay. Sophia closed her eyes briefly, wanting to keep hold of the moment.

'Here.' She pulled two folded squares of paper from her hand-muff: one for Miss Garth, one for Caroline. Garth took them, tucked them carefully inside the inner pocket of his scarlet coat and then held out letters for Sophia.

She knew she should hide them away, but she didn't. She gazed at her illicit treasures, running her fingers along the folds of the paper. They made her feel breathless, excited. Her palms tingled as she held them. 'Do you ever read them?'

Garth looked at her sharply. 'I beg your pardon?'

'The letters.' She was ashamed. Why had she said a stupid

thing like that? Perhaps she wanted him to read them, wanted him to admit he had an interest in her life.

'No, of course not.'

Sophia blushed and traced Caroline's writing with her index finger. Of course not. As if he would care about the scribbling of a foolish young lady.

'Please don't think I'm accusing you,' she said quickly. 'It's just . . . Letters are such private things, aren't they? All those secrets . . . I think I would be tempted.'

He laughed and shook his grey head. 'By the time you reach my age, your curiosity fades.'

That was not how she pictured him at all; old and jaded. 'Surely not. Does nothing surprise you anymore?'

He considered. The soft whinny of a horse vibrated through the silence. 'People surprise me,' he said at last. 'And . . . feelings.'

Sophia's heart kicked unexpectedly at the soft tone of his voice. Feelings for whom? She covered her confusion with a show of humour. 'Feelings? In Windsor? Sir, you may be my elder but I have to lecture you: such things are not tolerated here.'

She chuckled, but Garth turned to her with infinite sadness in his weather-beaten features.

'Poor Sophia. You wouldn't be a princess if you could choose it, would you?'

She froze. How did he know? 'No, I would not.' She felt naked, exposed. If he could glimpse her sentiments, surely he knew the other secret of her heart, the one it shouted every moment? Her voice quavered. 'But these things cannot be helped. It is like your profession: some are born to it, others are pressed into it.'

Garth leant over the stable door and clucked his tongue. Lazily, Traveller moved his head toward him and snorted.

Still wobbly, Sophia pulled a handful of hay from the net and fed it into the horse's velvety lips. 'What about you, General Garth? Did you choose to be a soldier?'

He looked round at her. 'Not exactly. A third son must make his living somehow – the army seemed a better option than the church or the law.'

A choice, all the same. He didn't know how lucky he was. 'There, see – I would love to travel with the army and cannot; you are forced to it! Yet we both serve the King. Shall we swap?'

He laughed. 'I fear I would ill become your elegant gowns.'

Sophia swallowed as he ran his eyes over her apparel. Did he think her elegant? No, no. He probably saw her as a daughter. 'Never mind. Let us hope you will marry your fortune one day and be free.'

Garth scratched Traveller underneath the forelock. 'I have left that a little late. I will be fifty-four on my next birthday.'

'A rich widow, sir?' she teased. 'You are too quick to give up hope.'

'Ah, but you do not know how exacting I am. Very few of your rich widows would match my high standards.'

She paused. Was this meant for her? A gentle hint, a caution to check her feelings? She hardly knew what to think. All she could do was match his jovial tone and pretend she had no interest in the state of his heart. 'Then list your requirements, sir! I will find someone for you. What qualities should I seek in your ideal lady?'

He gave her a wry smile. His eyes held hers just a little longer than they should. 'I had better not say.'

∼ Scharnhausen ∼

'I don't know. I do not want to worry Papa unless I have to.'

Royal stood on the driveway and watched Fritz heave himself onto a horse. He took his gun from a servant and slung it over his shoulder.

'You have to,' he told her, picking up the reins. 'No one can avoid this war – no matter how delicate their sensibilities.'

She bristled. Was that a slight against her father? She could hardly believe they were quarrelling already. It had all been going so well. They had spent a few lovely weeks away with the children, relishing their honeymoon period. The hunting lodge, Scharnhausen, was a gem of a palace, smothered in woodland with powdery cream walls. But now Fritz's friends had arrived and intruded on their solitude, talking politics, forcing the real world upon their notice.

'I know your sister urges you to fight the French,' Royal said, smoothing over her irritation, 'but she is in Russia, wife to a Tsar. Think of the size of her army, compared to ours! She does not realise what she is asking.'

'Which is why you need to persuade your father to take the duchy under his protection.'

She drew in a breath and bit back her retort. Fritz, like the King, was a man to be managed carefully. She could not make him out. Abrupt, yet tender; often laughing, but angered by strange, inconsequential things.

She watched him, looking for the affectionate Fritz who shared her bed, the urbane Fritz who kissed her hand over breakfast. He had evaporated like morning mist. What remained was an inflexible prince with a weapon in his grasp. The bulk of him dominated his steed, making it look a mere pony as his powerful presence filled the saddle and his firm hands gripped the reins.

'I will try.' Royal murmured. She had no choice.

Fritz took her by surprise. Turning in his saddle, he put the reins in one hand and blew her a kiss. Her cheeks burned with girlish pleasure.

'Thank you, *Engel*. Thank you.'

He kicked back his heels, wheeled round and cantered off with his hunting party, into a thick coppice of trees blushing with the first hues of autumn. Royal watched the foliage envelop him and sighed. Her feelings were tangled like a mess of embroidery ribbon.

One moment she was ready to throw herself at his feet, do anything for sheer love of him. The next ... exasperated. Afraid of his temper. Missing the King. Far away as she was, she still balanced on a tightrope, afraid what one false move would do to her father's mind. She could not banish him from her thoughts just because she no longer lived with him.

She turned toward the hunting lodge and ambled back past the columns to the colonnade. Laughter floated down from the windows upstairs, where the children studied. It lifted her spirits. Once she had written to the King, she could go and sit with Trinette and be happy again. It was the right thing to do. Her duty was to her husband now.

Royal entered the hallway and headed to her morning room, wondering what to write. The wording had to convey Württemberg's perilous situation, but not cause alarm. She had to persuade, appeal to her father's love, without stirring other emotions. It was a task as delicate as needlepoint – but with stitches that could not be undone.

In her room, all was tranquil and still. No fire burned in the grate, but she didn't mind. The air was cleaner and easier to breathe without the scent of wood or coal. She picked up her writing slope, selected a quill and took a chair next to the window. Words refused to come. Reluctance toyed with her, offering a variety of distractions. The woodland outside her window crisped at the edges. Before long, it would be winter again and the leaves would drop. What would her first winter in Württemberg be like? Trinette talked of sledging parties and ice skates. But no, she must concentrate. She smoothed out a sheet of paper. As her hands moved, she felt an odd flutter in her stomach, almost like nerves. She dipped her quill in ink and wrote a few lines, but the sensation kept interrupting her, a soft butterfly, drifting in and out of her consciousness.

She gazed out the window once more. Fields stretched before the house, sloping down to the woods. A wispy mist floated above the grass and a pheasant darted through it into the trees.

A light tap sounded at the door. Relieved, Royal threw down her quill and stood.

'Enter.'

Her Mistress of the Robes, Madame de Spiegel, shuffled in carrying a basket of sewing. 'I beg your pardon, princess. I thought you might like a little company.'

'Oh, yes! Please, sit down and talk to me. Talk of anything but this horrid war.'

Madame de Spiegel smiled and obeyed. She sat on the sofa with her embroidery hoop, chatting amiably about deer and grouse. Out in the distant woods, a gun popped. 'Ah,' said Madame de Spiegel, 'another bird for the table. Poor creature.'

Unease wrapped itself around Royal's chest like a pair of

tight stays. The cracking, hollow sound of the shot recalled summer days in England, watching the troops out for review in Hyde Park. Then, they had marched and fired for the sake of ceremony, but now the armies of Europe stalked across the land with a deadly purpose. What if the French descended on Württemberg and swarmed across it like a horde of blue locusts? What if her men ended up like the soldiers from the American war: missing limbs, reduced to begging on the street, gunpowder ingrained into their skin? Was she going to sit there and watch it happen? No. Fritz was right. She had to write to her father, she had to try and prevent it.

Picking up her quill with determination, she gave it a fresh coat of ink, laid it on the page – and jumped. The door banged open and a servant darted across the room. The speed of his movement sent her letter drifting to the floor. He gave Royal the briefest nod before flying to Madame de Spiegel and whispering in her ear.

'What is it?' Royal cried.

Ignoring her, the servant straightened up and sped out of the door, leaving it wide open behind him.

Madame de Spiegel stood, her movements stiff and deliberately calm. 'Apparently Prince Wilhelm wishes to speak with me.'

The fluttering in Royal's stomach returned with renewed force. 'What can he have to say that I cannot hear?'

'Probably a servant's quarrel. They work themselves into

a fuss over nothing. Do not worry, I will be back soon.'
Madame de Spiegel finished packing her needlework and
left, refusing to meet Royal's eye. She closed the door with
a tender softness, as if leaving a sleeping baby.

Royal felt sick. What was it? Something too horrible for
words. She recalled the last time servants had kept information from her: her father's illness. Nausea overwhelmed
her. It couldn't be a mere quarrel; something had happened.
Something to do with the soldiers, or with Fritz . . .

She heard shouts and carriage wheels splashing through
puddles. In an instant she was up, out of her chair, pressing
her face against the windowpane. She gripped the frame
with both hands. Nothing but a clump of dark trees met
her eyes. Pearly mist rolled toward them, retreating from
the autumn sun.

'Princess?'

Royal leapt at the sound and fell into the window seat.

Madame de Spiegel stood halfway across the threshold,
her hand wrapped around the side of the door. Her face
was soft and lined with pity.

'Oh, my dear madam! You look ill.'

'You f-f-frightened me,' Royal stuttered. 'What's happened?'

'Will you come into the garden?'

Oh, God. That wasn't an answer. What terrible secret had
to be told in the garden rather than right here, right now?
Images from the past swarmed around her. Madame de

Spiegel had the same look – yes, the exact same! – Lady Harcourt had given the Queen in her distress: soothing, commiserating. Royal reached out her hands and Madame de Spiegel clasped them. Limp as a wet feather, she leant against her attendant and stumbled from the room.

Her vision was speckled. Noise distorted; she couldn't make out anything around her until she felt a whip of cool air on her face and inhaled the sharp scent of decaying leaves. Madame de Spiegel pressed her onto a stone seat. It was damp against Royal's thighs and she shivered.

'What's happened to my husband? I'm sure it must be my husband.'

Madame de Spiegel chaffed her cold hands and made a hushing sound. 'It *is* your husband, madam.'

Royal gasped but Madame de Spiegel was quick to interject. 'It is nothing to alarm you. A fall from his horse, that's all.'

'That's *all*!' Royal echoed. 'That is enough! Is he hurt?'

'Only a little. Mainly bruising. Prince Wilhelm has sent for a surgeon, but we are a good three hours' ride from anywhere.'

The tracks of Royal's tears were cold against her cheeks. Fear and relief fought inside her chest, making it difficult to breathe. She had to move and do something. Anything to shake off the cold grip of horror. 'I must write,' she said. 'I must tell the duke and duchess what has happened.' Royal stood and felt how unequal her legs were to the task. Defeated, she slumped down again.

'All in good time,' said Madame de Spiegel. 'Sit here for a moment. When you are recovered, I will take you to the prince.'

What a weak, wretched thing Royal was. No support in a time of crisis; a fainting, hysterical wife. And not even an obedient one. She had argued with him, refusing to write to her father. Fritz could have been killed and her last words to him would have been angry ones. Less than a year as a wife and already she was unkind, rebellious. The shame was unbearable.

'I will go to him now,' she declared.

Her legs were like liquid, but she forced them to hold her weight. She had to prove her worth. Fritz was everything. Not England; not the King. Württemberg was her home now and her loyalty lay with Fritz. She had been an ingrate to think otherwise.

She stood up and propelled herself, toward the house and the man she loved.

CHAPTER TWENTY-FOUR

Queen's House, London
~ Winter 1797 ~

Charlotte shifted her granddaughter on her lap and placed the girl's small cheek against her breast. The child snuggled in closer and closed her coral eyelids. There were tiny blue veins, faint as gossamer, within them. She put a protective palm over the child's head. If only it could shield her from the war between her parents.

Was it Charlotte's fault? If she had encouraged and advised Caroline, would the marriage have turned out differently? She thought not. George was determined to get rid of his wife, even if he did not have a replacement to hand. Charlotte's letter to Mrs Fitzherbert had produced no effect; the Catholic still shied away from a reunion like a nervous filly. The marriage was disintegrating from inside, without her help, and nothing could suck the poison out.

It would be for the best, in the long term; little Charlotte would be safe from the influence of her wicked mother and fit to sit on the throne of England. But in the meantime, she must be batted about between enemy lines, not knowing whom to love or believe.

Charlotte dwelt upon her granddaughter's tiny, flushed features and soft, delicate eyelashes. Definitely a Hanover child – not a Brunswicker. She was so like George as an infant that it made Charlotte ache. Had it really been thirty-five years since she held him like this: a hot, squidgy little body in her arms? Desire stirred within her; not desire for another child, exactly – more a deep nostalgia – a fervent wish she could go back in time and do it all again. Do it better.

'The King!'

Charlotte and her ladies rose to their feet with a flap of their taffeta gowns. Little Charlotte opened her clear blue eyes.

'What a pleasant sight!' the King approached them with outstretched arms.

Charlotte noticed sheets of paper folded in his hand. News about the war? Lists of the navy's demands? She tried not to let the apprehension show in her face.

'So sorry I was detained. Has she been here long?'

'Only half an hour or so.' Charlotte gave the infant into his ready embrace.

He swept his granddaughter round and round, making her squeal with glee. Charlotte averted her eyes, trying not to remember him doing the same thing with her poor, dead

Octavius. So long ago now, yet the wound was still fresh, the scab easily removed.

'You have a letter to show me?' she asked.

The King stopped his game and turned. 'Hmm?'

She nodded at his hand, clutching the mass of crumpled paper.

'Oh! Yes. Lady Elgin, take the little love for me, will you?'

Their small granddaughter tottered off with her governess toward the other ladies, eager to play.

The King sighed. 'Such a good-tempered child. It's a bad business, my dear.'

'Have they come to an agreement yet? George and Caroline?'

He blew out his cheeks. 'Yes and no. Poor Caroline. My God, Charlotte, some of the things she writes to me . . .'

'Is the letter from Caroline?' It would be like the blasted girl to send another of her melodramatic stories and upset the King. Was she not content with making the prince miserable?

He looked at his hand again, as if surprised by it. 'Oh! No. This is from Royal.'

Charlotte frowned, allowing Caroline to float from her mind like a light fog. Royal had not written to her in weeks. She was just like the rest, always favouring her father.

'Another begging letter to use your influence for Württemberg?' she guessed. 'That husband of hers is shameless.'

George smiled. 'No, he won't be bothering me for a while. He's fallen from his horse.'

'Is he hurt?'

The King scratched his ear. 'Not much. A broken arm. Though the way Royal runs on, you would think him in mortal danger.' He chuckled.

'It must have been a shock.' Charlotte lowered her head, weighed down with memories. 'In a strange country with only a husband as your friend . . . the thought of losing him is terrifying.'

The King put his hand on hers and smiled warmly. If he really knew all she had suffered, he would not smile.

'And she hasn't her mother's nerves of steel. But it looks like old Fritz has been more than considerate. The first thing he did after the accident was get her away from the house; he didn't want the sight of him being carried in to distress her.'

Charlotte cocked an eyebrow. 'So says Royal. She is besotted – I would not take her word for it.' She was conscious of a horrible sneer as she said the word *besotted*. Fresh, hopeful love curdled her blood now, like bad milk. And she was still angry with Royal. Why would she not come to her mother with this? Charlotte was the one who could understand her feelings and give her sound advice.

'I hope it's true,' he said. 'She will need a kind husband now more than ever. She is with child.'

Blood rushed past Charlotte's ears. 'Really? She's sure?'

He nodded. 'Isn't it wonderful?'

It *was* wonderful. The child that grew inside Charlotte had a child growing inside her. All the perils of Charlotte's own first pregnancy came flooding back: the illness, the fears of death in childbirth.

'I won't be there,' she fretted. 'Royal will need me and I won't be there.'

George squeezed her shoulder. 'She will be fine. You had fifteen children without your mother's help! I am sure Fritz's parents will take good care of her.'

It was hardly the point – she'd need her real mother. Or would she? Charlotte paused as a stinging realisation dawned on her. 'She didn't write to me.'

The King shrugged. 'She knew I would tell you.'

So that was how it was. Charlotte was inconsequential, a person to be told by proxy. The wound was deep, but she could not let it show. 'Still. It's the kind of thing a girl tells her mother.'

The King observed the working of her face and smiled ruefully. 'Do you see what I mean, now? It is no good for me to take little Charlotte away from Caroline. A child always needs its mother. Do you not agree?'

A mean comparison to make. She slid her gaze to where her pretty granddaughter played with the ladies-in-waiting. It would be easy, as an unloved wife in a foreign place, to build your life around such a cherub. Charlotte recalled the agony of being prised apart from Alfred and Octavius; a pain so intense it echoed through the years. Did Caroline feel the same way? The answer was swift and ice cold: *no*. Such a woman was incapable of tender emotions. And she certainly did not deserve this angel of a daughter with rosy cheeks and a merry laugh. The need to possess the child, to keep it, throbbed through Charlotte until it made her eyes water. She would be her comfort, her solace. God knew she needed one.

She looked the King straight in the eye and dared, for once in their marriage, to tell the truth.

'No,' she said simply. 'No, I don't agree with you.'

～ *Ludwigsburg* ～

A baby. It hardly seemed possible to Royal that beneath her own unremarkable skin, new life was growing.

She attempted to concentrate on the sheet of paper in front of her, but her eyes kept falling to her stomach. Under her velvet dress, she was heavy laden like an apple tree in autumn. She bit the feather of her pen. It was important to finish her letter to England; war raged around her new home and both Austrian and French troops marched through Stuttgart daily, foraging and plundering. Already her beautiful new land had lost much. Fritz was relying on her to gain the King's support. And yet . . .

Royal's stomach was a gentle curve, perfectly round. It was a bubble, with just her and the baby inside; war and politics could clamour around them, but they heard none of it.

Madame de Spiegel looked up from her embroidery. 'What are you hoping for? A boy or a girl?'

'A girl,' Royal said too quickly. They laughed. 'Of course, I would still love a boy . . .'

Madame de Spiegel nodded. 'I understand. There is something special between a mother and her daughter, is there not?'

Was there? Royal wound her relationship with the Queen round in her mind like a skein of silk. She only recalled frustration and humiliation, shot through with odd strands of kindness. But she could not confess that to a servant. 'Yes. Of course.'

She put her hand on her swollen belly and felt a sharp point like an elbow. Why did she want a daughter so badly? She didn't like to admit it, even to herself. Part of her – a small part – believed having a little girl would put everything right – somehow make up for her own thwarted teenage years. She would be the type of mother her own should have been.

'The prince's friend Count Zeppelin has arrived,' Madame de Spiegel said, interrupting her thoughts.

Royal looked out of the window, framed with frost, to the park where thick snow coated the ground. The hedges stooped beneath the weight of their white burden and the lake had frozen over.

'Really? He came in this weather? Well. I'm sure I'll see nothing of my husband now.'

'Nonsense. You must not listen to the rumours.'

Royal turned in surprise. She had spoken in jest, but there was something in her companion's voice that was absolutely serious.

'What rumours?'

Madame de Spiegel coloured and concentrated on threading her needle. 'Oh, nothing. Foolish stuff.' She was clearly uncomfortable. Royal twirled her pen between her fingers and her mind turned too, rotating the rumours she had heard about Fritz. It was common knowledge that he and Count Zepplin were close – very close – almost inseparable. She wondered what else was whispered. It seemed everyone had a terrible story about her husband. Uneasiness stole around her, cold and prickly. She shook it off – she had no reason to complain. Fritz had done right by her. Not only had he rescued her from stagnant spinsterhood, he had given her the greatest gift it was possible to bestow: a child. She had to stop doubting him. The indissoluble knot was tied and the baby would cement the pact. A good wife should let rumours roll right off her shoulders.

Royal put her pen down with a sigh. 'I cannot do this now. Shall we walk?'

'Not outside?'

Royal laughed at Madame de Spiegel's shocked expression. 'In the gallery, then.'

'You have to rest, in your condition.'

'My mother had fifteen children. I never saw her sit down while she carried them.'

'You English are made of stern stuff.'

Royal put a hand to the small of her back and stretched. 'I hate it when pregnant women fuss. I'm growing new life, not dying.'

'All the same,' said Madame de Spiegel, 'you must take it easy.'

Before they had put away their things, quick footsteps sounded on the stairs. Alarmed, Royal looked at her companion. With a war surrounding them, a messenger could mean anything. She imagined bayonets and cannon, the smoke of battle. She clasped her hands around her stomach.

Fritz flung through the door, panting with exhaustion, his face a deathly white. His bad arm was still strapped across his chest with bandages.

Royal set her teeth, ready for the bullet. 'My love, what's happened?'

He took a deep, shuddering breath. 'My *Vater* is dead.'

Royal gasped and she started toward her husband. 'Oh, I'm sorry. I'm so, so sorry.' Tears misted her eyes, tokens of her own grief for the poor duke, but she put them aside. Fritz came first. She knew how she would feel under such a crushing blow. The loss of her father – whether to death or madness – would be the worst possible news.

But as she reached Fritz, he waved her away. 'I am all right.'

She recoiled, stung. She had no idea how to comfort him. 'How is your mother?'

'Terrible. She is in hysterics. They are sending Trinette to us.'

'Of course.' Royal hesitated. 'Is there anything I can do?'

He shook his head. 'Just look after the girl for me. I have much business to attend.'

Business. As she thought of the ledger books, the official seals and the blotted ink, clarity burst upon her.

'Of course you do. You are the Duke, now.'

He pursed his lips. 'Yes,' he said. 'It is all on my shoulders. And there is a war going on.'

More commotion in the hallway. Royal turned and saw Trinette stumble into the room. Poor child! Her eyes were big and red, her cheeks stained with tears. Instinctively, Royal opened her arms. Trinette had none of her father's pride. She flew across the floor, a black streak, and threw herself into Royal's embrace.

'Mama,' she said, for the first time.

Despite everything, Royal smiled.

CHAPTER TWENTY-FIVE

Lower Lodge, Windsor
∼ 1798 ∼

Mary and Amelia pored over music sheets, clunking out disjointed notes on the spinet. Sophia sat apart in the corner with a candle and scraps of blotted paper. The sight of her sisters playing and singing, so vital and full of health, filled her with dismay. Princes would come for them, marry them and take them to distant shores. Soon they would plump out, like Royal, with the first of many babies. Only Sophia, the invalid, would remain here. Her health had deteriorated yet again. At first she had been plagued with fits, then she struggled to swallow food. Now there were red hot cramps in her stomach. It felt like she would never be well again.

Pressing her forehead against the cool glass of the windowpane, Sophia glanced into the garden. Outside the shadowy castle rose, tall and magnificent above her. Did she really want a prince to rescue her from this place? She knew the answer, even before she asked the question: *no*. She only wanted General Garth.

Blushes stained her cheeks. It was shameful, absurd. He was not handsome, she knew that, and he was so old! His kindness, which she loved to dwell upon, probably stemmed from deference to her father, not regard for her. But logic was useless. He was the first man ever to notice her; the first man her heart had leapt to see. No reason could undo the magic of that.

Sophia closed her eyes as stomach cramps gripped with their burning hands and wrung her flesh together. Both her pains and her love for Garth were growing roots, taking possession of her as she sat clutching the fabric of the curtain. She felt nothing but the agony of her stomach, saw nothing but his face.

'Oh!'

Mary's fingers slid off the keyboard with a discordant twang. Sophia snapped her head up, startled, and saw Amelia drop to the floor on one knee.

'It hurts! Oh, God!'

Sophia recognised the expression of bitter pain on her sister's face. 'Your leg again?'

Amelia nodded, wordlessly, tears gathering in the corners of her eyes.

'Show me,' said Mary.

'I'd better fetch someone.' Sophia stood up, but she could not move fast with her painful stomach.

'No, ring the bell. You're not well yourself.' Mary prised Amelia's fingers away from her leg and lifted her figured muslin skirt. 'It's so swollen! It looks like a cricket ball.'

It was a vicious inflammation, angry and red. Sophia's eyes expanded. Hurriedly, she limped to the bell and pulled on the lever.

'It's become much worse.' Mary shook her head as Amelia whimpered and leant on her shoulder. 'I can't imagine what it is.'

Sophia met her anxious eyes and knew they were both thinking of the same thing, the thing their mother feared more than death: a taint in the family blood. Sophia shrank within the case of her body, which suddenly felt unreliable and foreign. She could sense it: a darkness stirring within her. But now it had come for Amelia too.

Frogmore, Windsor

The winter months faded away into a bright spring. Charlotte took out her book of pressed flowers and ran her fingers over the dried petals. Soon she would have live blooms to look upon, not just mummified stems. If only she could preserve other things with her fragile flowers. She would have bottled her optimism before it was pressed out of her like the juice from these leaves.

New signs appeared in the King daily; turnpike tickets on the road to madness. There was nothing Charlotte could do. Events had spiralled, from George's broken marriage to Amelia's sudden illness, until she could no longer see her way to the surface. No clawing or frantic activity would turn the tide back now. She was almost sick of trying. All she saw in the future was war and revolution. The Swiss had caught the fever and were convulsing with it. So far, the British had proven themselves loyal to the crown, but would it last? Not with a deranged monarch and a debauched heir to the throne.

She sighed and looked out of the window. Sophia, Ernest and George strolled up and down the gardens, taking advantage of the mild air. All at once they stopped beneath the budding trees, caught by something George said. Sophia bit her lip and furrowed her brow. Ernest was laconic as always, the rim of his hat practically over his eyes, but George made great gestures with his arms as he spoke.

Charlotte felt nauseous.

'You there,' she gestured to a footman. 'Fetch the Princes George and Ernest in here.'

The man bowed and walked outside. Charlotte watched his progress through the smeary glass. Why did her heart thunder? They could not have received alarming news about Amelia – that would have come to Charlotte first. Unless it went to the King. And if the King was alone, fretting about his darling daughter . . .

She shut the volume of flowers and hugged its weight to her chest.

Her sons trooped into the room and bowed before her. Petals spotted their whiskers and dishevelled hair, now cropped to match the fashion. Charlotte waved the servants away.

'What is it?' she demanded. 'What are you speaking of?'

'Rebellion,' Ernest returned blithely.

The word sent prickles down her spine. She stole a glance at her eldest son, George, and saw his cheeks flushed with worry.

'Not Amelia?'

'No,' George confirmed. 'Amelia is, I trust, recovering as I left her. But the Channel Fleet are on the verge of mutiny at Portsmouth.'

Stress squeezed against her temples, hurting her head. The King would be beside himself.

'Mutiny in wartime? Have they no sense?'

'They have no pay and no food. Hopefully the Admiralty will sort it out before the French can take advantage. But they don't have much time. Ireland is in revolt.'

Charlotte's hands fluttered nervously on the cover of her book. She couldn't think; she could only feel pain and flashing panic. 'Whatever for?'

'They want Irish taxes to go to Ireland. They want to be free of English rule.'

Charlotte snarled. 'Do they? Well, let them go. I daresay they'll come crying back.'

'I think not; the French have landed at Kilcummin.

They're marching and gathering recruits as they go.'

She barked an incredulous laugh, masking her terror. The King would run distracted. No one would rally behind George. They may as well raise the French colours now.

'So! They won't have the English but they welcome the French, with their beheadings and bloodbaths!'

George exhaled heavily. 'This is beside the point. If the French take Ireland, they're a stride away from invasion.'

The remaining colour seeped from Charlotte's skin. 'Pitt will save us,' she asserted.

'Pitt says we'll have to form a union – give the Irish franchise and trading rights.'

Ernest scoffed. 'The Catholics? Not likely! The old man will never break his vow to keep them out.'

George turned about desperately. 'But Pitt will resign if he doesn't.'

Charlotte licked her parched lips. 'How does the King take it, exactly?'

They looked at one another.

'Not well, I fear.'

⁓ *Stuttgart* ⁓

Royal bent her head in prayer, letting the veil slide over her face. She didn't close her eyes, but she was communicating something desperately to her God.

Her private Anglican chapel was painfully silent. The

dark evening sucked the life from the stained-glass windows, leaving them as vapid shapes. The wooden choir stands lay deserted. In front of the altar, hundreds of candles sparkled over the silver cross and communion cup. She pretended to pray for peace and the souls of her in-laws, but God knew the truth. Fear, not grief, drew her to the cool sanctuary of the chapel.

She ran a hand over her blooming stomach, remembering the doctor's declaration that it was a big, strong child. All very well for him: he didn't have to push it out. *Childbirth. Travail. Confinement.* The words swam around her, each with its own sinister whisper. How lightly she had dismissed them as a young virgin, eager for babies of her own. Only now, as the time drew near, she had to admit the possibility she had hidden like a dirty stain beneath a rug: she could die. These might be her last months on earth.

How could she prepare for the great trial of her life, the most intense pain she would ever know? First labours could last days. As kind and attentive as Fritz was, he would not be allowed in the birthing chamber and he certainly wouldn't be able to help her. If only Fritz's mother was still alive. Royal had been relying on her, but once the poor duchess lost her life's partner, she had withered away. Now Royal's mentor was gone; she had to face the childbed without a woman's advice.

The Queen never considered marriage and childbirth fit topics to discuss with her daughter. Why did she not write, like a proper mother, with advice and soothing words? Her letters were banal, useless – only imparting the news that she would send a pair of kangaroos from England, so that they could make a menagerie at Ludwigsburg. Royal needed reassurance, not damned kangaroos!

The pastor's voice resonated through the church and rumbled softly in her ear. It was like a warm liquid, soothing, reaching deep inside. A memory rose unbidden: Royal sitting on her father's lap, leaning her head against his chest and listening to him speak. If only she could feel his comfort now.

Once, she would have confided all her fears to the King. But how could she burden the poor man with more worry? He was having enough trouble keeping his own country under control. His letters had a cheerful air but his uneven, shaky writing gave him away.

Trinette sniffed, her face wet with tears. The cluster of distress inside Royal's head separated and reached out tendrils toward her darling stepdaughter. It was selfish to brood over her own misfortunes while Trinette suffered beside her. The girl was without her real mother or the grandmother who substituted for her. Only Royal remained for Trinette to rely upon. Wasn't now the time for Royal to show her worth? To do what she always vowed she would: be a better mother than the Queen? Easier said than done.

Royal stared at the pew in front of her, tracing the whirls

in the wood. Her marriage was in its infancy, and already two members of the family had faded away, blown out like the prayer candles flickering at the front of the church. It was her job to unite this sad, broken house of Württemberg. To reassure the public in a time of turmoil, to welcome the immigrants who came flooding out of Switzerland and other territories seized by the French. The weight of responsibility paralysed her.

The pastor, solemn in his black and white robes, called Royal forward for Communion.

Royal willed the strength of Christ into her body as she chewed the bread and swallowed the wine, but they were tasteless in her mouth.

CHAPTER TWENTY-SIX

Drury Lane Theatre, London
1798

Flickering candles lit the stage, throwing shadows over the wood and the thick, velvet curtains. Everything had a blurred, dream-like quality. It was hot, almost suffocating, and the close air reeked with the scent of cheap tallow lights and perfume. Charlotte hung back at the entrance to the royal box, barring her daughters with an outstretched arm. The King wanted to go first.

'No fear, Charlotte,' he said, clenching her hand within his own. 'I will not show them fear.'

His sanity dangled by a thread. Through dumb luck they had kept Ireland under control and placated the navy, but the political situation was fragile – and so was the King.

'Stand up straight!' Charlotte hissed at Mary. 'Your father wants us to look brave.'

Dutifully, Mary pulled back her shoulders.

The King strode to the front of the box and bowed.

Charlotte watched his profile, wondering when he would snap at last. Applause rang out in the stalls. Charlotte glanced at her daughters, preparing them to step forward. But as she moved her foot, white light flashed and a *crump* came from below. Her breath caught. She knew the sound of a pistol.

Hurried footsteps thundered behind her. Shouts rang out from the audience. Charlotte swayed and clung to the velvet curtain, her eyes fixed on the King. He took a single step back.

'George!'

To Charlotte's astonishment, he pulled out a quizzing glass and peered around the circle. 'Stay there. Just a squib backstage.'

Another shot. The audience roared.

'George!' she flew forward, pressing her hands to his chest, feeling desperately for wounds.

'Do be still,' he said. He hadn't even flinched. 'You make such a fuss.'

She didn't have time to react. The door opened, pushing the princesses forward. Mr Sheridan, the theatre manager, ran into the box, his face twisted in panic, sweat gleaming on his forehead.

'Your Majesty, Your Majesty! I have a carriage ready for you!'

Charlotte could have kissed him. 'Oh bless you, sir!'

The King turned and lowered his glass. 'You want us to leave?'

Sheridan stuttered. He looked to Charlotte. 'No – I do not *want* you to leave, Your Majesty. I fear for your safety. We've caught the man but he might have accomplices in the audience . . .'

'No, no.' The King dismissed him with a wave of his hand. 'We'll not stir. We'll see the entertainment out.'

Charlotte could not believe her ears. Her shoulders solidified with tension. Such foolhardiness, such flagrant disregard for the safety of his daughters! It was either bravery or madness – and she feared she knew which. She opened her mouth to protest but it was too late; George pushed back to the front of the box, showing himself unharmed to the cheering crowd.

'Come, Charlotte! Don't dawdle.'

With trembling legs, Charlotte inched forward and acknowledged the public. The audience went wild, standing on their seats and waving handkerchiefs in the air.

Charlotte couldn't bear to watch their mania. It was like a large-scale reproduction of the King's state of mind.

'Sit down, girls, sit.'

The princesses fell into their chairs, looking at their father in speechless admiration. Once again Charlotte felt the sting of their favouritism. He could risk their lives for his own pride, he could run mad, and they still worshipped him.

Fifteen years before, she would have worshipped him too.

⤙ Windsor ⤚

Sophia cowered in Traveller's stall, her arms stretched over his muscular neck, her face against his fur. She quivered uncontrollably from the horror of the assault. Why would anyone want to kill her father? What had he done to them?

Instinct told her it would be the final prod, pushing his mind over the edge – the last card laid upon the house they had built with such painstaking care. She had only to stand back, catch her breath, and watch it topple to the ground.

Traveller nickered softly, sympathetic to her tears.

She knew she couldn't go through it again: the King raving, the Queen poisoned by sorrow, spitting fury like an injured snake. But who would comfort her? Sophia's family were all too absorbed with their own misery.

She wished she could mount Traveller and ride, fast as a comet, jumping fences, pushing through hedges, on and on until fear and frustration were nothing but a memory.

'Sophia?'

General Garth.

Traveller tossed his head. Sophia cringed closer to him, twining his mane between her fingers. She did not want Garth to see her like this. Her breath accelerated – she felt like a child, caught in a forbidden act.

'Is that you, Sophia?' *Go away.* She couldn't plaster on a smile or put on a show for him. Another moment and he would see her weak soul, bare in its agony. Embarrassing, humiliating beyond belief. What better way to confirm herself as a fretful child in his eyes?

A boot crunched on the straw. 'Good God! What are you doing here, at this hour?' The bolt slid across the door. With a gentle creak, Garth let himself into the stable and placed a hand on Sophia's shoulder. Her flesh burnt under the heat of it. 'Won't you tell me?'

No. There were no words for such things. She would not show him a wet shining face, speak in whooping breaths or risk her nose running down her chin. She had at least *some* dignity.

'Sophy? I heard the King was attacked. He is not hurt?'

Concern sweetened his voice. It gave her a swooping sensation – the same she got when the carriage went over a hill too fast. As he moved closer, the heat of his body warmed her, slowed the trembling of her limbs.

'Do you want me to go away?'

She wasn't sure, now. She lifted an eye from Traveller's neck.

Garth was very close, only a breath away. Flecks of stubble sat above his top lip, drawing her gaze to his mouth. She wanted him. She wanted him so badly it was a physical pain that made fresh tears start to her eyes. Garth, in her arms, in her life. To cling to, to protect her.

'Wouldn't it help to tell me what's wrong?'

With a sob, she surrendered to the irresistible tug of her

flesh toward his. His body caught her like a pillow, firm yet soft, while his warm, strong arms formed a protective shield around her.

'Oh, poor dear!'

Bliss. Despite her misery, Sophia tasted the crackle of desire in her mouth. A man, holding her. It had never happened before. She had almost given up hoping it ever would. *Remember this.* This moment was hers now – no one would take it away. The dizzying closeness, the connection of his body to hers. The way she had to breathe through her mouth to keep air flowing to her brain.

'What is it, dear one?'

One arm circled her waist, the other patted her back. Carefully, she rested her head upon his shoulder and let her tears settle upon the epaulettes of his scarlet jacket. They became dewy beads of beauty there, emblazoned by gold.

'Come on, Sophy. What's wrong?'

'Everything.' Her voice bubbled. She hid her face in his lapel, not wanting him to see her tear-stained and blotchy.

Garth moved his hand from her back, sending tingles through her skin, until it settled on her nape. He stroked gently, a hypnotising caress. She melted into him.

'It's been a cruel time for you,' he said softly, 'what with Princess Amelia's illness and the war. . . I wish there was something I could do.'

For the first time, she raised her chin and gazed full into his face. There was no hiding it – the veil had to drop.

Adoration burned in her eyes, too vivid and naked to be ignored. Garth looked at her for a beat. Suddenly, his urgent arms pulled her to him. His mouth came down, warm and sweet upon hers. Surely it was a dream. It felt like one: engulfing her, washing her mind until there was nothing – nothing before or after, except this moment. Her body fell limp with ecstasy.

Time must have passed. She didn't notice it. At last his lips withdrew, slowly. She couldn't bear to let them go.

Her voice came out airy, hardly there at all. 'Don't stop.'

'But . . . The King.'

The King. How could she forget? His image crashed rudely into the stable beside her, chilling the air with his disapproval. What was she thinking? Just a moment ago she had been crying over him and now . . . Now . . .

'Yes,' she whispered. Her heart drummed, shouting over her scruples. It would not give in. She tightened her grip on the lapels of his jacket. 'My father . . .'

'I would never hurt your father,' he whispered into her hair, nuzzling at her ear, 'and I would never involve you in anything dishonourable.'

Her spirit screamed against the injustice of it all. She itched to tear things, knock over tables and send objects clattering to the ground. How could it be possible to want something this badly and not get it? There must be some way for them to be together. Her feelings were too powerful to be ignored, too strong to be submerged.

'But – then. . .' she started desperately. 'What shall we do?'

He focused his soft, love-drenched gaze upon her. 'I don't know, Sophy. I don't know.'

And he kissed her again.

⌒ Stuttgart ⌒

Royal lay in a dark, stuffy room for three weeks before the pains came. They began like menstruation: twinges that made her jump, as some diabolical puppeteer pulled strings inside her womb and made it dance.

She put down her book and forced herself to say the words. 'I think it is time.' They resounded against the walls, ominous as the drum roll before the guillotine dropped. Her ladies leapt into action. They closed the curtains, barred the shutters and pinned blankets over the windows. Everything fell into gloom, making Royal apprehensive.

This is it. The hot, damp room wobbled. Odd details stood out: a dusty windowsill, Roman numerals upon the clock. Before long even they vanished as the women drew heavy curtains around her bed and pinned them together.

'Tell Monsieur de Reder,' she panted. 'He must – he must go to England and inform my father.' Even as the pains tore through her belly she thought of the King, pale in suspense. It was her duty to lighten his anxiety by birthing a healthy, wailing baby.

It felt like her whole life, everything she had worked and

striven for, was a prelude to this moment. She braced herself and set her teeth. Only a matter of hours before her arms would be full and she would never feel empty again.

As daylight deepened to dusk, the hard, steady pressure in the small of her back grew into a spiky ball. A powerful force clawed to get out, threatening to rip her open. She didn't cry and she didn't shriek. She would get through this.

There were blessed moments when the hot pain subsided, like a wave drawing back from the beach, and she fell down on the crumpled bed to gasp for breath. At other times, distorted shapes came to her, embroidery on the curtains, the wooden bedstead, grim and ornate; attendants carrying silver bowls of water, her own arm glistening with sweat, clutching at the sheets.

The *accoucheur* gave her advice but Royal had lost the ability to interpret her adopted tongue; words and sentences meant nothing. Only the language of pain filled her head and it was all consuming. 'Oh, God! Oh, God!' Suddenly the agony jumped up a level, forcing cries from her mouth.

She took a breath of thick air – it was metallic with the scent of blood, tinged with sharp bursts of body odour. A wave of nausea hit her just as a fresh pulse of bloody discharge streamed out between her legs. Royal writhed and creased the bedclothes, her legs kicking out.

'Help me!' Her body heaved in a great spasm as something heavy fell away and rushed out of her. As it went, it took her last drop of energy with it. She tried, tried so hard to stay awake and hear her baby cry, but the swirling darkness reached out and claimed her.

Royal awoke on a bed of coals. Pain rose swift to greet her, beating inside like a pulse.

My baby. She knew it was no longer tied to her, but she could not hear or see it. The severance was unbearable. She struggled to raise her head from the pillow but it wouldn't obey. Movement flickered in the corner of her eye. *My baby. Bring me my baby.* She tried to call out but her voice no longer worked – she only slurred out an unintelligible stream of noise.

'There now, take this.' The voice echoed from far away.

Warm liquor trickled down her throat. It scalded and made her cough with its bitter taste. What was wrong with her? She was meant to be a proud new mother by now, cradling a bundle of pink, peeling skin in her tired arms. Instead she was paralysed. Her skin felt hot, but she shivered. She wanted her baby.

Strong as her desire was, she couldn't hold onto the thought. Once more, she drifted into the seas of unconsciousness.

Royal jolted awake. Her own voice echoed back at her from the walls. She winced and wished she hadn't sat up so fast. Every inch of her hurt, as if she had been caught under the hooves of a cavalry charge. But the pain was unimportant; there was something else, something . . .

Everything lay still around her. Early morning light bleached the objects in her bedroom of their usual colours, leaving her in a strange shadow world. She blinked at them. Was that Fritz? Yes, his large form sat slumped in a chair beside her, his chin upon his chest and a snore fluttering his cravat. Why wasn't he beside her in the bed? She thought she knew the answer, but every time she caught at a thread of memory it slipped from her grasp.

The baby. Of course! Where was the baby? She put her hand to her stomach and found it strangely deflated, tender and lumpy to the touch. Royal shivered and pulled up her quilt. A doleful wind sighed down the chimney as she sat, alone, waiting.

She didn't like to wake Fritz; it didn't seem right. She wasn't even sure if he was really there. She began to wonder, as she stared into the surreal half-light, if this was a dream and she was really in another bed, fast asleep, still pregnant. Somewhere close-by a clock ticked, whispering the time. Royal let the minutes pass in agonising uncertainty.

By and by there were footsteps. She clutched the covers. The door edged open and a servant girl peeped in, checking on the threshold as she saw Royal sitting up and awake. For a moment she disappeared, and then came back bearing a tray.

'Good morning, Your Grace.'

The glorious scent of tea wafted into the room. Royal

watched the girl set a cup down beside her bed. She didn't feel equal to drinking it – not yet – but she let the delicious fumes wash over and revive her.

Fritz did not stir.

The girl moved to the fireplace and scrambled about in the grate. Royal watched her dispassionately, trying to decide if she was an apparition.

No. The noises, the scents and feelings were real. As flames kindled, the comforting smell of woodsmoke infused the foetid air.

'Will that be all, Your Grace?' The servant turned from her task and rose to her feet. Orange light from the fire played on her young face and Royal started.

Tragedy was etched upon the maid's features. She stood, awaiting orders, her big brown eyes swimming with tears.

What is it? Oh God, what's wrong? Royal formed the words with her mouth, but her vocal chords were taut. No sound escaped her.

Taking her silence as permission to leave, the servant wiped her hands on her apron and hurried through the door. Royal thought she heard a muffled sob as the latch clicked behind her.

With wobbling arms, Royal took her cup of tea and held the warm china in her hands. A thick gruel of dread stirred in her stomach. Nothing made sense. She thought she was dying, but she wasn't dead, and the baby was nowhere to be seen, and the maid . . .

Fritz snorted in his sleep.

She sipped her tea, trying to calm her nerves. Anything could have caused the maid's distress. She might have received a scolding from the housekeeper or quarrelled with a sweetheart. It did not mean the baby was ill or deformed. Wasn't Fritz there, sleeping calmly by Royal's side? Would he be doing that if everything wasn't perfectly well? Of course not.

At last, rays of sunlight broke through the curtains and tickled at Fritz's face. He tried to brush them off and grumbled before opening his eyes.

It felt an age since she had seen him, heard his dear voice. When he finally looked up, his flabby features animated once more, the sight was so sweet that Royal wept. Discarding the tea, she held out her arms to him.

'Hush, my dear, hush. Stay down.' He put a hand on her clammy forehead and stroked away the curls plastered there.

Relief washed over her. No need to be brave now, no need to face anything alone. She had another human, an anchor to hold onto. 'It hurt so much.'

'I know.' He paused as she clung to his hand and laid her cheek against it. 'It is over now, *Liebchen*. Your ordeal is over.'

Yes. A ferocious battle, a long race . . . But where was her reward? The idea of a baby thrust itself into her consciousness again, wailing and screaming. She had almost forgotten in her delight at being held by Fritz.

'My love . . . the baby. What did I have?'

He cleared his throat. 'A girl. A big, beautiful girl.'

Royal's spirit soared. A girl. A daughter, a real daughter, not a counterfeit like Amelia or Trinette. They were the words she had longed to hear all her life. She couldn't believe they were really in her ears. If someone had told her, five years before, that she would escape England, marry and bear her own daughter, she would have thought them as mad as her father. But she had achieved the impossible. Suddenly all the pain, all the hours of torment were erased.

'Just like we wanted!' she cried. 'Now we have two boys and two girls . . .'

'My darling, she was born dead.'

Dead. It struck Royal like a blow about the face. Her weak faculties wrestled with his sentence, appalled.

'Dead?' she repeated.

A tear fell down Fritz's vast face. 'We thought you were going to die too. Thank God you were restored to us!'

Born dead. It didn't make sense to Royal, still weak and confused. Born and dead – those words meant opposite things. Was he talking about her baby? Surely not, surely he meant something else. Born dead?

'The people were so worried,' Fritz said. 'They are throwing a gala for your recovery.'

She didn't hear him. On some level, she understood the great tragedy that had befallen her, but it was too enormous to absorb. Numbness shielded her from the grief, letting it howl and scream at a distance, as if locked in a separate room.

'The people have never shown such concern for a duchess before! They truly love you!'

What did the people matter? She only cared about her baby, but her limbs had never moved, her eyes had never opened. The whole dream of her life evaporated. How could she just disappear, drift away like smoke from a musket? A cold, hard part of her brain answered her question with biting clarity: *you should have rested. They told you to rest.*

Fritz saw her staring away, eyes glazed over. 'My dear, shall I leave you?'

Royal nodded dumbly. She wished she had died instead.

Fritz stroked her hand. 'We can have more children,' he soothed. 'You are not past the age yet.'

Royal glared at him. He didn't understand. How could he? To him the dead daughter was just a child he had never met. But she was the intimate sharer of Royal's body, exchanging a constant internal communion; she was part of Royal. A part that had been amputated without opiates.

'Just remember the subjects and the children we have. Remember how much you are treasured.' He kissed Royal's wet cheek. 'I know it does not feel like it now, but we have much to be grateful for.' Fritz plumped up the pillows, tucked his wife back into the bed and left her to sleep.

Royal watched him all the way to the door, where his face changed. Unaware of her scrutiny, his pudgy features collapsed into pure agony. As she saw her own roiling emotions on his face, the truth thumped across her dull brain. She had caused all this misery; she would not rest. She would not rest and now her daughter was dead. Fritz shut the door softly and tears tumbled from her eyes.

Royal curled into a foetal position, hugging her knees to her heaving chest. It still hurt to move, but nothing was more painful than her grief. What had she done? How would she ever, ever atone? Her firstborn, her daughter, the little thing upon which she had built so much hope was dead. And it was her fault.

CHAPTER TWENTY-SEVEN

Weymouth
∼ *1799* ∼

A cloud of gunsmoke blocked the sun, its sharp scent lacing the wind as it whipped the sails into full swell.

Charlotte struggled to balance on the damp boards swaying beneath her feet. Salutes to the royal yacht had never made her dizzy with fright before. She ran a hand over her brow, smoothing the tight skin that clung around her eyes and stretched across her forehead.

'Did they really say it was English spies?' she whispered.

'Yes. English spies in the Assembly of France.' The King nodded a little longer than necessary. 'They used the excuse to dissolve the Directory at gunpoint.'

The ocean winked at Charlotte, as dark and cold as her frightened soul. If only she understood. She couldn't ask the King more questions – he had an indecent air of excitement about him. But if the French had overthrown their Directory, brought to power through the revolution, surely it was a good thing?

She chose her words carefully. 'And these men who mean to lead as consuls . . .'

'Cannot be trusted,' George confirmed. He sounded enthusiastic, as if he was telling her about his favourite play. 'Especially this General Buonaparte. He stormed the meeting – against their own laws – spouting his nonsense!'

'He didn't do it because he hates the revolution?' she asked hopefully. 'To end the bloodshed?'

George snorted. 'Oh no!' The thought seemed to please him. 'A man who takes power with six thousand troops isn't interested in peace.'

Another political development to keep her short of breath and stretched tight as a cello string. It was she who felt the strain of this country – not the King at all.

Amelia reclined in the special cot Prince George had sent over from Brighton. Her knee had improved, but she still kept it raised from the ground. She looked thin and pale in her cherry-coloured dress and hat.

Bunching her skirt in one hand, Charlotte picked her way around the puddles on deck and staggered toward her daughter. The planks rolled and groaned beneath her shoes. 'Are you well? Does the movement hurt you?'

'Only a little.' Amelia rearranged the folds of her red skirts over her knee. 'I am more troubled by Royal's news.'

A cavern opened inside Charlotte. Her poor girl, so far

away, in the worst pain imaginable. She could do nothing to help. What words, what empty messages of condolence could fill such a hole? Charlotte knew only too well that the spectre of this dead baby would haunt Royal all her life, taunt her with images of what could never be. 'Royal will conquer this,' she lied. 'She is brave and sensible. You do not remember, but she had to cope with losing two infant brothers before you were born. She will rally.'

Amelia offered a wan, angelic smile. 'I do hope so, Mama. I will write to her again.'

Wearily, Charlotte slouched to the side of the boat. She peered over the edge, where the sea, pierced by raindrops, tossed and swelled in distress. She stood there, watching it, for a long time.

⌒ Teinach ⌒

Everywhere Royal looked, the Black Forest rose up, dark and wistful, like her thoughts. The thermal baths, the lulling sounds of streams and waterfalls, did nothing to ease her misery.

It was as if she was stuck in a bowl of molasses – her movements, even her thoughts, were laboured and slow. For the first time in her life, she was well and truly beaten. No future glimmered above her dark cloud, no hope slipped in beneath her shroud of mourning. She had been insolent to think she could be a great leader and a model parent. Even the Queen, for all her faults as a mother, had brought every baby into the world alive. Royal couldn't even do that.

Fritz had behaved like an angel. When she was well enough to sit outside, he built her a flower garden, and now she could move about, he had sent her to the valleys of Teinach spa to revive her health. She knew she should be grateful, thankful that at least that she had a kind husband. But she wasn't. She did not want to recover her spirits. She certainly didn't want to move on.

Her family wrote awkward notes of condolence. Royal replied with as much bravery as she could muster, carving out false words with a small and shaky hand. Even in her despair, she knew she had to reassure the King and convince him that she was resigned to her loss. It was easy enough to persuade him – but she could not fool herself.

It was dismal, but true: this was a storm she couldn't weather. She knew the raw, screaming pain of her grief would not heal; she would just learn to conceal it. Perhaps it would turn into a form of self-denial.

She paddled the lukewarm liquid of the pool with her fingertips. Ripples distorted the image of her flabby body, sitting motionless beneath the water in a brown bathing dress. An empty cocoon. Only a few months ago, the curve of her belly had filled her with joy. Now it was a repulsive husk.

'We should go for a walk,' she said. She flinched at the

sudden memory of herself, looking at a snowy landscape, saying the same thing while the baby squirmed in her belly.

The water sloshed as Madame de Spiegel turned to face her. 'You need to relax.'

Tears crushed against the back of Royal's eyes, hot and spiky. Why didn't they realise she needed to move? Only activity, ceaseless activity, could pull her away from dark thoughts and banish the picture of her daughter's sweet, lifeless face.

'No, I need to walk. I am fat.'

Royal's attendant gave a weak, consoling smile. 'It is just the pregnancy. It will wear off on its own.'

'In England, I was the princess with the best figure.'

Madame de Spiegel placed a wet, wrinkled hand on her arm. 'You will be again. Then, you will grow plump once more, with another child.'

Another child. Royal pulled her arm away. They all spoke as if one human being could simply substitute for another. It was not as if she had spoiled a favourite gown and they could make up a new one. Royal didn't want another child; she wanted *her* child. She wanted her dead child to be alive. 'How close are the French?' she asked.

Madame de Spiegel started at the change of subject. 'To here?'

'No. To Ludwigsburg.'

Madame de Spiegel looked anxious. 'I do not know. But

the duke speaks of sending you and the children some-where safe.'

Royal bit her lip, calculating the days before she could reasonably expect to be shot by the enemy. It was too long.

Despair squeezed its icy fingers against her heart. Why had she not died in child-bed? She deserved to. It would be kind of a Frenchman to put a bullet through her head.

'My dear duchess,' Madam de Spiegel moved closer, her voice tender. 'These are no times for children. The little one ... she is safe from the miseries of this life and far happier with God than she could ever be on earth.'

Royal bowed her head and let her tears drip into the pool. The water made a gentle, trickling noise and a breeze set the trees whispering. Just as soft as the sound of a tiny soul, taking flight before it even drew breath.

'Amen,' Royal said. 'May He keep her safe until we meet again.'

She hoped against hope that it would be soon.

Frogmore, Windsor

Sophia ran beneath the long shadows of the plane trees, twisting and turning along the canal. Banks of kind foliage shielded her from the house and its many windows. She flitted across a stone bridge and vanished behind another wall of trees. A team of ducks waddled along by the water and she smiled at them, raising a finger to her lips. Only they knew her secret: she wasn't really ill today.

After all the misery it had caused, her weak health was turning out to be a blessing. Without it, she wouldn't be able to disappear with Garth, to have hours of delirious love while the world thought her tucked up safe in bed. For the other times, Ernest served as her alibi. She told him she was sneaking out to see Caroline and he agreed to cover for her.

Yes, of course, it was wrong. It was deceitful. It was playing on her family's honest, loving sympathy. Self-reproach squeezed her like whalebone stays and she had the same desperate highs and lows as an opium addict. Tonight, the remembrance of these hours would make her feel dirty. But now, so close to the man she loved, all the guilt sank beneath a deluge of champagne-like joy bubbling through her head.

There was no choice, really. She had to be with him.

The wobbling turrets of the Gothic ruin peeked out at her between waving green branches. It was the perfect scene for a romantic interlude. Mock crumbling arches, climbing ivy – just like a scene from one of Mrs Radcliffe's novels. Sophia ran inside, her stomach seething with anticipation. Garth was already there. At the sound of her step, he turned and took her into his arms.

Heaven. She never tired of the slide of his tongue against the inside of her cheek, or the soft, erotic whisper of his lips on hers. His kisses obliterated the outside world. Princess Sophia disintegrated, passing away into a cloud of fairy dust.

As Garth pulled her closer, she tasted longing in his mouth. How could she, little Sophia, inspire such love? More importantly, how had she lived a day without it? He let her go, gently, but she clung to him. This was her only chance to love someone with all her heart and she was going to relish every minute.

'I have a present for you.' His face was flushed, his birthmark barely visible.

'What?'

'Come and see.' He led Sophia to a chair and sat her down.

She smiled up at him. 'I don't need anything, you know. I just want to be with you.'

He planted his lips upon her forehead and fumbled with his inside pocket. At last, he found what he was searching for and brought out a clenched fist.

Sophia laughed. 'What is it?' It looked like the prelude to a magic trick.

Slowly, he eased his arm down and uncurled his clenched fingers. In the palm of his hand sat a thin gold ring.

Her heart skipped a beat. The crumbling walls and wooden floor whirled around while the ring remained, glowing and steady. Was it really what she thought it was? Her mind galloped, searching for alternative meanings.

'They will not let us marry,' he said. His voice was gruff, caught by emotion. 'The lawyers, Parliament, your father . . . But who are they to decide that?'

She held onto the chair. 'Thomas . . .'

'Stupid human laws are all that stop us. We are married to each other in our hearts, are we not?'

A smile seized Sophia's face; she couldn't stop it. 'Yes.'

He took the ring and slid it onto her finger. It was a perfect fit.

'When you wear this, you will know that I am married to you, that I have made those vows. What does the law matter if God knows we love each other?'

Sophia held her hand up to the light. The ring glimmered and sparkled, tempting her. This was all she had ever wanted. All that Caroline told her she could never have.

But the memory of the King at Royal's wedding tugged on her skirts like an impatient child. The way his limbs had trembled. The pale, cold sweat on his face as he gave his daughter away. 'If Papa found out . . .'

Garth stroked back her hair. 'He won't. I promise.'

Easy for him to say. It wasn't his father standing on the precipice of madness, just waiting for a push. She tried to picture what would happen if the King found out his daughter had married an equerry, but even her mind recoiled, refusing to form the image. She considered for a moment, twisting the ring round and around her finger, where it felt so right.

It wasn't fair. This was her chance – her only chance – for love and happiness. She could not turn it down. It would break Garth's heart, not to mention her own.

But accepting would break her father's.

'Perhaps . . .' she stumbled. 'Perhaps we should wait? One day, my brother George will be King.'

'Would he acknowledge our marriage?'

'Yes. Yes, I think so.' Of course he would. George was always good to her, despite her friendship with Caroline. It might be a long time to wait for George's reign, and the Queen would still hate her, but it was something to hope for.

'Well then. Let that happen when it happens. But Sophia, I can tell you now . . . I take you as my wife.'

She nuzzled her head under his chin. Her heart glowed. 'You are my husband,' she confessed. 'I already think of you as my husband.'

'Then we are married. God has heard us.'

Garth cupped her face and raised her lips to his. The kiss was sweeter, more meaningful than any they had shared before. He was right. This was a marriage. In the eyes of God, they were one, and not even her father could claim authority over Him.

Gently, Garth drew Sophia from the chair and pulled her down with him onto the floor.

CHAPTER TWENTY-EIGHT

Ludwigsburg
1800

The journey home from Teinach opened Royal's eyes to a reality that had been there for a long time. Through the dull fog of grief, she had failed to notice the tenacious fingers of war, creeping across her new country. But she saw them now. She saw them all in the stark light of day: fields tilled with the tracks of cannon wheels, cows lying in bloody heaps, thick clods of flesh severed from their bones by enemy troops.

The children ran down the palace steps and pulled her out of the carriage, into their embrace. She still called them children – they were fifteen, seventeen and nineteen now. The moment they put their arms around her and said they were glad she had come home, she knew she could not disappoint them. She couldn't be like the Queen, wallowing in despair. Although her baby was dead, she was still a mother with people relying on her. She forced herself to go on for them.

The cogs of the palace turned, miming normality, but it was clear that a change was coming fast. The household held its breath, sensing the French troops circling them like a pack of wolves. Day and night, Fritz's raised voice travelled through the veins of the palace, increasingly desperate in tone.

Post was scarce. A few intrepid letters trickled in from Amelia, but Royal could hardly bear to look at them. How insufferably petty her sister's cares seemed now! No one in England was forced to dissolve Parliament because they suggested making peace with the French. Amelia wasn't afraid to go outside the bounds of her palaces – and she did not open her eyes every day to the memory that her daughter was dead.

Royal folded away the letters and put them in her workbox, ready to read when she was in a better frame of mind. Heavy footsteps beat in the hallway. She looked up as Fritz burst into the room, looking more dead than alive.

She raised her chin, steeling herself for more bad news.

'Tell your ladies to pack your things. You are going to Erlangen.' His words reeked with the stench of defeat.

She shook her head so forcefully her earrings jangled. 'No. You need me here to help you.'

He huffed. 'Do you say no to your husband? You are going. And the children also.'

'I cannot leave you alone!'

'Wilhelm will stay with me. We will go to Vienna and make the Holy Roman Emperor listen.'

Royal hesitated, her lower lip jutting stubbornly. Packed away with the children. She had always meant to be a great leader, a beacon for her people in times of trouble. The old ambition sizzled inside her, refusing to be doused. In this mood she was prepared to risk all, give all, for the good of her country. She could serve her people, if Fritz would only let her. 'I would rather stay with you.'

Fritz threw up his hands, angry now. 'Your life was not spared in childbirth for you to die needlessly in a war! I tell you, you will go and look after Paul and Trinette. My sister evacuated from Russia weeks ago.'

Royal considered her husband, perspiring and raging before her. His large face was pale, his eyes red-rimmed. Her stomach lurched with a blend of pity and disdain. Her father would not have run away, but Fritz had none of the King's poise. His terror blinded him, making him seem angry. His clawing, nervous energy needed to go somewhere and he channelled it into fury. She had to tread gently. 'I'm sorry. I'll worry about you, that's all.'

He sighed. 'You will only cause me trouble if you stay. You forget you are a Princess of England – a valuable hostage.'

Royal felt her hopes slip through her fingers. How could she reason with him? He would make her go and she was duty bound to obey. She hung her head, trying to look penitent. 'I will do as you say, of course. But I will miss you.'

He came up and embraced her. Royal rested her cheek against his chest. His shirt was damp with sweat. She willed him, willed him with all she was worth, to change his mind and let her stay. But he was determined. 'You will be safe,' he murmured. 'I must have you safe. And you can take the kangaroos with you to amuse the children.'

Royal baulked at the idea of hiding in exile with kanga-roos while her husband fought the French. What had she been reduced to?

She had set out to be a better mother and a better leader than the Queen. The very thought was laughable now.

Fritz released her and mopped his brow with a hand-kerchief. 'Oh, there is one more thing.'

'Yes?'

A change came over him: he was suddenly hard and duke-like again. 'Send a letter to your father, if you can get one out.' He turned away, tossing the words over his shoulder. 'Tell him of the danger you are in. He has been no friend to us, refusing to send troops or funds. Perhaps he will take this seriously.' He swept out of the room with his bevy of attendants, not giving her a second look.

Royal felt the sting – its poison dripped down to mingle with the disappointment seething in her stomach. Did he really dare to criticise the King? She balled her hands into fists and waited in furious silence for the door to close.

When she was alone, she spoke under her breath. 'My father is twice the leader you will ever be.'

Some two hours later, Royal squeezed her way through an avenue of trunks and bandboxes. The preparations were well under-way and the vast corridors of Ludwigsburg seemed cramped, obscured with parcels and trunks. It helped to pour her frustrated feelings into the task of packing up. If she could not steer the country, she would at least plan the evacuation perfectly.

It was a complex mission. There were not enough servants to help with the workload, so she had to join in, folding up a linen package for Trinette while she walked up and down, inspecting the progress. She was already buttoned into her travelling dress, the hood of her cape up around her curls. It would be good to get in the carriage and start moving.

A door banged. The ladies dropped what they were packing and fell into curtseys as Fritz strode toward them.

'The carriages are here,' he barked. 'Why are you not packed yet?'

Royal tied a final knot in the string of Trinette's bundle. It hurt to have him so snappish. They were all stressed and afraid – he needn't take it out on her.

'These things take time, love.'

'Time we do not have. Stop that! Stop it, all of you!' he waved at the servants. 'You will go as you are.'

So now she was not even allowed to direct the move! It was too much.

Royal trotted after him down the hallway, tossing her finished package to one of her ladies.

'But Fritz, the children need . . .'

He cut her off. 'You should have thought of that earlier. There is no time.'

'But—'

'I assume you have written to your father. Is that why you are tardy in packing?'

Anger flashed before her eyes, but she had no time to express it. She struggled to keep pace with his long steps, dodging attendants as she went. The hood flew off her head.

'Why . . . I . . . no—'

'No, that is not why you are late? Or no, you have not written?'

'I *haven't* written,' Royal cried, stopping still. 'I won't! There is nothing Papa can do. It would only worry him to—'

Fast as lightening, Fritz turned and slapped her. Hot pain rang around her ear and up her cheek. The servants fell silent. 'Your duty is to me, not your father!' he roared. 'You have failed me!' He panted, glaring into her face, flecks of spittle on his lip. Then, in a lower, weary tone, 'You have failed me, Charlotte.'

Everything was still. Royal's right cheek burned from the sting of the blow and the heat of shame. *Failed.* It was one thing to upbraid herself for weakness, quite another to hear the accusation on Fritz's lips. A failed wife. Struck and scolded before the whole household. Tears made her vision shimmer.

He moved toward her again and she tensed. But he only planted a quick, dry kiss on her untouched cheek. 'You must go. Goodbye.'

Trinette and Paul thumped down the stairs with portmanteaux and boxes. Royal rubbed the back of her hand over her eyes and roused herself. 'Well then. Are you ready? Say goodbye to your Papa.'

They left in a bustle, with a confusion of trunks. Royal did not have a moment to dwell upon what had happened. She completed the preparations and put the children into the carriage in a state of shock, feeling nothing, thinking nothing.

It was only when they drew away from the palace, waving to Fritz and Wilhelm, who stood outside, that she realised her eyes were on her husband's powerful arm. An arm that was meant to protect, but had struck.

She raised a hand to her injured cheek.

⤙ *Kew* ⤚

How could it have happened? Sophia dashed along the path, her legs shaking. She never even dreamt it was possible.

Garth had been so sure. She had trusted him implicitly with her body – he seemed to know everything. He had a sheath of animal gut with a ribbon to secure it in place, he had a lemon rind to block the entrance to her womb – he even had a special method of making love to a rhythm. But he had been wrong.

Not only had she missed courses but there were strange motions in her belly, rippling across the skin like a breeze across a lake. She pulled her pelisse around her burgeoning stomach and felt a wave of panic as the fabric stretched. Had anyone noticed?

Thank God the current fashion favoured loose-fitting gowns with a high waist, which concealed the bump. If the Queen were to see . . . or even worse, if the King found out! The scandal, the betrayal of his favourite equerry, would surely kill him.

Babies had always seemed like sweet, innocent cherubs. But not this one. Its spectre followed her, a dark shadow gripping on the hem of her skirt with sticky little fingers. It was relentlessly ploughing toward her and there was no way to change its path. What could she do? She looked at the young women passing her: society misses, simpler beings who could perhaps disappear and drop a baby discreetly in the country. Princesses did not have that option. Sophia was in the public eye and the truth would out . . .

It was a death sentence for her and her family.

She stopped and leant on a tree. Its bark was rough

against her aching back. How could she have been so foolish? Suddenly her marriage to Garth, which she had believed in without question for so long, seemed a weak and flimsy thing. The world would not accept lovers' vows swapped without a vicar – and it certainly would not accept her child.

There was no help in sight on the green. Children chased hoops with sticks along the paths and boats raced down the river without a care in the world. Further off, cows grazed, humming gently into the spring air. Sophia felt like a stain in their simple presence – dirty and guilty.

Disconsolate, she watched a governess take her little charges down the river bank. They chattered in high-pitched voices. The eldest boy threw bread to the ducks and they swarmed thick and fast around him, jostling one another out of the way.

Sophia longed for the days she had spent like these children – running around Kew as if it were a magical playground, seeing the exotic plants and the foreign animals, fighting with her brothers and sisters. What she would not give to be free of burdens once more, trotting behind Miss Gouldsworthy in the crocodile of royal children . . .

Miss Gouldsworthy. She stood up straight, galvanised by the idea. Surely her governess, of all people, would help her? She might be angry, having raised the princesses so carefully, but she would keep the secret. Sophia took a step and hesitated. Revealing the truth would lay her open to attack.

She had to be sure. A sharp kick from the baby winded her. Such force! It must be big and strong already. She imagined it; a menacing, muscular baby, growing huge just to spite her. Dear God, she needed to take the chance and tell someone, or she would give birth alone in a ditch. It had to be Miss Gouldsworthy. There was no one else.

She picked up her skirts and ran as fast as she could across the park.

Miss Gouldsworthy let her in at once. Sophia leaped out of the sunlight and shut the door fast behind her heels.

'Are we alone?'

Her governess looked around, perplexed. 'My brother is upstairs. Why, what is wrong?'

Sophia did not know how to start. Her courage buckled before Miss Gouldsworthy's kind, familiar face. This wasn't like the other times when she had run from Mama's scolding or begged pardon for not learning her lesson. Sophia stared at Miss Gouldsworthy's gentle eyebrows, slanted in concern, and thought what a blow of disappointment she was about to deal. She closed her eyes and took a deep breath. 'I need to talk to you.'

Miss Gouldsworthy put a hand upon Sophia's shoulder and guided her toward a chair. 'Won't you have some tea?'

The very thought made Sophia queasy. 'No. Thank you.'

They took their seats and looked at one another in silence.

Miss Gouldsworthy leant forwards – an invitation to confide – but Sophia could not start. She couldn't articulate the words that bounced around her mind with cries of terror.

'Sophy, you are scaring me. What is it?'

She stared at her hands, squeezing and nearly ripping the fabric covering her lap. 'I think . . .'

'You think . . . ?'

She had to do it. It was like leaping from the bathing machine at Weymouth; she just had to screw up her courage and plunge in. 'I think I'm . . . with . . . child.' Her squeezed lungs almost suffocated the last, fateful word.

Miss Gouldsworthy's chair squeaked across the floorboards. 'What?'

Sophia hid her face in her hands, but she could imagine the disappointment taking hold of Miss Gouldsworthy's features. 'With child.' Now the terrible words were out of her mouth they expanded, filling the room with dark consequences. 'It's not as bad as you think,' Sophia gabbled. 'I am not a slut. I am married, but Papa doesn't know. He cannot know.'

Miss Gouldsworthy laid a hand on her back. It trembled lightly on her spine. 'Are you sure?'

Sophia wiped her nose. 'I'll show you.'

They didn't look at one another as they drew the curtains and bolted the door. The tension was unbearable.

Part of Sophia hoped that Miss Gouldsworthy would

look at her, laugh and tell her she was wrong. But even as she felt her own pulse hammer in her neck, she was vaguely aware of another heart, pounding in the pit of her stomach. Sophia untied the ribbons of her pelisse. A gentle hump pushed out the muslin of her day gown, barely noticeable between the loose folds of fabric.

Miss Gouldsworthy considered her, unsure.

With grim determination, Sophia squatted and picked up the hem of her skirt, lifting the material to reveal her ankles and white stockings. Gathering her petticoats, she pulled everything up until the bottom of her chemise was visible. Carefully, she held down the edge of her undergarment and lifted the folds of her dress and petticoats right over the bulge. The moment Miss Goldsworthy gasped, she knew she was lost.

'My dear! How long has it been?'

The words pressed painfully against Sophia's ears. 'I – I don't know. My illnesses often make me miss a course or get strange feelings in my stomach. I thought it was dropsy.'

'Dropsy!' Miss Gouldsworthy repeated, incredulous. 'Surely the father – surely your husband noticed?'

Sophia dropped the swathes of her gown and smoothed them hurriedly. Her big, bulbous stomach was a brand of the deepest shame. She wanted to hide it, make it disappear. 'No. He only officially comes here three months a year.'

'An equerry, then?'

Sophia nodded, desolate. Her cheeks were cold and damp – she realised she was crying. 'Oh Gouly, what will I do?'

Miss Gouldsworthy drew her into her arms. The comforting smell of her only made things worse. 'Don't worry. We'll figure something out. I do not know how, but we will. Does anyone else know?'

'I hope not.'

'Not even the father?'

Sophia swallowed. Neither of them thought she *could* conceive. They had taken precautions, but with little fear. After all, was that not why the princes of Europe steered clear of her? *Incapable*. That had been Caroline's word. 'I do not want him to know. He'd be so angry.'

'Angry?' Miss Gouldsworthy peered into Sophia's face. 'Surely not?'

'It is not a normal pregnancy, Gouly. We are both in a lot of trouble.'

'Your first child. It should not be like this.'

Sophia pressed her hands to her ears. 'Don't say that,' she whispered fiercely. 'Don't make me think of it as a person.'

'But . . .'

'I can't. Don't you understand? I cannot see it and I cannot go anywhere near it. It has to be given away. For the sake of the King.'

'Oh, my dear.'

Sophia's throat filled with fluid. 'It would be better for the poor thing if I miscarried now. What sort of life will it lead?' She let out a wet sob. It was one thing to toy with her own reputation by taking up with Garth. But now she had destroyed her own child's prospects before its life even began.

Miss Gouldsworthy wrapped her in another maternal embrace. Sophia slumped into it, paralysed by sorrow.

'Don't you worry. You leave it to me.' Miss Gouldsworthy stroked Sophia's hair. 'There is just one thing for you to do alone: you must tell the father.'

CHAPTER TWENTY-NINE

Hyde Park, London

⤙ *1800* ⤚

Charlotte stood in a bright pool of sunlight, watching red-coated soldiers march to the beat of a drum, when she heard it. Beneath the drum's steady rhythm, a sound cracked out like a whip. She turned her head, but glinting metal dazzled her eyes. She positioned her fan like a visor, shading her face from the sun.

Her gaze fell upon the King just as the man next to him winced and crumpled to the ground. A terrific scream tore through the air. Before Charlotte knew what was happening, guards pressed down around her, moving her.

'The King!' somebody cried. 'Save the King!'

The floor was a tangle of Hessian boots and ladies' slippers. A dark red substance trickled into a puddle at the King's feet. It couldn't be. Not after all she had been through to protect him . . . 'George!'

Someone clutched at her hand – perhaps one of her

daughters – but she shook them off and scrambled through the crowd. She had to get to her husband. In their desperation to flee, the people barely noticed Charlotte amongst them. Those that saw her parted to let her through, but she had to push and shove with the best of them.

Over the tall military hats she made out George's wig. If he was standing, he couldn't be hurt. Could he? Relentless in her terror, she beat out a path and dove into the King's arms – live, warm arms! He was safe. She clung to him like a drowning woman. Blood spotted the fine lawn cotton of his shirt and she dabbed at it, eager to brush away any trace of a wound.

'None of this, none of this. Have courage!'

Charlotte was aghast as her husband pushed her off. He folded his hands behind his back and calmly surveyed the body on the ground.

'Poor man. Naval clerk, did you say, what?' he asked his attendant.

'Yes, Your Majesty.'

Charlotte had not even noticed the body – she must have hurdled it to reach George. She stared at the sickening sight, wanting to feel pity – but she could only thank God that it wasn't the King lying there.

The man was bent at a strange angle, an expression of shock carved on his face. There was a small puncture, just under his right breast. Blood bubbled through a ragged hole in his shirt, but the real damage was in his back, where the ball had exited.

Charlotte turned her face from the mangled flesh. 'For goodness' sake!' she cried. 'A man is dead and you just stand and look at him? That shot was meant for you, George. We must leave.'

He shook his head. 'No, no. The surgeon will come and fetch him and we'll carry on. See, the soldiers are still here. Doesn't bother them, a bit of gunfire.'

Charlotte swept her eyes over the park, the treetops, looking for a sharpshooter. 'At least send your daughters home! Look at them.'

Her five girls clustered together in a knot, struggling for breath. They were as stone; still and almost bloodless.

'No, I wouldn't have them stir for the world.'

A bolt of anger flew through Charlotte. It was his choice to risk his own life, but not that of her children. 'What? Are you—' She stopped. She had almost said *mad*.

Two men arrived with a stretcher and heaved the bleeding corpse onto it, staining their breeches.

Charlotte looked away, letting the terrible seed of suspicion grow in her brain. Madness. It had to be. No one in their right mind would disregard their children's safety.

'There now,' she heard George say. 'Let's get back to it, shall we?'

Charlotte took his proffered arm with reluctance. Her flesh shrank from him, as if his touch could taint her with his madness. She couldn't keep a wicked question from her mind: would it have been better for her family if the marksman had hit his target?

⌒ *Queen's House, London* ⌒

Sophia could not catch her breath or calm the crazed reel of her heart. It was so close – just like that time at the theatre. A few inches to the left or the right and her life would have been transformed.

She pressed her head against the cool blue silk lining the wall. She could not bounce back with the ease of her mother and sisters. A week had passed since the assassination attempt and they had found distractions to push it from their thoughts. Only she sat, trembling still, clutching a dose of laudanum drops mixed with wine and spices.

Of course, it wasn't just the attack making her jittery. She had written the fateful letter to Garth and received his startled response. Odd snatches of it ran through her mind. *Nothing could astonish me more.*

He didn't speculate if their baby would be a boy or a girl, he didn't wonder who it would look like – of course he didn't. He knew, just like Sophia, that they had to push it from their lives. *Your idea of a poor family seems practical. It is the only option. Acknowledging the marriage would do nothing – the King would simply dissolve the union and dismiss me, and then who would pay for the child's upkeep?*

The writing was illegible in places, smudged, crossed through, evidently written in haste. *I suppose there is no predicting the date of these things – when the child is to arrive? How can we contrive to keep you from sight? I think you'll have to tell Amelia. We need someone in the family looking out for us.* More humiliation. Amelia would judge, blame her for putting the King's mind at risk. She would be right. A good daughter would have flirted with Garth and no more.

Sophy, if you can swear upon your word of honour it is mine, I might have a plan. Not for the birth. For the future. Trust me. Sophia wanted to trust him. But alone, cloistered in the sickroom, she only felt vulnerable.

Garth didn't understand what it meant to be a member of the royal family; he didn't feel the mixture of rebellion and guilt welling inside his chest. She loved the King. She loved Garth. How could she possibly choose between them?

Sophia tossed back the laudanum in one gulp. Dizzy and wretched, she let the glass slip from her hand and dropped down upon the bed.

CHAPTER THIRTY

Erlangen
⁓ *1801* ⁓

'Paul, come away from the window.'

Royal's stepson didn't respond to her voice.

'Paul.'

'But I'm *bored*,' he whined, without turning round.

He did not look much like a Prince of Württemberg in this wretched place. Fingers of dust streaked his back and his coat hung oddly on his skinny shoulders. Royal pitied him, but it was no time for a teenage strop. She strode across the room and seized his arm. 'I *said* come away.' God only knew what he was staring at out there. Flat, colourless sand surrounded their refuge, stretching on for miles. Here and there a mangy brown conifer varied the scene. It was a wasteland, a purgatory, and they were stuck there.

Royal dragged Paul to the sofa and pushed him down next to Trinette.

'You let Madame de Spiegel go to the village,' he flared

at Royal. 'Even the bloody kangaroos are allowed outside.'

'The kangaroos do not have a price on their heads,' she snapped. 'No one wants to capture them and no one wants to shoot them. I do not think you realise there are people out there who want you dead.'

'I am one of them,' Trinette said cheerfully.

Royal went to the table and sat on a threadbare chair which rocked on uneven legs. She put her head in her hands. This wasn't what she imagined when she walked down the aisle. She never dreamt she would be a fat woman cowering in a paper house with squabbling stepchildren. No matter what she did, she was imprisoned somewhere; if not Windsor, Erlangen.

The separation from Fritz was the hardest part. When she thought of him, it wasn't the angry, stressed man who had slapped her about the face. It was the Fritz who had nursed her after the stillbirth, caressed her in bed. She missed him. With the distance of time and space, even that slap seemed like a trivial thing. It was a cry for help, not an attack.

Hadn't her father been angry and almost crazed with anxiety during the American war? He had turned it inward and injured his humours. Fritz hit outwards – that was the only difference.

Poor, tired Fritz. Her heart went out to him, across the violent continent, all the way to Vienna.

There was little choice now but to make peace with France. The Austrian troops had thrown down their arms and only seven thousand men stood at Württemberg's defence. She wondered how Fritz would bear the humiliation. Trying to keep her little family safe in this house was an easy trial compared to what Fritz and Wilhelm suffered. She needed to stop wallowing in self-pity and think about her husband.

The front door slammed and Royal wobbled on her ill-balanced chair. Madame de Spiegel dashed in, her eyes wide and flashing, and pressed her back to the door.

'Close the curtains. Close everything up.'

Her tone left no room for argument. Royal obeyed without question, shutting and bolting the windows.

Suddenly, Madame de Spiegel cried, 'The kangaroos! The kangaroos!' She ran out to fetch them. Once the animals were inside and the door was locked with a grind of metal, the small house appeared hopeless and dull.

Royal shuddered. It was like being sealed in a tomb. 'What is it?' she whispered.

'French troops. In the village. I saw a patrol so I turned and I ran.'

Royal grabbed Madame de Spiegel's hand. 'Thank God you are safe. What –'

A low rumble cut her off. The children clutched at her gown to hold themselves steady as the furniture shook. Fine white powder drifted from the ceiling and settled on Trinette's hair.

'Cannon,' Paul breathed.

It had finally happened: the French were coming.

Royal ran toward her bed, pulling Trinette with her, and pushed the girl down on the mattress. 'Come quickly. Everyone. Stay away from the windows.'

Back in the spa, after her daughter's death, Royal had longed for the French and their artillery. She didn't now. Her instinct to live beat to the surface, bright and demanding. What would the children do without her?

The small household curled up on the bed. Royal pulled the heavy curtains shut, protecting her loved ones in a shell of grey light. Outside, the cannon boomed and thundered.

'Mama, are they coming for us?'

Royal clutched Trinette and buried her nose in her sweet brown hair.

'I won't let them touch you,' Royal swore. But they would be here soon. She wondered, fleetingly, what the King would do if she was killed.

Shots rang out. The household winced as a body; even the kangaroos shuffled their feet. The play of light and sound was strange, like a discordant storm.

'I'll kill old Boney if he comes anywhere near us,' said Paul, with the pitiful bravery of youth.

It was not just the thunder of artillery now – they heard shouts, screams and the frantic whinnies of horses.

Trinette looked up, her dark eyes swimming. 'Are those shots killing people, Mama? How many of our men are dying out there?'

Royal shivered. She could almost smell the bitter gun smoke, see the troops biting their cartridges. 'I don't know sweetheart.'

But she did know something. Now that the village had fallen, the country was done for. Far away in Vienna, Fritz would be convulsing in the last throes of political death. They would have to join the French – there was no choice.

And what would that make Royal? The enemy of England, of her father, and all she held dear. A traitor. She closed her eyes and gripped Trinette tight as another cannon ball fell and shook the floorboards.

⤙ Salisbury ⤚

They had been on the road for hours. Outside, a watery moon rode in the sky, painting silver streaks across the trees and hedgerows. In the low light of the carriage, Sophia saw Amelia's face looking over her, all blonde curls and blue eyes like an angel. Sophia was relieved she'd confided in her sister at last. Amelia was a sweet girl and had not judged. On the contrary, she treated Sophia's predicament as a romantic adventure.

'Are you well?'

Sophia wriggled, pushing her belly out. 'The usual stomach pains.'

Actually, they were worse than the normal cramps, but there was no point in making a fuss. She should have realised the movement of a carriage would cause her agony. Thank God she had persuaded the Queen to let her and Amelia travel to Weymouth a day ahead of the rest. It would have been impossible to hide the truth if she had travelled with the family. The Queen, having endured sixteen pregnancies, would be able to spot Sophia's all too easily.

'We're nearly there now,' Miss Gouldsworthy said to reassure her.

They planned to go slowly and stop at General Gouldsworthy's house, where, God willing, Sophia would have the baby.

She had barely dwelt on the idea of giving birth – she was more afraid of discovery. What if it decided to cling on to her womb? What if it was days late? They would have to make up an excuse to stay.

She settled her head against the cushions. There was a good chance she would get away with it. The Queen was preoccupied, all her care tied up with the poor King. His nerves had been torn to pieces by the resignation of his trusted Prime Minister, Pitt, followed swiftly by Royal's surrender to the French, and he was showing worrying signs of delirium. If there was any time to drop a baby, unnoticed, it was now.

Sophia dozed on and off, listening to the endless creak of the wheels on the road. Every time she started to drift into sleep, a blast of hot pain snapped her eyelids open. She thought, and not for the first time, that the baby was objecting to her actions. Whenever she tried to put it from her mind and sever the link between them, the child flared up again, strong and violent inside her.

Would it ever understand, when it was older? Would it realise that she did this for its own good – that she had tried to give it a chance? She hoped so. Far better to be the child of Sharland the tailor than the illegitimate grandson of a King, infamous for driving him over the brink of sanity. Despairing of repose, she glanced out at the deepening darkness and wondered where Garth was, and what he was thinking.

They had written, but hadn't seen each other since she found out about the baby. In Weymouth, probably in front of the King and Queen, they would meet again and Sophia would have to look into his sorrowful eyes and wonder if their baby had the same ones. Temptation teased at the corners of her mind, telling her she might sneak one look at her child before they sent it off to its adopted family. Just one. But if she saw it, she would love it, and then how would she part with it? No, she had to break her heart to save her little one. And to save the King.

The countryside loomed through Sophia's window, menacing and dark. Again she shuffled, trying to get comfortable. The cushions were warm as she moved against them. Hadn't the hot bricks cooled yet? She heaved a sigh of irritation, too tired to think about it. The heat spread, through her lap, behind her thighs. Sophia wondered vaguely if someone had thrown a blanket over her legs.

Gradually, she became aware of a slow, dripping noise. 'Is it raining?'

Even as Sophia spoke, there was a violent shift inside her. A tide of fluid rushed out of her travelling cloak and splashed on the carriage floor. Amelia screamed and pulled her feet up on the cushions. 'What's happening?'

'Her waters.' Miss Gouldsworthy's words came out strangled. 'She's having the baby.'

No. Not here. Not now. Pain splintered across Sophia's stomach; she gasped but didn't cry out.

'What do we do? Do we stop the carriage?' Amelia squealed.

'I don't know!' Miss Gouldsworthy peered out the window. 'I don't think we're far now.'

'We can't help her in the carriage while it's moving!'

'But wouldn't it be better to give birth in a house than by a roadside?'

Keep going. If Sophia could speak, she would insist upon it.

She concentrated on the rhythm of her breath; if she knew how to deal with anything, it was crippling pain. The beat of the carriage helped her to time gasps of air; she could predict the next wave of torture when she counted the click of the horses' hooves.

'It's all right, Sophy.' Amelia gripped her sweating hand.

She was no comfort. Where was Garth? Why wasn't he

here, mopping her brow and speaking words of reassurance? Sophia was suddenly enraged against him. It was all his fault.

The horses stepped up into a canter. The ladies slid along the slick, bouncing seats, the moon racing beside them in the night sky. Time passed and the pains came closer together. All at once, the wheels screeched and Sophia flew forward. Amelia and Miss Gouldsworthy caught her with a sharp jolt just before she hit the floor.

'We're here, Sophy. Don't worry, we're here.'

The carriage door burst open. Lamps flickered above her and a dog barked somewhere nearby. Sophia quivered as General Gouldsworthy looped his arms around her and lifted her out into the night air. Her wet gown clung to her legs with icy claws.

Colourful shapes spun before her eyes as they swept through the house, up the stairs and into the bedchamber. Everything moved except the fixed funnel of fire between Sophia's lower ribcage and the back of her knees. She grappled with the contractions, wearying under the constant demand to push, push, push. Heavy boulders rolled back and forth over her stomach, squeezing her breath out.

Hours passed.

At last, a cry awoke her from her stupor. 'It's coming, it's coming!' With one final sword thrust of agony, the weight pressing down on her lifted. She pushed again. Suddenly she was a fountain, a waterfall — new life flowed from her thick and fast.

'It's a boy!'

Don't tell me. Don't tell me.

Sophia pulled the sweaty pillow over her head, but the wail of her newborn son penetrated the feathers. She pressed the stuffing hard against her ears. Still, the dreaded sound was only muffled, not erased.

She should have known better. She didn't need to see her son to fall in love. She heard his voice, the cry of life formed of her own flesh, and her heart returned his call.

⤙ Weymouth ⤚

Charlotte watched the face of her husband as he slept. He was peaceful now the warm hops were under his head; his face a perfect stone carving above the quilt.

His straight, alabaster nose flared as he breathed, setting the candles aflutter. Pungent vinegar and musk sickened the air, but they didn't disturb him. Dawn crept in through the curtains and highlighted his innocent, blank eyelids, his pinched cheekbones.

Was it wrong to hope he would stay this still and serene forever? To pray that death would set him free, leaving her infuriating, frustrating but still hopelessly dear son with a kingdom at last?

She did not think it was wrong. She wanted to remember him as he was now, tranquil on a pure white pillow. But she knew she was losing him again; she heard it in his rasping breath, she saw it in the flickering muscles of his cheeks.

The previous week he had drunk enough water to drain the Thames and rolled up a hundred handkerchiefs. Even now, in his dreams, he clenched his teeth.

She could not go through it again. Many years ago, she lost the real substance of her beloved husband, but at least he had left a friend, a shadow of the man she once loved. What part of him would disappear this time? Which of her slender comforts must she make up her mind to lose? Had she not lost enough?

No one dared tell the King that Prussian troops had invaded his precious Electorate of Hanover – he was still reeling from Württemberg's surrender – but he had to find out sometime.

George stirred in his sleep. His blistered, wigless head tossed on the pillow and he croaked out, 'I am perfectly well.'

Tears blinded Charlotte's eyes.

Her side of the bed stretched out, empty and unruffled. She looked at it and felt the chill of a marital bed that had turned cold. There were nights in her youth when they couldn't lie beside each other without succumbing to desire. Those years were gone, and maybe George would be gone soon too.

She had written to Dr Willis, begging him and his sons

to meet them when they returned to Kew. Once there, they would confine the King to the White House, while Charlotte and her daughters stayed in the Dutch House. He would think of it as a betrayal; Charlotte didn't doubt that. But the George she married would understand why she had to do it. If she spent another night watching him pray until the sweat poured down his face, or listening to him get in and out of bed to close the shutters every hour, she would die of grief.

Charlotte reached out and stroked his damp hair. The motion soothed him and his features relaxed. There he was again, her George. She would stay, watching him and loving him, until the very last moment, this wonderful mirage of the George she once knew. And she would keep hoping, so ardently, for his sake, that he never woke up.

CHAPTER THIRTY-ONE

The Dutch House, Kew
∼ *Winter 1801* ∼

Sophia and her sisters clustered round a weak fire in the Queen's boudoir. Nobody spoke and nobody moved. It was like being locked in an ice house: the blue-green walls, the dim light, the bitter cold and the frigid expression of the Queen. Her large mouth dominated her face, collapsed into a frown. No doubt she was thinking of the poor King, locked up with the Willises in the White House. The doctors had to take him by force, in the end. They had to chase and corner him like a dog, and drag him to captivity.

But Sophia's mind didn't stalk up and down the quiet corridors of the White House with him. It was beached upon the Weymouth sands, searching for her boy as the tide rolled in and out. They had taken her baby away. He would stay with a good family of tailors called the Sharlands and spend his life living a lie on the coast. She ought to be glad. She had done her duty, the boy was safe and yet

... She was empty. Beyond empty. Stripped out, scoured clean. The fire spat and scattered sparks. Sophia stared hard into the dying flames, wanting to burn her eyes out. Right now, it was miserable to exist.

'It all started when Pitt resigned.' Elizabeth observed. The sound of her voice made them jump. 'The newspapers say—'

The Queen rounded on her. 'We do not read the newspapers, Elizabeth. We do not pay attention to their drivel.'

Elizabeth bowed her head. 'I wish he hadn't resigned as Prime Minister. That's all.'

'Pitt had to resign,' Sophia mumbled. 'It was a matter of principle. Over the Catholics.'

The Queen turned baleful eyes upon her. She was terrifying and ghostly, with her white hair gathered up on her head, but Sophia didn't shrink back. No mere scolding could hurt her now. She had felt pain beyond pain.

'He's a fool to have those principles,' the Queen snapped. 'He has no idea what he is talking about. Do you not know what happened the last time we tried to give the Catholics a concession?'

'Yes.'

The Queen carried on regardless, seething with anger. 'The people stormed the city! Set fire to churches, carriages and prisons! What do you think they will do if we grant complete emancipation?'

Sophia shrugged. She did not care what happened to her.

'They'll throw your father off the throne, that's what. You know they would. They have tried to kill him already. If we do not keep the Catholics in their place, you may as well hand the crown to the House of Savoy on a plate.'

It was true, of course. The King's Protestant religion was the only thing that put his claim to the throne above scores of pretenders. But what did it matter now?

Sophia threw up her hands in defeat. She couldn't stand this cold prison of a room for a moment longer. She surged up and strode out the door without looking back. There would be hell to pay for her desertion later, but later was a very long time away in this toy palace, where the minutes ticked by like years.

She stomped through the drawing room and down the passageway. It felt good to move.

If her baby was there, she would have something to wake up for every morning. But the moment they took the child from the room where Sophia gave birth to him, a great cavity opened up inside her soul.

Now that he was out of her belly, in the world, she was no longer afraid of him. She just wanted to hold him. Her feet hammered down the staircase, punishing the maroon carpet. She turned on the landing, took the last flight at a run and bumped headlong into General Garth.

'Sophy!'

'Oh, Thomas!'

She went to fling herself into his arms, but something in

his manner made her pause. His face was grave; he did not look pleased to see her.

'Is it mine?'

'What?' She was so flustered that she didn't catch the meaning of his words.

'The baby. You never did reply to that part of my letter. I told you I had a plan. So swear to me – is it mine?'

Sophia turned cold. 'What a question!'

'Still, you have not answered it.' There was no apology in his face.

No; this was all wrong. Everything was meant to be right, now Garth was here again. But Sophia didn't know this man standing in front of her – he wasn't the kind, smiling lover to whom she had promised herself.

'Of course it's yours!' she hissed. 'Who else's would it be?'

He shook his head. His brow wrinkled. 'I have heard rumours. And I was always so careful . . .'

'Not careful enough, clearly.'

He looked away. Sophia could not believe it. Why did he not put an arm around her shoulders or speak a word of comfort? Who had been whispering to him, poisoning him against her?

'I must deliver this bulletin to the Queen. It is from Dr Willis.'

She put one hand on the wall and one on the banister, blocking his path. 'Have the Sharlands written? How is our son?'

'He is well, I hear. I will call on him soon.'

'You can't!' Sophia cried. 'He must get on with his life. People will not believe he is the child of a tailor if we visit all the time!'

'Anyone would think you were ashamed of him.'

Furious, Sophia flushed up to the roots of her hair. 'No. No, it is not fair to our son. He must have his life ... And the King! What if the King were to hear of us visiting?'

Garth shrugged. For the first time Sophia saw pain in his face. 'I don't know. I'll write to you about it. I have to see the Queen.'

A murmur of voices in the hallway: servants returning from the gardens. They jumped apart from each other.

'Thomas ...'

'I will write,' he said again, and disappeared up the stairs.

Sophia felt as if someone had ripped a layer from her skin, leaving her burning and raw. The servants could not see her like this.

She dove down the corridor, through the anteroom and into the wood-panelled library. She shut all the doors, turned the keys in the locks and sank to her knees. Just like that, she had lost everything. No son, no father and no husband. Silently, she wept. Even now, in her great distress she had to hide herself, stifle all signs that she existed and felt. She was so desperate for someone to hold her that she wrapped her arms around her chest. Then she recoiled and looked down in astonishment. A thick, creamy liquid pushed its way through her stays and onto the patterned muslin of her dress. She dabbed at the substance but it welled up again, irrepressible. Then Sophia realised she was lactating – producing milk for the baby who could not drink it. Who would never drink it.

She stretched out flat on the floor, pushing her face close to the dusty boards. Under the gaze of towering bookshelves, she wrenched out a silent scream.

CHAPTER THIRTY-TWO

Kew Green

↢ *1802* ↣

The people were jubilant. Despite the chill, they waved ribbons, raced boats along the river and danced reels. Several children capered across the path, narrowly avoiding the hooves of Charlotte's black horses. A hog roasted on the green, spreading the scent of meat and woodsmoke.

How could the subjects cavort and celebrate like this while their King lay ill? It was indecent. She resented being dressed up and put out in the open carriage to wave at their happiness.

Nearly a decade of bloodshed in Europe had come to an end through the Treaty of Amiens. But for Charlotte, little had changed. She had nothing to smile about, save Royal's escape from Erlangen. Even then, it was a hollow victory. Württemberg had surrendered long before the peace.

The foolish new Prime Minister, Addington, had cut down

army lists and taxes as if he would never need them again. He was dangerously optimistic. If the King were well, perhaps he could impose some restraint. But as things stood . . .

The flags flew at full mast as she descended from the carriage. Her gown of royal purple swept down the steps. Large diamonds glistened in her hair and pearls hung from her neck. In the centre of her bodice nestled a pure white rose. She looked every inch an elegant Queen, as the people wanted. She bared her teeth in a false smile and curtseyed. She was about to retire from the painful spectacle when one of her pages dashed up to her.

'Your Majesty. The Princess of Wales is here.'

Charlotte gritted her teeth. 'Tell her to go away. You know the King becomes impassioned by the sight of her.' She ran her eyes over the windows, half-expecting to see the King pressed up against one of them, banging on the glass and demanding to speak with his niece.

'I did, Your Majesty. But she was quite insistent. She gave me this . . .'

He presented a sealed note. Charlotte removed one glove and ripped it open.

No doubt Caroline would be play-acting again, appealing to Charlotte's sense of pity. She would be keen to take advantage of the strange thoughts that galloped through the King's head on bad days, such as building a new wing on her house in Blackheath and letting her keep little Charlotte under her sole care.

Charlotte scanned the scrap of paper. Only two lines met her eyes – in Caroline's blotched writing and terrible English.

I have heard rumour the King must not. I come warn you.

She screwed the paper up in a fist and held it tight against her lips. A lie, surely. But how could she be certain?

'Let the princess into my chambers,' she said, walking toward the door. 'She will not be staying to take refreshment.'

⤙ *Between Lorch and Ludwigsburg* ⤚

Cold blue skies formed a bright arc above Royal and her travelling party. Birds wheeled overhead as the sun kissed her face – a wonderful sensation she had not felt for a long, long time.

Although Royal and the children had surrendered to the French, they had been forced to stay in their retreat for safety. It was only with this new, international peace that they dared return home. The land had slumbered in the months of Royal's absence. Now the trees shot hopeful buds and the crocuses were up, tasting freedom after exile in the cold, dark earth. Trinette and Paul blinked in the sunlight, their skin paler than the early daffodil buds. Behind them, the kangaroos beat out a steady thump with their feet, a wary-eyed baby hanging from the female's pouch.

Royal insisted on walking over the uneven, muddy roads. A carriage was torture to her after being cooped up at Erlangen, but the children stumbled like new-born foals unused to their legs.

'Mama,' Trinette called.

'Yes, love.'

'We will not have to go away again, will we?'

Royal looked past her stepdaughter's dark curls, which now framed the blooming features of a young woman.

'I don't know. I hope not.' But Royal knew the Treaties of Amiens and Lunéville were hardly secure – Britain had lost too much land to abide content. They would never give up Malta as Napoleon desired and even if they did, he was not a man to be trusted.

Trinette halted, screening her eyes with her hand. 'Look! Over there!'

Royal followed her stepdaughter's gaze across the horizon. Shapes swarmed in the distance: tiny carriages and twig-like soldiers. In front of them, two figures tripped over the churned road: Wilhelm and Fritz.

Trinette gathered up her muddy skirt and ran, Paul galloping after her. Royal laughed at their shrieks of glee and picked her way over the mud. It had been so long. Nerves slithered in her stomach at the thought of meeting her husband – she was as shy as a virgin, as giddy as a girl. Would he be proud of her efforts? Would he return to the genial, flabby Fritz of old?

Self-conscious, Royal looked down at her gown and saw dirt circling the hem. She remained fat from her stillborn child; the pregnancy weight never left her, just as the weight of grief would never leave her. But, back in Fritz's bed, perhaps she would conceive another child, a child of her freedom, born in peace time. The dizzying thought made her stumble.

As she neared her family, Royal realised it wasn't just Fritz's entourage that filled the road – the people of Württemberg lined the track and cheered at her return. Wind whipped their shouts up to the banners rippling above their heads.

Fritz lifted his lips in a weary smile. He looked older than Royal remembered, and tired. Without saying a word, he took her in his arms. The people whooped, filling Royal with a wonderful sense of belonging. She was home, nestled in Fritz's soft arms, loved by her people.

Her exile had earned her this devotion. A year in Erlangen had melted and shaped her into a woman of Württemberg – the leader and the wife she wanted to be. She was Princess Royal no more.

⌁ *Queen's House, London* ⌁

Charlotte had blushed for the conduct of her sons many times, but a daughter – to be ashamed of a daughter was much worse.

How had she failed to notice? It all made sense now; Sophia's obsession with Garth and the stables, her sudden symptoms of dropsy. Then she had departed for Weymouth a day before the royal carriages and spent the holiday moping.

At the time, Charlotte thought Sophia grieved for the King's state of mind, but now she knew better. If only Charlotte had paid more attention. To have the shock sprung on her – from blasted Caroline, of all people in England! It was humiliating. London gossips knew more about Charlotte's daughter than she did.

She sat on her red-and-gilt throne and counted the seconds of Sophia's absence. She pretended to listen to Monsieur De Luc on his lectern, reading a publication on the revolution in France.

In her mind, she pictured Sophia making her way through the pale grey passageways downstairs, Mercury's basket balancing on one hip. With every imaginary step she took, Charlotte's resentment mounted. Had she not raised her to be a model of virtue? Did she not teach her to control her own petty desires?

Now Sophia would be walking down the avenue of Corinthian columns, placing her foot on the first broad stone step. Charlotte visualised her in the echoing stairwell, the painted figures on the wall reaching out for her. She imagined a trail of dark, polluting sin leaking from beneath her skirt.

A guard edged the door open and Sophia crept in, her dimity dress whispering over the carpet. She set down the dog's basket and Mercury trotted straight over, turning round a few times before settling with his head over one paw.

Monsieur De Luc paused, leaving a space for Charlotte to grant Sophia permission to sit down. They all looked to her expectantly, but she said nothing. If Sophia could get herself pregnant, she could stand up. Monsieur De Luc was forced to carry on with his reading.

Who would believe the thin, sylph-like Sophia was wanton? Not just wanton – breathtakingly selfish. The King was recuperating, but if he found out his fifth daughter was a harlot, the shock of it would kill him. Charlotte would have to hush it up. Give Sophia a chance to redeem herself and adopt the right course of behaviour. It was more than she deserved. At least Garth had the decency to pay for his bastard's keep. If Charlotte sent money to Weymouth herself, it would lend credence to the rumours.

From what Caroline said, Charlotte gathered there was wild speculation about the baby's parentage. Some wicked tongues even suggested the King had attacked Sophia in one of his mad fits. Charlotte shuddered. To think of the King's good name, tarnished like that because Sophia couldn't keep her skirts down!

Sophia sagged against the wainscot, pain carved in her

face. Charlotte shot her a glare and she snapped to attention again.

It was a meagre revenge for the hurt Sophia had put her through, but it pleased Charlotte nonetheless.

CHAPTER THIRTY-THREE

Ludwigsburg
Summer 1802

Royal dashed out into the gardens, breathless. She passed the statues, skipped down the steps, ran around the parterre and made straight for the canal, where Fritz walked with the English ambassador Sir Thomas Tyrwhitt.

It was cool and tranquil by the water. Insects skipped across the surface, darting in and out of orange rays cast by the setting sun. Royal slowed her step and fell into pace beside the men. She waited for them to finish their conversation, bursting with impatience.

'I think the duchess would like a word,' said Sir Thomas, peering around Fritz's stomach. He looked tiny at the best of times, but next to hefty Fritz, the Englishman was absolutely comical.

Fritz attempted a smile, but it was strained. 'Sir Thomas has been explaining our income, *mein Schatzi*. The interest on your settlement is skewed by the exchange rate. Out of each five thousand, we never receive more than one.'

Royal schooled her radiant face into a serious expression. 'That's terrible. But won't the currency recover in peacetime?'

'We can only hope.' He looked down to pick up her arm and saw the piece of paper clamped in her hand. 'What have you there?'

A bird called from across the water. Royal used the pause to still her heart and moderate her emotion.

'A letter from my brother George. He wants me to come and stay with him in England. While there is peace and my father is well . . .'

Fritz snatched the paper from her fingers. 'Let me see that.'

The breeze sent the trees shivering. Royal waited, wringing her empty hands together until she made red marks on her palms. *Please, please.* She wanted this so badly, it made her sick and dizzy with apprehension. Surely there could be no question. He must let her go.

The minutes passed, marked only by the splash of ducks in the canal. Why did he take so long to read it? Royal did not dare look into his face; she couldn't bear to see a denial written there.

Finally, he moistened his lips with his tongue. 'It does not mention me. Or the children.'

She faltered. 'No. I – I imagine he thought you would be too busy. But if I write and say–'

'In fact,' Fritz interrupted, 'it ignores me completely. Why would he address such a request to you and not your husband? The husband ought to direct the wife. I ought to have been consulted.'

Pink patches appeared under his ears. Royal sensed the anger boiling inside him and took a step back.

'If he had written to me, I would have been agreeable to the idea. But I see how it is. I am set at naught by your Englishmen. I know what they say of me in your blasted gazettes. Well, I assure you, I can feel my dignity as well as an English sovereign.'

Sir Thomas, with a delicate ambassadorial flourish, ventured to interject. 'Your Grace, I deeply regret the mistake. I am sure it is no slight. The duchess's family only love her too sincerely to think of etiquette, when their heads are dizzy with the pleasurable notion of seeing her once more.'

Fritz turned on him, a quivering hulk of indignation. 'They mean to take my wife – *my* wife! – out of the country without a by-your-leave! And you say they do not aim to wound my authority? I know their game. The minute she lands they will pour poison into her ears about me, blame me for surrendering to the French. Well, what have the English done for us? Nothing! They sit there and they judge and they do not lift a finger to save their own daughter's family! They only remember her when it is convenient to do so!'

How dare he? Royal opened her mouth to protest, but

anger, disappointment and fear formed a wedge at the back of her throat. She choked on her words, throttled by emotion. Would he really not let her go? Her father – would she never see him again? Giddy, she crouched on the grass and buried her fingers in the peaty earth. Fritz looked down at her. Surely he would reconsider when he saw her misery? Yes – the hot colour drained from his face and he stepped away from Sir Thomas.

'You see how it is, sir,' he said coolly. 'Observe my wife.' He gestured to Royal, on her knees and struggling for breath. 'She is far too ill to travel. Could I, as a loving husband, send her to England in this state?'

What? This could not be happening, Royal couldn't let it happen, but she had no words to put it right.

Fritz yanked her to her feet and wiped the tears from her face. She was utterly dumbfounded. 'There, now. No need to cry. We cannot have a baby with the Channel between us.'

Royal winced as the trap clicked. He had caught her. He knew, as well as she did, that it was the only thing she would ever put before her father: a baby. A child of her own. There was even a veiled threat that he would not come to her bed, wouldn't give her another chance to conceive, if she disobeyed.

'I am too ill,' she repeated, tasting the treachery on her tongue. 'I am too ill to see my family.' She buried her head in her hands and sobbed with raw grief. She had pictured herself there, beside her father, embracing her sisters. In her joy at the King's recovery, she had forgotten how this other man in her life needed to be managed, coaxed, tip-toed round on egg shells. She would never forget again.

Fritz placed a protective arm over her shoulders. 'Never mind, *Liebling*. I will look after you.'

Weymouth

Sophia sat in a window seat, watching the early morning riders clatter home across the cobbled streets. She peered through her spectacles, hoping what she saw would prove her suspicions wrong. But sure enough, Charles Fitzroy hung back to ride at Amelia's side.

Amelia glanced at him under her eyelashes, her cheeks pink. Sophia swallowed, recognising the signs all too well. It was just as she feared; her little sister was in love.

Fitzroy was an equerry, like Garth, but he was no short, ageing man with a deforming birthmark. He was tall and handsome with a chiselled face, dark eyebrows and gently curling hair. Just the kind to steal Amelia's heart.

Sophia stood, ran to the door and jammed a bonnet on her head. This had to stop. Heaven only knew what she would say, but she had to say something. She could not watch her sweet baby sister, so adorably old-fashioned with a lace ruff at her neck, burn with passion and despair.

The air was balmy and scented with salt. Sophia charged

into a haze of golden sunshine, her eyes on the lovers. She could almost taste their desire. Fitzroy swept his elegant body out of his saddle and helped the bashful Amelia dismount.

Suddenly, something like a wall appeared and stopped Sophia short. Squinting up through her spectacles, she realised it was Ernest, jerking his horse to a halt. A lick of foam wetted the animal's neck, a sure sign of heavy riding. Her stomach dropped.

'Good God! What's happened?' she cried.

Ernest threw down the reins and swung out of the saddle in one fluid movement. There were creases between his eyebrows and patches of sweat under the arms of his coat.

'Ernest?'

Roughly, he seized Sophia by the wrist and dragged her away from the riders and servants. When they were out of earshot, he wheeled her round.

'Who've you been talking to?'

The question was so strange that she gasped at him. 'What?'

'Sophia. What have you been saying?'

Sophia racked her brain for one incriminating sentence that had passed her lips. She shook her head, dumbstruck.

'Well you must have said something. All of London knows you've had a baby.'

Everything moved. Sophia no longer stood on the grass but on a boat, tossing about on the waves. How did Ernest know? She hadn't told him. 'What do you mean?'

His scarred eye glared at her beneath its hooded lid, unimpressed. 'All those times I lied for you. You said you were seeing Caroline. Think how foolish I felt when I heard the truth.'

There was no denying it, then.

'How? How did anyone find out?'

'I thought you'd know. The rumour's spread like gangrene,' he growled through clenched teeth.

Waves rushed in against the shore and seagulls called. Sophia put her head in her hands. Her fears streamlined, focusing to a single point. 'The King?'

'He doesn't know, yet. If we are lucky, no one will dare tell him.'

'What if they do? His mind won't stand it!'

Ernest shook his head. 'It does not bear thinking about. No one would be so foolish.'

She shivered. 'What about the Queen?'

'She hasn't said anything.'

'But you think she knows?'

'Yes.'

Of course she did; that was why she wouldn't let Sophia sit in her presence.

The papers would print it, if she and Ernest failed to buy up the articles and caricatures in time. Everyone would shun her. Nobody would know or accept that she and Garth had made their marriage vows in private – the dark shroud of a fallen woman would cover her.

'You have to help me,' she gabbled. 'Have you any money? The Queen will cast me out. The King will run mad.'

Ernest pushed a hand through his tousled, sandy hair. There was something else.

'Ernest?'

He coloured. 'Garth's been making enquiries – I gather Garth is your man?' He could not look at her. 'Because they're saying – those damned people are saying that I'm the father.'

Vomit pushed hard against the back of her throat. She swayed, but Ernest snatched her out of the swoon with one strong arm.

'Who says? Who says it?' She couldn't imagine spite dark enough to prompt slander like that.

'Lots of people. My political enemies.'

Ernest leant Sophia against a stone wall, where she tossed her head like one in a fever. A pulse beat loud in her temple, drowning out the crash of waves, the horses passing by and the excited chatter of onlookers.

No wonder Garth was so strange and suspicious. Someone must have whispered to him, convinced him their baby was nothing but a monster.

'What will we do? What will we do?' Her poor son. She had to stay away from him – now, more than ever. No one could know he was hers. Being dubbed a royal bastard would taint his life, but if people thought he was the product of incest . . .

Ernest's voice came to her in disturbed patches of sound. 'Deny it. All you can do is deny it. Refute every rumour. Insist there is no baby, there was never a baby.'

She could do so with a clear conscience. It would not be a lie. There was no baby in her life – and now there never would be.

CHAPTER THIRTY-FOUR

Queen's House, London
1803

'You must let me have a command now! Surely you see that?'

Charlotte ducked beneath the blast of George's voice as he shouted at the King.

The King shook his head. 'I will take away that toy regiment you *do* have if you carry on.'

George swiped his jewelled ceremonial sword through the air. He was practically spitting with rage. 'You are too old! You're too old and too ill to ride at the head of your troops. There are a hundred thousand men waiting to cross from Boulogne! This is not a game!'

He was right. Boulogne had become an impenetrable coast of iron and bronze. Rumour had it that Bonaparte was assembling a fleet to rival the Spanish Armada – strange bulbous ships, rafts, floating fortresses and hot air balloons. Every English village drilled its citizens, from the labourers in their smocks to the clerks who practised three hours a day before work. A tattoo of drums and fifes pounded along the coastline, erecting sentry towers and beacons as it went. The walls in Chatham were now thirteen feet thick, mounted with guns.

Royal would never be able to visit now. The small window of time for sailing the Channel in safety had slammed shut, barring Charlotte from her girl. And since blasted Fritz favoured the French these days, it was unlikely Royal would receive her family's letters from England.

Charlotte exhaled, ruffling the fur of her dog, Phoebe. War had one advantage, at least: it kept the press busy. The King wouldn't hear of Sophia's misadventure while a bugle blared across the nation.

'I am not too old to command. I should like to fight Boney single-handed. I'm sure I should. I should give him a good hiding. I'm sure of it.' The King's eyes glimmered with the determination of a child. His white, queued wig wobbled as he emphasised the foolish words.

George raised a bergamot-scented handkerchief to his forehead. 'Listen to yourself! This is war – the Treaty of Amiens has failed! Buonaparte is a formidable commander and he has taken Hanover already. We're next on his list! You need a younger man at the head of your troops. You need *me*.'

The King rose to his feet, vibrant with anger, and drew back his stooped shoulders. 'I do *not* need you. Pah! I'll ride into battle myself, like my grandfather before me. I'm not a yellow-belly like that fool of Württemberg – I won't roll over and give in. I'll fight.'

Charlotte pulled Phoebe close and concentrated on a deep red jewel in her bracelet. Once again, she was stuck in the middle, torn apart like a piece of meat between two starving curs. Usually, she would take George's part, but with the King in this excited state it was dangerous.

'I'm not disputing your right to fight,' George explained. 'I want you to fight. I want to help you.'

'You can review the volunteer corps with your brothers.'

'Papa—'

'And I'll expect you at my side on the field of battle when the invaders land. That's all. No command. You're not king yet, you know.'

George sliced the King with resentful eyes. The poor boy never had free rein.

'What about us?' Charlotte asked.

A pause. They turned to look at her.

'Hmmm?'

'The ladies. What will we do, while you're off on this battlefield?'

'You will go to Worcester, dear. I've arranged it.'

Insufferable. Charlotte foresaw her future: crouching in hiding with no idea of what was going on – no idea whether her husband and sons were alive or whether she was still Queen. She looked back to her bracelet and the dark red of its jewel filled her eyes, filled her mind. So much rage and resentment she could never express. She tried to pour the poisonous feelings into the ruby with the intensity of her gaze.

'Go on now, George, go,' said the King. 'Can you not see your mother is distressed? Be off with you.' He made a shooing motion with his hands.

Glowering, George picked up his hat and gloves. Charlotte's darling son was not the beautiful, florid boy he used to be; disappointment, frustration and downright foolish living had taken their toll.

'Mama.' He bent over to kiss Charlotte's hand, reeking of pomade and eau du cologne.

Their eyes met.

He was always a clever boy. He knew, as well as she did, that they were doomed. He knew the King was off with his strange fancies again, at the worst possible time, and Britain would either have a legitimate, mad King or a false, French Emperor.

CHAPTER THIRTY-FIVE

Ludwigsburg
1804

The evening was overcast with dark clouds marbling the moon. Royal knelt between the window and her bed, deep in prayer.

She possessed all she had longed for as a girl – a family of her own and a palace at her command – but she was not the fulfilled, confident woman she had envisaged; she was in pieces. What must they think of her back home? It was bad enough being parted from her relations by distance, but to lose their good opinion too was intolerable.

Württemberg was not neutral in this war; they had made a pact with the devil. The French had crossed the Rhine. The duchy could only fight on to certain death or surrender and become a member of their Confederation.

Fritz had made the decision her father never would: he had given up. The King's greatest foe, Napoleon, was on his way. Royal would have to meet him, offering friendship and politeness, in just two days. Driving her fingernails into the back of her clasped hands, she begged God for the courage to perform her duty: to curtsey to the usurper of France.

For her husband, for Württemberg, she had to make a good impression. Napoleon wasn't simply a general now; he was an Emperor with Spain and Italy on his side. He could not be beaten.

Royal squeezed her hands together and entreated Christ to intercede for her husband and her father. Hopeless, really. One's victory would mean the other's defeat. It was a cruel, cruel position. Would the King understand? Or would he view this surrender as a personal betrayal? Heaven knew Royal would sacrifice much for her dear Papa, but she could not put her family and her people at risk to protect his feelings. As a good sovereign, he must see that. She prayed that he would see that.

She started as the door opened and shut. *What could this be?* She had ordered her ladies to leave her alone for prayer just a moment ago. She opened her eyes, a scold on her lips.

A dark shape passed quickly beside her. Before she could turn, a rough hand gripped her hair and wrenched her to her feet. Needles of pain pricked her scalp as she twisted helplessly, her neck bent at an unnatural angle.

'Let go of me!' she shrieked, but something heavy collided with her teeth. She tasted blood. Her nose cracked and bright spots sprang up before her eyes. Pain reverberated through her skull until she dropped onto the bed, limp as a ragdoll.

Royal opened her eyes to glare at her attacker. They flickered into focus, the double images sliding back into a single frame. A man towered over her, his face scrunched and red as tears poured down his cheeks.

It was Fritz.

For a moment she was so stunned that she fell back against the coverlet. Of all the people sworn to protect her, it was Fritz. She would rather have seen a masked assassin. She would rather have been stabbed through the heart.

Hiding his face in both hands, he bellowed and slumped down beside her. 'I am sorry,' he gasped into the sheets. 'I am sorry. I just . . . I cannot . . . I am so sorry.'

For a while she remained still, breathing in and out, staring at the ceiling. The bed trembled beneath her husband's sobs.

What had he been reduced to? Had the war really crushed him into this pathetic beast? His presence turned her skin cold. Instinct told her to jam shoes on her feet and fly from the room. But there was no way out of the situation. She was tied to him, on the wrong side of a war, hundreds of miles from England. And what about the children? She could not run from the children. This violence, this weakness of Fritz's was just another thing she would have to cope with.

She tried to make way for it in her mind, winding it

round and through her love for him without quite stifling it. Maybe it was a trait of all leaders, this double personality. She pictured her father, so genial and kind playing with the children one moment, then foaming at the mouth and groping Lady Pembroke the next. He had outbursts, he had hit pages. It did not make him a bad man. Royal had blamed her mother for collapsing under the swings of the King's temper, yet here she was, doing the same thing.

Blood trickled down her nose onto her lips. Its bitterness filled her mouth. After all she had been through, she was no better than her mother. She hadn't learnt. And she was such a poor wife that her husband beat her. She shuddered as the idea surfaced: was it her fault? She had always been difficult, disobedient.

Images and arguments flashed through her mind: the hunting lodge, his slap before she left for Erlangen, the scene by the canal. She had not been an easy, biddable wife. Her birth had shackled him to England long after it became necessary to side with France, and her refusal to write to the King had left Fritz without an ally. Shame burned through her, leaving a sick trail of guilt. There was another sin, far greater: her carelessness had killed their baby. No wonder he hit her.

She put out the hand that bore her wedding ring and let it hover above Fritz's head. His hair was tangled and clogged with powder. It did not look like the head of a monster, or a fiend. Despite everything, it was the same. It was just Fritz.

She planted a kiss upon her palm and laid it flat against his skull. She would do better than the Queen. She would learn to forgive. She would be the real stability and power holding this duchy together. It would be her hardest lesson yet.

Another stream of blood ran across her cheek and spotted the coverlet.

'I am sorry,' Fritz repeated.

~ *Kew* ~

Mist shrouded the morning, winding its tendrils around the plants. Sophia ambled along, holding Amelia's hand and wished the swirling clouds would swallow her up. How could Garth believe it? How could anyone believe such a sick, vicious rumour?

Losing a child was bad enough; she hadn't expected it to drive a wedge between her and Garth too. Estranged, barely speaking or writing, it was as if they had never meant the world to one another. She felt it like an internal rupture. Something had burst and bled profusely, but she had nothing to staunch the flow. Sophia sighed, the smoke of her breath blending with the fog.

Amelia turned concerned blue eyes on her. 'Have you spoken to Garth yet?' she whispered.

Sophia shook her head. 'I don't think I could bear to. I hate him. I hate him for believing that about me and Ernest.'

Amelia glanced over her shoulder. 'Sophy, I am not sure he *does* believe it. I've heard something else. People say Garth is thinking of adopting a child – a poor child – and making him his heir.'

Sophia squeezed Amelia's gloved fingers. She focused hard on staying upright and walking straight. 'My child?'

'Who else's?'

He could not do that. The only reason Sophia let them take her boy away was to give him a fresh start, free from the slander surrounding his birth. Had it all been for nothing? All her self-denial, the wrenching age spent torn from her own flesh and blood? 'He can't,' she insisted. 'He can't.'

'He is the father. He can do whatever he wants.'

Sophia shook her head fiercely. Her brain burned as she racked it for a solution that would protect both the boy and the King. 'If I stay away from them both, there's a chance that no one will guess I am his mother. Isn't there?'

Amelia shrugged. 'Unless the papers discover your affair with Garth.'

'They don't *want* to discover that. Half of London thinks I gave birth to Ernest's baby. They're happy with that twisted story. If I don't go and see Garth, maybe they won't associate the boy with me. Perhaps they'll believe he really is some pauper, adopted out of the goodness of Garth's heart.'

Amelia gave her a pitying look. 'Perhaps.'

Perhaps. A stake through her chest, a life spent in mourning – an awful lot to risk for a perhaps. But if there was a chance, even a chance, that Sophia's pain could help her child, she would bear it. Of course she would – she was his mother.

When Sophia thought of helping others, it suddenly occurred to her that she'd forgotten to question Amelia about Fitzroy. This business with the baby had blown it clean from her mind. Yet, perhaps Sophia didn't need to caution her sister after today's conversation. Amelia was intelligent; surely she would see the agony Sophia had endured and take a warning from it? But then again, love blinded the wisest minds . . .

Sophia blinked as a dark streak hurtled toward her through the mist. A man ran, full pelt across the lawn, unable to cut a clear path through the fog. He stumbled, cried out, lurched forward and nearly collided into the back of Amelia.

'Excuse me! Your Royal Highness!' The messenger pulled himself up, panting.

'What is it?'

He tried to catch his breath. 'The Queen has summoned you.'

Sophia turned cold. The Queen knew about the baby – Ernest had been sure. She clenched Amelia's hand until her knuckles turned white.

'Only the Princess Amelia,' the messenger explained.

The girls exchanged a glance, Sophia's fright seeping out of her features and flowing into Amelia's.

'Are you certain?' Sophia asked.

'Yes, Your Royal Highness.'

Sophia released her sister and almost dropped to the ground with relief. 'What could it be?' she whispered.

Amelia shrugged guiltily and followed the messenger across the dew-soaked lawn. Sophia watched her disappear, gradually, into the mist.

⤝ The Dutch House, Kew ⤜

The princesses' old English teacher, Miss Gomm, scuttled into Charlotte's quiet drawing-room. She slammed the door shut and froze for a moment, her hands pressed upon it. What now? 'Miss Gomm?'

The lady dropped to her knees in a pool of green silk. 'Your Majesty, forgive me.'

Charlotte peered down at her. 'What on earth has happened to you?'

'Nothing; nothing to me, Your Majesty. Only – oh! I do not know what to do.'

Charlotte was silent, unable to feign interest. Another disaster? What did it matter? Her life consisted of bouncing from one calamity to the next. There would only be something worse next week, even worse the week after that.

'It is Princess Amelia,' Miss Gomm gasped. 'I have been remiss in my duty. I've been very, very remiss.'

Low sunlight filtered through the scarlet curtains onto Charlotte's face, but she felt no heat. Everything was dead to her.

'I believe the princess has fallen in love with Charles Fitzroy,' Miss Gomm confessed.

Charlotte inspected her nails. 'I observed to you last year, several times, that she fell behind to ride with him.'

Miss Gomm nodded, her face a mask of contrition. 'I should have listened. But it is far worse now. God forgive me, I let them spend time together, under my watch. I pitied them as young lovers. I was very wrong.'

Charlotte sniffed. 'What do you want me to do about it?'

The governess widened her eyes. 'I thought you might speak to her, Your Majesty. She won't listen to me, not now.'

Charlotte made a moue of distaste. She had polished over Sophia's indiscretion without even mentioning the matter to her – the girl was clever enough to give up Garth herself, when she saw what their relationship would do to the King. Amelia would follow the same path.

'Can we not just let the romance run its course? They'll tire of each other soon enough. Just make sure there is no – physical contact.'

Miss Gomm wrung her hands. 'Oh, Your Majesty, she will be ruined! There are already such rumours! I am afraid the King will hear of it. I am afraid that she'll elope with him.'

An ember of anger burnt through Charlotte's torpor. She was relieved; it proved there was something left inside her. 'Would she really forget her duty so far?'

Miss Gomm threw out her hands. 'She is bewitched.'

'Bring her to me.'

'I have already sent a messenger, Your Majesty. The princess will be waiting in the next room.'

While Miss Gomm ran to fetch Amelia, Charlotte waited, staring at the marble chimneypiece and feeling her anger mount. She cherished the life-giving power it carried as it flowed through her veins – veins that were otherwise dead.

As Amelia bustled in through the door, her chin erect, Charlotte rose up, a Queen once more, forceful and terrible in her rage.

She made no preamble. 'So! What is this I hear about Charles Fitzroy?'

Amelia drew herself up. 'I love him, Mama.'

Charlotte wanted to spit. Impossible, while Amelia was young and hot-blooded, to persuade her that love was not enough – that love could fade as easily as a handsome face. 'And what about your father? Do you not love him?'

Amelia's lips parted. For an instant, Charlotte saw the winning little girl who brought the family such joy. 'Of course I love Papa.'

'Then you must know this will kill him when I speak of it. Or perhaps that is your plan? You would be free to marry then. George would give his consent.'

Amelia flinched as if scalded. 'No!' she cried. 'No, I would never wish harm on Papa.'

'Well then, I expect to hear no more of this unpleasant business.'

Amelia bristled, her sweet blue eyes turning sharp as daggers. 'He is not an *unpleasant business*. He is the man I love.'

Charlotte scoffed.

'You don't know what it is like,' Amelia hurried on. 'You were married to Papa straight from the schoolroom. You had no choice. You do not know what it is to wait and wait for love.'

A low, unpleasant laugh escaped Charlotte's clenched teeth. It amused her when Amelia spoke of boredom and neglect; she did not understand the meaning of the words. All her life, she had been petted and spoilt. She would not have coped with Charlotte's childhood, marooned in the crumbling Schloss of a war-scourged duchy.

Tears of frustration spilled over Amelia's lashes. 'Please, Mama, please. Have pity.'

Perhaps Charlotte would have done, once. But now she only saw the disobedience and selfishness of her youngest daughter, and she used it to fuel her molten rage. 'You're a fool, Amelia. Princesses do not get to choose. You will marry or stay single as your father pleases.' Charlotte gazed out of the window, looking into the past. She chuckled drily. 'Love! My sister loved a man once, back in Mecklenburg-Strelitz. An English duke. He would have been a good match for her. Do you know what happened?'

Reluctantly, Amelia shook her head.

'My brother struck a deal to marry me to the King of England. Suddenly everything changed and my sister couldn't have her man. It was written in the terms of the contract. She never saw her lover again.'

Amelia's mouth hung open. 'But that's not fair!'

'No, it's not. Life is not fair.' It certainly wasn't fair when it stole her darling husband's mind, when it killed her baby boys.

Amelia put her hands to the curls at her forehead. 'I won't give him up,' she murmured. 'I won't.'

'You will.'

'No!' she screamed.

Lord bless her, she still thought she could win. She thought she could beat Charlotte in a struggle of wills. There could be no hints with this girl, no coercing half-measures. Charlotte would have to be cruel. 'You'll give him up,' she said slowly, 'or I'll tell your father. It will send him mad – for good, this time. And it will all be your fault.'

Without a word Amelia turned on her heel and strode from the room, showing Charlotte her back, as if she were an ordinary woman, not a Queen entitled to respect. She shut the door with a reverberating bang.

Charlotte was strangely satisfied.

⤳ *The Dutch House, Kew* ⤶

Sophia stared at the mound of dishes on the table, wondering which one to risk. She had to bolt something down – her lack of appetite was attracting notice. Plates of cutlets, pies, jelly and fish lay before her, all displayed beautifully, some fanned out with a decorative garnish. But the thought of eating made her gag.

She had received a letter through her trusted messenger, Robinson, just before going in to dress. At first she was relieved Garth had answered her frantic enquiries, but now, sitting down to dinner in a room as white as her drained skin, she wished she had never asked him.

Knives scratched against the Dresden china. Mary's glass of wine chinked as she picked it up to take a sip. No one spoke. Sophia thanked God for it. In this state, she could not feign conversation. Garth had gone behind her back. Her baby, whom she meant to save with a life of obscurity, would be his. An adopted nephew, Garth said. He thought no one would suspect, this long after the birth. He was a fool.

Sophia swallowed against the taste of soup. Her stomach felt full of liquid, sloshing, seething. At last, she took a mutton chop offered to her and winced as it hit her plate with a wet, meaty slap. All Garth had been waiting for was her word of honour; her assurance the baby was his. Now he could see it resembled him, not Ernest, he had no hesitation. He did not think of the King.

I was at fault, I was scared and you have every reason to hate me. But I beg you will not. I am willing to forget what has passed — say you are too.

I told you I had a plan, and I always did. I have saved enough money now to put it into action. Come away with me, Sophy. Let us be a family. Of course we cannot stay here, but there are homes outside of England. Would not America receive us with open arms?

There are places on the coast where the sun shines all year round. I know you would be fit and well there. I know our boy would thrive.

Sophia surveyed the room, taking in the hefty fireplace, the organ, the self-portrait of Van Dyke. What a liberating and terrifying experience it would be, leaving Kew forever. There would be no heavy red curtains in an American home, no Tudor rose carved into the ceiling. Plain living on Garth's slender savings, with her son in her arms.

Reason closed the shutters on her imaginary scene with a snap. It was every bit as foolish as a daydream. How would she escape, where would she run to without being recognised? She was chained to this palace, this family. Garth was talking like a Bedlamite.

Long ago, in a stall sweet with the smell of hay, he promised he would never hurt her father. He had forgotten, but Sophia did not find it so easy to sponge the poor King from her mind.

She planted her fork into the mutton and watched juice run out of it. The thick scent turned her stomach once again. A voice whispered in her ear, teasing at her mind like sin. It told her the King was already mad. He had gone. No actions of hers could make him worse. She should run, now, and seize happiness while she had the chance.

But would she really be happy? Guilt would weigh like a cannon on her chest. Each time she took her boy into her embrace, she would trace his features and find the King looking back at her. Every kiss of Garth's would damn her, blight her.

She cut the meat carefully into equal squares. Stabbing a piece on her fork, she willed herself to eat it. It had been the only way, all her life: forcing her body into acts it did not condone. Pushing herself beyond the limits of human endurance to be a perfect, dutiful princess. She would have to tell him *no*. She would have to slam the door on the prospect of sunny days and long, loving nights.

Sophia placed the mutton cube on her tongue and slowly, painfully, ground it in her teeth. Fighting against her gorge, she swallowed the chewed meat down.

Later, Robinson brought Sophia a response from Garth under the cover of darkness. She took a candle and broke the seal.

The contents were brutal. Garth mocked her fears about the adoption. He denied it was foolish to parade their son – whom he had named Tommy – about the town. He branded Sophia as selfish and affected, an unnatural mother who never expressed a desire to see her own boy.

The candle dripped and sputtered as the words scalded Sophia's heart. God knew, she had only kept away for the sake of her son and for her father. She continued to hurt herself to protect her family, to protect Garth. She had acted for the good of everyone except herself. There would be no hope of reconciliation with Garth now. She knew, as she stared up at the brooding sky with tiny stars picked out beneath the clouds, that she was ruined.

She threw the letter onto the dying fire, where it curled and blackened before catching light. As a dark stream of smoke rose from the flaming words, Sophia saw a shadow fall over her future. Black – nothing but black.

Windsor

'Your Majesty, do you understand?'

'I understand,' Charlotte replied, 'but I can't do it. How can I treat him as if he's well? He is not well. He has not been well for many, many years.'

Dr Heberden inclined his head respectfully. 'Your Majesty, it does the King no good to see how nervous you are in his presence. He needs your strength.'

She rounded on him. 'I can tell you Dr Heberden, it does *me* no good to *be* in his presence.' They always blamed her and treated the King's illness as if it was her fault. No one spared an ounce of pity to think how she felt. With a clatter, Charlotte threw down her knife and fork. 'I cannot eat that now. I'll go to my bed. Girls, come.'

Grimacing, her daughters fell in line behind her like sheep. The vanquished doctor bowed them out of the room.

Charlotte looked out of her tall, thin window across the rolling hills. Dusk spread its wings over the long walk. The red, glimmering sun touched the path where it met the horizon. It looked like a slender chip of hope. On the other side of the lodge was a different view: the sturdy curtain wall of the castle. Encasing her inside this asylum. Charlotte sighed heavily and sat down to her dressing table.

If only her son George would come. He understood what it was to be mewled up, tethered fast to a mad spouse.

Her darling boy had fought hard over the past years, against Napoleon and against his wife. Thanks to Nelson and the Battle of Trafalgar, Napoleon was at bay, but Caroline . . . No matter what her outrages, no matter how much evidence George produced against her, the King would not give way. George grew too tired to battle on.

Charlotte was tired, as well.

She thought of the document with its great swirls of black ink, locked, waiting, in her desk. All she had to do was sign it. One little flourish and the King's treatment would be decided by the cabinet, not her. The burden would lift. Could she do it? Even now, it felt wrong. The final kiss of betrayal. But God knew she couldn't carry on much longer.

In the glass, she saw the reflection of her five daughters standing perfectly still, expressionless like the porcelain ornaments that littered the windowsills.

'I tried to get you out of this,' she told them. 'My nephew wanted to come from Mecklenburg-Strelitz and claim one of you for his bride. But even when the King is well he gives me nothing but excuses. The Hereditary Prince will stop waiting and marry someone else.'

The mirrored images drooped like candles melting to their wicks. Charlotte turned on her stool and put out her hands. 'Come. We are better off together. Heaven knows what I would do without you, my girls.' They laid their hands in hers. Their fingers were icy cold. She squeezed them and looked up, staring pointedly between Amelia and Sophia. 'It is a fine thing to have an establishment of your own. But in the end, men will only bring you pain. Remember that.'

Charlotte sensed Amelia raise her hackles. She was still young and romantic. But Sophia seemed to hear the truth in her words. A single tear slid down her plump cheek and dripped onto the satin breast of her gown.

Suddenly, Charlotte heard a bump and a holler upstairs.

She dropped her daughters' hands and twisted back to face the mirror. Her own eyes greeted her, huge and terrified. 'You will stay here,' she panted. 'You will stay here until I dismiss you.'

Hot blood hammered through her body, making her thoughts swim. Another scene – another attack. He would try to come to her bed again.

She could not bear it, she could not stand an instant alone with him. Why would he not stay away and leave her with the memories of him, young and sane?

Ladies swarmed over to her dressing table and removed the large, square diamonds from her hair. It was thin and coarse now. As her locks fell down around her shoulders, Charlotte noticed liver spots on her face and neck. She focused on them, fixed points mooring her to reality. She schooled her breath into regular, heavy gulps.

The King burst into the room with the chime of the clock, panting and red faced. An enormous, old-fashioned periwig swamped his head and nearly covered his chest. He looked like a rabid bear. Charlotte steeled herself. Any show of emotion would only excite him. She raised her thin eyebrows a fraction in the looking glass. 'Your Majesty.' She was impressed by the clear, crystal cold sound of her voice. 'What is that on your head?'

He laughed. 'Thought you'd like it. Going to wear it for the Knights of the Garter Ceremony, what?'

She pulled a face – tried to make it clear he could not

discompose her serenity – even though her pulse knocked at the back of her throat. 'As you wish.'

The King watched her in the mirror, carelessly wiping powder from her face. Then, inexplicably, he began to sob.

Sophia and Amelia rushed to comfort him. Charlotte did not move. This melancholy could switch to violence with a snap of the fingers.

'Papa?'

His elbow bore down on Sophia's shoulder. One hand shielded his eyes. 'Oh, Sophy, he's dead!' he wailed.

'Who is dead?'

'My brother, the Duke of Gloucester. He's dead!' He bent over with grief.

Sophia held him gently. 'Yes, Papa. For a few weeks now, I think?'

He wept wordlessly. The ridiculous wig slid to the floor as his thin ribcage heaved with sobs.

Charlotte watched Sophia stroke his small, stubbly head and realised she would have done that, once. But she couldn't now. She couldn't even swivel on her stool.

'Mama? What do we do?'

Charlotte inhaled and addressed the King in a bright, clipped voice. 'Come, sir, it will look better in the morning. Now you must go – it is time for bed.'

Sophia gaped at her. 'He is not well! He needs some comfort.'

'By all means, Sophy, take him outside and comfort him.'

The King snuffled against Sophia's shoulder. 'I want to stay here,' he whined. 'I want to stay with the Queen. Let me stay.'

Horror gave Charlotte the impetus to stand and face them. 'No. Absolutely not.'

'Mama! For pity's sake! Look at him!'

She did. He was as innocent as a bawling toddler, wet beneath the nose with shining, pleading eyes. But she knew how quickly this mood could turn. She couldn't explain to Sophia – she could not begin to describe the terror of those nights, alone with him.

'Your husband, Mama! The King! How can you deny him anything?'

Anger surged through her. How dare Sophia criticise? How dare she scold her own mother on horrors she knew nothing about? Charlotte pounced on Sophia and twisted a pinch of flesh hard between her fingers, making her gasp.

'We all know *you* will not deny a man anything, Sophy,' she hissed. 'Take him away.'

Sophia dragged her bewildered father from the room, all wet with tears. Charlotte held the door for them, her nostrils flaring. 'Sleep, sir,' she managed to say. 'You will feel better.'

Father and daughter fell into the corridor and Charlotte snapped the door shut behind them. With shaking hands, she slid three bolts across the wood and turned the key in the lock.

CHAPTER THIRTY-SIX

Ludwigsburg
⌒ 1806 ⌒

Royal's suite of rooms buzzed with the excitement of Twelfth Night. Her ladies had gathered raisins and brandy for snap-dragon, and a pail of water and some apples for bobbing. They splashed each other and ran, shrieking, to the corners. Royal smiled and shuffled a pack of cards in preparation for the family games.

All in all, she was content. She had done her duty – for the children, as well as Fritz. Paul was married to Princess Charlotte of Saxe-Hildburghausen and Trinette, darling Trinette, was engaged to Napoleon's brother.

She shivered, despite the warmth of her furs. Ghostly memories stalked her. She saw a library long ago, and a King sitting opposite his daughter as she begged him for the chance to marry. Trinette would never feel that desperation. She would not have to stagnate in a prolonged spinsterhood. Royal had done the best she could for her.

Still, there was something in it that smacked of treachery. It was an alliance of pure politics – not a love match.

Outside, church bells pealed through the frosty air. She tapped the pack of cards on the table. She understood, now, the King's reluctance to let her go. Fears for Trinette's future ate away at her. Would Royal cope without her girl, without Paul? Just her, Fritz and Wilhelm.

In spite of their efforts, no second baby quickened in Royal's womb. She spent days on her knees, bruising them against the hard stone floor of the chapel, praying it was not too late. The fertile years were running out, but surely she would bear a child soon. A live child. She had to. If she did not, and her courses stopped, it would all have been for nothing. Betraying her father, spending time in exile, enduring Fritz's temper . . . All for nothing.

Shaking off the terrible thought, she put down the cards and went to join her ladies. She could not waste time with regret. The King was too deranged to understand she was on the other side now. Without his disapproval, how could she repent? The war was over for Württemberg. In a bitter winter, she was warm and safe inside her luxurious palace with its marble corridors and swagged curtains. If they hadn't joined Napoleon, she would not be supervising the placement of holly or savouring the tang of orange peel in the air; she'd be preparing for another winter in exile.

The door crashed open and Fritz strode into the room with an entourage of jubilant men. 'Charlotte, get changed at once.'

Obediently, Royal stood and her ladies flew to the closet. 'What shall I wear?'

He beamed at her. 'My love, wear your most magnificent gown.'

She couldn't read his face. She had never seen him this happy, not even when she told him she was with child. 'Where are we going?'

'To church. We must give thanks.'

'What for, my dear? Tell me what for!'

His strong hands gripped her shoulders and pulled her straight. 'Stand tall, Charlotte. Today you have been made Queen of Württemberg.'

The ladies gasped. Royal stood, stunned. 'Queen?'

'Yes. Emperor Napoleon has made us a kingdom. We are King and Queen.'

Dizziness swept over her. It was too good to be true, too wonderful for words. Queen Charlotte of Württemberg! All those years and now she had finally done it – she had beaten her mother. The Queen of England could look down on her no more – Royal was her equal. Despite the attendants, she flung herself into Fritz's arms.

His belly rumbled with a hearty chuckle. 'Go on then, dress, dress! I expect you to look every inch a queen.'

The men bowed to Royal before escorting Fritz back out of the room. The instant the door clicked shut, the ladies erupted in a giggle of hysterical joy.

'A queen!' cried Madame de Spiegel. 'I will call you *Your Majesty*!'

Royal laughed. 'Oh yes,' she said with mock severity. 'Make sure you start at once!'

'Gracious, what will we put you in? I have never dressed a queen before!'

Royal thought of her mother and the time she spent on her clothes; the way she controlled the princesses' outfits, making them dress in matching, inferior versions of her own gown. 'I will let you choose,' she said. 'I have something to do.'

While they pulled dress after dress out of Royal's wardrobe, agonising over velvet, satin or watered silk, she ran to her writing desk. Driven entirely by impulse, she seized a piece of paper, dipped her pen in the ink and wrote:

To my very dear mother and sister Queen

She fell back in her chair, laughing. The Queen would hate it, she would absolutely hate it. The very thought of her mother's outraged face made her shriek with joy.

⚮ *Weymouth* ⚮

'Chin up, Sophy! Carry on, carry on!' The King pulled his horse alongside Sophia's and slapped her forcefully on the rump. She tensed as fresh bites of pain gnawed through her muscles. The streets blurred in a laudanum haze. She was drugged up to the hilt and far too ill to ride, but the King paid no heed.

Only the memory of what he once was, and the hope of what he would be again, kept Sophia beside the red-faced, leering man who hung from the saddle with saliva running down his chin. He had raised her from the cradle. Could she love him less, now?

Amelia kept her horse near Fitzroy's – for once, not for flirtation, but for protection. 'Won't the Queen expect us back soon?'

The King shook his head vigorously. 'Oh, no, no. I'm not going back there.' Once again he aimed his mount at Traveller, riding so close to Sophia that his boots kicked her stirrup. Traveller huffed with discontent. 'You are my friend, Sophy, so I can tell you. I can't go on with her like she is. She is not my Queen, and they refuse to let me go to Lady Pembroke, although everyone *knows* I am married to her. That scoundrel Dr Halford was at the wedding, you know, and he has the effrontery to deny it to my face!'

Sophia's vision flickered. She took a clump of Traveller's

mane in one hand and the pommel of the saddle in the other to steady herself.

'But it doesn't matter. I will find someone else. What do you think, eh?'

'I lament it,' she told him. With her little remaining strength, she raised her face to his. Horror surged through her as she caught him staring down the front of her dress. She pulled Traveller away. She had sacrificed her happiness for this – chosen mad ravings and salacious looks instead of Garth and Tommy. Regret stole her breath. In her giddiness, she feared sliding from Traveller's back. An avenue of trees arched over the riders' heads, shading them from the heat. The path fell away and declined into a hill. Sophia leant back in her saddle, ready to help Traveller balance his weight.

'We'll canter!' The King whooped a halloo and dug his heels into the flanks of his horse.

Before the riders could react, their mounts charged after the King's horse. Scrambling hooves clattered against gritty cement. Wind rushed past Sophia's ears, knocking her hat off, and she bounced dangerously in the saddle. Her foot flew out of the stirrup. This was it. She was going to die. The road was far, far too steep.

Her weak fingers clung to the reins for all they were worth, forcing Traveller to sense the pressure on his mouth. He slowed, but she felt his hooves slide beneath her. The other horses jostled past Traveller, knocking painfully against Sophia's legs. She watched them fly forward like a quiver of arrows, their shoes scraping on the ground. Suddenly a scream rent the air. Not just the shriek of a girl, but the throaty groan of a terrified animal. Sophia's head snapped up.

Amelia's horse wheeled his front legs uselessly in the air, no longer in control of them. In the next instant he plunged, fell to his knees and scraped them on the stones with a pitiful cry. Amelia cart-wheeled over his head, flew into the air and landed flat on her face. Sophia gasped, her stomach plunging in time with Amelia's body. A volley of shouts rang out from the other riders – they yanked back their reins, screeching their horses to a halt just before trampling over the inert princess.

Amelia's horse recovered his feet, stumbling. His knees were badly grazed. Amelia did not move.

The equerries surrounded her in an instant, turning her over, rubbing her temples. The only person who did not swing out of his saddle and charge to her side was the father that doted on her.

Fitzroy propped Amelia's head up in his lap. Dark streams of blood poured from her nostrils and ran over her lips.

A sob bubbled out of Sophia and she raised her hand to catch it. A broken neck? A shattered skull?

'My house is nearby,' said Mr Rose. 'Let's take her there and lay her down.'

Amelia's eyelids flickered open.

'Thank God!' Sophia cried. 'Let's go at once.'

'No.' The King's hard voice cut through their plan, shattering it to pieces. He sat straight and tall, staring down at Amelia as if she were no more than an insect.

Mr Rose stammered. 'S-Sir?'

'She'll get back on the horse.'

'But Your Majesty . . .'

'She's fine,' the King insisted, his colour rising. 'Look. She's awake.'

Sophia could not believe her ears. She gaped at Mr Rose and saw her despair reflected in his pinched face.

'Please God she will be well, Your Majesty, but to prevent any ill effects from this accident we should. . . '

'She'll get back on the horse, I tell you.' He slashed his riding crop in fury. 'I'll be damned if any of my children lack courage.'

Amelia raised a shaking hand to quiet the equerries. With phenomenal effort, she pulled herself into a sitting position. The blood welled up scarlet over her face. 'It's all right,' she said in a thin, feeble voice. 'It's all right. I'll get back on.'

The King nodded his approval. He did not see her grope blindly for her horse, did not hear her moan of suppressed agony as she heaved herself into the saddle. The road was dark and slippery with her blood.

'There is only one of my children who wants courage,

thank God,' the King announced. 'But I won't name him, no, no. What a cursed fate he should be the one to succeed me!'

No one listened to him. They watched the poor, un-steady Amelia and the red dripping from her nose.

CHAPTER THIRTY-SEVEN

Windsor Castle

✒ *1809* ✒

The costume of a queen lay folded on Charlotte's bed. A deep, sapphire silk gown, foaming with lace and tight, restrictive sleeves. Stays and stomacher, their laces lined up with military precision. A black shawl to drape over her shoulders and blot out the chill.

Cold floorboards pressed against Charlotte's stockinged feet. She was not allowed a carpet, or even a rug, because the King said they harboured dust. Even in his lunacy, his word was rule. Charlotte longed for the day when all she had to worry about was dust.

Her ladies prepared to perform their morning ritual. Each of them sized up the articles on the bed, working through the complex puzzle of which pieces came first and who would pass what to whom. As if it really mattered, now.

They were shaking out her clean shift when a reluctant tap came at the door. Dread clenched her insides. There was no good news, no messenger with joyful tidings these days. She nodded to Lady Townshend. 'Tell them to come back later.'

The whole palace knew she dressed at this hour. She kept her routine regular as clockwork, just as the King liked it. But Lady Townshend came back, apology cringing in her face. 'It is the Princess Sophia,' she explained. 'She insists on admittance, Your Majesty.'

Charlotte closed her eyes. She didn't want another argument. 'Very well. Show her in.' She held out her arms for the ladies to drape a peachy silk powdering robe over her shoulders. 'And leave us.'

Sophia shuffled into the room with her face turned down and her hands curled together. Charlotte watched her with a mother's eye and nearly wept. What a waste.

With that round, babyish face and big blue eyes, clear as a summer sky behind her spectacles, Sophia should be full of light and life. But she never stood a chance. She was what – eleven – when the King's malady began? Sadness and illness had stripped the buoyancy from her skin, dirtied her straw-blonde hair. Blighted her, just like the rest of them.

Without looking up, Sophia curtseyed. Charlotte saw that the action made her legs tremble violently.

'Go on, then. Sit down.'

As always, Sophia perched on the very edge of the chair, gripping the seat with her fingers.

'What is it?' she asked, but she thought she knew. It

would be a plea about the baby or Garth, perhaps an entreaty to be kinder to the King. Another petition she would have to refuse and look like a vile monster.

'It's Amelia.'

Charlotte stumbled back to the chaise-longue and sat down. 'What has she done now? Eloped?'

Sophia tilted her chin up. Worry possessed her face, holding the features taut. 'She is ill, Mama. She's so very ill. I saw her cough up blood.'

Everything swirled. It couldn't be. Amelia was young, healthy. She still possessed enough spirit to argue about Fitzroy. And yet . . . Charlotte ran over her recent memories, scanning them frantically for signs of illness. Amelia had grown thinner. Her high-necked chemisette could not hide the ribs and collar bone that jutted through her chest.

'Mama, someone has to tell the King. She needs treatment. Someone has to break it to him. I thought you the proper person.'

No. She pictured him wringing his white hair, wailing in agony. Blaming her. 'Must I?'

'Yes. I think we need to get her out of Windsor. Maybe to the sea.'

Images of the rolling tide filled Charlotte's mind. Last time, with Amelia's bad knee, they had sent her to Worthing. She frowned, lines wrinkling her brow. That was where Amelia fell in love with Fitzroy. A flaming arrow of suspicion shot through her.

'Do you think me a fool?'

'What?'

Charlotte curled her lip. 'Oh, do not play the innocent. What is it she needs the time for? A secret marriage? Baptising a bastard child?'

Colour rushed to Sophia's wan cheeks. 'No – Mama, no! She is really ill! I swear it!'

Charlotte rolled her eyes. 'I thought you, of all people, would know better than to encourage her.' She wished the words back at once. It was like she had slashed her daughter with a sabre. Sophia curled into herself and her shoulders shook. Poor child. The business with Garth was her own fault, of course, but Charlotte understood her agony. Separation from a baby. Charlotte heard Sophia's lonely sniffles and felt the pain in her own body. Was that how she had looked, mourning Octavius and Alfred?

With an awkward motion she stood and patted Sophia's back. She hadn't practised playing the mother for a long while. 'You did the right thing, you know,' she said softly. Despite everything, Charlotte was proud of her for that. A truly noble action, a strength of character she had not expected in her frail daughter.

Sophia gazed up, warily. 'So you *did* know.'

'Yes.' Charlotte smiled. 'Who do you think told the King you had dropsy and were cured by roast beef?'

Fresh tears cascaded down Sophia's cheeks. Her voice broke. 'My baby . . .'

'Would have caused you pain sooner or later. Made you regret the sacrifices you made for him.'

Sophia shook her head.

'He will grow up loved,' Charlotte insisted. 'Garth will take care of him. He was always a man of honour. And you . . . You and I will look after the King.'

Sophia raised her eyes. Tears made them burn with a turquoise flame. 'As always.'

'Yes. As always.'

Sophia took the handkerchief Charlotte gave her and blew her nose. 'He'll need us more than ever now. Amelia really is ill.'

Charlotte sighed. Did she believe it? Not in her heart. The girl was ambitious, hungry for love. She would stop at nothing to get her way. 'I think Amelia has fooled you, Sophia, as she is trying to fool me.' Sophia opened her mouth, but Charlotte cut her off. 'Nonetheless, I will talk to the King.'

Sophia swallowed. 'What will you say?'

Charlotte opened and closed her mouth. What *would* she say? There was a time she would have deposited all her secrets in the King's gentle ear. Now she could barely form a sentence in his presence.

'I'll think of something,' she sighed. 'I always do.'

CHAPTER THIRTY-EIGHT

Windsor Castle
⌁ *1810* ⌁

He knew her. Even after all this time, Charlotte felt a surge of hope. He could not see her clearly, but he knew her voice, knew her touch. It was a good day – a gift from Heaven. They were so rare. The King peered into her face. His eyes were swollen, with little snowdrops of skin peeling at the corners where leeches had sucked. 'Charlotte?'

She gripped his hand, as if her grasp could hold his mind and tether it to the shores of sanity. 'It's me. I'm here.'

'I want to talk to you about Amelia.'

The name was like a blow to the face. *Amelia.* Always Amelia, whether lucid or mad. Charlotte dropped his hand.

'She must come home,' the King insisted. 'Weymouth does her no good, no good at all.'

'It is that foolish Quaker doctor who does no good. Send her Dr Millman for God's sake, he will do the trick.'

'She likes Pope.'

'Then she's a fool,' Charlotte retorted.

'She wants to go to Kew, to convalesce.'

Of course she did. Little Kew, so removed from the world, would be the perfect place to meet Fitzroy or drop an illegitimate child. There could be no other motive. Why else would Amelia refuse to see a royal doctor, take Mary away with her and entreat them to return her to a secluded palace? She always was an extravagant, heedless girl. 'Why Kew? There is no need for that. She can come here.'

Strain pulled the King's features. 'Dr Pope says she cannot stay in the castle. It is too elevated and the rooms face east.'

'I am sure he does,' Charlotte said. 'Can't she stay somewhere else, close by? If she is as wretched as you say, we should have her near us.'

The King weighed this. 'She is in such a sad way, Charlotte. I do not like to deny her anything.'

He never did.

Jealous anger built to an intolerable degree. Charlotte wanted to shout, scream, blister him with words. But there was no vent for her, no gap of air to let the hot rage escape. She had to swallow her frustration and gloss over it until it became loving support. All to keep him lucid for a few more hours. Charlotte tried to keep the irritation from her voice. 'She is not your only daughter. Think of Mary! It is not fair for her to be carted about the country waiting on Amelia. The poor girl is bearing all this on her own.'

The King gave her a warning look. 'I have told you already, I will not have them separated.'

'I'm not suggesting that. Only, if she must be with Amelia, she needs her family in easy reach. Augusta might take over nursing if she gets too tired.'

'That's true,' he admitted. 'That is true.' He sat, put his hands together and rested his fingertips against his lips. 'I would prefer to keep her here, close to me. God knows I would.'

'Then do it. Kew indeed! Get her down to Windsor and send her Dr Millman. I have never seen a child so whimsical and selfish. Does Sophia make this fuss? Did she ever?'

A growl rumbled in the King's chest.

Amelia, always Amelia, even in his first great illness. Rather than clinging to his wife when their little sons died, the King gave himself to their new daughter and turned her into this spoilt and wilful child.

As Charlotte thought it over, she began to hate the very sight of the King; his useless eyes, his long nose, the stupid Windsor uniform and that massive forehead. She hated the castle he had caged her in, the life he had made her lead, and she hated this England where he had trapped her, like a pheasant in a net, and never, never taken her home.

Charlotte heard the dry sound of his lips part.

'The woman I married was so full of pity, she wept to see the poor and the wounded struggling through her country. She wrote to the King of Prussia himself to beg for mercy.

Now she cannot spare a penny for her own daughter.'

Indignation pulled her to her feet in a rustle of silk. How dare he? How dare he accuse *her* of changing? 'The woman you married died of a broken heart.'

He acknowledged the hit with a deep sigh. 'I miss her.'

So did Charlotte.

∽ *Augusta Lodge, Windsor* ∾

The air was close and moist with the promise of rain. Sophia and Augusta quickened their steps.

'You must brace yourself,' Augusta warned.

It was all Sophia did, these days. First a valet attacked Ernest in his sleep, scratching more battle scars into his skin. Now Amelia collapsed. When Sophia visited her injured siblings, she yearned for a sickbed herself; somewhere to rest and escape from the cruel world. She wound her fingers around Augusta's arm. 'Is Amelia as bad as Papa was, during his fits?'

Augusta adjusted a bell-shaped cage, which she carried in her other hand. 'Worse,' she said quietly. 'I think she is worse.'

They reached the lodge just as the first drops of rain fell from the sky. Footmen opened the door and the groom of the chamber took their things with solemn pageantry. Nobody smiled or raised their voice above a whisper.

Amelia's maid opened the door to the sickroom. Putrid

air swam out and forced its way up Sophia's nostrils – a noxious smell of unwashed hair, dirty linen and sweat.

Amelia lay marooned on a bed in the middle of the room, propped up on a mountain of pillows. The instant Sophia saw her face, all hope fled.

The happy, smiling Amelia of her childhood evaporated; she knew this pitiful image, and this image alone, would remain in her memory.

Sharp cheekbones made Amelia's face pointed and angular. A burning rash covered every inch of her skin. Here and there, stark welts stood out, glowering over the scabbed blisters. Oozing wounds peppered her cheeks and nose.

'Dear heart, it is us. Augusta and Sophia, come to see you.'

Amelia's eyes, glassy with opium, struggled to focus. 'Thank God. I thought it might be the Queen. Don't let her come, will you? I can have no pleasure in seeing her.' Her bony features contorted with rage. 'She can stay locked up with Elizabeth. A pair of old hags together. Do you know, neither of them believe I'm ill?'

More accurately, they did not *want* to believe Amelia was dying. Sophia recognised the Queen's tactics; she had used them herself as a child, when her little brothers died. *Close your eyes, pretend it isn't real.* If she didn't see the truth, how could it hurt her?

But the age of pretending had past. Reality burned through Sophia's spectacles with painful clarity: Amelia was doomed. Dazed, Sophia followed Augusta across the room to kiss her sister. She applied her lips very carefully, avoiding the excruciating sores. Amelia's skin carried the creamy, sickening scent of pus.

Mary sat by the window, rigidly controlled. Her gaze did not shift from Amelia. She was like a tiger guarding its young.

'Look what I have bought you, dearest.' Augusta unveiled her cage to reveal a canary, hopping and scuttling about. 'His note is so sweet. It won't hurt your ears. I want you to have your music.'

Amelia moved her face into a jagged grin. The little life remaining lit up her eyes. 'Oh, thank you!'

The bird cocked his head from side to side behind the golden bars of his cage. He fixed his beady gaze on Amelia and chirped.

'No, don't try to sit up,' Mary rose swiftly, but it was too late. Amelia flinched and held herself taut, bracing her feeble body against bullets of pain.

'Oh. Oh.' Amelia's eyebrows arched high into her forehead. 'Have I broken something?' she wailed. 'I am sure my arm is broken.'

Both Mary and Augusta positioned her back against the bed.

'No, my love,' Mary soothed. 'No. Just wait, it will feel better.'

Sophia could not look at them. She could not watch

Amelia's features and wonder when they would cease to move, or run her eyes over Amelia's burning skin and imagine the blood beneath stilling. That fatal, Gotha blood.

Amelia wept, wincing every time a salty tear entered a blister on her face. 'Oh God, I will never see him again! I will never see my Charles before I die.'

Mary spoke to the others in an undertone. 'She has been like this all day. She keeps saying she wants her gravestone to say Amelia Fitzroy.'

'Surely Papa would let us marry now, legally?' Amelia asked, pathetically hopeful. 'What harm can it do? It will not be for long.'

They did not answer her. Which of them was cruel enough to speak the truth? It would always matter to their proud father who his children married, living or dead.

Augusta fixed her gaze upon the happy little canary, so out of place, and balled her hands into fists. 'I'll bring Fitzroy to you, my love,' she said. 'You will see him again. I swear it.'

Charlotte waited in the airless antechamber while the King occupied Amelia's precious moments. She was too ill to see her parents together, so they took turns visiting. Charlotte acknowledged that she had not earned the right to go first. Once she and Amelia shared a body, but now they shared nothing.

The door clicked but Charlotte did not look up. She did

not want the moment to arrive. How could she go in there, knowing it would be the last time she laid eyes on her daughter? How would she ever say all she needed to?

Footsteps scuffed across the carpet. Charlotte heard the King sniff up his tears and whine in misery. This would be the orchestration of her life from now on. He would cry for both of them. 'Am I to go in?' Ludicrously, Charlotte hoped he would say *no*. But he nodded his drooping head in a hopeless, heavy gesture.

She stood and struggled toward the door. Her heavy gown held her back as if it was clogged with water. She couldn't cope. She was drowning, sinking in the swirling currents of stress and pain, but still her feet went on. Asphyxiating heat engulfed her the moment she entered the sickroom. It pressed close against her face, along with a meaty smell from the cups of beef tea sitting discarded on the table.

Amelia lay in her tangled bed dozing; five minutes with the King had drained her slim vial of energy. Charlotte's stomach twisted. What could she say to comfort her daughter? There were no words, no magic spells to keep her with them. Mother couldn't make it better.

'No,' Amelia murmured through her blue lips.

Charlotte wondered what she dreamt of – the life she wanted with Fitzroy, the children she would never have, or the places she would never see.

'No!' Amelia jumped up with a gasp.

Charlotte grabbed the bedpost. It wasn't her girl who awoke but a thin ghost with giant eyes and dark rings beneath them. Amelia's blonde ringlets were cropped short like a victim of the guillotine, and her downy scalp showed through the thin hair. Her skin was as delicate as when she was a babe in arms.

'Mama? Is that you?'

Black spots threatened Charlotte's vision as she approached the bed. She noticed a beaten volume of Richardson's *Clarissa* splayed out on the sheets and pushed it to the floor, remembering the tragic death of the heroine at the end. 'Yes. It's me.'

'Thank God. I thought ... I thought I was in prison.' Amelia pressed her fingertips against her eyelids.

'No.' Charlotte wanted to take Amelia's hand and hold it for dear life, but it was so thin and tiny – almost transparent. If she touched it, it would break.

Awkwardly, Amelia shuffled up on the pillows. Her wet lips gagged and twisted into a retch.

'Are you all right?'

Amelia's eyes flashed, mocking the stupidity of the question.

'No.' Charlotte's cheeks blazed. 'Of course not.'

'I have something for you.'

'Please, Amelia, sit still. Don't trouble yourself.'

Amelia rummaged in the cabinet beside her bed. For once, her disobedience did not anger Charlotte.

'Here.' Amelia's fragile hand closed upon an object. 'Put out your hand.'

She placed a smooth, cool object in Charlotte's palm. It was an oval locket on a long, delicately wrought chain. At the centre sat a coil of Amelia's hair, already cut off from her, already dead.

Charlotte sensed the importance of this moment, this memory, and the consciousness took her breath away. Soon this locket would become her relic; an object she stared at in wonder. The blonde curl at its heart used to move against Amelia's shoulders and shine in the sunshine.

Amelia's eyes, her father's eyes, pierced Charlotte. 'I hope your own suffering and anxiety will soon be over. I only ask that you take this and remember me.'

Guilt spread through Charlotte like a scratchy, blistering rash. Why had she let envy and despair wade between her and this dear daughter? She still remembered carrying her in the womb, fearing for her safety. How had they grown so far apart? Even now, even this last time, Charlotte did not have the words to ask for forgiveness.

CHAPTER THIRTY-NINE

Windsor Castle
⤿ *Winter 1810* ⤾

Stars shone in the ebony sky of a bitter November night. Sugary frost dusted the grass.

Charlotte shivered in her rooms in the Upper Ward, imagining Amelia in the stone-cold crypt. Etiquette forbade her and the princesses from attending the funeral; as always they had the harder task of sitting, waiting and imagining.

It was all over now. Already, Charlotte felt the deadness of her depression steal over her, a worm gnawing at her soul. There would be no recovery this time. The family would not pick themselves up and start again as they tried to do after Alfred and Octavius passed. The King would not rally. Even now, as they lowered the body of his favourite daughter into the royal vault of St George's chapel, he lay prostrate in a drugged sleep. In the morning he would wake and rave about how she had risen from the dead. It wasn't just Charlotte's daughter they buried tonight; they were committing to the ground the last remains she had of a husband.

Dear Prince George would have his way: the Regency would come at last. The war, the expense of a Regent's court and the King's medical care would diminish, if not expunge, Charlotte's household. Come morning she would give notice to dozens of loyal, well-loved members of the staff. Her musicians would go and they would sell the horses. She would have nothing left to remind her.

As the bell tolled, Mary and Sophia grew still. They knew the sound signalled the entrance of the hearse. Without thinking, Charlotte rose to her feet and prowled by the window. Only the orange gleams of flambeaux reached her across the ward, but it didn't matter – she knew all the arrangements and her imagination supplied the rest.

In her mind's eye, she saw the solemn carriage led by eight black horses, dark feathers fluttering between their ears. She saw the troop of Royal Household Blues, their swords glinting in the moonlight as they raised them in salute. Her sons would be there, dark cloaks drawn up against the cold, wearing black boots. They would weep in the torchlight, watching the Yeomen of the Guard lift the coffin down onto their shoulders.

A log shifted on the fire. The princesses jumped as it hissed and fizzed but Charlotte's nerves remained untouched. She had been here before; she had ridden the waves of misery, coming up for snatches of air before plunging back into the depths of dismay. But this time there would be no second dawn. Not for the King, not for Charlotte.

∼ *Windsor Castle* ∼

A feather bolster supported Sophia's weak body. Warmth coated her skin, spreading out from the many quilts and sheets heaped upon her bed. She could live her life like this, she realised; give into the tug of her body and exist as a spoilt invalid. Why not retire from the world and stay where it was safe? All fire and struggle had departed with Amelia's death. It brought Sophia a strange relief. The worst had happened: the King was mad beyond cure. George took up the reins as Regent. There was nothing left to fear. A great weight of suspense had lifted and left her lighter, free.

A soft knock came at the door. She blinked as a servant shuffled in.

'The Prince of Wales – I mean, the Prince Regent, Your Highness.'

Delight flooded her as George appeared, dressed in black velvet. He was the princesses' world now, their comfort.

'My dear! Do come and sit down. How good of you to visit a sad old cat like me.'

He lifted his flabby cheeks in a half-hearted smile. Strain

pulled at his eyes and brow. After many years longing for
the crown, it seemed he found it a burden. 'You are
precious to me,' he said, his eyes misting over. 'All my remaining sisters are infinitely precious.'

Sophia bowed her head, replaying Amelia's death. She
saw Sir Henry holding up the candle to her thin, white lips
to see if the flame flickered. It didn't. Then he'd drawn the
curtain, closing out her little sister and an era of Sophia's
life. 'Amelia was brave right to the end. She was not afraid.
She did not want us to mourn for her.'

George sat in a chair beside the bed. The cushions
creaked beneath him as he crossed his legs. 'All the same, I
cannot sleep since it happened. I need candles in the room
with me.'

Sophia clasped his big hand in her own. 'We must look
forward.'

A cloud cleared from his brow. 'Yes, you're right. That is
why I am here – to cheer you.' His blue eyes sparkled as he
reached into his pocket and produced a small box wrapped
with ribbons. Smiling, Sophia accepted it and opened her
gift. A pendant shaped like a pansy sparkled back at her.

'Another present? You are so kind to me. To all of us.'
She leaned forward and let him fasten the necklace around
her throat.

'You need me.' George blew out his breath. 'The whole
family is in a sorry state. I have just been to see Ernest. He
recovers well, but he is still shaken up. Fancy being slashed

by your own valet! That's what he gets for employing foreign rascals.'

The rascal in question, Sellis, had slit his own throat with a razor shortly after the failed attack. But as always with Ernest, there was gossip.

'And those awful rumours that it was all staged? That Ernest . . .' she hesitated, unable to say the disgusting words, '. . . killed Sellis himself?'

George scowled. 'They still fly. He will have to lay low until they settle.' His eyes met hers, intent with meaning. 'There will always be rumours about Ernest.'

She blushed and looked down. Surely George didn't think . . .? 'Have you visited Mary too?' she asked to change the subject. After tireless hours of nursing, Mary was laid low in a nervous collapse. They blistered the back of her head and told her to sleep, but she couldn't obey. As soon as she closed her eyes, she told Sophia, Amelia was there, watching back.

George shifted in his chair. 'Yes. In fact, I have called on Mary, Augusta and Elizabeth to tell them what I'm about to tell you.'

Her heart dropped. 'What now? Not more bad news?'

'No – good news.' He stroked her cheek. 'You have all been held captive for too long. I'm making you independent. I've asked Parliament to grant you eight thousand a year each – and they have agreed.'

The mattress shifted beneath her. Eight thousand

pounds! It was enough to keep a house of her own, it was the key to freedom. 'George,' she breathed. For a moment, happy images of the future danced, weaving their magic spell. Then a sour face appeared and sent them plummeting down. 'The Queen will hate it if she cannot keep us close. She will spit fire.'

George's lips twisted in a wry smile. 'It does her good to rage. Give her something to fume about and she comes alive again.' He cleared his throat. 'Seriously, though. I will look after the Queen. I've failed her once – I will not do it again.'

It felt like a long time ago, the first Regency crisis. George was a different person back then. It made Sophia sad to think he still blamed himself for the recklessness of youth. Who could say they had not been a fool, years ago? Not Sophia; not the Queen.

'Thank you.' Sophia shook her head, fighting down the sentimental tears that tickled her throat. 'I know you struggle for money, and you give this out of your own Civil List. To four old spinsters who should be put in a bag and drowned! You are an angel. I will never forget it.'

George coloured with pleasure. Whatever his faults, he had a soft heart that glowed when it gratified others. 'Our sisters are making plans,' he said. 'Mary talks of marrying Cousin William. Well, he always had a soft spot for her. Elizabeth hopes to find a husband in a German province.'

He fixed her with his azure blue gaze. 'What are your plans, Sophy?'

Sophia swallowed a hard bud of regret. 'You know marriage is impossible.'

'Garth wouldn't have you?'

Pride scorched her belly. She couldn't think of Garth without antipathy now. He had believed disgusting gossip and blamed her for loving the King. He was not the man she thought he was. 'No. He thinks me heartless.'

He had resented her from the moment she turned down his plan to run away. If he had waited, if he had realised they just had to bide their time until the King passed into lunacy, it might have been different. But now that door was closed. At ten years old, Tommy would never open his arms to her and call her *Mama*. She had missed too much.

George grimaced. He leant forward in the chair and plaited his fingers. 'I'm sorry, Sophy. I thought there might be hope. If I had known . . .' He squirmed. 'Look, I've given Garth a place in my daughter's household. Just say the word if it makes you uncomfortable, and I will remove him.'

Part of her yearned to do it – cast him out from the family. But she knew he would serve her niece well.

'No, keep him on. It will benefit the child.'

George stared at her, as if he knew she meant Tommy and not Charlotte. 'It is a good allowance,' he said.

Sophia nodded. Tommy deserved the best. Lord knew, he had lost much.

She stirred from her thoughts as George laid a warm hand upon hers. 'I've brought her with me, you know. Little Charlotte.'

The mist retreated from Sophia's head. Magical Charlotte, who even managed to make the dour old Queen laugh. She was only a few years older than Tommy; another child parted from its mother.

'She asks after her Aunt Sophy. You're the favourite.'

Joy glowed inside her. Such a simple thing, the affection of a child, but what a difference it made.

'She will need a lady to guide her,' George prompted. 'She is just a girl and heir to the throne. She has no one to look up to. Her mother is . . . unsuitable.'

A spark of rebellion flickered through her. Poor Caroline. But although Sophia still felt for her sister-in-law, she didn't cleave to her like she used to. The Wales marriage was no longer black and white. A government report had exposed Caroline's shocking behaviour whilst living apart from her husband, and Ernest swore that she had fuelled the rumours about his supposed incest. Sophia didn't know who to believe, but while George sat there holding her hand and promising her protection, she would be a fool to turn him away.

'It will be an honour to help Charlotte.'

George released her hand and beamed. 'Good! I'll go and fetch her, shall I?' He rose, groaning, to his feet and made his way to the door. He checked on the threshold. 'It will be all right, you know. You, me and Augusta will care for the Queen and raise little Charlotte. Your life won't be wasted; you must never think that.'

Sophia leant back against the bolster and closed her eyes. George spoke the truth. It was her duty to care for her mother and a privilege to assist a future sovereign. Especially if that future sovereign was a child who could fill the gap in her heart.

Yes, that was her destiny. God never closed a door without opening one. Sophia would devote herself to Queen Charlotte – this one and the next.

CHAPTER FORTY

The Dutch House, Kew
1818

The room in Kew was small and unpretentious. Charlotte kept a modest, white bed and a few pictures of her children on the walls. It was here she would die. After so many years longing for the release of death, it stood at her shoulder, stroking her hair, and she was terrified. Judgement day had come, and she had much to answer for.

Mary moved to the little table in front of her and plumped the cushion upon it. Charlotte could no longer lie in bed. Here, in her favourite black horsehair chair, she was as comfortable as she would ever be in this life – she did not dare to speculate about the next.

Augusta came to hold her hand. 'There's nothing to worry about, Mama. George and Frederick will be here soon.'

Charlotte pressed her cheek to the pillow, where it lay slick with perspiration and tears. Her dim eyes searched the room for Elizabeth. Of course they would not see her, far away in Bad Homburg, where she had finally found a husband. She would never see her favourite daughter again, nor Sophia, too sick to travel from Windsor.

'What is it, Mama?' Mary laid a hand upon her cheek.

Charlotte's voice cracked. 'I wish to God I could see your sisters and your brothers! Tell them I love them.'

'They will be here, Mama. They will be here soon.'

Charlotte always imagined she would die holding her husband's hand. But, ensconced in Windsor, he was oblivious to her illness. Her name was an empty word to him. The old, balding head retained no memories of their wedding, their children, their life together. Only dreams and fantasies played behind the blind, cloudy eyes.

Charlotte remembered him as he was, her handsome King, and her long dead love revived, triumphant like the phoenix. Memories waded around her, swallowing her. She didn't mind – when she saw them, she didn't feel pain.

A rumbling noise stirred her back into the present.

'Mama,' Augusta said from a distance. 'George and Fred are here.'

Boots pounded up the staircase and Charlotte heard them as if she were underwater. She had to stay awake to say goodbye, but she was so, so tired. She had laboured hard to be strong and queenly in the years since she had washed up on England's shore, a poor princess the people scoffed at. Now she must die with becoming grace, while the petrified wings of her soul beat against her failing body.

'Mama!' A voice that always had power over her: her firstborn George, her dearest son. She blinked away the settling haze and his face floated into her vision. The Prince Regent was an ageing man now, some fifty-six years old. So why did Charlotte see his face radiant with youth and chubby as a toddler? Why did she see long, curling hair and the blue eyes of his father when he took her hand?

She tried to smile. Her four children sheltered her in a loving circle. Someone kissed her.

'I love you, Mama.' The words came in a childish lisp. Suddenly, Charlotte understood everything. Time was unwinding. In death, she would get her final wish.

When she fell asleep she would awake as Charlotte of Mecklenburg-Strelitz once more, with amber flames warming her grey hair and smooth skin. She would see Octavius, Alfred and Amelia.

'Mama?' Her son's voice, a soft lullaby in her ears.

'George,' she breathed. The real King would come to her again – she only had to close her eyes and dream.

'George.'

She saw the silhouette of a young man with his back to her, standing before a setting sun. He was lean and athletic with leather boots up to his knees. Instead of a wig, he wore his own light brown hair pulled back into a queue.

'George?'

He turned at her voice. A ray of warm, orange light

illuminated the features she knew so well: the high, proud forehead, long nose, globular eyes, pendulous lips.

He smiled. 'My love.'

He was so young. No hints of madness tainted his handsome, radiant face. She ran to him and he opened his arms wide.

'George!'

His embrace enveloped her; the familiar, comforting scent of his skin filled her nostrils. A perfect dream.

Mary reached out to touch the Queen's arm. 'Mama. Mama!'

But she was already gone. The folds of her cheek pressed down against the pillow, sapped of life. No pulse beat, no breath flowed, yet on her aged lips there sat the faintest trace of a smile.

Ludwigsburg
~ *1818* ~

When the letters arrived on black-edged paper, Royal knew her mother was dead. She did not break the seal, but sat with the folded paper in her hands, looking out across the sunlit gardens of Ludwigsburg, and waited for the tears. They did not come.

It was not a life to wish prolonged. Thirty lacerating years trying to save one man – a man who played his flute and ate cherry tarts through the long months of her final illness.

Royal gazed at the bare trees, remembering her mother. Every trace of her would blow away with the dead November leaves. Her servants, her dogs, her music. Nothing left but the sad princesses and a twilight King.

The fountain tinkled gently. Instinctively, Royal's hand strayed to the locket at her neck. Fritz in one side, the King in the other. Both far beyond her reach. She unwound the chain from her neck and popped the locket open. Her father's portrait had faded with age. She ran a thumb over it, remembering.

What would become of him without the Queen? His small remnant of royal dignity must evaporate. Parliament would not pay to keep a madman in style – even one who devoted his life to the nation. He would live out a shadowy existence, blind, deaf and lame. In essence, he was already dead.

At least her father wouldn't endure the torture of losing a spouse. He was safe from the world in his own delusions. There would be no washing of the body for him; no dressing of the corpse, no walking round the coffin as it lay in state, a gilt crown resting at its head, with candles lighting the waxy, dead skin.

Royal closed her eyes to the winter sunlight and said a prayer for Fritz's soul. She missed him, on days like this, sitting in the gardens he made for her. But she had no cause for complaint. Wilhelm was in charge, the land was recovering from many years of war and the people, Royal's people, remembered she had been there through it all.

The palace door closed and Royal looked up from her devotions. Footmen marched across the gardens to take her back inside. Her body, never blessed with another child, had run to fat. She could not walk on her own and needed them to carry her on a chair with four poles.

She kissed the locket and clasped it back around her neck.

She would have young ones clamouring around her the moment she entered the palace. Paul and Wilhelm's children loved her more than their own mothers.

The men closed in and heaved up her chair, raising her aloft in the cool air. She bobbed along above the box hedge, surveying her beautiful land. There was no reason to despair. The time for regret was over. She had a palace full of joy and affection just waiting for her to enter it. She needed to move on.

The King and Queen may be gone, but they would live on through Royal: a blend of their passion, of their love. They gave her the gift of life; she owed it to them to live a full one. Free.

AUTHOR'S NOTE

In retelling the story of Charlotte, Royal and Sophia I have mingled fact, speculation and fiction. In some cases I have moved events forward or backward to aid the narrative flow.

George III survived Charlotte by less than two years. He suffered a massive fit around Christmas 1819 that left him unable to sleep or eat. He died aged 81 on 29 January 1820. Medical historians now believe that he suffered either from bipolar disorder or acute porphyria, a hereditary metabolic condition. His physical symptoms make the later more likely.

Royal visited England one last time in 1827 for an emotional reunion with her surviving siblings. Massively overweight with gout in her feet and hands, she made a slow progress through her native land before returning to Württemberg. She died just one year after her return. Her adopted grandchildren were present at her death and showed the depth of their affection by refusing to leave her body. Royal always refuted the claims that her husband ill-treated her, but accounts from English ministers and

Napoleon suggest she was lying. Given Fritz's violent relationship with his first wife, Augusta, I suspect there was some abuse in his second marriage. However, this did not change the couple's love for one another.

Sophia proved a true friend to young Charlotte up until the girl's tragic death in 1819. Her affection then moved on to another niece, Victoria, and her mother the Duchess of Kent. Always swayed by a handsome face, Sophia soon fell under the spell of the infamous Sir John Conroy. She purchased him several residences, but at least her investment was repaid by Conroy's support in later years. She was sorely tried by Tommy Garth's continual demands for a royal annuity and threats that he would publish documents revealing the truth about his birth. She lived the last few years of her life blind, partially deaf and unable to move from her seat without being carried.

Although there are historians who reject the idea that Sophia gave birth to an illegitimate child, I believe Tommy Garth was her son. It is certainly worth noting the speed with which the royal family were willing to pay him off. That Sophia had an affair with General Garth and exchanged rings is clear from her correspondence, although the suggestion she considered the relationship as a marriage is my own. It seems likely, however, given the family's religious nature and Sophia's own protestations of innocence, that promises were made. The rumour that Ernest fathered Tommy would follow Sophia to the grave.

It is an interesting and deliciously scandalous theory, but one I believe is false. Though Ernest was certainly a rake by contemporary standards, it seems all too probable that the rumours were vicious whispers from his many political enemies.

Laura Purcell, 2014
www.laurapurcell.com

ABOUT LAURA PURCELL

Laura Purcell lives in Colchester, England's oldest recorded town. She met her husband while working in a bookshop and they share their home with several guinea pigs.

She is a member of the Historical Novel Society, The Society for Court Studies and Historical Royal Palaces. She appeared on the PBS documentary: *The Secrets of Henry VIII's Palace*, discussing Queen Caroline's life at Hampton Court.

Her novels explore the lives of royal women during the Georgian era, who have largely been ignored by modern history.

Laura writes a history blog at www.laurapurcell.com

Coming soon ...

LAURA PURCELL'S
Mistress of the Court

Orphaned and trapped in an abusive marriage, Henrietta
Howard has little left to lose. She stakes everything on a
new life in Hanover with its royal family, the heirs to the
British throne.

Henrietta's beauty and intelligence soon win her th
friendship of clever Princess Caroline and her merc
husband Prince George. But as time passes, it beco
clear that friendship is the last thing on the hot-blood
young prince's mind. Dare Henrietta give into his advances
and anger her violent husband? Dare she refuse?

Whatever George's shortcomings, Princess Caroline is
determined to make the family a success. Yet the feud
between her husband and his obstinate father threatens all
she has worked for. As England erupts in Jacobite riots, her
family falls apart. She vows to save the country for her children to inherit — even if it costs her pride and her marriage.

Set in the turbulent years of the Hanoverian accession,
Mistress of the Court tells the story of two remarkable women
at the centre of George II's reign.

978-1-910183-07-6 Paperback
978-1-910183-08-3 Ebook